MACAQUE ATTACK

GARETH L. POWELL

SOLARIS

First published 2015 by Solaris
an imprint of Rebellion Publishing Ltd,
Riverside House, Osney Mead,
Oxford, OX2 0ES, UK

www.solarisbooks.com

ISBN: 978 1 78108 286 7

10 9 8 7 6 5 4 3 2 1

A CIP catalogue record for this book is available from the
British Library.

Designed & typeset by Rebellion Publishing

Printed in the US

For my sister, Rebecca, with thanks.

IN SEPTEMBER 1956, France found herself facing economic difficulties at home and an escalating crisis in Suez. In desperation, the French prime minister came to London with an audacious proposition for Sir Anthony Eden: a political and economic union between the United Kingdom and France, with Her Majesty Queen Elizabeth II as the new head of the French state.

Although Eden greeted the idea with skepticism, a resounding Anglo-French victory against Egypt persuaded his successor to accept and, despite disapproving noises from both Washington and Moscow, Harold Macmillan and Charles de Gaulle eventually signed the Declaration of Union on 29th November 1959, thereby laying the foundations for a wider European Commonwealth.

And now, one hundred and three years have passed...

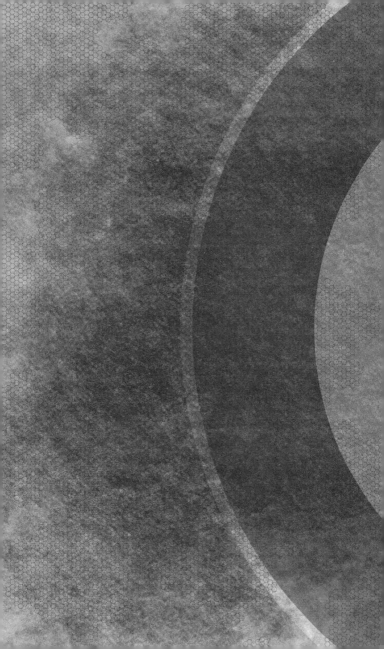

PART ONE

PERSONAL FRANKENSTEIN

Of all the animals, man is the only one that is cruel.
He is the only one that inflicts pain for the pleasure
of doing it.

(Mark Twain, *The Lowest Animal*)

BREAKING NEWS

From *B&FBC NEWS ONLINE:*

King to mark second anniversary of invasion

LONDON 15/11/ 2062 – A service of remembrance will be held in Parliament Square tomorrow to mark the second anniversary of the Gestalt Invasion.

During the invasion, heavily armed airships appeared over major cities across the globe, and government buildings and seats of power were destroyed in an attempt to 'decapitate' international society. The Gestalt were eventually beaten, but not before thousands of civilians and military personnel lost their lives.

His Majesty, King Merovech I, ruler of the United Kingdom of Great Britain, France, Ireland and Norway, will dedicate a memorial to those who died in London, including his fiancée, Julie Girard, Princess of Normandy. Similar services will be held simultaneously in Cardiff, Oslo, Manchester, Dublin, and Paris.

Two years on from the events of 16th November 2060, the whereabouts of those responsible for halting the invasion remains a mystery. Captain Valois and the crew of her skyliner, the *Tereshkova*—including the famed monkey pilot, Ack-Ack Macaque—vanished shortly after defeating the Gestalt forces in the skies above the British capital. It is believed they may have used the hive mind's own machinery to 'jump' to a parallel dimension.

Whether they went to avenge the attack, or on some other undisclosed quest, their fate remains unknown.　.

Related Stories:

Controversial light-sail probe reaches Mars.

A look inside the rebuilt Palace of Westminster.

From protester to princess: the life of Julie Girard.

Gestalt prisoners reveal chilling details of 'alternate Earth'.

World leaders sign mutual defence pact in Moscow.

Global warming: sea level rise may be faster than predicted.

CHAPTER ONE
INSTANT KARMA

"ARE YOU SURE we should be doing this?" The driver's sharp green eyes met Victoria's in the rearview mirror and she looked away, twisting her gloved hands in her lap. She was being driven through Paris in a shiny black Mercedes. The parked cars, buildings and skeletal linden trees were bright and crisp beneath the winter sun.

"I think so."

At the wheel, K8 shrugged. She was nineteen years old, with cropped copper hair and a smart white suit.

"Only…"

Victoria frowned, and brushed a speck of dust from the knee of her black trousers.

"Only what?"

"Should it be you that does it? Maybe somebody else—"

"She won't listen to anybody else."

"You don't know that for sure."

"I really do."

They passed across the Pont Neuf. Sunlight glittered off the waters of the Seine. The towers of Notre Dame stood resolute against the sky, their solidity a direct counterpoint to the ephemeral advertising holograms that stepped and swaggered above the city's boulevards and streets.

"Look," Victoria said apologetically, "I didn't mean to be snappy. I really appreciate you coming along. I know things haven't been easy for you recently."

K8 kept her attention focused on the road ahead.

"We are fine."

"It must have been tough for you." During the final battle over London, the poor kid had been assimilated into the Gestalt hive mind. For a time, she'd been part of a group consciousness, lost in a sea of other people's thoughts.

"It was, but we're okay now. Really." There were no other members of the Gestalt on this parallel version of the Earth. For the first time since the battle, the girl was alone in her head.

"You're still referring to yourself in the plural."

"We can't help it."

The car negotiated the Place de la Bastille, and plunged into the narrow streets beyond. Their target lived in a two-room apartment on the third floor of a red brick house on the corner of la Rue Pétion. When they reached the address, Victoria instructed K8 to park the Mercedes at the opposite end of the avenue and wait. Then she got out and walked back towards the house.

With her hands in the pockets of her long army coat, she sniffed the cold air. This morning, Paris smelled of damp leaves and fresh coffee. Far away and long ago, on another timeline entirely, this had been her neighbourhood, her street. Even the graffiti tags scrawled between the shop fronts seemed just as she remembered them from when she lived here as a journalist for *Le Monde*, in the days before she met Paul.

Paul...

Victoria squeezed her fists and pushed them deeper into her pockets. Paul was her ex-husband. In the three years since his death, he'd existed as a computer simulation. She'd managed to keep him alive, despite the fact that personality 'back-ups' were inherently unstable and prone to dissolution. Originally developed for battlefield use, back-ups had become a means by which the civilian deceased— at least those who could afford the implants—could say their goodbyes after death and tie up their affairs. The recordings weren't intended or expected to endure more than six months but, with her help, Paul had already far exceeded that limit.

But nothing lasts forever.

During the past weeks, Paul's virtual personality had become increasingly erratic and forgetful, and she knew he couldn't hold out much longer. In order to preserve whatever run-time he might have left, she'd found a way to pause his simulation, leaving him frozen in time until her return. She didn't want to lose him. In many ways, he was the love of her life; and yet she knew her attempts to hold on to him were only delaying the inevitable. Sooner or later, she'd have to let him go. Three years after his death, she'd finally have to say goodbye.

Scuffing the soles of her boots against the pavement, she wondered if the woman inhabiting the apartment above had anyone significant in *her* life. This woman still lived and worked as a reporter in Paris, was registered as single on her social media profile, and had somehow managed to avoid the helicopter crash that had left Victoria with a skull full of prosthetic gelware processors.

Victoria reached up and adjusted the fur cap covering her bald scalp.

This would have been my life, she thought, *if I'd never met Paul, never gone to the Falklands...*

She felt a surge of irrational hatred for the woman who shared her face, the stranger who had once been her but whose life had diverged at an unspecified point. Where had that divergence come? Who knew? A missed promotion, perhaps, or maybe something as banal as simply turning right when her other self had turned left... Now, they were completely different people. One of them was a newspaper correspondent living in a hip quarter of Paris, the other a battle-hardened skyliner captain in league with an army of dimension-hopping monkeys.

At the front door, she hesitated. How could she explain *any* of this?

For the past two years, she'd been travelling with Ack-Ack Macaque, jumping from one world to the next. Together, they'd sought out and freed as many of his simian counterparts as they could find, unhooking them from whichever video games or weapons guidance systems they'd been wired into, and telling them they were no longer alone, no longer unique—welcoming them into the troupe. But in all that time, on all those worlds, she'd never once sought out an alternate version of herself. The thought simply hadn't occurred to her.

Here and now, though, things were different.

K8 had tracked the most likely location of Ack-Ack Macaque's counterpart on this world to an organisation known as the Malsight Institute. It was a privately funded research facility on the outskirts of Paris, surrounded by security fences and razor wire. While trying to hack its systems from outside, K8 had discovered a file containing a list of people the institute saw as 'threats' to their continued operation. Victoria's counterpart had been the third person named on that list. Apparently, she'd been asking questions, probing around online, and generally making a nuisance of herself. The first two people on the list were already dead, their deaths part of an ongoing police investigation. One had been a former employee of the institute, the other an investigative journalist for an online news site. Both had been found stabbed and mutilated, their bodies charred almost beyond all recognition. Hence, the reason for this visit. If the deaths were connected to the Institute, Victoria felt duty-bound to warn her other self before the woman wound up as a headline on the evening news, her hacked and blackened corpse grinning from the smoking remains of a burned-out car.

From the pocket of her coat, she drew her house key. She'd kept the small sliver of brass and nickel with her for years, letting it rattle around in the bottom of one suitcase after another like a half-forgotten talisman. She'd never expected to need it again, but neither had she ever managed to quite bring herself to throw it away.

She slid the key into the lock and opened the door. Inside, the hallway was exactly as she remembered:

black and white diamond-shaped floor tiles; a side table piled with uncollected mail, free newspapers and takeaway menus; and a black-railed staircase leading to the floors above. She closed the front door behind her and made her way up, her thick-soled boots making dull clumps on the uncarpeted steps.

The feel of the smooth bannister, the creak of the stairs, even the slightly musty smell of the walls brought back memories of a time that had been, in retrospect, happier and simpler.

In particular, she remembered an upstairs neighbour, a woman in her mid-forties with a taste for young men. Often, Victoria had found she had to turn up her TV to hide the bumps and giggles from above. One time, a lump of plaster fell off the ceiling and smashed her glass coffee table. Then, in the morning, there would usually be a young man standing in the communal stairwell. Some were lost, some shell-shocked or euphoric. Some were reassessing their lives and relationships in the light of the previous night's events. Victoria would take them in and make them coffee, call them cabs or get them cigarettes, that sort of thing.

She liked their company. In those days, she liked being useful. And sometimes, one of the boys would stay with her for a few days. They used her to wind down, to ground themselves. Sometimes, they just needed to talk. And when they left, as they inevitably did, it made her sad. She would rinse out their empty coffee mugs, clean the ashtrays, and fetch herself a glass of wine from the fridge. Then she would settle herself on the sofa again, rest her feet on the coffee table frame, and turn the TV volume way up.

*   *   *

SOMEBODY SCREAMED. THE sound cut through her memories. It came from above. Reaching into her coat pocket, Victoria pulled the retractable fighting stick from her coat and shook it out to its full two-metre length. Was she already too late? Taking the stairs two at a time, she reached the third floor to find the door of the apartment—*her* apartment—locked, and fresh blood spreading from beneath it, soaking into the bristles of the welcome mat.

She'd been around the monkey long enough to know she'd only hurt herself if she tried shoulder-charging the door. Instead, she delivered a sharp kick with the heel of her heavy boot, aiming for the edge of door opposite the handle. The lock would be strong, but only a handful of screws held the hinges in place. She heard wood crack, but the door remained closed. Leaning backwards for balance, she kicked again. This time, the frame splintered, the hinges came away from the wall, and the door crashed inwards and to the side.

Victoria pushed through, stepping over the puddle of blood, and found herself on the threshold of a familiar-looking room. A body lay on the floor by the couch. It had shoulder-length blonde hair. A tall, thin man loomed over it, a long black knife in his almost skeletal hand. His shoes had left red prints on the parquet floor, and there was a long smear where he'd dragged the body. As she burst in, he looked up at her. His face was set in a rictus grin, and she swallowed back a surge of revulsion.

"Cassius Berg."

His expression didn't change, and she knew it couldn't. His skin had been stretched taut over an artificial frame.

"Who are you?"

Victoria swallowed. She felt as if she was talking to a ghost. "The last time we met, I dropped you out of a skyliner's cargo hatch, four hundred feet above Windsor."

He tipped his head on one side. His eyes were reptilian slits.

"What are you on about?" He stepped over the corpse and brandished the knife. "Who are you?"

Victoria moved her staff into a defensive position.

"I'm her."

She couldn't bring herself to look directly at the body. As a reporter, she'd seen her share of violent crime scenes, and knew what to expect. Instead, she looked inside her own head, concentrating on the mental commands that transferred her consciousness from the battered remains of her natural cortex to the clean, bright clarity of her gelware implants.

Berg's posture tightened. He glanced from her to the body, and back again.

"Twin sister?"

"Something like that."

"Lucky me."

The first time she'd fought him—or at least the version of him from her own parallel—he'd been superhumanly fast and tough, and he'd almost killed her. She'd been left for dead with a hole punched through the back of her skull. She tightened her grip on the metal staff. This time would be different. This time, she knew all about him, knew his methods and limitations, while he remained blissfully unaware of her capabilities.

Visualising her internal menu, she overclocked her neural processors. As the speed of her thinking increased, her perception of time stretched and slowed. The traffic noise from outside deepened, winding down like a faulty tape. In slow motion, she saw Berg's muscles tense. His legs pushed up and he surged towards her, black coat flapping around behind him, knife held forward, aimed at her face. His speed was astonishing. A normal human would have been pinned through the eye before they could move. As it was, Victoria only just managed to spin aside. As momentum carried him past, she completed her twirl and brought the end of her staff cracking into the back of his head. The blow caught him off balance and sent him flailing forwards with an indignant cry, through the remains of the front door and out, into the hallway.

He ended up on his hands and knees. Victoria stepped up behind him, but before she could bring her staff down, Berg's spindly arm slashed backwards, and his knife caught her across the shins, slicing through denim and skin. The pain registered as a sharp red alarm somewhere at the back of her mind, way down in the animal part of her brain, and she tried to ignore it. It was a distraction, the gelware told her, nothing more. Her heart thumped in her chest, each beat like the pounding of some great engine. He'd hurt her before; she wouldn't allow him to hurt her again. She stabbed down with her staff, pinning his wrist to the hardwood floor, and leant her weight on it. She ground until she felt the bones of his hand snap and crack, and saw the knife fall from his fingers.

Berg's head turned to look at her. Although the grin remained stretched across his face, his eyes were wide and fearful.

"Who *are* you?"

"I told you." Victoria could feel blood running down her shins, soaking into the tops of her socks. She glanced back at the dead woman in the apartment, and saw blonde hair mixed with wine-coloured blood, and an out-thrown hand with torn and bruised knuckles. The poor woman hadn't stood a chance. She'd been butchered, and all Victoria could do now was avenge her.

"I'm Victoria Valois." She stepped forward and raised her weapon high over her head. She wanted to bring it down hard, driving the butt end into the space between his eyes. She wanted to feel his metal skull cave beneath her blow, feel his brains squish and perish. He had killed at least three people, probably more, and would kill her too if he got the chance.

He deserved to die.

And yet...

CHAPTER TWO
UNCLEAN ZOO

TAKING OFF FROM a private airstrip on the outskirts of Paris, Victoria and K8 flew across the English Channel in a borrowed seaplane, with Cassius Berg handcuffed and gagged in the hold. They were heading for a sea fort that stood a few miles off the coast of Portsmouth. When the old structure came into sight, they splashed the plane into the waters of the Solent, carving a feather of white across the shimmering blue surface, and taxied to the rotting jetty that served as the fort's one and only link with the outside world.

The seaplane was an ancient Grumman Goose: a small and ungainly contraption with which Victoria had somehow fallen grudgingly in love. The little aircraft had two chunky propeller engines mounted on an overhead wing, and the main fuselage dangled between them like a fat-bottomed boat bolted to the underside of a boomerang.

When she stepped from the plane's hatch, Victoria found a monkey waiting for her, fishing from the end of the jetty. It wore a flowery sunhat and a string vest, and had a large silver pistol tucked into the waistband of its cut-off denim shorts. Overhead, the sun burned white and clean.

"I'm Valois."

The monkey watched her from behind its mirrored shades. She couldn't remember its name. A portable transistor radio, resting on the planks beside the bait bucket, played scratchy Europop.

"So?"

Behind the monkey, at the far end of the jetty, the fort rose as an implacable, curving wall of stone. Victoria swallowed back her irritation. The breeze blowing in from the sea held the all-too-familiar fragrances of brine, fresh fish, and childhood holidays. Considering it was November, the day felt exceptionally mild.

"Where's your boss?"

"Does he know you're coming?"

"Don't be stupid." She slipped off her flying jacket, pulled a red bandana from her trouser pocket, and wiped her forehead. Keeping hold of its rod with one hand, the monkey produced a rolled-up cigarette from behind its ear. The paper was damp and starting to unravel. It pushed the rollup between its yellowing teeth, and lit up using a match struck against the jetty's crumbling planks.

"I don't think he'll want to see you."

Smoke curled around it, blue in the sunlight. Victoria sighed, and raised her eyes to the armoured Zeppelin tethered to the fort's radio mast.

"Is he up there?"

"Yeah, but he ain't taking no visitors."

"We'll see about that."

She went back to the Goose and pulled Berg out onto the jetty's planks. He blinked against the sunlight. Victoria slipped a loop of rope around his neck, and jerked on it like a dog chain. Leaving K8 to secure the plane, she led her prisoner past the startled monkey, along the jetty, and into the coolness of the stone fort.

The corridors were dank with rainwater, and she was surprised to feel a sense of homecoming. Despite the frosty welcome, this little manmade island felt more like home than anywhere else on this timeline. She'd spent the past six weeks in Europe, but it hadn't been her Europe. Everything about it had been different and, to her, somehow wrong. She looked forward to getting back to the familiar cabins and gangways of the armoured airship, and Paul.

Would he even remember her?

Dragging Berg, she stomped her way across the fort's main flagstone courtyard.

Standing in the English Channel, several miles off the coast of the Isle of Wight, the circular fort had been built in the 19th century to defend Portsmouth from the French. Made of thick stone and surrounded by water on all sides, the structure had lain derelict until the turn of the millennium, when an enterprising developer had converted the stronghold into a luxury hotel and conference centre, complete with open-air swimming pool. Fifty years, and two stock market crashes, later, the weeds and rust had returned; and now that the place had been 'liberated' by the monkey army, it more resembled an unclean zoo than an exclusive resort. The water in the swimming pool lay brown and stagnant, its scummy surface speckled by shoals of empty beer cans and the wallowing bleach-white bones of broken patio furniture. Shards of glass littered the patio area.

The steps up to the base of the radio mast were where she remembered, still overgrown with lichen, grass and mould. The grass whispered against her leather boots, and she knew suspicious eyes watched her from the fort's seemingly empty windows.

Stupid monkeys.

She'd only been gone six weeks.

ONCE ABOARD THE airship, Victoria led Berg to the artificial jungle built into the vessel's glass-panelled nose. Cut off from the rest of the craft by a thick brass door, this leafy enclosure formed Ack-Ack Macaque's personal and private sanctuary and, at first, the monkeys guarding it didn't want to let her in.

"He's in a foul mood," warned the one wearing a leather vest.

Victoria tugged at the rope around Berg's neck, making him stumble forwards.

"He'll be in a worse one by the time I'm through with him. Now, are you going to let me past or not?"

The monkeys exchanged glances. They knew who she was, yet were obviously nervous about troubling their leader. Finally the older of the two, a grey-muzzled macaque with a thick gold ring in his right ear, stood aside.

"Go ahead, ma'am."

"Thank you."

Victoria pushed open the heavy door and stepped inside. The chamber was a vast vault occupying the forward portion of the airship's main hull. The floor had been covered in reed matting, on which stood hundreds of large ceramic pots. Palm trees and other jungle plants grew from the pots, forming a canopy overhead, and it took her a minute or so to make her way through the trees to the wooden verandah overlooking the interior of the craft's glass bow. Birds and butterflies twitched hither and thither among the branches. The air smelled like the interior of a greenhouse.

ACK-ACK MACAQUE STOOD at the verandah's rail, hands clasped behind his back and a fat cigar clamped in his teeth. He didn't turn as Victoria walked up behind him.

"You're back," he said.

"I am."

From where he stood, he could see the sea fort and the blue waters of the Channel.

"Any luck?"

"Some."

She took her prisoner by the shoulder and pushed him down, into a kneeling position on the planks at his feet. Ack-Ack Macaque looked down with his one good eye.

"Who's that?"

"Cassius Berg."

The monkey gave the man an experimental prod with his shoe.

"Didn't you kill that fucker once already?"

"Not on this timeline."

Ack-Ack frowned at her. Her face was pale despite

her exertions, and her eyes were red and tired-looking. He could see she hadn't slept well in several days. "And your other self? Did you find her?"

"We were too late."

A wrought-iron patio table stood a little way along the verandah. Behind it stood a wheeled drinks cabinet filled with bottles of all shapes and sizes. Victoria left Berg kneeling where he was and walked over and helped herself to a vodka martini.

A parrot squawked in one of the higher branches, its plumage red against the canopy's khaki and emerald.

Six weeks ago, Ack-Ack Macaque had tried to talk her out of getting involved with another version of herself but, predictably, she hadn't listened—and he'd had more than enough to do trying to keep control of his monkey army. The problem with being the alpha monkey was that they all looked to him to tell them what to do and arbitrate all their pathetic squabbles. When faced with any kind of decision, they were more than happy to pass the responsibility up the chain of command until it dropped into his lap. It was the way primate troupes worked; it was also the way the military worked, and he didn't like it. It was a pain in the hole. He was used to being a maverick, a grunt, an ace pilot rather than an Air Marshal. Being a leader cramped his style.

Considering the figure at his feet, he said, "What are we going to do with him?"

Victoria took a sip from the glass, and wiped her lips on the back of her gloved hand.

"He's a cyborg, same as before. A human brain in an artificial body."

Ack-Ack Macaque twitched his nostrils. The man smelled like an old, wet raincoat. He gave the guy a nudge and, arms still cuffed behind him, Berg tipped over onto his side.

"It's definitely him, though?"

He watched as Victoria swirled the clear liquid in the bottom of her glass.

"*Mais oui,*" she said. "And you realise what this means, don't you?"

Ack-Ack Macaque scowled at her.

"Should I?"

"It means Nguyen's on this parallel, too."

Ack-Ack Macaque's hackles rose. His scowl turned to a snarl, and his fingers went to his hips, where two silver Colts shone in their holsters.

"Where is he?"

"Paris, I think. An operation calling itself the Malsight Institute. I had K8 pull up some information on it."

"And?"

"Officially it doesn't exist. There's nothing about it until two years ago. Rumours, conspiracy theories, that sort of thing. Very secretive, government money. Black research. Heavy security."

"Sounds familiar."

"If he's there, and he's building another robot army, we have to stop him."

Ack-Ack Macaque growled, deep in his throat. Doctor Nguyen had been the man responsible for creating them both in his laboratories—their own personal Frankenstein. He took the cigar from his lips and rolled it in his fingers.

"We leave in an hour," he decided. He was overdue

for some action, and, after spending the last six weeks trying to sort out the complaints and squabbles of a troupe of irritable, irresponsible monkeys, he was itching to bust some skulls. "Reactivate your husband and recall the crew."

"What are you going to do?"

"What do you think I'm going to do?" His lips curled back, revealing his sharp yellow fangs. He clamped the cigar back between his teeth. Leathery fingers bunched into fists. "If Nguyen's here, I'm going to grab the bastard by the ears and rip his fucking head off."

CHAPTER THREE
ASSHOLE VARIATIONS

ON THE AIRSHIP's bridge, Paul shimmered into apparent solidity. He blinked, removed his rimless spectacles, and rubbed his eyes.

"Ah, Vicky."

His image was a hologram projected by a small drone, about the size and shape of a dragonfly, which hovered behind his eyes. It portrayed him as he had been before his death: spiky peroxide hair, gold ear stud, and a loud Hawaiian shirt under a long white lab coat.

"How are you feeling?"

"Me? I'm perfectly, um—" He frowned down at the glasses in his hand, as if seeing them for the first time.

"Fine?" she suggested.

He jumped, as if startled. "What? Oh yes. Fine. Perfectly fine."

"Are you still hooked into the main computer?"

"I am."

"Then warm up the engines, we're leaving."

She walked over and lowered herself into the captain's chair. She knew Ack-Ack Macaque wouldn't mind.

Below, the members of the ragtag monkey army emerged from the doors and windows of the sea fort.

Some were clothed, others were not; but all carried weapons, either slung on their backs or gripped in their teeth. She watched them swarm up the mooring ropes and suppressed a shiver.

"As soon as they're all aboard, head for France," she said. "And tell K8 to leave the plane and get her butt up here, or she's going to get left behind."

"And Cole?"

"*Merde.*" She'd forgotten the writer. "Where is he?"

"The Lake District."

"And Lila's with him?"

"Lila?"

"His daughter."

"Ah yes, of course. I think so."

"Can you get a call through to them?"

"I'll do my best." Paul's image wavered and froze as he turned his attention to the airship's communication systems. Victoria sat back in her chair, allowing her coat to fall open around her. After a few seconds, one of the screens blanked, and then cleared to show the face of a middle-aged man with wild grey hair.

"Hello, Captain, what can I do for you?" The picture was shaky and showed the man's face from below. Cole was hiking in the hills above Lake Windermere, and talking into a handheld phone. His cheeks were red and he was out of breath.

"We're moving the ship, Cole."

"And you want us to come back?'

She shook her head. "There isn't time. We're going to Paris. We'll try to pick you up afterwards."

William Cole stopped walking. The air wheezed between his lips.

"Don't hurry on our behalf," he said. Behind him, Victoria glimpsed sunlit hills curled with brown autumn bracken and, far below, the waters of the lake.

"We'll be back," she promised. "But maybe not for a while."

"What are you going to do?"

"Something illegal."

"Well, don't worry on our account." He scratched the grey fuzz on his chin. "We're happy enough here. We found Marie and everything's great. In fact…" He looked away from the camera and the wind ruffled his hair.

"What?"

"Well, we were thinking of staying here," he said. "Permanently."

Victoria felt a pang of disappointment. "Is that what you both really want?"

"I think so. I mean it's quiet here. Things are going well with Marie. We've found a cottage, and I've started writing again."

Victoria took off her fur cap and ran a hand over the bristles of her scalp. Thrown together by chance, she and Cole had become friends over the past two years, and she'd be sad to lose him—especially as he was one of the last humans left among the airship's crew. With him and Lila gone, only Victoria and K8 remained, the only two women on a Zeppelin full of primates.

"Then I wish you luck." She drew herself up in her chair. "You and Lila. After everything that's happened, you both deserve some peace."

Cole smiled.

"As do we all, Captain. As do we all."

*   *   *

FIFTEEN MINUTES LATER, the gigantic airship rose from the fort and turned its two-kilometre hull eastwards towards France. Once, it had belonged to the leader of the Gestalt; now it belonged to the monkey army, a prize taken in battle and rechristened in honour of its new masters. At first, the monkeys had simply called it 'Big Sky Thing'. It was only recently, at the urging of the troupe's more erudite members, that Ack-Ack Macaque had officially renamed it *Sun Wukong*, after the monkey king of Chinese myth, who was born from a stone and went on to rebel against Heaven itself. Reclining on the bridge, Victoria watched the blue waters of the English Channel wheel beneath. The coast of France lay against the horizon like a green and purple cloud.

Back we go…

She gripped the arms of the chair. Unlike the world she called home, on this parallel France and England were separate countries, and she guessed the French wouldn't be too keen at the prospect of a heavily armed dreadnought ploughing through their airspace.

Still, it's not as if they've got anything big enough to shoot us down.

For a moment, her thoughts turned back to the apartment, and the blonde woman lying dead on the parquet floor.

Just let them try…

Over the past two years, she'd seen dozens of worlds, each a little different to the last. She'd seen versions of Europe riven by war and famine;

versions ruled over by resurgent British, German or Roman Empires; and versions controlled by every '-ism' under the sun, from capitalism to communism to religious fundamentalism. She'd walked their streets listening to the *put-put-put* of steam-driven cars; seen gleaming supersonic airliners cleave the skies; watched gigantic Soviet hovercraft patrol the Thames Estuary; and taken a ride through a Transatlantic Tunnel wide enough for four lanes of traffic. And in all that time, on all those worlds, had encountered nothing capable of putting more than the most cursory of dents in the *Sun Wukong*'s armour plate.

"All engines online and showing green," reported Paul.

Victoria glanced around at the bare metal walls with their lines of rivets. She'd been away for a month and half, and now saw the cold, spartan interior with fresh eyes. She knew the monkeys didn't care about the lack of décor, but she missed the shabby elegance of her old skyliner, the *Tereshkova*. At least she had the bridge of this vessel pretty much to herself. Paul could run the ship, it didn't need a crew; and none of the monkeys were all that interested in acting like one. To them, the airship was simply a moving home—a means to get from one adventure to the next. Even Ack-Ack Macaque came up here only occasionally. He was happy in his potted jungle, and could issue commands from there as well as anywhere.

Victoria tapped her nails against the chair's armrests.

"Then, full speed ahead, all engines."

"Aye."

At the rear of the dreadnought, on a forest of engine nacelles, huge black blades began to turn. Moving slowly at first, they gradually increased their speed until they blurred into whirring grey discs, and the vast craft to which they were attached began to slide reluctantly forwards, slowly picking up momentum. Sunlight glimmered from its gun turrets and sensor pods. Two thousand metres in length, it moved like an eclipse across the world's busiest shipping lane, its rippling shadow dwarfing even the largest of the Channel's car ferries and container ships.

Victoria Valois felt the vibration of the airship's engines through the gondola's steel deck and smiled. Even though they were riding into battle, it was comforting to be airborne again, and to know that she rode the largest flying machine this particular version of the Earth had ever seen.

STANDING AT THE window of her cabin, K8 looked out through a ten-inch thick porthole. Despite her exertions with the seaplane, she still wore her habitual white skirt and blouse. It was her uniform now, as seemly and natural as blue jeans and a black t-shirt had been to her younger self.

"We're not a child any more. We're nearly twenty."

Beside her, Ack-Ack Macaque scratched at the leather patch covering his left eye.

"Yeah, but—"

"You can't stop us."

"I fucking can."

She looked him in the eye. "No, you fucking can't."

He watched her cross her arms across her chest, and turn back to the window. Her hair looked bronze in the light; her freckles like sprinkles fallen across her nose and cheeks. He pulled the cigar from his mouth and rolled it between finger and thumb.

"So, what am I supposed to do?"

She didn't look around.

"Just take us somewhere we can connect back into the hive mind."

Ack-Ack sighed. He watched the smoke twisting in the cabin's air.

"This is partly my fault, isn't it?"

K8 made a scornful noise. "Of course it's your fault. It's your *entire* fault. You gave us to the hive."

"I didn't have a choice."

"We never said you did." She hunched her shoulders. "We just need to get back, to reconnect."

"But why?"

She hugged herself, gripping her upper arms. "You wouldn't understand."

Ack-Ack Macaque frowned. He could see sweat on her lip.

"I thought you'd be better off here," he said, "cut off from the rest of them."

"You were wrong."

"Well, excuse me."

K8 winced at his sarcasm. She passed a hand across her face, and turned to face him. "Look, we're sorry, okay? We know you were trying to help. It's just tough for us now, to be alone."

"Tell me about it."

"This is different."

Ack-Ack Macaque sat heavily on the edge of the

bed. "I don't see how. So you're the only Gestalt drone on this rock. Big whoop. I spent years as the world's only talking monkey."

"But now you have an army."

He grinned. "Yeah, but most of them are assholes."

K8 looked him in the eye, expression serious. "Most of them are variations of you."

"Asshole variations."

"Well, imagine losing them." She straightened the hem of her jacket with a tug. "Imagine going back to being the only one of your kind after being surrounded by all those others. How do you think that would feel?"

Ack-Ack Macaque shifted his position on the bed, getting more comfortable on the mussed blankets.

"Pretty shitty," he admitted.

"Well, that's what we're going through. The majority of the Gestalt aren't fanatics. Only the leaders were evil. Most of the drones are ordinary, decent people caught up in something bigger than themselves. And they welcomed us. They took us for who we were and welcomed us. For the first time in our life, we felt truly accepted; truly part of a family."

"The 'first time', huh?"

"Don't be like that." She stuck her chin forward. "We come from a broken home. Our only friend was a talking monkey."

"I thought we were doing okay."

"We were." She rapped the side of her head. "But now it's too quiet. We can't stand it."

Ack-Ack Macaque looked down at his hairy hands.

"I'm sorry," he said. "If I could get that computer stuff out of your head..."

"We don't want it out."

He pulled a cigar from the inside pocket of his flight jacket.

"Then what should I do? I can't just give you back to the hive."

"It's what we want. We need to be whole again."

"But, Nguyen—"

"We'll help you with Nguyen. But after that, you take us back, okay?"

He huffed air through his cheeks. He could tell she wasn't going to drop the subject, and he couldn't be bothered to argue any more. Best just to agree now and deal with the consequences later.

"Okay," he said.

"You promise?"

Ack-Ack Macaque screwed the cigar into his lips and lit it. All he wanted was some peace and quiet. "Sure."

"Then we have a deal."

"Thank fuck for that."

K8 uncrossed her arms and perched beside him. "What do you need us to do?"

Ack-Ack suppressed a yawn. "I need you to get on the jump engines and plot our escape. I don't want to hang around after we've trashed Nguyen's lab. I can do without a run-in with the French air force."

K8 raised an eyebrow. "That doesn't sound like you, Skipper."

"Maybe I'm getting old."

"Seriously?"

"We're about to attack a civilian government

contractor." He blew at the tip of his cigar, watching the cherry-red ember flare. "The French are going to take that as an act of terrorism. They'll send planes."

"They don't have anything that can hurt us."

"Not straight away." Ack-Ack Macaque got to his feet and shambled to the door. "But as soon as we shoot one of them down, they'll send ten more. We'll be fighting a war and, frankly, I'm just too tired for all that crap." He scratched his belly. Some mornings, he ached all over, and he had to get up at least twice every night to take a piss.

"So, you want us to go in fast, hit them hard, and then vanish?"

"Bingo." He turned the handle and stepped out into the gangway beyond. "Oh, and K8?"

"Yes, Skip?"

"Try to find us somewhere nice, okay?"

"Define 'nice'."

"Ah, you know." He waved a hand. "All the usual shit. White sand, blue sea, coconut trees. *No incoming fire*."

"You want us to plot a course back to Kishkindha?"

Ack-Ack Macaque let his shoulders and cigar droop.

"If you must."

MEANWHILE, AS THE *Sun Wukong* crossed the coast of France, Victoria stood on the verandah inside the airship's glass nose. Paul's image stood beside her. Together, they watched the craft's shadow pass over the white waves and yellow beaches of the Normandy shore, and Victoria caught herself wondering how many human bones lay forever buried in those deceptively welcoming sands. Was there anywhere in Europe that hadn't been a battlefield at least once? She squeezed the verandah's bamboo rail. Behind her, in the potted forest, birds chirped and squawked.

"So," she said.

Paul gave her a sideways glance. "So?"

"This forgetfulness…"

He made a face. "I know what you're going to say."

"You're supposed to be running this ship."

"I know, I know." He looked down at his red baseball boots, and rubbed the side of his nose with the index finger of his right hand. "It's just, I get these headaches."

Victoria blew air through pursed lips. "*Merde.*"

"What?"

"You're the expert, you tell me."

Paul looked up at the sky. "You think I'm de-cohering?"

"You've lasted a lot longer than most."

He sighed. "Maybe you're right."

"Seriously?"

"Don't think it hasn't occurred to me. Don't think that, since I found I was a back-up, I haven't thought about it every single minute of every single day." He waved his arms in exasperation. "How do you think it feels to realise you have a built-in expiry date?"

Victoria watched as his image walked to the wrought iron table and appeared to flop onto one of its attendant chairs.

"What can we do?" she asked.

He gave an angry shrug. "How the hell would I know?"

"You know more than most."

"Still not enough."

They fell silent. Below, the beaches had given way to brown fields and winding lanes.

"I don't want to do it," Victoria said quietly, "but, if you need me to, I can always switch you off, permanently."

Paul's eyes widened. "No. No, absolutely not. Why would you say that?"

She walked over and crouched in front of him, wishing she could take his hand in hers.

"Then, I'll be here for you," she promised, "as long as you need me."

Paul looked down at her. His forehead wrinkled. "Do I sense a 'but'?"

Victoria rocked backwards on her heels. "But I think we should disengage you from some of the airship's more vital systems."

She let out a breath.

There, I've said it.

The apparition on the chair blinked at her from behind his spectacles. "You think I can't handle this?"

"It doesn't matter what I think."

"Of course it does." He leaned forward. "Vicky, I need to know that you believe in me."

"Of course I believe in you." She felt flustered. "But you've lasted so long, so much longer than anybody else in your position. I just—"

"What?"

"I think we need to take precautions."

His chin dropped to his chest, and his eyes closed. When he finally spoke, his voice was small and tired. "Look, I know you're right. But, not just yet, okay?"

"Then, when?"

He raised his eyes to her. "I don't know. I want to be useful. I know I'm deteriorating, but there's something I want to do first, before..." He coughed, stumbling over his words. "Before the end."

"What?"

"It's a surprise. I just need a bit of time. Can you give me that?"

Hands pressing on her thighs, Victoria pushed herself back up onto her feet. "I don't know. If you start to—"

"If I endanger the ship, you can cut me out of the loop. I'll rig up a protocol."

She chewed her lower lip. The *Sun Wukong* was a monster: two thousand metres of gasbags, aluminium struts and thick armour plating, powered by dozens of nuclear-electric turbines. If something went wrong and it crashed into a populated area, the devastation would be appalling.

Paul looked at her over the rim of his glasses. "Please?"

Victoria took a deep breath. She couldn't refuse him; she never could. He was like a little boy. "Okay, for now. But the second you start to have any doubts, you tell me."

"I love you."

She felt her cheeks redden. "I know. I love you too."

Paul's nervous smile was like the sun coming out from behind a cloud. He jumped to his feet. "In that case, let's go and cause some trouble."

Victoria grinned despite herself. She wiped her eyes on the back of her wrist, and drew herself up to her full height. Further discussion could wait. For now, it was time to focus on the task at hand.

"Right," she said, "give me full speed ahead and don't stop for anything."

"There isn't anything that *can* stop us, short of a nuclear blast."

"Well, let's hope we don't run into any of those."

"Amen to that. Now, hold on tight. I'm putting us on an…" He clicked his fingers, searching for the right words. "Um…"

"Attack approach?"

"Yeah." He looked sheepish. Victoria rolled her eyes.

"Oh, *mon dieu*."

CHAPTER FOUR
PHOENIX EGGS

FROM THE WINDOW of his office on the third floor of Buckingham Palace, Merovech watched the rain falling over London. On the mahogany desk behind him, sheaves of paperwork awaited his attention and his inbox bulged with unanswered email. He wasn't in the mood to pay either more than a cursory glance. He'd rolled up his shirtsleeves and loosened his black tie. A glass of single malt nestled, half forgotten, in his hand.

At first, he'd intended to remain king only as long as it took to restore national calm following the death of his parents and the revelation of his mother's complicity in an attempted coup d'état. But that had been three years ago, before the Gestalt invasion and the death of his fiancée. Since then, everything had changed. The world had become stranger and more threatening than anybody could have guessed, and his Commonwealth needed him. They needed a figurehead and a sense of continuity, and he was the most qualified to offer both. Whatever the secret truth of his origins—that he'd been cloned in a lab from one of his mother's cells—he'd been raised to be monarch, and nobody else had his level of training or preparation. His people needed him and, truth be told, he needed them. With Julie gone, he had nothing else.

The rain blew across the Mall, shaking the leafless trees lining the road. Car headlights shimmered through the gloom. To the east, a twin-hulled skyliner thrummed its way upriver, following the twists and turns of the Thames. Its navigation lights blinked red and green. As he watched, it passed behind the forest of cranes towering over Westminster, where the government buildings were still being rebuilt, rising like misshapen, blocky phoenix eggs from the craters left by the Gestalt's bombardment.

How many times had this city rebuilt itself? The inhabitants seemed used to chaos and ruin; in fact, they seemed to revel in their resilience. From the destruction wrought by Boudicca, and then the Great Fire of 1666, through to bomb attacks by the IRA and Al Qaeda, via the Zeppelin raids of the First World War and the Blitzkrieg pummelling of the Second, Londoners had always been fiercely proud of their ability to keep calm and carry on, even in the most trying of circumstances. And these past two years had been no exception. Faced with a baffling multiverse of potential threats, the capital was doing what it had always done: going about its daily life with scarcely more than a shrug and tut. As long as the Tube ran, the people were happy. Whereas other cities such as Pompeii, Petra, Hashima Island, and Detroit had fallen by the wayside during London's two thousand years of history, the Mother of All Cities had simply endured, and always would.

Looking down, Merovech remembered the glass

in his hand, and raised it to his lips. Set against the ravages of the past, the damage left by the Gestalt—a few dozen bomb craters, some demolished buildings—seemed minor and ephemeral, a hiss and a pop in history's sizzling pan; but that was only until you remembered the three thousand dead bodies that had been pulled from the rubble. Three thousand innocent men, women and children who had been caught in a conflict they couldn't possibly have foreseen or understood, killed in a surprise attack.

He rinsed the whisky around his teeth. His wife had been among them. At least, she would have been his wife if she'd lived. The date of their wedding had been set, and the preparations had been under way. Then a Gestalt dreadnought appeared in the skies over London and showered missiles on Whitehall.

When the assault came, Julie had been in a car, on her way to shelter. She'd been crossing Westminster Bridge at the exact moment the parliament buildings took their first hit. A swerving lorry crushed her car through the stone parapet, into the Thames.

Merovech drained his glass.

She hadn't stood a chance.

With her gone, he had nothing. He had no mother or father, no brothers or sisters, hardly any friends. He felt like a refugee from a vanished land—alone, and the last of his kind. Even the damned monkey had disappeared. All that kept him going was his duty; the same duty he'd once spurned and sworn to resign.

Three thousand had died in London, but similar numbers had also been killed in all the other cities that had been targeted. In the aftermath of all that tumult and loss, the survivors craved stability. They desperately needed a leader they could count on; somebody whose familiarity would provide permanence and comfort in a world turned outlandish and unsafe; somebody to be a focus for their grief, and embody their hopes for the future. And so he toured the cities that had suffered in the attack; he cut ribbons at construction sites and waved for cameras; he visited schools and factories and spoke about hope and faith and the importance of rebuilding the country; and then, when he came home, he locked himself in his office, away from the public gaze, and drank whisky until the footmen came to pour him into bed.

He watched the twin-hulled skyliner until it disappeared. Then he turned to the bottle on his desk, ready to refill his glass. As he unscrewed the cap, he heard a soft knock at the office door.

"Come in."

The door opened and his personal secretary stepped into the room.

"Your Majesty."

"Amy?" The neck of the bottle clinked against the rim of his glass as he refilled it. "What are you doing here so late?"

"We have a bit of a situation, sir."

Amy Llewellyn still wore the same clothes she'd been wearing earlier in the day, but now she'd discarded her suit jacket, loosened her collar, and pushed the sleeves of her blouse up to the elbows.

"A situation?" Carefully, he replaced the bottle on the desk and fastened the cap. Then he picked up his drink. "I thought I'd asked to be left alone."

"This won't wait, sir."

Fatigue clawed at him. He gave them body and soul during the day. Why couldn't they leave him in peace in the evening?

"What is it?"

Amy blew a loose strand of hair from in front of her face. "We've received a message."

He sighed. "Are you sure it can't wait?"

She swallowed, and shook her head. "It's from your mother, sir."

Merovech's fingers tightened on the glass. "My mother's dead."

"Quite so."

"Then what are you talking about?"

"She made a back-up, sir."

Merovech felt his knees begin to shake. He'd seen his mother die, blown to fragments by her own hand grenade. He leaned against the desk. "Where is it? Where's it calling from?"

Without asking, Amy turned over a clean glass and poured herself a drink.

"You're not going to like this, sir."

He watched her put the top back on the bottle, and noticed her hands were shaking.

"Just tell me."

Amy swallowed nervously, and cleared her throat.

"The transmission appears to have originated on, um, Mars."

CHAPTER FIVE
HAIRY FRIENDS

CASSIUS BERG'S SPINDLY frame lay strapped to a bunk in the airship's infirmary. Victoria looked down at him with distaste. Even in sleep, his leering smile remained fixed and permanent.

The Smiling Man.

Once, on her world, he'd been a figure of nightmare and terror, a killer with the face of a clown and the dead eyes of a snake. He'd haunted her nightmares. He'd killed Paul and tried to kill her. And then she'd thrown him out of the *Tereshkova*'s cargo bay, and thought it was over. She'd thought he was gone for good, little suspecting she'd run into another version of him, in an alternate version of Paris, on another timeline altogether.

This new version of Berg looked even more like a corpse than the first one had. His skin was pale almost to the point of translucence, and had been stretched tightly across his scalp and cheekbones. Metal staples held it in place, each at the centre of a circle of red and puckered flesh. His black overcoat reeked of mildew and stale cigarettes.

She looked around at the dozen or so monkeys crowding the bed.

"Wake him up," she said.

A grizzled capuchin tapped Berg on the forehead with the flat side of a meat cleaver.

Victoria looked down and straightened her tunic. It was a red one with gold buttons and a silver scabbard on a white silk sash, and it had once belonged to her elderly Russian godfather, the Commodore. It was the only thing of his to have survived the crash of his old skyliner, the *Tereshkova*; and it had only survived because she had been wearing it at the time, having donned it for luck in the battle against the Gestalt.

For this confrontation, she had left her head bare, displaying her scars—scars the other Berg had given her during their first clash.

On the bed, the new Berg's eyelids flickered. He blinked up at the hairy faces and bared fangs around him and jerked against his restraints.

"What's happening?"

"I'm happening, Mister Berg." Victoria stepped forward and bent slightly, bringing her face a little closer to his. "I trust you remember me from this morning?"

"Let me go."

Victoria shook her head, keeping her expression immobile and unfriendly. "I'm afraid not. I have some questions for you."

"I mean it. I have powerful friends. If—"

"As you can see, I have angry, hairy friends, Mister Berg, with sharp teeth and bad tempers. Now, let's take all your bluster as read, shall we? Because, from where I'm standing, you're in no position to be making threats."

He glared at her.

"When I get free from these straps, I *will* make it my business to kill you."

Victoria wagged a finger. "If you get free from those straps, Mister Berg, these guys will *eat* you."

She brushed at a speck of dust on her tunic, making the medals clink and jangle, and let her other hand rest on the pommel of her sword. Around the bed, the monkeys chattered and whooped, and did their best to look fierce and hungry. They brandished swords and knives. One, a brawny howler monkey, carried an old fire axe.

Berg looked around at them, and stopped straining against his straps.

"I won't talk."

"Yes, you will."

He cocked his head. "How can you be so sure?"

"Because we've done this before, you and I." Victoria tried not to shudder at the memory. "Last time we spoke, you were dangling out of the back of a skyliner and, when push came to shove, you told me everything I needed to know."

Berg's brows furrowed. "What on Earth are you talking about?"

"We've met before, Mister Berg, on another timeline. You may have killed the Victoria from this world—you may have killed a whole lot of people for that matter—but, where I come from, *you're* the one who's dead." She rocked back on her heels and folded her arms. The overhead light twinkled across the frayed gold braid on her cuffs. "So, keeping that in mind, I want you to tell me about your boss, Doctor Nguyen. We know he's at the Malsight

Institute; I just need you to tell me on which floor to find his office."

Berg licked his lips, his tongue darting like a lizard's, scenting the air.

"Go to hell."

Victoria sighed. "Please, Mister Berg. This is your last chance to be helpful." She looked around at the motley troupe of primates assembled around the bed. "Otherwise I'm going to have to ask my friends here to start getting creative with you."

She gave a nod to the capuchin. The little creature had a swollen head, deformed by the artificial processors crammed into its skull, and a row of sturdy input jacks protruding from its back like the spines of a dinosaur. At her signal, it inched forward, raising its cleaver above the captive's forehead.

Berg's flat and expressionless eyes looked up at the blade.

Then, with a roar of anger, he sat up. The leather straps at his wrists stretched and snapped. With the speed of a striking snake, he clamped a hand around the little monkey's neck and snapped its spine like a used match.

Aghast, Victoria threw out a hand.

"Stop!"

But it was too late. With an angry shriek, the rest of the troupe fell on him. Berg writhed and lashed out with his hands and feet, but they were too numerous, too close. Blades flashed. He used his forearm to block one sword, but two more skewered him through the ribs. He cried out, sounding more indignant than hurt, and tried to swing his legs off the table, but that only exposed his back, and a gibbon with patchy fur took the opportunity to sink a foot-long carving knife into the hollow between his shoulder blades.

Victoria stepped backwards to the door, hands covering her ears.

"Stop," she cried again, but they couldn't hear her over their own frenzied screeching. Horrified, she watched Berg sway to his feet. He had a sword stuck right through his chest, and she could see both ends of it. However, it didn't seem to be slowing him down. With a single bone-crunching backhand, he slapped a Japanese macaque against the wall, crushing its skull.

"Stop!"

His smile turned in her direction and their eyes locked. The monkeys were just an inconvenience to him. He had promised to kill her, and he intended to make good on that vow. As if in a nightmare, Victoria drew her own sword. Berg moved towards her as if moving through water, monkeys hanging from his arms and legs, weighing him down. As she watched, he reached around and pulled one of the knives from his back. He held the red, slick blade by the point, and drew his hand back, ready to throw it.

"Goodbye, Miss Valois."

Victoria flattened herself against the door. She didn't have time to access her internal clock. She'd have to rely on her natural reactions. But he moved so *fast*...

Behind him, the howler monkey leapt from the bed. Still in the air, it swung its axe. Howlers were among the largest of all monkeys, and its arms were twin cables of elastic muscle. Hearing its cry, Berg glanced around, and the blade caught him across the bridge of his nose. The top of his skull came away like the top of a boiled egg, and he collapsed, dragged down and submerged beneath a tide of biting, clawing, stabbing beasts.

CHAPTER SIX
KISHKINDHA

BALI SAT CROSS-LEGGED on a sun-warmed rock, waiting for the leopard. His tail twitched. He knew the big cat was stalking him, and had been for some minutes now. He was at the upper limit of the jungle, where the trees grew sparse and petered out like a green wave breaking against the volcano's curving flank. Below, he could see most of the island and, beyond its treetops, the narrow strait dividing the island from the rest of the peninsula. Sunlight danced on the water. A couple of miles from where he sat, smoke rose from a clearing, marking the position of the stockade where the other members of the monkey army, gathered and brought here by Ack-Ack Macaque and the *Sun Wukong*, awaited him.

Humans, it seemed, had uplifted at least one primate on every parallel world visited by the airship. As soon as they had the technology, they created an intelligent ape or monkey. Privately, Bali wondered if they did it because they were lonely. Once, the humans had shared their worlds with other intelligent hominids, such as *Homo erectus* and the Neanderthals; but then those species had died away, leaving *Homo sapiens* home alone, with only themselves to talk to.

It must have been terribly lonely for them, he thought. No wonder their stories were filled with fairies, pixies, vampires and other half-human creatures.

But was that loneliness what had driven them to upgrade other primates?

Life for most of the uplifted creatures had not been pleasant. Some bore lingering pain from the surgery that had increased their intelligence; others simply pined for more of their kind, or for a release from captivity. Some, like Ack-Ack Macaque, had been plugged into virtual reality environments, such as games or targeting systems; while others lived out their days in laboratories or cages.

Now, thanks to Ack-Ack Macaque, they were all free. They had this island, which they'd named after the monkey kingdom in the story of the *Ramayana*; and they had each other. And, while Ack-Ack Macaque was away with the *Sun Wukong*, Bali had command. In the big guy's absence, he was the alpha male.

And so it had fallen to him to kill the leopard.

He could feel it behind him in the shadows, and imagine it edging closer and closer, its belly brushing the leaves of the forest floor, haunches trembling, muscles coiled and ready to strike, spotted fur quivering.

Not today, mon ami.

In his lap, Bali held an automatic pistol and a hunting knife. All he needed was to draw the animal to him, and bring it close enough for a clean shot, or a deft strike with the blade.

The beast had been hanging around the camp for

a couple of weeks. In that time, it had taken a lamb and half a dozen chickens. Then, last night, it had attacked and killed one of the chimps as they were out gathering firewood. How it got onto the island, nobody knew. Bali's best guess was that it must have swum across the strait from the mainland, but he had no idea what could have driven it to attempt such an arduous feat, unless it had been drawn by cooking smells and the promise of fresh monkey meat.

He glanced down at the knife in his left hand. When he killed the leopard, he had decided he'd gut it and wear its skin as a trophy. He would walk back into the stockade draped in the pelt and blood of the vanquished beast. A display like that would impress the rest of the troupe, and strengthen his position as alpha. It might even convince a few of them that he should be running the show, rather than Ack-Ack Macaque. After all, where was their precious leader now that they needed him? Swanking around the multiverse in his dreadnought with the women, while the rest of them were here in the jungle, facing down predators and building a civilisation from scratch, with little in the way of luxury—and no females.

Bali felt his lips draw back from his sharp incisors. If he were in charge, things would be different. Good lord, yes. Less crude, more forward thinking, more *businesslike*. And there would be females! Even if he had to raid a zoo, he would find some.

To hell with trying to build a homeland of our own, he thought. What could be more inefficient? With their numbers and the dreadnought, they could take one by force, rather than carving it from the jungle by hand. There were so many human worlds. Surely they could find a lightly defended one that was ripe for a management takeover, with plenty of human slaves to do their bidding? After everything they'd suffered at the hands of the humans, surely they were owed a modicum of revenge, not to mention compensation?

Before being picked up by the *Sun Wukong*, Bali had been kept in a temple, chained to a wall and fed by the monks. They had taken him in following his escape from the laboratory that created him. The monks revered him as an aspect of their monkey god, Hanuman, and he'd enjoyed being pampered. Despite the chain, he had been looked after and respected, and he missed that. He had liked being a god. His grip tightened on the knife. He would be one again. When he became the true and undisputed alpha, he would fashion himself as a fearsome leopard god, falling from the skies to plunder world after world. Instead of hiding here, on an empty parallel devoid of humans, he and his brethren would avenge themselves on their creators. They would gather riches and power—and, most importantly, females—and he would be the true, one-and-only alpha, forever.

His nostrils quivered. On the breeze, he caught the barest hint of cat; a fleeting waft of spice, sweat and blood. The beast must be close now. Slowly, so as not to startle it, he rose to his feet, gun held out to his right, knife to his left, naked save for the elasticated straps of his shoulder holster.

He felt invincible.

"Okay, *mon ami*, I am here, and I am ready." His eyes swept the shadows and dapples between the trees, his ears strained for the stealthiest sound.

"Now, where are you?"

CHAPTER SEVEN
SHITS AND GIGGLES

STILL SHAKEN BY the killing frenzy in the infirmary, Victoria summoned the *Sun Wukong*'s command crew to the airship's briefing room. They sat in the front row of chairs, and she leant on the lectern before them. Outside the porthole, dusk had begun to lower.

"Okay," she said, "Let's review what we know about Nguyen."

Ack-Ack Macaque stirred in his seat.

"He's a fuck-head?"

Victoria ignored him. The gelware in her skull had been pumping sedatives into her bloodstream to calm her after the incident with Berg, and she felt lightheaded and in no mood to spar with the gruff old monkey. Instead, she nodded to K8.

"S'il te plaît?"

The white-suited teenager gave a tight smile, and unrolled a keypad. She tapped in a command and a screen lit behind Victoria. It displayed a photograph of a short, balding, middle-aged man with a stethoscope slung around his neck.

"Doctor Kenta Nguyen," K8 said, reading from her notes. "Surgeon and gelware specialist. On our parallel, he was born on the seventh of December 1989, in Osaka, Japan. Mother Japanese, father from Vietnam. He graduated from university in Tokyo in June 2014; went to work on the Human Genome Project; and then went to work for the Céleste Institute, where he helped develop soul-catcher technology and became a pioneer in the field of gelware neural prostheses."

"Blah, blah, blah." Ack-Ack Macaque made talking motions with his hands. "And then in 2059, he tried to blow up the world and turn everybody into robots. Yeah, we know the story." He sat back in his chair. "I just don't see what good talking about it's going to do. I don't need to understand the guy." He made his fingers into the shape of a gun and took aim at an imaginary target. "I just need to know *where* he is."

Victoria put her hands on her hips. "And then what are you going to do? You just want to shoot him?"

Ack-Ack Macaque's grizzled face frowned in puzzlement.

"Well, yes." His expression split into a toothy grin. "Something like that, anyway. You know the old saying, boss: revenge is a dish best served hot, from ten thousand feet."

"You want to bomb the place?"

"I figure we cruise over and drop half a dozen missiles on the lab. That ought to do it."

"Aerial bombardment?" Victoria shook her head. "That's your answer to everything. Besides, we couldn't be sure we'd got him, and there'd be a lot of innocents caught in the explosions. No, if we're going to do this, we're going to do it face-to-face.

Up close and personal. Before he dies, he's going to know who we are and why we're there to stop him."

The monkey huffed, and stuck out his bottom lip. "Then what do you suggest?"

Victoria drummed her nails on the edge of the lectern. "I suggest you take a small team and infiltrate the lab. Find Nguyen and bring him back on board."

"A quick smash and grab?"

"Precisely."

Ack-Ack Macaque stroked his hairy chin, considering. Then he shrugged.

"Okay, you got my vote. I'm happy as long as I get to wreck stuff and hurt people." He pulled out a fresh cigar and ran it under his nose, savouring the smell.

"Who will you take?"

"Lumpy and Cuddles have commando training. Erik and Fang are handy in a fight."

"*D'accord.*" Victoria folded her hands on top of the lectern. "Take them to the armoury and get what you need. We'll be in position in thirty minutes."

Ack-Ack Macaque stuck the cigar in his mouth, rose to his feet and threw her a floppy salute.

"Aye, boss." He shambled out and K8 followed him, leaving Victoria and Paul by themselves.

Victoria looked at her ex-husband.

"What?" she asked.

Paul shrugged. "Nothing."

"Don't give me that. I know that look. What's wrong?"

Paul pushed his glasses more firmly onto the bridge of his nose.

"I'm just a bit concerned, that's all."

"About what?"

He looked down at his hands.

"About killing Nguyen."

Victoria walked over and sat in the chair next to his. She thought of Berg, and shivered.

"In what sense?"

"In the moral sense." He shifted around to face her. "I mean, I know the Nguyen on our world was a bastard and all, but does that justify us killing his counterpart on *this* parallel? For all we know, the man might be innocent."

He looked so worried that Victoria felt a rush of affection, and had to consciously stop herself from putting an arm around him. She kept forgetting he was only made of light and that, if she tried to touch him, her fingers would pass right through his hologram body, saddening them both.

"I think I understand what you're saying," she said. "But you didn't see Cassisus Berg. He looked exactly as he did before, with human skin over a metal skull. Which means Nguyen's pursuing the same goals he was last time. He's trying to build cyborg bodies for human brains."

Paul looked unconvinced. "But that doesn't mean he's going to try to start a nuclear war, does it?"

"We can't take that chance."

"But what if he's innocent?"

Victoria clenched her jaw. "He's not."

"How can you be so sure?"

She crossed her legs. "If he had nothing to hide, he wouldn't have sent Berg to kill me. The other me, in Paris."

"I suppose."

He still looked doubtful. She let him mull her words over for a moment, then asked, "How are you feeling otherwise?"

He gave her a wary look. "I'm fine."

"Are you sure? Because I'm counting on you to fly this thing."

He looked away. "I won't let you down."

Victoria clasped her hands on her knee.

Merde.

She took a deep breath, and made a decision.

"I'll try not to let you down, either."

"What do you mean?"

Fingers still interlocked, she tapped the ends of her thumbs together. "We won't kill him."

"Seriously?" Paul sat up straight.

Victoria exhaled. She had seen more than enough killing and death for one day—for one lifetime, even—and it disturbed her that assassinating the elderly scientist had been her default response. The man had done some terrible things on her world, but unthinkingly condemning his doppelganger to death put her on dubious moral ground.

"Seriously. Well, we'll try. If we capture him in one piece, then instead of killing him, we can stick him in the brig until we find somewhere safe to maroon him, where he can't do any harm. How about that?"

Paul swallowed.

"Thank you." He looked about to cry.

"No." Victoria gave him a smile that was part affection, part relief. Her conscience might have been asleep at its post, but his was as reliable as ever, and he'd saved her from making an irrevocable decision she might later have regretted. Killing Nguyen on this world would have made her no better than the monkeys in the infirmary, lashing out for vengeance with no thought for morals or justice. "Thank *you*."

HALF AN HOUR later, the *Sun Wukong* reached the outskirts of Paris. Ack-Ack Macaque and his team dropped from its underside, and their black parachutes flowered in the darkness. Below, the Malsight Institute was a large, smoked glass building surrounded by lawns and fountains, and a gradually emptying car park. The time was six o'clock, and workers were packing up for the day and leaving.

"Does this bring back memories, Chief?" Erik called. He was an orangutan, with arms made of sinew and covered in carrot-coloured hair.

Ack-Ack Macaque glared at him with his one good eye.

"Shut up and concentrate."

They came down in a small, square courtyard at the centre of the building. As Ack-Ack Macaque's boots hit the flagstones, he let out a grunt.

I really am getting too old for this crap.

He rolled over and hauled at the lines connecting him to his 'chute, pulling it towards him in great bundled armfuls. By the time he had it gathered, the rest of the team had done likewise, and were stuffing their 'chutes into the courtyard's fountain. He crammed his in as well, and shuffled over to a fire escape.

"Cuddles, get this open."

"Right away, Skip." The young gorilla stalked

forward on his knuckles. He was almost twice the size of Ack-Ack Macaque, and wore a gold chain and a set of specially adapted Ray-Bans. Without preamble, he punched his fist through the thin aluminum door and hauled back, ripping it from its frame.

"Good work." Ack-Ack Macaque drew his revolvers. "Now, the rest of you, inside."

He could feel his lungs heaving in his chest. He wasn't as young as he'd once been, and all those cigars had taken their toll. He was happy to let the younger primates take the lead as he followed them into a corridor lined with offices.

"All right, split up, just like we planned. Cuddles, take the first floor; Lumpy, the second; Erik, the third. I'll check out this one."

He watched them go, scattering startled office workers as they charged towards the stairwell. Then he struck a match against the doorframe and lit his cigar.

Okay.

He knew the younger monkeys thought he'd picked the ground floor in order to avoid tiring himself on the stairs, but that wasn't the reason; at least, not the *only* reason. He thought he knew Nguyen. He'd fought the man before, and had seen what a control freak he was. The old man liked to oversee everything. He wouldn't be stuck away upstairs, he'd be down here, close to his minions and machinery.

Victoria wanted Nguyen alive. Ack-Ack Macaque drew his guns. He wasn't so fussy. He'd happily plug the bastard as soon as look at him. And 'alive' didn't necessarily mean 'intact'.

He was at the corner of the building. The corridor led off in two directions. His team had gone left, towards the stairs, so he set off right. Men and women in white coats manned the offices and laboratories he passed, with pens and surgical instruments sticking from their pockets. They smelled of anesthetic and disinfectant, and cowered back when he snarled at them.

"You!" He waved one of his Colts in the face of a young man carrying a pile of box files. "Where's Nguyen?"

The files clattered to the floor and the man raised an arm.

"That way," he stammered. "In the lab. Last door, at the end."

Ack-Ack Macaque grinned around his cigar.

"Thanks, kid."

As he stalked towards the laboratory, Ack-Ack Macaque took an earpiece from his pocket and thumbed it into his left ear.

"We're inside," he said.

The earpiece hissed, and then Victoria's voice came on the line.

"Understood," she said. "Deploy the drone."

"Aye, aye."

Ack-Ack Macaque fished the drone from the pocket of his flight jacket. The tiny machine looked like a jewelled dragonfly with a lens instead of a head. He held it in the palm of his hand and bent his face in close, focusing on it with his single eye.

"Are you getting this?"

"Urgh!"

"What's the matter?"

"Don't get so close to the lens."

"What? Why not?"

"You're holding a high definition camera, and I really don't need to see the inside of your nose in that much detail."

Ack-Ack Macaque huffed, and tossed the little machine into the air. It whirred away in a clatter of miniature blade-like wings.

"Just keep it out of my way," he grumbled.

He heard gunshots and screams from the floors above, followed by the shrill of a fire alarm, and he grinned. He'd handpicked his crew for their expertise at making noise and causing chaos—and it seemed they weren't letting him down.

Ahead, the door to Nguyen's lab remained closed. He holstered one of his guns and tried the handle. Inside, the lab smelled of disinfectant, fear, and monkey shit, and Ack-Ack Macaque felt the hackles rise at the back of his neck. Until Merovech and Julie had busted him out, he'd lived in a lab just like this one, strapped into a couch with wires plugged into his brain.

How many monkeys had he since rescued from a similar plight? It must be getting on for a hundred and fifty now, and yet the smell, with its overtones of surgery and terror, still bothered him. It was a sharp, chemical reminder that he was an artificial, made thing—a prototype weapon manufactured as a proof of concept, and then plugged into a video game because, hey, waste not, want not.

He stepped through the door, and the drone buzzed

past his shoulder. It rose to the ceiling and scanned the room. The lab was a long, narrow and brightly lit room, with an adjoining office. Workbenches lined the walls; medical equipment stood on stainless steel trolleys; and six couches stood in a row down the centre of the room, each with its own simian occupant. Ack-Ack Macaque gripped his guns. At the far end of the lab, two white-coated technicians were bending over the last couch, ministering to the monkey strapped into it. One was a tall, blond man; the other was, unmistakably, Nguyen.

"Hey."

They looked up. For a second, their mouths hung open and their eyes popped. Then the big guy went for his hip pocket and Ack-Ack Macaque shot him. The Colts were deafening in the narrow laboratory. The blond took two bullets in the chest and crashed backwards against a workbench, scattering scalpels and other instruments.

Ack-Ack Macaque and Doctor Nguyen regarded each other through a blue haze of gun smoke and tobacco.

"Remember," Victoria buzzed in Ack-Ack Macaque's ear, "we want him alive."

Ack-Ack swore under his breath. It would be so easy to waste this fucker. All he had to do was pull the trigger...

But then he'd get Victoria mad at him, and the last thing he felt like was an earful from her. With a snarl, he lowered his guns.

"Get your coat, doc; you're coming with me."

Nguyen straightened his back. A bloody catheter dangled, forgotten, from his fingers. With his other hand, he gestured to the sedated primates on their couches.

"You are one of mine?"

"Yeah, something like that."

"And you wish revenge?'

"Me, and the rest of these poor bastards."

The old man swallowed visibly, then narrowed his eyes. "I don't remember you." His lip curled. "But what does it matter? Stupid monkey. You should be thanking me."

"For what?"

"I made you a man."

"Big whoop." Ack-Ack Macaque chewed his cigar from one side of his mouth to the other. Nguyen's fists were clenched at his side. The elderly doctor drew himself up to his full height.

"I gave you the gift of consciousness. I raised you to sentience."

"And I'm supposed to be grateful?"

"I don't care if you are or not. I did what I did for the betterment of mankind, and I have no regrets. Can you say as much, I wonder?"

Ack-Ack Macaque waggled his guns.

"Shut the fuck up. You're coming with me."

"You're insane."

"Yeah, and whose fault is that?" Pointing the gun in his right hand at the bridge of Nguyen's nose, Ack-Ack Macaque holstered the one in his left. If he was going to have to drag Nguyen out, that was fine. He might even bounce him off a few walls while he was at it, just for shits and giggles. With a growl, he reached out. But, before his leathery fingers could close around the knot of the old man's tie, he heard the flat snap of a pistol shot and Nguyen fell, poleaxed by a round to the left temple.

VICTORIA SCRAMBLED TO her feet.

"What the hell was that?" She was on the bridge of the *Sun Wukong*. Paul's image stood beside her; K8 sat at a console, controlling the dragonfly drone. In front of them, the main screen displayed the feed coming through from the drone's camera. Doctor Nguyen lay slumped in a splatter of blood. Ack-Ack Macaque crouched behind one of the couches, Colts in hand.

"Get the rest of the boys down here," he snarled.

"What's happening?" Victoria shouted. "Who's shooting?"

The monkey didn't reply. He stood upright and fired both guns through the open office door, then ducked back as his shots were answered.

"Fuck and blast," he muttered, crouching.

"Can you see who it is?"

"No, they're behind something. See if you can get the drone in there."

Victoria glanced at K8.

"Do it."

"Aye." The young woman's fingernails tick-tacked the keys of her console, and the view on the screen trembled. Slowly, the drone advanced, keeping close to the ceiling and out of the line of fire.

"What sensors do you have on that thing?"

"We have everything. Microphones, thermometers, spectrometers, the works."

"Turn them all on."

Another click of the keyboard, and a dozen sub-windows opened around the edges of the display, showing the same view filtered through the drone's various onboard instruments. Victoria leant forwards, squinting at them. Some were dark and fuzzy, others simply readouts of temperature or humidity. When she reached the infrared view, she stopped.

"*Merde.*"

Something in the office glowed like a miniature sun, swamping all other heat signatures.

"Some sort of machinery?" Paul ventured.

Victoria shrugged. Whatever it was, it seemed to be getting steadily hotter.

"We are picking up some noise," K8 said.

"Let's hear it."

A rising whine filled the bridge.

"That's coming from the office?"

"As far as we can tell."

Victoria touched the headset attached to her ear. "Hey, monkey-man. Are you hearing this?'

"Yeah." He had to raise his voice. "Sounds like they're firing up a jet engine in there."

Paul put a hand to his bristled chin. "I don't like this at all. You should get him out of there."

A sickly white glow shone from the office door, casting a beam across the laboratory floor.

"Yes," Victoria said, "I think you're right. I'll—"

Ack-Ack Macaque leapt to his feet. In one fluid move he vaulted the row of couches and, firing both Colts, charged the light.

"*Merde!*" Victoria turned and barked at K8. "Get the drone in there, now!"

The picture on the screen tipped forward as the dragonfly dived at the open door. For a second, everything disintegrated into a whirling medley of gunshots and bright light. Then she caught a glimpse of an armed figure silhouetted against the threshold of a bright, circular portal. It was a woman. Whoever she was, she looked up as the drone clattered into the room, taking her eyes from the door. As she did so, Ack-Ack Macaque barrelled into the room at full pelt, and shoulder-charged her. He hit like a rugby player, knocking them both into the gaping portal. Victoria had an instant to see their bodies puff apart in bursts of dust, and then the screen flashed white, and died.

She cried out in frustration.

"Power spike," K8 said, voice flat. "Drone's dead."

CHAPTER EIGHT
A NECKLACE OF LEOPARD'S TEETH

THE *SUN WUKONG* loomed over the jungle, its armoured glass bow moored to a mast on the summit of the island's volcano. In its briefing room, Victoria Valois stood with her arms crossed. Her tunic hung open and her scabbard hung crooked. K8, Cuddles and Erik sat in the front row of the theatre-style seats. Paul's image hovered at the back, glowing gently in the low light. Wrapped in an animal pelt, Bali leant against the door, a twine necklace of leopard's teeth draped around his neck.

Nobody wanted to be the first to speak.

Finally, Victoria walked over to the brass porthole and considered the blue ocean stretching away to the horizon. Below, between the trees, she could see the thatched roofs of the log cabins in the monkeys' stockade.

"So," she said, hugging her upper arms, "did we salvage *anything*?" She looked questioningly at them all, one after another—all except Cuddles. One thing she'd learned about male gorillas was that, no matter what, you never looked them in the eye. Not unless you wanted your arms ripped off and your head stomped into paste.

Erik coughed and squirmed in his seat. "Not much. By the time we got into the lab, there was no trace of the Skipper, and the machine had pretty much melted. It must've had a destruct setting." From his shoulder bag he pulled something sticky and covered in dried black crusts of flaky blood. He held it pinched between thumb and forefinger in much the same way Victoria imagined he'd have held the tail of a dead, plague-sodden rat.

"We did get this, though." He stretched his lower lip over his upper. "It's the doctor's soul-catcher."

Victoria glanced at the dangled fronds of hair-fine wire, and then at the bayonet sheathed in the orangutan's belt. She didn't need to ask how they'd extracted the device from Nguyen's skull.

"Is it intact?"

Erik dropped it onto the empty seat beside his, and wiped his long, hairy orange fingers on the bare plastic arm.

"We pulled it out by the root, Captain."

"Anything else?' She addressed the room. "Anything that can tell us what the hell happened back there?"

After a moment, K8 raised a hand.

"We've been analysing the drone's telemetry."

"And?"

The teenager stood and walked over to the wall screen. She tapped the upper right hand corner, and it flashed into life.

"These graphs represent readings taken from the machine immediately prior to its self-destruction." Her index finger traced a sharp upward curve. "As you can see, there's a spike here, indicating an energy profile similar to that of the *Sun Wukong*'s jump engines."

Victoria raised an eyebrow. The lines and words on the screen were squiggles to her.

"You think it might work the same way?"

"Almost definitely."

Victoria blinked away a mental image of Ack-Ack Macaque's body apparently exploding into dust. "Then he could still be alive?"

K8 gave a small, tight smile. "We think so."

"How do we find him?"

The young woman returned her attention to the screen. "There's a clue in the visual footage." She tapped a few commands and the graphs disappeared, replaced by a blurred close-up of the black-clad figure in the office, caught in the instant she glanced up at the dragonfly. Victoria walked up to the screen, screwing her eyes into slits in an attempt to glean as much detail as she could.

"She looks familiar, but…"

Behind the figure, the portal presented as a disc of shimmering light.

K8 said, "We can enhance the image."

She pressed a control and a line moved across the screen from left to right. As it tightened the pixels and sharpened the picture, Victoria felt her eyes widen with surprise. She put a hand to her chest. Behind her, everybody started talking and shouting and gibbering at once. She waved an arm to shush them. Even though the woman's hair had been closely cropped, and she now wore a coal-black military uniform, the face on the screen was undoubtedly and unmistakably that of Lady Alyssa Célestine.

K8 said, "It must be another version of her, another iteration, from another parallel."

"Can we follow them?"

"We don't know where they went. They could be on any one of a billion possible timelines."

"So, we've lost him?"

K8 blanked the screen and looked down at her white shoes. "In all likelihood, yes. We're afraid so."

The temperature seemed to drop a couple of degrees. Victoria rubbed the bridge of her nose. "I hate this parallel world shit."

Across the room, Bali straightened up. With a shrug of his leopardskin-covered shoulders, he pushed himself away from the doorframe against which he'd been leaning.

"He's gone?"

Victoria didn't answer. She couldn't trust herself to speak. Bali seemed agitated. His bare feet shuffled on the steel deck.

"Then we should choose a new leader," he said.

Erik looked him up and down. The orangutan's eyes narrowed. "And I suppose you want the job?"

Bali drew himself up. "Who else is there?" He cast around, as if looking for someone to challenge him.

Victoria took a deep breath. "You know who else."

"The old lady?" Bali frowned as if genuinely puzzled. "Surely you can't be serious?"

"She should be consulted."

"She's a psychopath."

"Nevertheless, Ack-Ack trusts her."

"And what gives you the right to decide that, *human*?" Bali fingered his necklace of teeth. "You may have been a captain on your own airship, but that doesn't confer any authority here. You're in Kishkindha now, and don't you forget it. This is our world, not yours."

Victoria flexed her fists. Her stomach felt hollow.

"Half of this airship's mine," she said defiantly. "Ack-Ack and I had a deal."

The monkey's lip curled. He held her stare. Heart in her throat, she wondered if he meant the eye contact as insolence or direct physical challenge. He was shorter than her, but wiry and powerful, the same as Ack-Ack Macaque, and she honestly didn't know if she could beat him.

Perhaps the fear showed in her face. Maybe it was in her scent or body language. Bali's eyes widened. His lips peeled back, exposing his incisors. Then, just as Victoria was tensing for an attack, he dropped onto all fours and, with a snort of triumph and disgust, knuckle-walked out of the room, tail held high and proud.

THE 'OLD LADY' occupied a cabin at the rear of the *Sun Wukong*'s main gondola, guarded by a gibbon with a shotgun. As Victoria approached, the gibbon gave a languid, long-limbed salute, and opened the door.

Victoria stepped through. The room smelled of lavender, incense, and musty books. The Founder was sitting in a wicker chair, using an e-reader in the light from the cabin's porthole. She wore a lacy black Victorian dress. Pearls clung to her hairy throat. Hearing the door, she looked up at Victoria and adjusted her monocle. "Good evening, Captain Valois."

"Miss Haversham."

The Founder clicked her tongue in irritation.

"Don't be facetious, dear, it doesn't suit you." She smoothed down the folds of her skirt. "Leave that sort of thing to our mutual friend."

Victoria helped herself to a chair. "It's him I've come to talk to you about."

The female monkey made a steeple of her fingers, and gave a theatrical sigh.

"What's he done *now*?"

Once, she'd been the head of the Gestalt movement. For the past two years, she'd been confined to this room, alone with her books and her sewing, cut off from the outside world in more ways than one. The Gestalt had installed this cabin when they'd built the airship. It was designed for isolation, impervious to radio or WiFi—a place to put damaged or infected drones, where they couldn't infect the rest of the hive—and therefore perfect for imprisoning the hive's queen, to keep her out of mischief and completely incommunicado.

"He's charged off and gotten himself lost somewhere."

The Founder gave a sigh. She placed the e-reader on the arm of her chair.

"How lost is 'lost'?"

As succinctly as she could, and reporting purely the facts, Victoria outlined the events at the Malsight Institute. The Founder listened, and scratched the greying hairs on her muzzle. When Victoria had finished, she said, "It's really quite simple, dear.

Célestine and Nguyen were quite obviously working together. You tell me you've recovered Nguyen's soul-catcher; in which case, all you need do is interrogate the back-up it contains."

Victoria tapped her forehead.

"Of course!"

"I'm sure his ghost will be able to tell you where they've gone."

"Thank you." Victoria turned to leave, then hesitated. "There's something else."

"One is, as ever, all ears."

"Bali wants to appoint a new alpha monkey, right now. And he thinks it should be him."

The Founder put her hand to the pearls around her neck. "Bali is a child. He wants to be the head of the pack but he has no appreciation of what it means to be a leader."

"And Ack-Ack does?"

The monkey smiled. "No, not really. But he never *wanted* to be a leader—which, in my book, makes him ideally suited to the job."

"So, what do we do?"

"About Bali? Well, dear, there's not much I can do from here." The Founder peered around at the walls of her cabin. "Now is there?"

"I can't let you out."

"Why ever not, dear? We're in the monkey kingdom now. There are no Gestalt here. I've no one to interact with. What harm can I do?"

Victoria raised an eyebrow.

"I'm sure you could do plenty, if you put your mind to it. And anyway, there's K8 to consider."

"She's still one of the hive?"

"Only just. We're trying to rehabilitate her."

"And you don't think I'd be a good influence?"

"Would you?"

The Founder raised her chin. "In the hive," she said haughtily, "K8 shared her every thought with thousands and thousands of individuals; and they shared theirs with her. Now, she's alone in her head." She paused to adjust her monocle. "I know something of that pain. And besides, you need my help with Bali. I can talk to him, make him see reason."

"Why would Bali listen to you?"

"Because I'm the alpha female."

"You're the *only* female."

"Same difference." The monkey frowned. Her lips became a horizontal slash. "And besides, there's something else."

"*Quoi?*"

The Founder gripped the arms of her chair and heaved herself up into a standing position, revealing a bulge in her midriff that stretched the lace of her dress. She put a hand to it.

"I'm with child."

Victoria spluttered. "Y-you're pregnant?"

"Very much so."

"But how? I mean… *Who?*"

"I think we know the answers to both those questions."

"Ack-Ack?"

"Indeed."

"Does he know?"

"Of course not."

"Then why are you telling me?"

The monkey exhaled regretfully. "Mostly because I'm not going to be able to hide it much longer. And besides, it could be to our mutual advantage."

"How so?"

"Family bonds are important, Captain, especially in a troupe with only one female. In human terms, I'm carrying the heir to the throne. I expect most of the macaques will side with me. Many of them are other iterations of Ack-Ack, close enough genetically to recognise the child as kin."

"Including Bali?"

"We'll have to see." Her face became thoughtful. "His ambition clouds his judgment. But even he must realise that, without children, Kishkindha's future looks bleak."

Victoria shook her head and smiled. "I still can't believe that you and Ack-Ack... I mean, I knew he spent a lot of time down here talking to you, but I never realised you were, you know. Doing It."

The Founder glowered through her monocle.

"I'll have you know that it only happened the once."

"And you got pregnant first time?"

The elderly monkey straightened her dress and turned to the porthole. "What can I say? The boy's an exceptional shot."

Victoria put a hand to her mouth to stifle a smile. "But you're two hundred years old. I wouldn't have thought—"

"Neither would I, but it appears we were both wrong. Apparently, the treatments I've taken to retain my youth have been more effective than even I could have suspected." Still at the porthole, she looked back over her shoulder. "So, do we have an agreement, Captain?"

Victoria gripped the pommel of her sheathed sword.

"I turn you loose?"

"And in return, I calm things down in the monkey camp."

"And K8?"

"I help her too."

Victoria let out a long sigh.

I know I'm going to regret this.

"*Oui, d'accord.*"

"Is that a yes, Captain?"

"As long as you keep Bali out of my face."

The Founder placed her palm against the porthole's glass. "And in return, I'm free to go down to the surface, to walk in the jungle, to feel the earth beneath my feet and the sun on my face?"

"I suppose." Absently, Victoria scratched at the long ridge of scar tissue at her temple. "But I'll need to know where you are at all times."

"Naturally."

"You'll be on probation."

"I'd expect nothing less."

"Fine, then."

The Founder gave a courteous nod. "Thank you, Captain. And not just from me." She gave her distended abdomen a gentle and affectionate pat. "But from these two, also."

CHAPTER NINE
IN VIRTUAL VERITAS

K8 DIDN'T HAVE time to create an entirely new virtual environment, so she stole one, lifting the code from a popular combat game. Looking over her shoulder, Victoria made a face.

"An oil rig?"

"It's the best we could do on short notice."

"Is Paul ready?"

"We're loading him in now." K8 entered a command and Paul's image appeared on the rig's helipad. Victoria saw that he'd dressed for the part. In his olive green combat fatigues, black beret and silvered sunglasses, he looked like a South American revolutionary.

K8 donned a headset and passed another to Victoria.

"You can speak to him through this," she said. She turned back to the screen and pulled her mike closer to her mouth. "Okay, Paul, we're going to load in Nguyen's back-up in a moment. First, there are a few things you need to know."

Paul walked to the edge of the helipad and leaned over, looking at the gantries and waves below. The rig was in a rendering of the North Sea, out of sight of land. A stiff wind blew from the northeast, ruffling his clothes.

"I'm listening," he said.

"This might be a sim, but it's based on real world physics. Things work the same in there as they do out here. So, don't try to walk off the edge of the rig or anything stupid like that."

Paul stepped back from the edge. "Gotcha."

"Also, you'll be able to feel pain."

"Jesus." Paul flinched. "What kind of game *is* this?"

"A hyper-realistic combat game. Special forces versus oil pirates."

"Sounds dreadful."

"Actually, it's pretty cool. But the point is, if you thump Nguyen, he's going to feel it."

"Okay." Paul shivered and wrapped his arms across his chest. "Couldn't you have found somewhere a bit warmer?"

K8 smiled and glanced at Victoria.

"The only alternative was a magical fairy castle, and we didn't think that sent out the right message."

"What?" Paul grumbled. "That we're bloodthirsty torturers who'll kill him if he doesn't cooperate?"

"Exactly."

"I don't know if I can go through with this."

Victoria activated her mike.

"You won't really be hurting him," she said reassuringly. "Remember, he's just a bunch of pixels."

"Yeah, but so am I."

"You'll be fine. Just remember why you're doing it, and try your best."

Beside her, K8's index finger clicked a key.

"We're uploading Nguyen now," the girl said.

Pixels rippled in the simulation, and the old man appeared in the centre of the helipad, looking much as he had in the lab. He wore a white coat over a blue business suit, a striped tie, and a pair of horn-rimmed spectacles. He stood, blinking in the sunlight, one arm raised to shade his eyes.

"Okay, Paul," she whispered. "You're on."

PAUL'S EYES WERE still on the slate-grey horizon, his thoughts lost in the simulated distance. At the sound of Victoria's voice, he gave a start.

Where am I?

Oh yes, Nguyen.

He cleared his throat and pushed back his shoulders.

"Welcome, Doctor."

Nguyen ignored him. He was peering around at the rig's pipes and derrick.

"Crude."

"I beg your pardon?"

The doctor waved an arm at his surroundings. "The simulation. It's very crude. I expected something far more sophisticated."

Behind his mirrored shades, Paul raised an eyebrow. "You were *expecting* to be killed?"

"Not at all." The old man looked over the top of his glasses like a disappointed schoolteacher. "But the whole point of wearing a soul-catcher is that, if you do die, you anticipate revival." Nguyen frowned. "And I expected to be revived somewhere altogether more luxurious than this."

"Well, I'm sorry to disappoint you."

Nguyen's expression soured. "You're not one of Célestine's people, are you?"

"I'll ask the questions, Doctor Nguyen."

"No." The man gave a small, tight shake of the head. "I don't think so."

Paul opened and closed his mouth. In his ear, he heard Victoria come on the line.

"Tell him to cooperate, or you'll torture him."

Paul grimaced. He drew a deep breath.

"Look, Doctor. You'd better answer our questions, or I'll hurt you." Even to his own ears, he sounded hesitant. To try to reinforce the point, he tapped the leather holster dangling from the webbing belt at his waist.

The corner of Nguyen's mouth twisted in a skewed smile. "No, I don't believe you will."

"Why not?"

"Because I've always been a very good judge of character and you, my young friend, you're not the type."

"You don't know anything about me."

The old man held up a gnarled finger. "Ah, but you're wrong. I know you very well. Or rather, I know the version of you that lives on my world. As a matter of fact, he's on my surgical team."

Paul felt his stomach flip, as if he was riding a plane in turbulence.

"He's still alive?"

"Of course, why shouldn't he be?" Nguyen removed his spectacles and regarded Paul with narrowed eyes. "Ah, I see." He gave a nod of understanding. "You are dead. You are a back-up."

The words were like icicles in Paul's gut.

"So are you," he blurted.

Nguyen shook his head sorrowfully. "Alas, I surmised as much. Tell me, how did I die?"

"You were shot."

"By your people?"

Paul forced a smile. "By Alyssa Célestine."

Nguyen sighed. For a moment he looked old and genuinely sad. "How… disappointing."

"And now I need you to tell me how to find her."

"Ah, so she got away, did she?"

"She fell through some kind of portal." Paul drew his gun. "And she took a friend of mine with her."

"I see."

"Will you help me?"

"Probably not."

A cold wind blew across the platform. High above, gulls cried.

"Then you leave me no choice." Paul raised his weapon.

"What are you going to do, shoot me?" Nguyen chuckled. "What good will it do here? I have already *been* shot."

Paul levelled the gun and swallowed. It was a light, compact pistol.

"This is your last chance," he said, voice wavering.

Nguyen laughed at him.

"You can't kill me," he said.

Paul clenched his jaw. His finger tightened on the trigger.

"Maybe not," he admitted. The gun fired with a savage jolt. Nguyen fell to his knees. His hands went to his stomach. Blood welled between his fingers.

"But I'll bet that hurts."

The old man groaned.

"I need the coordinates of Célestine's world," Paul insisted. Nguyen looked up at him helplessly. Blood dribbled from his lips.

"What's the matter?" Paul asked. "Can't you talk?"

Nguyen shook his head. He opened his mouth and retched ropes of thick, red gore. Disgusted, Paul stepped forward and pressed the gun barrel to the doctor's temple. The hot metal sizzled against the old man's mottled skin.

"Better luck next time."

Victoria watched as Paul pulled the trigger. She really hadn't believed he'd actually do it, and she didn't know whether to be relieved or horrified.

Beside her, K8's fingernails rattled against the console's keypad.

"Okay," she said, "we're re-spawning Nguyen in five, four, three, two…"

Doctor Nguyen reappeared at the exact centre of the helipad to find himself standing astride his own dead body, facing his killer, who brandished a still-smoking pistol.

"We can do this all day," Paul said. "And it's going to hurt just as badly every time."

Nguyen put a hand to his stomach. Slowly, he looked up to meet his own reflection in Paul's mirrored lenses.

"Perhaps we could come to some form of arrangement?"

Blam!

Nguyen tottered back on his heels, half-blinded by the muzzle flash. A hot, red pain skewered his chest. His pulse roared in his ears.

"Sorry," he heard Paul say. "No deals."

"RE-SPAWNING IN FIVE, four, three..."

CHAPTER TEN
CLAP OF SILENCE

PAUL'S HOLOGRAM STOOD at the edge of the wooden verandah. He'd changed out of his military fatigues, back into his Hawaiian shirt and white lab coat. His head was down, looking out through the *Sun Wukong*'s nose at the island of Kishkindha, and his hands were in the pockets of his jeans. The sun slanting in from the glass panels above rendered his peroxide blond hair a dazzling white.

"Are you okay?" Victoria walked over to stand beside him.

He shook his head. "I don't know."

She gripped the bamboo rail. "Look, I'm really sorry. I expected him to give up much sooner than that."

"Stubborn old git." Paul looked ready to spit. "I think he was hoping I'd get sick of it before he did."

Victoria wanted to hug him. "Is there anything I can do? I mean, I can't offer you a stiff drink or anything, but if there's something…"

"I'll be all right." His fingers worried at the gold stud in his ear. "I just need some time. I just need to forget."

"It *was* worth it, you know."

"Was it?" Paul kicked the toe of one trainer against the back of the other.

"He told us how to find Ack-Ack."

A shrug. "Yes, I suppose."

"Come on." Victoria tried to sound cheerful. "The monkey would have done the same for you."

"Would he?" Paul's shoulders slumped even further.

"Yes, of course he would." Victoria smiled. "Only more so."

They stood side by side, looking down at the steep, tree-covered slopes of the volcano and the clustered huts of the monkey village. After a few minutes, Paul said, "I want to go home."

Victoria looked at him. He sounded like a lost child, and she wanted desperately to take him in her arms.

"I'm serious," he continued, as if she'd spoken. "As soon as we've got the monkey back, I want to go home, to our world, to our London. I want to see my flat again."

Victoria bit her lip, all attempts at forced jollity abandoned.

"*Pourquoi?*"

Paul looked up at the sky and clicked his tongue behind his teeth.

"I don't think I have much time left, and I'd rather be somewhere familiar, somewhere I remember, when it runs out. I don't want to die in a strange place."

Victoria felt her eyes prickle. Her vision swam.

"Okay," she said.

"You promise?"

"Whatever you want, whatever I can do."

Paul walked over to the edge of the potted jungle. A blue butterfly flapped between the trees.

"And I want you to promise me something else," he said.

"Anything."

He stopped beside a vine, and tried to cup his hand beneath the bloom of a large white flower, but his hologram fingers passed through its petals without disturbing them.

"When I'm gone, I want you to go back to the world where we left Cole and his daughter."

"The one we've just come from?" Victoria shook her head. "After all the chaos we've just caused, I don't think I'd be very welcome."

"Nevertheless, you have to go back," Paul maintained. "Sneak in, go in disguise, anything."

Arms folded, Victoria walked over to him.

"But why?"

Paul's hand dropped from the flower.

"Nguyen said that the Paul on his world still lived." He gave her a sad, sly look. "And we already know Berg killed the Victoria that was there."

"What are you saying?"

"Do I have to spell it out? You'll be a Victoria without a Paul; he'll be a Paul without a Victoria. You'll need each other. You'll need to be together."

Victoria's cheeks burned. A tear ran down her face.

"No," she said.

Paul looked crestfallen. "I think you should do it, for me."

Victoria shook her head again. "No, it wouldn't be the same. He wouldn't be you."

Paul pursed his lips. "He'd be close. Maybe too close to tell apart. Cole managed to find another version of his dead wife. Why can't you do the same with me?"

Victoria felt her cheeks flush. "I don't want another version, you idiot. I want you."

"I'm just a recording."

"You're more than that!" She paused, letting the anger subside. "You've changed, you've grown." He was now, she thought with a twinge of guilt, a far more caring and considerate person than he'd ever been while alive. Dreadful as it was to admit to herself, his death had, in some ways, improved their relationship beyond all recognition and, after everything they'd been through over the past three years, she couldn't imagine starting again with a stranger—even a stranger with his face and mannerisms.

"No." She wiped her eyes on the back of her sleeve and sniffed. She hadn't cried properly in years, and she wasn't about to start now. "No, that's not going to happen. You're my Paul, and I don't want anybody else." She swallowed down the lump in her throat. "I'm not going to lose you."

He watched her as she straightened the collar of her tunic, brushed the medals into place, and gripped the pommel of her sword.

"Now, pull yourself together," she said, straightening her back, unsure if she was talking to him or herself. "We've got a monkey to rescue." She walked back to the edge of the verandah and looked out at the island. "Are the crew all aboard?"

Paul joined her.

"The Founder recalled them as soon as we had the coordinates."

"She's still here?" After the monkey's long

detention, Victoria had expected her to be down on the ground, enjoying the daylight and open space.

"She's as interested in finding Ack-Ack as we are."

"Very well. Sound the alarm. We jump in thirty seconds."

"Thirty *seconds*?"

"There's no telling what sort of trouble he's in," Victoria said. "The sooner we find him, the better."

Paul gave a nod. He clicked his fingers and alarms wailed in the corridors and open spaces beyond the indoor jungle.

"I'm going to bring the engines online," he said. He became very still, like a figure in a paused video, and Victoria knew his attention had moved elsewhere, focused on the *Sun Wukong*'s navigation systems. She looked down, over the bamboo rail, to where dark machines bulked in the verandah's shadow. As the power rose, she felt the vibration through her hands and feet.

"Five," Paul's voice said over the ship-wide address system. "Four."

Blue static danced over the machines.

"Three."

A rising whine came from below, building rapidly, like the sound of an approaching train. Victoria braced herself.

"Two."

The airship's skin crackled with a green aurora.

"One."

Victoria's ears pulsed with a noise beyond hearing: a silent detonation. She felt her stomach turn itself inside out.

And they were gone.

BREAKING NEWS

From *B&FBC* NEWS ONLINE:

Message received from Mars Probe?

LONDON 17/11/2062 – Government sources are staying tight-lipped this evening regarding earlier reports of a possible message from the surface of Mars.

First mention of the message came at 04:20 GMT this morning, when an anonymous operator at the Parkes Observatory in Australia posted a report on the observatory's website, as well as on a number of online message boards, claiming to have received a radio message from the Céleste probe. This report has since been taken down, and all references to it have been deleted.

At 06:40, NASA's press office released a statement saying that they were monitoring the situation and, while 'an anomalous signal' had been received, it was 'most likely natural in origin', and 'no cause for alarm'.

Céleste Technologies launched the probe three years ago, to coincide with celebrations to mark the centenary of the union of Great Britain and France. However the company, which was owned by the Duchess of Brittany, was disbanded following her foiled plot to assassinate her husband, King William V, and seize control of the Franco-British throne.

The controversial probe reached the red planet yesterday, carrying a cargo of allegedly stolen 'souls'.

When it was launched, Céleste Technologies claimed the probe carried only scientific instruments, but according to recently unearthed documents, the probe actually carried 'back-up' personality recordings of the Duchess and other high-ranking members of Céleste Technologies staff, as well as several hundred personalities harvested from former employees, including some from murder victims. In addition, it also carried machinery capable of turning material from the Martian soil into cyborg bodies designed to house those stored personalities.

A spokesperson for the ESA said, "Mars is 225 million miles from the Earth. Even if these cyborgs exist, and I'm very far from being convinced that they do, there's almost nothing they could do to threaten us from that distance."

However, inside sources tell us the agency will be allocating additional funding to its experimental nuclear engine programme, designed to create boosters capable of pushing craft through interplanetary space.

When confronted with this information, the ESA spokesperson said, "While it is true that the project exists, and a number of test engines have been built, we have neither the resources nor the funding to construct a spacecraft capable of making the journey to Mars."

Read more | Like | Comment | Share

Related Stories:

Parallel worlds: How likely are we to be invaded again?

The King cancels royal visit to Canada.

Is there life on Mars?

Troubled 'Ack-Ack Macaque' film to premiere at Cannes.

Crew of the Tereshkova declared officially 'lost'.

CHAPTER ELEVEN
TOUGH TO KILL

ACK-ACK MACAQUE TOOK shelter in the front room of a burned-out cottage, and peered through a broken window at the bridge. If he was right, the river it spanned was the Seine, and he was a few kilometres south of Paris. He could see a small town on the far bank, and a distant church tower. At each end of the bridge, barbed wire had been strewn across the road. The middle section of the bridge had collapsed into the water, leaving a tangled mess of girders and concrete. If he could somehow get across, he might be able to shake off his pursuers. Even a temporary reprieve would give him time to take stock, to look around and figure out how he'd get a message to Victoria. He was sure she'd be looking for him, but had no idea how she'd find him. Even if she somehow traced him to this new world, how would she know where he was hiding, and how could he let her know without giving his position away to the cyborgs on his trail?

He shivered, and pulled his sodden jacket tighter. The cottage smelled of damp and ashes. A few sticks of charred furniture remained. Every time he moved his feet, his boots crunched on shards of broken glass and crockery. Outside, rain fell from a bruised sky, pocking the surface of the river. The wind whipped dead leaves across the road. Thunder rumbled in the overcast.

When he'd woken up this morning, getting trapped in a post-apocalyptic wasteland hadn't been high on his list of things to do—and yet, here he was. One instant he'd been charging the figure in the office, keeping low to avoid bullets. The next, he'd been rolling and sprawling on the shiny white floor of a different laboratory, on a different world altogether. The black-clad version of Célestine lay beside him on the tiles, winded, sucking in air. Behind them, the portal died, its light sputtering out like a dying candle. For long moments, Ack-Ack Macaque lay looking up at the strip lights. Then a squad of soldiers entered the room and he took flight, leaping through a window and hurling himself away, into the ruins of an industrial park.

Now, hours later, he was wet, cold and hungry, and the bastards were still chasing him.

"I should have stood and fought," he grumbled, but he knew he couldn't have won. The soldiers hadn't been human. Each had displayed the unnaturally smooth features, the waxy, sepia-coloured skin and tall, graceful builds he remembered from the last time he'd tangled with one of Nguyen's cyborgs, back on his own timeline. They were human back-ups running on gelware brains, housed inside bodies equipped with titanium skulls and carbon fibre skeletons. One of them had been tough to kill; a whole squad would have been next to impossible. And so he'd run, and kept running.

Now, he needed food, ammunition and allies, and

he needed time to think, to work out where he was and how he could find his friends—but he couldn't do any of that until he got away from his pursuers.

He'd skirted several villages and suburbs, crossed half a dozen major roads, and had yet to meet a single human. Where was everybody? Thunder cracked and rolled, almost directly overhead. He could feel the rumble of it in his chest. He scratched at the leather patch covering his left eye socket, and yawned. If his geography was correct, the forest of Sénart lay a kilometre or so east of the river and, if he could only get to the trees, they'd never catch him.

First, though, he had to get across the river. It was too wide to swim, and looked to be running fast, swollen with rainwater. The broken bridge was his only option. It was a modern, two-lane highway with little in the way of cover, only steel railings on either side.

Well, I can't stay here.

He stood and slithered over the windowsill, back out into the rain. Nguyen's cyborgs were fast, and he'd have to keep moving if he wanted to stay ahead of them.

Before him, the bridge looked empty and wide. If he tried to run across, he'd be plainly visible to anybody on either bank, and exposed to whatever weaponry they cared to turn in his direction.

But did he have to go *over* the bridge? Seized by a sudden idea, he ran on all fours, scampering to the edge of the carriageway and down a slippery grass slope to the towpath running along the riverbank. From underneath, the bridge was made up of six long steel I-beam girders lying side by side, with the road running atop them.

Behind him, in the direction from which he'd come, he heard the *thud-thud-thud* of military helicopters.

Damn. Another moment, and he'd have been caught in the open. *Don't these guys ever stop?*

As the sounds of pursuit grew louder, he jumped up and heaved himself into the space between two of the girders. The gap was about a metre wide. From here, he'd only be visible to somebody looking up from directly beneath. With his hands and feet braced against the girders' lower flanges, and his tail whipping around to keep him balanced, he could cross the bridge on all fours without being seen by the choppers or, when he got out over the water, anyone on the bank or roadway. The collapsed middle section might prove tricky, but he'd deal with that when he reached it. Right now, his priority was to get across the river without being caught, and without falling in.

Muttering obscenities to himself, he started crawling.

CHAPTER TWELVE
VAST AND COOL

As if opening an old fashioned scroll, Amy Llewellyn unrolled a flexible display screen and placed it on the desk before Merovech, weighing down its corners with coffee mugs and books.

"She's waiting for you."

Merovech exhaled. He had a hollow, churning feeling in his stomach.

"Will this be live?"

"Yes, sir. We've repurposed one of the largest dishes at Goonhilly. She wants to speak to you, and you alone." She tapped a spot at the side of the flat screen, turning on the power.

"Of course she does."

"But that doesn't mean other people won't be listening. Most of the news networks will be casting this live."

"I'm sure."

"All you have to do is touch this button here to connect, and touch it again to disconnect." She leant over him, pointing to the appropriate control, and he could smell the shampoo in her hair: a hint of mint and berries.

"This one?"

"Exactly." She straightened up and tugged down

the hem of her silk blouse. "But don't forget, there'll be a delay on the signal."

"What sort of delay?"

"With Mars at the distance it is from Earth, it'll take your signal about six minutes to reach her, and another six minutes until you receive her reply."

"Twelve minutes?"

"I'm afraid it will make for rather a slow conversation." She reached into her pocket and produced a large, silver-plated stopwatch. "This will help you keep track."

Merovech took it from her and put it on the desk in front of him. His hands felt jittery.

"Okay," he said. "I think I can manage this by myself."

Amy raised her eyebrows. "Are you sure you don't want me to stay?"

"No." He waved her away. "No, thank you. I want to do this by myself."

"But, sir."

"No, really. It's better this way." He would be self-conscious enough just knowing the world's media were eavesdropping. He didn't think he could bear to have anybody else in with him, watching and listening and trying not to meet his eyes. "I'll be fine."

She put her hands on her hips.

"Well, if you're sure."

"I am."

She tugged at the cuffs of her blouse. "Then I'll be right outside. Just call me if you need me."

Merovech rose to his feet.

"I will," he said. "Thank you."

She went to the door. He listened to her heels clack on the oak floorboards. When she'd gone, he considered his reflection in the ornate, silver-framed mirror that hung on the wall above the fireplace. As he was in mourning, he'd chosen to wear a black shirt and tie with a charcoal-grey jacket. It was the same suit he'd worn to his father's funeral, three years ago. But, of course, the previous king hadn't been his *real* father—and, although she'd carried him in her womb, his mother hadn't really been his mother, either. He was a clone, cultured from one of her cells and turned male through the use of prenatal hormone injections—an artificial creature grown with the sole purpose of furthering his mother's dynastic ambitions. Now that Julie was dead, only three people in the world knew the truth, and two of them—Victoria Valois and Ack-Ack Macaque—were missing, presumed lost.

He clenched his fists and swallowed. The whole world would be listening to his conversation—at least, those agencies, governments and broadcasters with the equipment and ability to intercept signals sent to and from Mars. Would the Duchess blurt the truth? Would she accidentally or deliberately expose him as a fraud? The disclosure would be a disaster. It would undo his attempts to unite and hold together his Commonwealth in the aftermath of both the Duchess's attempted coup and the Gestalt invasion. The last thing his people needed right now was another crisis; and yet, in a deep and selfish corner of his heart, he knew the revelation—despite the accompanying scandal and disgrace—would come as something of a relief. For the first time in his life, he wouldn't be playing a part; he would have responsibility for nothing but himself.

It was all he'd ever craved: the simple freedom to be himself. But suppose he ended up in jail, or was cast out as an exile, with the media hounding his every move? From childhood, he'd been trained and shaped for leadership and, for the past three years, he'd worked hard to keep the United Kingdoms together in the face of attack and economic turbulence. To have his efforts go to waste… Well, it was more than he would be able to bear.

His thoughts turned to Julie. She had respected but never really understood his sense of duty. What would she say now? From somewhere, she'd found the courage to confront her abusive father. Surely, she'd expect the same courage from him.

With a dry mouth, he turned to the desk and held his finger over the button.

"Okay." He took a long breath. "Let's get this over with."

And let the cards fall where they may.

THE FACE THAT appeared on the screen before him bore a passing resemblance to his mother, the Duchess, but its features held the smooth, passive lines of a waxwork. Behind it, Merovech could see the rusty pink glow of a Martian sunrise.

"I'm here," he said, and reached for the stopwatch.

Twelve minutes. The lower drawer of his desk held the bottle of 15-year-old single malt that he'd been enjoying earlier, and a clean set of crystal tumblers. He picked one and sloshed in a generous measure, and then sat back to await his mother's reply. When it came, he saw her eyes narrow and her posture harden. The ghost of a smile crept across her lips. A faint breeze disturbed her synthetic hair.

"I see you survived."

Merovech felt his jaw clench.

No thanks to you.

On the screen, the Duchess raised a hand to indicate the boulder-strewn Martian plateau behind her. Tall, spindly figures bestrode the cratered surface, picking their way between the rocks. Some carried tools, others weapons. They cast long, black shadows across the regolith.

"So have we."

"What do you want, mother?" Merovech spoke without thinking, and then sighed and restarted the stopwatch. He got up from his chair and walked over to the window, and looked out at the cranes and scaffolding of a city in the process of reconstructing itself.

If she'd had her way, this would all be radioactive ash.

Twelve minutes crawled past.

"Straight to the point, I see." Was that a hint of pride in her voice? Merovech returned to his seat.

"I am calling with a proposition," the cyborg continued. "I am aware of your recent brush with the Gestalt, and I'm here to offer my protection."

"Your what?"

"You see," she continued, as yet unaware of his interruption, "I have an army of my own here. A thousand cyborgs with human minds. We are stronger, faster and more intelligent than you could ever be. Our technology is years ahead of yours, and we have all the resources of this red planet. Just think what we can achieve."

Merovech clunked his tumbler onto the desk.

"Get to the point," he muttered.

Two hundred and twenty million kilometres away, the Duchess smiled.

"I know the world listens to our conversation," she said. "And I'm here to make you this offer. Any country that pledges us their fealty and support will receive in return our protection. There are an infinite number of parallel worlds out there. Who knows when the next invasion may come?"

She paused expectantly. Merovech chewed his lower lip.

"You tried to trigger a nuclear war," he said. "And now you expect us to believe you have our best interests at heart?" He sat back and shook his head. "I don't buy it. I won't believe it."

A dozen minutes later, the Duchess laughed.

"What you believe scarcely matters, my son. The simple fact is, the Earth is under threat and only we can save it."

"Save it by destroying it, you mean? By bending it to your will?"

"Spin it however you like, Merovech, but know this: Your world is being watched by intelligences greater than your own, intelligences vast and cool and deeply sympathetic. Spurn us at your peril."

She fell silent. Merovech cleared his throat.

"Is that a threat, mother?"

Twelve minutes later, the Duchess narrowed her eyes. "Every carrot has a stick, my son. When we return to Earth—and return we shall—the weapons we will have built to defend our supporters will be turned against those who have denied us." Her eyes flicked up and to the right, as if consulting a display he couldn't see. "You, and all the nations of the Earth, have one hour to decide. Our forces grow by the minute. Within days, we'll have weapons capable of reaching the Earth. Join us now, or suffer the consequences."

CHAPTER THIRTEEN
CARBON FIBRE BONES

IN THE COLD grey light of a damp false dawn, Victoria stood at the edge of the village, her thin frame wrapped in an old army greatcoat like one of the ones the Commodore used to wear in the winter. Leaves blew around her feet, which were wrapped in rags. Her clothes were drab and tattered and she'd left her head bare to the glowering sky. Only a torn and grimy length of cloth, wrapped around her forehead and tied at the back, hid the input jacks set into her temple. Shambling from their ruined houses, the villagers ignored her. She looked like one of them. Moving like emaciated shadows, their feet dragged through the mud and rubble and their eyes remained lowered and hopeless. As they formed up into ranks at the edge of the main road, she shouldered her way in among them, keeping her head down, hoping her disguise would be enough to fool the guards at the laboratory.

In the corner of her eye, she saw Paul's image. He hung above the cracked and weed-pocked tarmac of the road like a spectre, invisible to everyone except her.

"I still say this is a bad idea," he muttered. Victoria said nothing. She hadn't wanted to leave him behind, so she'd uploaded him into her neural gelware, as she had three years ago after first activating him. Now, he was a ghost overlaid across her vision. She nestled her hands deeper into the pockets of her coat, squeezing them for warmth. Around her, the villagers huddled into themselves. Unkempt, stale and unwashed, they stank. None of them spoke; they simply stood there, swaying slightly, as they waited for the sun to rise and the truck to appear.

Paul looked around at them.

"These people are starving," he said. "And covered in sores. And I don't like the way some of them are missing clumps of hair."

Victoria sidled to the edge of the group.

"What do you think?"

"I don't know. I'm a surgeon, not a general practitioner."

"If you had to guess."

"Radiation poisoning, maybe."

"*Merde.* You really think so?"

"I could be wrong." He considered the drab sky and shivered. "But I wouldn't recommend staying here a moment longer than absolutely necessary."

Victoria swallowed. Her mouth felt suddenly dry.

"*Oui, d'accord.*"

Despite his pessimism, she was glad to have him along for the ride. In this drab and forlorn landscape, it felt good to have a friendly face to offer moral support.

A fat drop of rain fell onto the road, followed by another, and another. From the left came the grunt and rumble of an engine. Belching smoke, the truck came around the corner at the end of the village.

It was an eight-wheeled military model painted in autumnal urban camouflage. With a squeak of brakes and a hiss of hydraulics, it pulled to a halt in front of the villagers. They clambered up to join the other workers already huddled on the benches inside. Victoria hauled herself up behind them, and sat on the bench with her back against the canvas wall. Someone banged the side and the vehicle lurched forward, throwing everyone against each other. Then they were under way and, through the flap at the back, she could see the unrepaired road spooling away behind them.

In a field beyond the village, a fairground lay rusting.

"What happened here?" she whispered.

Paul shrugged. "Something bad." He jerked a thumb at the truck's other occupants. "Why don't you ask them?"

Victoria glanced sideways, and gave a tight little shake of her head. She didn't want to do anything that would make her stand out as being different, or not from around these parts. To do so would be to risk getting turned in for a reward. Instead, she turned up her collar and hunkered lower on her seat. The truck bumped and rattled along the road, jolting her spine.

Eventually, after a seeming eternity of discomfort, they came to a wire fence and a pair of anonymous-looking cyborg guards, who waved them through with scarcely a glance. Through the rear flap, Victoria saw the barrier and its coils of barbed wire receding behind them.

No turning back now.

They were in the grounds of the laboratory. If Célestine were anywhere, she'd be here, overseeing the activities of Nguyen's cyborg master race. All Victoria had to do was find her, and then get her to lead her to the monkey. Victoria's fingers curled around the plastic casing of the tracking device in her pocket. Once she got within a few hundred metres of Ack-Ack Macaque, she'd be able to locate him via the microchip she'd hired a vet to implant under his skin.

That's if he's still alive.

The truck pulled up in front of a pre-fab industrial unit, and the workers clambered out. Keeping amongst them, Victoria allowed them to lead her to a large canvas marquee, which had been erected at the side of the building, and which housed a couple of rickety trestle tables, from behind which dispirited-looking men and women dispensed cups of water and bowls of thin porridge. Accepting a bowl and a tin mug, Victoria stood on the edge of the group. The other workers ate and drank with listless, automatic movements. They showed no relish or urgency in the slaking of their hunger. They were like machines taking on fuel. Holding the plastic bowl to her chin, Victoria sniffed.

"That looks tasty," Paul said.

"It smells like wallpaper paste."

"You're not going to eat it, then?"

"Shut up."

The last thing she'd eaten had been a simple egg-white omelette, some hours before, in the commissary of the *Sun Wukong*. Now, the giant airship lay somewhere out in the Bay of Biscay, out of sight of land, its vast bulk floating half a dozen metres above the water—hopefully beyond the range of any radars Nguyen's troops might bring to bear, and hidden from the few civilian vessels brave or foolhardy enough to set forth upon the dead, polluted sea.

She swilled the gloopy muck around, and then tipped it into some weeds growing up against the side of the building.

"How did I get here?'

Paul looked confused.

"The truck…?"

She shook her head and sighed. "I mean, how did I get *here*." She looked around at the low, functional buildings, the miserable workers, and the dark, sullen sky. How had she made the progression from that apartment in Paris, from a promising career in journalism, to this post-apocalyptic wasteland? She thought of her other self, lying dead in that apartment, and almost envied her.

"Maybe I should have died in the crash," she murmured, thinking back to her accident in the South Atlantic. Everything that had happened, all the weirdness, had come about as a direct result of that crash. From the moment, four years ago, when she stepped onto the chopper and strapped into the seat next to the then-teenage Prince of Wales, her course had been fixed, her life changed. She'd climbed aboard as an up-and-coming reporter, and then woken four weeks later as a technological freak—a woman kept alive by the artificial neurons that now did most of her thinking.

And here she was on a parallel timeline, in a

possibly radioactive dystopia, searching for her best friend—a rude, violent, ungrateful monkey, who smelled like a wet dog and drank like a fish—with only the electronic projection of her dead husband for company.

Why couldn't they have just let her drown?

She pulled her coat tight, and muttered curses under her breath. After a few minutes, the doors to the laboratory opened, and she followed the thin, shivering villagers to a production line, where industrial robots assembled artificial cyborg bodies in showers of welding sparks, and humans simply fetched and carried, swept and sorted. For an hour, she tried to blend in but had no idea what she was supposed to be doing and kept getting in the way. The sight of the arms and legs that lay, awaiting attachment, in hoppers beside the conveyor belts unnerved and sickened her. Their carbon fibre bones had already been partially covered in cultured skin, giving them the look of severed human limbs. It made her feel like a worker in a death camp. Especially as she knew that, somewhere nearby, real arms and legs were being carved off and discarded as brains and nervous systems were stripped from frail flesh-and-blood bodies and implanted into waiting cyborg shells.

When the two tall, expressionless guards came to arrest her, she felt almost relieved.

"Take me," she said as bravely as she could, "to your leader."

CHAPTER FOURTEEN
WRATH AND MALICE

ACK-ACK MACAQUE KEPT moving. His stomach grumbled and tiredness clawed at him. He'd been on the run for hours now and was, frankly, knackered. But, even though he'd made it to the forest, he didn't dare stay still for more than a few minutes at a time—just long enough to catch his breath, drink some water from a stream, or take a shit. After all, who knew what kind of heat-seeking tech those metal bastards packed? For all he knew they'd be able to pick him out at a hundred yards, and he had no intention of sitting around waiting for them to find him. Better to keep low and stay nimble, scampering through the undergrowth on his hands and feet. His plan, such as it was, involved finding a police station or army base, or maybe even a country sports store—anywhere that might have a stock of guns and ammunition. He only had four bullets left in his Colts, and there was no way in hell he'd be able to force his way back into Célestine's facility without some serious firepower.

And when I get inside, I'm going to shoot her ladyship in the kneecaps, he vowed to himself, *and then keep shooting bits off her until she agrees to send me home.*

He paused for a moment to catch his breath, and leant against a tree, chest heaving. All he'd wanted was to save the world—and it hadn't even been his world. How had he ended up here, in this cold and windy hellhole? Still wheezing, he spat into the grass, regretting each and every cigar he'd ever smoked.

From behind, he heard the thud of clawed feet on mossy ground, and the rustle of lithe bodies crashing through bracken and underbrush.

Dogs!

They were close, and their cyborg masters wouldn't be far behind.

"Shitballs."

The trees in this part of the forest were mostly young saplings, with thin springy branches that wouldn't bear his weight. Even if he managed to swarm up one, he'd be trapped in it, treed like a cat—unable to swing to the next because it'd snap beneath him.

The sounds of pursuit grew closer, and he looked back. From the undergrowth, a pair of Dobermans flew at him like slavering suede missiles. His hands dropped to his holsters; but he knew that if he fired, he'd be giving away his position to his pursuers *and* using the last of his ammo. Instead, with no other choice, he dropped into a fighting crouch and let his lips peel back from his teeth.

"All right, mutts, let's play."

The dogs were almost upon him. He could see breath steaming from their mouths and powerful muscles rippling like pistons under their hides. He curled his hands into claws and thrashed his tail. Then he let out the deepest, most guttural snarl he could muster—an outpouring of rage and frustration that welled up from the soles of his boots. It was the cry of a challenged alpha male, an expression of wrath and malice so potent it could have stopped a charging gorilla.

The two Dobermans slithered to a halt, their paws scrabbling at wet leaves and moss. It was a fair bet that, living in France, they'd never seen a monkey before—especially an enraged male almost the size of a human being. They took one look at the creature in the clearing—at its yellow incisors and baleful eye—and, whimpering in terror, fled back the way they had come.

Ack-Ack Macaque scowled after them.

"Yeah, you'd better run." He put a hand to the small of his back and straightened his spine. Something clicked and he groaned. "Goddammit." The roar had taken much of his strength. He felt emptied out. Much of the fear and anger that had been driving him had vanished, having vented away into the damp autumn air like steam from a safety valve. Now, he felt overwhelmingly tired.

What I wouldn't give for a coffee right now. He scratched his stomach. He couldn't afford to linger. With a sigh, he turned and loped deeper into the forest, heading away from the distant sounds of pursuit.

Soon, he came to an older part of the wood, where he scaled the first tree that seemed capable of holding him. Once up in the tangle of bare branches, he started swinging from tree to tree. The going was slower than running on the forest floor, but at least he wasn't leaving a scent trail for the dogs to follow. They wouldn't be able to track him through the air.

*   *   *

HALF AN HOUR later, as the light of the afternoon began to fade and his arms started to feel like overstretched rubber bands, he came to an area where the trees were blackened and charred. An airliner had crashed into the heart of the forest. Parts of the wings and fuselage were clearly visible at the centre of the burned-out area. Cautiously, he crept closer. There hadn't been many jet airliners on Victoria's world, where skyliners accommodated the vast majority of aerial passengers. Neither had there been any in the game world he'd once inhabited, based as it had been on a fictionalised version of World War II.

Stupid way to travel, he thought, regarding the wreck. Blasting through the air at half the speed of sound, crammed into a thin metal tube, more payload than passenger. Why go through all that when you could have the comfort and relative spaciousness of a skyliner cabin? Sure, the journey would take longer, but if your only concern was time, why not simply strap yourself onto a missile and have done with it?

Something white caught his eye. A thighbone. Now that he'd seen one, other bones seemed to leap out at him. They lay strewn around the wreck like the leftovers of some hideous feast, some half-buried and sticking up from the earth, others piled in heaps where they'd fallen. He frowned. The plane had fallen here, and nobody had come to collect the bodies.

What the hell? This wasn't the Amazon rainforest; the wreck lay less than ten kilometres from the centre of Paris. Why hadn't anybody come? They must have been able to see the smoke and flames. He thought back to the ruined village, the collapsed bridge. Whatever had happened here must have happened everywhere else as well. Some calamity had hit the whole country—maybe the whole world—and nobody had come to investigate this plane crash because they were all too busy dealing with their own dead and injured.

He shivered.

A couple of years ago, he'd fought Célestine and her plan to provoke a nuclear war. The crazy old cow had wanted to cleanse the world, leaving it free for her cyborg armies to inherit. Eventually, she'd been defeated and killed; but this was a whole different timeline, with a whole different Célestine. What if, in this reality, the Duchess had succeeded? Ack-Ack Macaque cast his eye at the darkened clouds and leafless trees.

"Ah, crap." He felt his skin crawl at the thought of radioactive fallout. The hairs on his neck and arms prickled. What was safe? Was he breathing the stuff now? Then he remembered Célestine. When they'd fallen through the portal, she hadn't been wearing a protective suit. She hadn't taken any precautions. Maybe things weren't so bad.

"Either way, there's fuck all I can do about it now."

He crawled along the branch he was on, and jumped into the waiting arms of the next tree. He was going to give the crash site a wide berth; and, unless he dropped dead of radiation poisoning in the next couple of hours, he'd just have to go on assuming there *was* no contamination—or, at least, not enough to hurt him in the short term. He had to assume he'd go on living.

After all, what choice did he have?

CHAPTER FIFTEEN
THAT VILE PRIMATE

THE TWO GUARDS marched Victoria across the windswept campus, past row after row of workshops and assembly lines; past racks of artificial torsos, crates filled with disembodied heads, and, at the back of one particular building, a conveyor belt leading to a row of dumpsters filled with discarded human remains. Arms and legs stuck out at uncomfortable, unnatural angles. The bodies had been cored like apples, their brains and spinal cords having been cut out and pasted into new cyborg bodies. Flies swarmed over the cooling meat. The workers tending the conveyor belt turned to watch her pass with dull, frightened eyes.

At the end of the row of structures, they came to an exposed area that had once been a car park but which was now empty, save for a couple of rusting Citroëns and a large military transport helicopter. The helicopter's twin rotors turned lazily. The craft had been painted the same dull, oppressive grey as the sky. Warm yellow light spilled from the ramp gaping open at its rear. The guards led Victoria to the base of the ramp and pushed her forward. She took a couple of steps, and then looked back.

"You're not coming?" she asked.

They regarded her with blank, impassive expressions, their faces betraying all the verve and personality of shop window mannequins.

"You go on," one of them said. "We'll be here when you're finished."

The breeze whipping across the car park smelled smoky and autumnal, laced with the scents of wet earth and rotting leaves. In Victoria's head, Paul said: "I don't like this." The helicopter's tail rotor towered above them. The ramp was wide enough to accommodate a tank.

"I don't blame you." She hadn't been a fan of helicopters since that crash in the South Atlantic, a lifetime ago.

She walked up the ramp and paused at the top, where she used her arm to shield her eyes, blinking as they adjusted to the contrast between the twilit gloom outside and the brightness within.

The helicopter's cargo hold had been outfitted as an art gallery. There were expensive-looking carpets on the deck, and tapestries hanging from the bulkheads. She recognised a number of famous paintings and carvings. In the centre of the space, a long metal box had been covered in candles, each of which was lit. There were votive candles, tea lights, lanterns, and gothic candelabra. Their glow gave the place the feel of a church, and their flames flickered brightly in the cold air swirling in from the open ramp. At the back of the room, near the hatch that led through to the cockpit, Alyssa Célestine sat behind a desk, face like a scowling cat. Back on Victoria's timeline, the woman had been the Duchess of Brittany, companion to the King of the United

Kingdoms, and mother to Merovech, the Prince of Wales. Goodness only knew what rank or title she held on this world.

"Come in." Célestine had unbuttoned her tunic. A squat black pistol lay on the desk in front of her. Victoria glanced back, at the guards at the bottom of the ramp. They were watching her. How could they stand to live in those metal shells? For a second or two, she pitied them. Then a wave of nausea splashed over her as she remembered her own situation. However artificial they might be on the outside, at least they still had their own brains. They weren't running on slippery, lab-grown gelware. Their limbs and organs may have been replaced but their minds were still their own, still the product of greasy human neurons. For all their physical alteration, they remained human in a way she never could. And it was all Célestine's fault. Célestine and Nguyen. Victoria should have died of her injuries, but they'd saved her. Nguyen had used her to test his techniques and theories. She had been an early prototype for his cyborg soldiers, her brain a testing ground for the gelware that allowed human consciousness to be copied and transferred into a metal body. They'd turned her into a guinea pig, and she'd been pathetically grateful—at least, until she'd realised the full scope of their plans. Then she'd killed Nguyen and helped Ack-Ack and Merovech finish off Célestine.

Yes, back on her timeline, the Duchess was dead. On this one, she wasn't. Victoria swallowed. Mouth dry and heart twitching like a caged animal, she turned to face the woman.

Lady Célestine glared at her.

"Do you speak English?"

"*Oui.*"

"Why have you come here?"

"To find my friend."

"The monkey?"

"Yes."

"He tried to kill me."

Victoria drew herself up. "As I recall, *you* opened fire on *him*."

The woman's gnarled fingers brushed the stock of the pistol on the desk.

"He broke into my lab."

"Is it your lab or is it Nguyen's?" Victoria narrowed her eyes. "And, talking of Nguyen, why did you shoot him, anyway?"

Célestine pursed her lips. She wrapped her fingers around the gun.

"He allowed himself to be captured. His death was necessary."

"In case he talked?"

"Because he disappointed me." She raised the weapon. "But now it's your turn to talk. Where are you from?"

"Paris, originally."

"Which Paris?"

"How the hell would I know?"

"Your name?"

"Victoria Valois."

"Valois…" Célestine's lip curled. "Of course. You're the woman from the helicopter crash."

"You know me?"

"I remember Nguyen operating on you."

Victoria blinked in surprise. "You were there?"

"I have made contact with alternate versions of myself and the good doctor on a dozen parallels," she said, "and on each, I have given them the tools to create new bodies, new societies." Keeping the gun's narrow barrel trained on Victoria, she rose stiffly to her feet. "The iteration you killed two years ago was one of my most promising students. We had never been so close to success. But then you ruined everything. You and that vile primate."

"You were trying to start a nuclear war."

"We were trying to save humanity. To improve it."

"By killing most of it."

"So what? Your world was dangerously overpopulated. You could have stood to lose some of the dross, the deadwood." Célestine gestured to the open ramp behind Victoria. "As we have done here."

Victoria's mouth felt dry.

"There was a nuclear war *here*?" A droplet of sweat tickled as it ran into the small of her back.

Célestine waved a dismissive hand. "A small one. Inconsequential, really."

"Somebody stopped you again?'

The woman smiled. "We just developed more subtle methods. Biological methods. Diseases genetically tailored to target certain subsets of the population, leaving only a percentage of the adults."

Victoria had to stop herself from turning away in disgust, appalled by the implied slaughter. "Enough to create your brave new world?" she asked, almost spitting the words.

"Enough to provide the slave labour to build it."

Victoria felt her cheeks growing hot. Rage bubbled up like stomach acid. "Who elected you ruler of the world?"

Behind her, she heard the ramp closing. The deck trembled underfoot as the helicopter wobbled into the air. Braced against the desk, the Duchess straightened her arm, and aimed the gun directly at Victoria's face.

"And who elected you its saviour?"

Beneath the anger, Célestine looked tired. The fingers holding the weapon were starting to gnarl, the backs of the hands blotchy with liver spots and ancient scars.

"Do you think this has been easy?" she asked, regarding Victoria with glittering eyes. "All these years, all these worlds? This has been my life's work."

"Turning people into robots?"

"Trying to save the human race!" She shook the gun and Victoria cringed. If she could keep the Duchess talking, she might have time to access her internal menus and dial up her speed and strength.

"You could just stop now, and walk away," she suggested, stalling for time.

Célestine shook her head. "No, not now. I've spent too long at this. I've invested too much time, too much of myself—too much of all my selves."

"Perhaps we could help you?"

"No." She motioned Victoria over to a porthole. They were climbing slowly, rising over the campus of workshops and warehouses that made up the laboratory. Victoria braced herself against the inside of the hull and bent to the window. Below, in the fields beyond the barbed wire fences, immense armoured vehicles sat in ranks.

"Are they tanks?" They were bigger than any kind of tank she'd ever seen.

Lady Alyssa buttoned her black tunic. Her close-cropped hair and bright eyes gave her the look of a Siamese cat.

"They are my Land Leviathans."

Victoria cupped a hand around her eyes and pressed her face to the glass. Bristling with guns, and with sparks shooting from their smoke stacks, the Leviathans resembled armoured locomotives, or battleships plucked from the sea and given caterpillar tracks. In the corner of her vision, she saw Paul's image superimposed across the scene.

"There are *hundreds* of them," he said.

For a moment, Victoria regretted her decision to allow Paul to ride in her head. If she got herself killed—and it seemed increasingly likely that she would—he'd also die. If her heart stopped pumping the oxygen her gelware ran on, he'd fade away like a computer program in a power cut. She could have left a copy of him running on the *Sun Wukong*'s processors, but that would have run contrary to their pact. In the aftermath of the Gestalt invasion, they'd made each other a promise. She wasn't backed-up, and Paul didn't want to live without her, haunting the memory banks of a captured airship. If she died, he would follow. On this trip, they were sharing the risk, and there would be no second chances.

Victoria stepped back from the window. Célestine let her pistol drop demurely to waist-height, but kept it aimed. "What do you think?"

"Does it matter what I think?"

"Perhaps not, but I wanted you to see them." She walked around the heavy metal box occupying the centre of the hold, putting it between them. In the candlelight, her eyes seemed to smoulder.

"You say I kill people? Before I came to this world, it was a totalitarian dictatorship, a fascist nightmare. There were death camps, torture houses. Now, because of me, many of the formerly downtrodden are free, and equipped with bodies that may serve them for a thousand years. I killed all the generals."

"And most of the people."

"They would have died anyway." Célestine's jaw clenched. "What do a few casualties mean in the grand scheme of things? Everybody dies sooner or later; nobody survives. The point is that I achieved my objective: I made it possible for a few to transcend the limitations of the flesh."

Victoria tasted sourness. "But all those deaths—"

"Think how many have died throughout history. Millions upon millions of bright, sparkling intelligences doomed to rot in a prison of meat. And only I can stop it all. I can make their lives worthwhile, because I have it in my power to halt death."

Victoria stepped back, away from the candles. "You're insane."

"Insane?" The gun waved above the flames. "Of course I'm insane. You would be too, if you'd had to do and see the things I have."

"Then why not stop? Why not put an end to it all?"

"Because humanity needs me. It needs what only I can do." Célestine drew herself up to her full height.

"I invented the soul-catcher, you know. Thanks to me, a hundred timelines use it. The people on them record their personalities as electronic back-ups, little realising the true purpose of the thing, its true potential."

As she spoke, Victoria called up the menu that enabled her self-defence routines—routines she'd been practising and refining for the past three years.

"Which is?"

"When the time comes," the Duchess said, "most of its users—at least, most of those worth saving—will already have a copy of themselves digitised and ready to load into one of my cyborg bodies."

In her mind's eye, Victoria triggered a threat evaluation subroutine. Slowly, the gelware in her head began to accelerate its processing rate from the speed of thought to the speed of light.

"So, you've built an army?" She tried to keep her voice steady, her tone neutral.

"Indeed." With the end of the pistol, Célestine pointed through the window. The helicopter had turned, bringing into sight something that looked like the sort of giant lighting rig you saw at open air music festivals: an arc of metal forming an archway big enough to easily accommodate one of the Leviathans. The centre glowed and rippled like a luminous heat haze. Its edges sparkled with rainbow light.

"Oh no," said Paul.

Victoria frowned, trying to make sense of the skeletal structure. Then realisation hit her, and she gaped at Lady Alyssa.

"That's a portal."

The woman's expression hardened.

"I have unfinished business on your world, Miss Valois." She motioned Victoria back to the desk and into a chair, then took up position across from her. "My spies tell me that, back on your timeline, the Céleste probe reached Mars. It was a success. Even as we speak, it will be busily constructing its own army of enhanced humans."

"You mean cyborgs."

Uniform fastened, Célestine raised the gun. Her eyes went to the scar tissue at Victoria's temple.

"You are in no position to make such distinctions."

Victoria focused on the barrel of the pistol, which was about a metre from her face. Her neural prosthesis tagged the weapon as a threat and dialled her adrenal glands up to maximum. At the same time, her mental clock completed its acceleration, and the world around her slowed to a glacial pace. She felt her chest rise like an old set of bellows, and the indrawn breath pass across her tongue into her throat. Her heart thumped and the blood roared in her ears. Her thoughts, which had been racing, hardened and clarified.

"But why do you need my world," she asked, "if you already have this one?"

Célestine looked scornful. "This world is ending," she said. "The seas are poisoned, the vegetation dying off. It's useless. Soon, only bacteria will remain." She took a step back and closed one eye, sighting the gun at the bridge of Victoria's nose. "On your world, we already have Mars—an unspoiled canvas upon which to build—and soon, we will have the Earth as well. With the red planet in our hands, we are halfway there. We just need the final push, and then we'll found a society that will last an aeon, spreading from world to world through space, and from timeline to timeline on Earth. A society that will outlast the sun itself."

Victoria tensed. She knew she could move quickly, but could she move quickly enough to dodge a bullet?

"It'll never happen," she said, buying time.

Lady Alyssa looked pityingly at her.

"My Leviathans cannot be stopped. I will fly this helicopter right into the heart of London and land it on the lawn of Buckingham Palace. Merovech will surrender to me personally."

"You'll be shot down before you get within a mile of the palace."

"Don't be so sure." The Duchess moved sideways and tapped the toe of one of her military boots against the metal box holding all the candles. "Do you know what this is?"

Victoria glanced down. Whatever the box might be, there were power cables plugged into it, and it gave off a faint, almost subliminal hum, easily missed against the racket of the helicopter's engines.

"I haven't the faintest idea."

Célestine smiled triumphantly, and thrust out her chest.

"It's a field generator. It creates an invisible energy shell around the aircraft. It can stop bullets, even tank shells."

"Bullshit."

"No, I assure you, it's true. It's even impervious to air and water. If we had the right propulsion system, with that shield in place, we could fly this helicopter under the sea."

"And your Leviathans have them?"

"Most, yes." She brought her free hand up to grasp her other wrist, steadying her aim. "But enough of this chatter. You have seen all I wished you to see, and now, I'm afraid, it's time to say farewell."

CHAPTER SIXTEEN
THE BONE PIPE

ACCORDING TO THE luminous dial of Ack-Ack Macaque's wristwatch, it was midnight when he first glimpsed the campfire. From where he hung, in the upper branches of a tall conifer, the flames danced invitingly, illuminating the trees and throwing long black shadows through the forest. He sniffed. His limbs were tired, his belly empty. Along with the wood smoke, he could smell something else. Something that smelled like an unwashed human, or perhaps…

Moving as stealthily as possible, he worked his way towards the quivering light, keeping to the high branches. Eventually, he came to the edge of a clearing and there, in the centre, was the fire. A figure crouched beside it, wrapped in old blankets, poking the glowing embers with a long stick. At first glance, it resembled a monk, or an old woman in a shawl, but on closer inspection, he saw that copper hair covered the backs of its hands, and its fingers were thick, leathery sausages. Ack-Ack Macaque wrinkled his nose. He'd been right about the smell. The figure wasn't an old woman; it wasn't even human. As he watched, it pulled back the blanket covering its head, revealing the deep brown eyes and greying muzzle of an elderly female orangutan.

"You may as well come down," the orangutan said. "I know you're there. I've been listening to you crashing around for the last ten minutes."

She waited patiently as Ack-Ack Macaque lowered himself to the forest floor and edged towards the campfire, one hand resting on his holster.

"Who are you?" he demanded.

The orangutan smacked her lips.

"My name is Apynja. Use it wisely." She reached into the folds of her blanket and pulled out a battered steel canteen. "I expect you're thirsty."

"You escaped from Célestine's place too?"

"It doesn't matter where I come from. My journey is of little consequence." She tossed the flask to Ack-Ack Macaque. "Now, take a drink."

Suddenly, Ack-Ack Macaque's tongue felt like an old flannel. He unscrewed the lid of the flask and took an experimental sniff.

"Is this vodka?"

"Vodka, and a few medicinal herbs." Apynja tapped her stick against one of the stones ringing the fire. "Strong stuff, too. It'll keep out the cold."

Ack-Ack Macaque swirled the liquid around in its container.

"What are you doing here, Apynja?"

"Waiting for you."

"For me?"

"You, or somebody like you. You see, if you're running from the laboratory, these woods are the closest of any appreciable size. I knew that if I waited here, you were bound to turn up sooner or later. You or somebody like you, at any rate."

Ack-Ack Macaque took a sip from the canteen.

The taste drew his lips back against his teeth. The fumes made his eye water.

"How long have you been here?"

"A short while."

"What about the cyborgs?'

"They don't worry me." Apynja smiled through thick, rubbery lips. "You can hear them coming a mile off."

Ack-Ack Macaque stepped closer to the warmth of the fire. His arms and legs felt like overcooked spaghetti.

"They were chasing me."

"I don't doubt it." She gave the fire a final prod, and then settled back on her haunches. "Now, why don't you sit down and join me." She reached behind her and threw a handful of dry leaves onto the embers. They crinkled and curled as they burned, giving off a sweet, oily smoke.

Ack-Ack Macaque glanced back, into the blackness beneath the trees.

"Listen, lady—"

"I'm no lady. And you can relax; you're perfectly safe here, as long as you're with me."

Ack-Ack Macaque opened his mouth to respond, then wondered why he was arguing. He let his shoulders slump.

"Whatever you say." He took a draught from the flask, and felt the vodka burning its way down to his belly. He was exhausted; he'd been running and swinging for hours. The internal warmth, combined with the heat from the fire, made him drowsy.

He watched as Apynja produced a dirty yellow pipe that looked as if it had been carved from the shinbone of a largish animal, and filled it from a drawstring pouch she kept tucked into the sleeve of her robe. With delicate fingers, she fished a burning twig from the edge of the fire and used it to light the mixture. After a few puffs, she got it going and gave a sigh of satisfaction.

Ack-Ack Macaque took a deep sniff through his nostrils, breathing in as much of the fragrance as he could catch, trying to identify it. She saw what he was doing, and held the pipe out to him.

"Would you like some?"

"Is it tobacco?"

"Something along those lines."

"Then hell, yeah. Pass it over."

The elderly ape paused. "It might be more… potent than you expect."

"Listen, lady, I've only got one cigar left, and I've been trying to save it. I'm gasping. The way I feel right now, I'd smoke a used teabag if I had to."

He accepted the pipe from her hands, and took a long, noisy suck from the business end.

Stars exploded behind his eyes.

"Whoa."

"Quite." Apynja smiled. In the firelight, wreathed in blue, sticky-smelling fumes, the hairs on her arms and face seemed to shimmer like molten gold. Ack-Ack Macaque blinked. His head felt deliciously light and airy, like a dusty attic with the skylight open, and he could feel all his aches and pains bubbling away into nothingness, as if he'd just slipped into a hot bath. He pulled back his lips and let the smoke curl out between his teeth.

"That," he said, his voice like boots treading a gravel path, "is some *seriously* good shit."

*   *   *

HE WAS BORN *in captivity, in slavery. For the first years of his life, all he knew was cages. Other monkeys were unknowable smells and shrieks in the darkness beyond the bars, trapped behind bars of their own. The only time he met them in the flesh was when he was put in a ring with one of them, their feet scuffing sawdust, weapons clenched in their paws, human faces howling and chanting around them.*

The victors were rewarded with fruit, cigarettes and beer; the losers died, coughing their last breath on the floor of the ring.

His owner, a rake-thin Malaysian, stank of coffee, sweat, and back-alley deals. All the man cared about was money. As long as Ack-Ack Macaque kept winning, his owner stayed happy and the treats kept coming. If he was wounded, there were no treats, just a slap across the head. If he lost... Well, Ack-Ack Macaque didn't need to lose in order to know his owner would walk away without a second glance. So he made sure he never lost. He channelled all his hurt and rage into the fights, taking on larger and larger opponents; sometimes two or three primates at a time; sometimes dogs or large cats. He had no morality or conscience, and could only dimly sense the suffering and pain he caused. In order to survive, he killed everything they put in front of him and, in the process, earned some scars and lost an eye.

Later, he was sold to a lab. They opened up his head and filled it with plastic. They gave him a voice box capable of human speech, then lengthened his spine and extended his arms and legs. He spent six

*months in a motion-capture suit learning to walk
and talk like a human. New skills and attitudes were
loaded onto the processors that filled his skull, and
then they dropped him into their virtual reality war
game and let him think it was real...*

THE MOVIE OF *his life went dark.*

*He felt himself unspool into the obscurity of the
void. The remains of the world reeled around him,
reduced to fragments of memory, glimpses of other
times, other places...*

Through the maelstrom, he heard Apynja's voice.

*"Close your eye," she said, "and tell me what you
see."*

*"Do what?" He struggled against the darkness,
flailing like a drowning monkey.*

"Indulge me."

AT FIRST, ALL *he perceived was the light of the fire
flickering through the skin and blood vessels of his
closed eyelid, turning his world a deep rosy pink.
Then, out of the colour, a pattern emerged. It was like
television static, but every blip and pixel contained an
image of the whole. Every scratch and shadow was
a world in itself, and all the worlds were connected.*

*"I see... everything," he said, his tongue thick like
a dead thing in his mouth. "The whole multiverse. All
the timelines."*

"And what else?"

*He tried to look closer, but the picture seethed,
always just out of focus. He got the impression*

there were forces moving beyond the limits of his perception, mighty struggles being played out just beneath the surface tension of his understanding.

"War," he said.

Apynja pursed her lips and nodded gravely.

"You are a creature of violence," *she said,* "in a world laid waste by violence—lost in an endless ether of chaos and suffering."

"It's not my fault."

Apynja's laugh filled the skies like the derision of an unkind god. "But of course it is."

The giddy sensation passed. Ack-Ack Macaque found himself standing on something that felt like sand or ashes. His toes sank into it and he shivered in the wind.

"Where am I?"

He raised his eye to a sky grown dim with the burned-out embers of dying stars, and knew he stood on a lifeless planetoid at the conclusion of all things, at the dusk of the universe.

"At the Eschaton. The place where one story ends and another begins."

Recoiling from the emptiness, he flailed his arms and legs, lashing the void around him, kicking up dust.

"Let me go!"

"Hush now." *The old orangutan's voice seemed to come from everywhere at once.* "Concentrate."

"Fuck you."

Apynja sighed like a tired parent.

"Why must you always make this so difficult?"

And then everything spiralled away, like water down a plughole.

* * *

SOME TIME LATER—he had no way of guessing exactly how many hours had actually passed—Ack-Ack Macaque realised he was back in the familiar discomfort of his own body. Opening his eye, he looked up through the black, almost leafless branches at the edge of the clearing. He was lying on his back and the clouds seemed to flex and roil above him like the skin on the belly of a dragon.

He sat up, and had to put his palms flat against the forest floor to stop the world from spinning. The trees around him seemed to bend and straighten in time with his breathing.

"What fuckery was that?" The dregs of his dream were fading. On the other side of the fire, Apynja watched him with shining eyes.

"You saw things as they really are. Now, tell me, what do you believe?"

Ack-Ack Macaque's head throbbed and he groaned. He hated hangovers. "I don't believe in anything."

The orangutan looked disappointed.

"How about good versus evil?"

With a hand to his brow, Ack-Ack Macaque snarled. "Good and evil, heaven and hell, humans and monkeys. I'm sick of all of it."

"Really?" The faintest suggestion of a smile brushed across the elderly ape's lips.

Ack-Ack Macaque took another pull on the pipe. The smoke seemed to calm him, seemed to stop the world from trying to sway and tilt. "Yeah, I'm sick of being told to choose sides all the time. I'm sick of people messing with my head; people trying to take over or destroy the world; sick of *fucking robots trying to kill me.*"

"Then what are you prepared to do about it?"

"Me?" He gave a snort. "What can I do, except look out for myself?"

"Ah!" Apynja held up a wrinkled finger. "So you *have* chosen a side?"

"Yeah, I guess I have." He looked into the flames. "My own side. Just me, because I'm sick of all the other bullshit."

"Always the same." Apynja scratched her cheek with dirty fingernails. "But would it surprise you to learn you're not alone?"

He glanced up at her with his one good eye.

"What does that mean?"

"There are a lot of humans who feel the same as you. They don't care about politics or war; they just want to be left to get on with their lives in peace. Look around you. There used to be eight billion people on this world, now only a tiny fraction remain." She pulled her blankets tighter around her squat frame. "You should have seen it when it happened. The corpses were rotting in the streets. Millions upon millions of them: men, women and children who wanted nothing more than to live their lives, to go to school, fall in love and care for their families."

Ack-Ack Macaque growled, deep in his throat. The silence seemed to press in against his ears.

"What are you trying to say?" He took another hit to steady the ache in his brainpan, and passed the pipe back across the fire.

"Look at the way you're dressed," Apynja said. "You're a soldier. A rebel. But have you ever asked yourself why? What is it you've been fighting all this time?"

Ack-Ack Macaque closed his eye again. He saw Spitfires and Messerschmitts wheeling across bright blue virtual skies; three-legged German war machines stomping through ruined villages; and Gestalt airships raining fire and death on London.

"Bad guys," he said. "All my life, I've been fighting bad guys. First, the Nazis, then the Céleste conspiracy, and then the Gestalt."

He looked at Apynja and she nodded.

"You've been fighting tyranny, Napoleon," she said quietly. "You always have, right from the beginning. Don't you remember? Even way back then, you had a problem with authority. The trouble is, the way things are set up at the moment, there will always be another would-be dictator. However many you defeat, others will always rise. It's human nature. They're primates like us. Their behaviour's ruled by the same power dynamics as ours. Someone always wants to dominate. They want more sex, more food and more money than the others, and they always want to rule the world—or as much of it as they can get their grubby little hands on."

"And now Célestine's trying to conquer two worlds?"

"If not more."

Ack-Ack Macaque felt the dead grass beneath him. The stillness beyond the fire's crackles seemed oppressive and sad, and spoke of murder and death. Another growl worked its way up from his chest, curling his lip.

"Fine. You want to know what I believe? Well, I

believe in a person's right to be free to get on with their life without all the bullshit, without other people trying to rip them off and kill them. Not to have to put up with governments and corporations and megalo-fucking-maniacs."

The elderly ape placed the bone pipe on the ground beside her.

"Then, I'll ask you once more, Napoleon. What are you prepared to do about it?"

Ack-Ack Macaque shrugged. "What can I do? I'm outnumbered, outgunned…"

"I thought you liked it that way."

"What are you saying, lady?"

Apynja raised her snout. "Somebody needs to bring order to the multiverse, to stop the killing, stop the chaos."

Ack-Ack Macaque frowned.

"Me?"

"Who better?"

Ack-Ack Macaque felt his lips peel back in a savage grin. For the first time since coming to this benighted hellhole, he felt some of his old fire return. Maybe it was exhaustion; maybe it was the vodka and the smoke, but right then he felt ready to take on the whole of Célestinc's cyborg army—one by one, or all at once.

"Eight billion people died here," Apynja said. "If you had the power, would you avenge them?"

He looked around at the empty forest, and thought of the bones littering the wreck of the crashed airliner.

"Damn straight."

"Would you find those responsible?"

"Yeah, I'd find them. And I'd fuck them up, too."

"Like the Lady Célestine?"

"Especially her."

"Good." Using her stick for support, Apynja levered herself into a standing position. "You need to make an example of her. You need to show the rest of them, all the would-be dictators, where the line is, and what will happen to them if they cross it."

"Yeah."

"You need to keep them in order, Macaque. You need to stop them killing their populations, stop them breaking out of their timelines."

For a queasy moment, Ack-Ack Macaque's head spun. He felt light and dry, like an autumn leaf.

"Hell, yeah," he mumbled.

Apynja gave a nod. She looked pleased. "That's what I was hoping you'd say." Leaning on her stick for support, she made off towards the trees at the far side of the clearing. "Now," she called over her shoulder, "come with me."

SHE LED HIM through the forest until they came to a large gnarled oak. To Ack-Ack Macaque, in his addled state, it resembled an ancient forest god, wrinkled and patient in its eternal vigil. Using her stick, Apynja hacked at the undergrowth surrounding the trunk and exposed an opening—a black maw in the half-light, like a vertical mouth, or the entrance to a womb.

"Here we are," she said.

Ack-Ack Macaque frowned.

"I may be stoned, but I'm not climbing in there." Spider webs draped the entrance, and who knew what other creepy crawlies lurked inside? "No fucking way."

Apynja made a rude noise.

"I don't want you to *get in there*." She spoke slowly, as if to an idiot. "I want you to *reach* in there and pull out the box."

"What box?"

"The one in the tree." She jabbed her stick at the hole. "And be quick about it."

Ack-Ack Macaque swore under his breath. He handed her the steel canteen that he'd been carrying, and stuck an arm into the orifice. Grimacing, he waved it around until his fingers made contact with something hard and rectangular. There seemed to be a rope handle affixed to the end. He gave it an experimental tug.

"Christ, this weighs a tonne."

"It should do." Apynja rapped her stick against the tree trunk. "It's full of guns."

Ack-Ack Macaque's tail stood on end. He turned his head to her.

"No shit?"

"Guns and bullets, and a few hand grenades."

Grinning, he gave another heave, and the wooden box slid out into the open. It was the length of a coffin, but narrower and not as deep. When he pulled up the lid, he found himself staring at a veritable arsenal of machine guns, pistols and spare magazines. There were a few knives taped to the inside of the lid, and even a couple of hatchets and a solid-looking chainsaw. He took a deep breath in through his nostrils, savouring the smells of cold metal and gun oil.

"Oh, momma. Where did you get them?"

Apynja sniffed. "At the start, the humans resisted. Célestine had the elite—the world leaders and major industrialists—in her pocket. She bribed them with promises of eternal life and eternal power. But the real people, the everyday men and women—the doctors, soldiers, teachers and police—they resisted. Even as they fell sick and died, they tried to fight Nguyen's metal men."

"What happened?"

"They died. These are their weapons. I've been collecting them from battlefields and mass graves. I thought they might come in useful." She tapped his boot with her cane. "I trust you know how to use them?"

"Do you shit in the woods?"

"I don't see how that—"

"It means yes." He picked up an automatic rifle. It was sleek and black, and reassuringly heavy. The fug in his head began to clear and he felt wired and energised and... just fucking ready to kick some fucking arse.

"Can you take me back to Célestine's lab?" he asked.

Apynja worked her lips together, looking pleased. "Of course."

"Good." He snapped a magazine into place. "Because my only way home's through her portal."

"You'll need her to operate it for you, Napoleon."

"I'll persuade her."

Apynja smiled. "Of course, you realise that the

only way to get to her will be by fighting your way through Nguyen's soldiers?"

Ack-Ack weighed the gun, judging its balance.

"That's what you're counting on, isn't it?"

Apynja's hands folded over the top of her cane. "Of course. If you can kill the woman and destroy Nguyen's creations, the surviving humans here might just stand a chance."

"Leave it to me." Hefting the rifle in one hand, Ack-Ack Macaque reached into his jacket and pulled out his last cigar. He looked at it for a moment, wondering if it really would be his *last* cigar; then he screwed it into the corner of his mouth and grinned. "Cos when I shoot a fucker, that fucker stays shot."

He heard a grunt of contentment.

"Why do you keep calling me Napoleon?" he asked.

"Because that's your name."

"No it isn't."

"Yes, it is. It's your *real* name..."

He felt the air stir, and his hair prickled with static. When he looked up, through a blue haze of cigar smoke, Apynja had gone. She had evaporated into the damp forest air as thoroughly as if she had never been there at all.

CHAPTER SEVENTEEN
TITANIUM CRANIUM

CÉLESTINE'S KNUCKLE TIGHTENED against the trigger. In her accelerated state, Victoria saw every movement as if in extreme slow motion. She saw the tendon in the woman's wrist stiffen like a violin string. She saw the skin of her knuckle stretch and blanch, and the way her jaw clenched in anticipation of the bang. Then, below, on the ground, something exploded. A fireball blossomed among the laboratory buildings. Distracted, Célestine's gaze flickered to the porthole, and Victoria had her chance.

Now.

Using all her pent-up energy, she threw herself across the metal box that lay between them, scattering candles in all directions. As she did so, the gun went off with a bang and a flash. The bullet passed somewhere above her, still aimed at the spot she'd just vacated. The recoil rocked the Duchess back on her heels. Victoria hit the floor with her shoulder and rolled. Her weight smashed into Célestine's legs. The gun flew from the woman's fingers, spinning a lazy parabolic course through the air. The Duchess cried out in indignation and surprise, and fell forwards onto her hands and knees.

Victoria climbed to her feet. She walked over

and picked the pistol from the deck. Her hands felt shaky. Crisis over, her neural circuits were powering down, draining the dangerous levels of adrenaline from her system and returning her time perception to something more akin to normal human experience. Behind her, Célestine was on all fours among the fallen and rolling candles, cursing the pain in her arms and legs.

Paul's ghost hovered in the air.

"Oh God," he said, hand over his mouth. "Oh shit, Jesus."

"It's over," Victoria told him.

"You were so *fast*."

"It's over. Send the signal."

"What signal?"

"To the *Sun Wukong*. Tell them to come and get us."

"Ah yes, of course. Sorry. I'll do it now."

Victoria remembered the pistol in her hands. She pointed it at the woman on the floor.

"Don't move." With her other hand, she rummaged in the pocket of her ragged coat, and pulled out her monkey detector. Paul watched her.

"Is it him?"

"Of course it's him." She risked a peep through the nearest porthole. A battle raged beneath. "Who else would it be?" The tracker beeped its confirmation. "He's at the far end of the compound," she said. "How long until the *Sun* gets here?"

"At least half an hour."

"*Merde*."

*   *   *

ACK-ACK MACAQUE LAY flat against the corrugated roof of one of the industrial units. He was panting. In one hand he gripped a matt black Desert Eagle—a semi-automatic pistol big enough to blow a tunnel through a mountain—and, in the other, the chainsaw. Grenades filled the bulging canvas satchel at his hip. Below, in the narrow gap between his building and the next, he heard heavy footsteps. The cyborgs hadn't considered that he could climb as well as he could run, and they were still looking for him on the ground. On the edge of the compound, a gas cylinder burned. The explosion had covered his entrance through the fence, and he'd been running and sniping ever since. He couldn't take on Nguyen's robot army and win in a stand-up firefight, but that was okay, because he had no intention of playing fair. The .44 Magnum cartridges in the Desert Eagle's clip were powerful enough to take down elk or buffalo, and the diamond-tipped chainsaw would make short work of even the sturdiest metal limb. If he could keep the action on a one-to-one basis, using the guerilla tactics of ambush and surprise, he might stand a chance.

For some moments, he remained where he was, ears straining. Then, when the noise of pursuit had died away, he rolled onto his stomach. His pistol had a fat silencer screwed into it that, while unable to actually silence the noise the gun made, would deaden the sound, making it harder for Célestine's troops to work out exactly where it was coming from. If he could stick to the rooftops, he might be able to take out a decent number of them before they located him.

Wriggling forward on his elbows, he took up position behind an air-conditioning unit and sighted along the pistol's barrel. Tall, spindly figures moved back and forth in the darkness, rifles gripped in their metal hands. He picked one that was out by itself, in the weeds near the perimeter fence, and lined up his sights.

"Say goodnight, dickhead."

The gun gave a low, flat crack and jumped in his hands. His target dropped into the long grass, a fist-sized hole punched through its titanium cranium, and he grinned.

One down, several hundred left to go.

He rolled away from the air-conditioner and scampered across the roof, in the opposite direction, seeking another vantage and another victim. If he could keep the robots guessing long enough, he might be able to slip into Célestine's sanctum unmolested.

Beyond the far edge of the laboratory compound, a large military helicopter wallowed in the air, only a few hundred feet above the scrubby ground. Its twin rotors filled the night with a low, guttural throb. Was it looking for him? It didn't seem to be executing any sort of obvious search pattern; in fact, it seemed to be wobbling around as if a fight were going on in its cockpit. He frowned at it in puzzlement, then turned his attention elsewhere, to more pressing matters. If the helicopter wasn't an immediate threat, he didn't have time to waste on it. He had better things to worry about.

The chainsaw had a leather strap, so he hooked it over his shoulder and slid the pistol into the waistband of his trousers. From where he stood, he could see the laboratory building that housed the portal that brought him here. It was the next building but one. To get there, he'd have to jump from this roof to the next—a gap of at least fifteen feet, over a drop of thirty.

To his right, a half-track troop carrier rumbled along the row of buildings, using a searchlight to peer into the alleys between.

Ah, fuck it. Sorry Apynja, but we both knew this was a suicide mission.

He backed up as far as he could. Then, when the searchlight had passed the alley he intended to jump, he took three grenades from his satchel and pulled their pins. An underarm toss sent them tumbling over the edge of the roof, towards the sound of the half-track's engine. While they were still in the air, he started to run. His boots slapped on the corrugated roof. The gap ahead yawned like a chasm.

By the time he realised he wasn't going to make it, he was already airborne. The alley between the buildings was simply too wide, the chainsaw too heavy.

"Fuuuuck!"

VICTORIA STOOD BRACED in the doorway of the helicopter's cockpit, holding Célestine's pistol to the pilot's head.

"Circle around," she told him. "Set down at the end of the row."

"Then what?" Paul asked. From her point of view, he was sitting in the vacant co-pilot's chair.

"Then we find the monkey and attract his attention."

"What if he shoots at us? If he sees a helicopter swooping at him, he's bound to assume it's hostile."

Victoria pursed her lips.

"Look, I'm improvising. If you've got any better suggestions, don't keep them to yourself."

In front of her, the pilot, who could only hear her side of the conversation, cleared his throat.

"If there is going to be shooting," he said in a strong French accent, "we could always activate the field generator."

Victoria and Paul looked at him, then at each other.

"Do it," Victoria said.

The man gave a shrug. "Only the Duchess can make it work."

Victoria considered this. Then she pressed the pistol hard into his shoulder. "If I leave you here for a moment, you won't try anything stupid?"

"*Non, Madame.*"

"Good boy."

With a tired sigh, she went aft, back into the helicopter's cargo hold. She'd left Lady Alyssa tied to the leg of the desk, but she wasn't there now. A wind whipped though the hold, extinguishing the candles. Célestine had opened the cargo bay's side hatch. She was a black figure framed against the night. Victoria whipped the gun up and squeezed off two shots, but Célestine had already gone, allowing herself to fall away into the wind, and Victoria wasn't sure whether or not she'd been hit.

"*Putain!*" She kicked her boot against the deck in frustration, and marched over to the hatch. The noise of the rotors was deafening. Below, the roofs of the factories wheeled beneath them in the darkness—but of the Duchess, there was no sign.

ACK-ACK MACAQUE'S CHEST hit the lip of the opposite roof with a crunch that blew the wind from his lungs. His knees smacked against the side of the warehouse. In a panic, his fingers scrabbled at the rusted metal roof.

Behind him, the half-track exploded.

He ended up hanging by one hand from a broken sheet of corrugated iron, his boots dangling over a thirty-foot drop, the chainsaw swinging on its strap from his shoulder. If one of the cyborgs saw him, he'd be a sitting duck.

Q: Why did the monkey fall off the roof?
A: He was shot.

With a snarl, he reached up and took hold of the gutter with his other hand. He couldn't pull himself up. The iron pipe was cold and its edges sharp, and he simply didn't have enough strength left in his arms. The breath heaved in his chest and, not for the first time, he began to regret his cigar habit.

If I get out of this, he promised himself, *I'm going to take up jogging. I'm going to join a gym. I'm going to…*

Oh, who am I kidding?

He kicked off his boots and let them fall. One after the other, they spun end-over-end to the muddy floor of the alley, landing with hollow thuds. If two hands weren't enough, he'd try four. Using his tail as a counterbalance, he swung his feet up, and gripped the roof with his toes. His legs were stronger than his arms. Using them to bear most of his weight freed his hands to seek firmer purchase, and he was eventually able to heave himself up, out of danger.

He lay on the roof, cursing softly under his breath. Voices came from below. Another few seconds, and he would have been seen.

"Too close," he muttered.

Overhead, the helicopter wheeled toward him; or at least, towards the car park at the end of the row of buildings. Light spilled from an open hatch in its side. A figure stood braced on the threshold, tall, thin and feminine. For a moment, it swayed. Then it fell, arms and legs spread out in a graceful swallow dive. Ack-Ack Macaque elbowed himself up into a sitting position. That was Célestine! What was the Duchess playing at? Was she trying to kill herself? He could see she was too low to use a parachute.

"Pavement pizza," he muttered glumly, wondering how he'd ever get home without her to operate the portal.

Then, as the falling woman hurtled towards the cracked surface of the parking lot, two of the spindly cyborgs leapt ten metres into the air. They caught her between them and fell, cradling her in their interlocked arms. As they hit the ground, their carbon fibre legs flexed, absorbing the force of the impact and the weight of the woman they'd rescued. They set her feet gently onto the shattered tarmac of the car park, and stepped away, giving her space.

Watching the Duchess, apparently unharmed and dusting herself down, Ack-Ack Macaque felt his jaw drop open. He blinked his solitary eye. Célestine had been falling from a helicopter, and two of her cyborgs had *jumped up and caught her*.

"What the *fuck*?"

Beyond the barbed wire of the perimeter fence, massive vehicles were coming to life. Their engines growled and their weapons swung back and forth as if scenting the air. Fire and smoke belched from their chimneys. Tall, spindly figures raced toward them, climbing into their cabs or piling into hatches along their lengths. Célestine and her saviours followed at a brisk walk. Ahead, through the gloom, the metal arch had begun to glow brighter than ever. Blue sparks flickered like sprites amidst the metal latticework of its frame. The warped space at its centre swirled and sparkled like a whirlpool, throwing off shards of rainbow light.

It was another portal, Ack-Ack Macaque realised, and all these giant tanks were lining up to pass through it.

"Holy shitballs." Even to his own ears, his laugh held an edge of panic. "It's an invasion!"

CHAPTER EIGHTEEN
A VIEW OF THE RIVER

THE CROWD STOOD in Parliament Square, solemnly contemplating Big Ben's ruined tower. Rather than being rebuilt along with the rest of the Palace of Westminster, the scarred and shattered clock face had been repurposed as a permanent memorial to those who had died in the Gestalt attack. The pockmarked sides of the tower had been inscribed with the names of more than fifty thousand Commonwealth citizens, from more than a dozen countries, who had perished during that initial assault on the major cities of the world. As well as civilians, the names included those of politicians, civil servants, and members of His Majesty's armed services.

Dressed in a ceremonial uniform, Merovech stood on a specially constructed stage and looked up at the tower. Today, it stood battered but proud against a backdrop of blue sky and high, white cloud. He wondered exactly where on its ornate surface Julie's name had been carved. He hoped it was somewhere near the top, with a good view of the river.

Around him on the platform sat heads of state from most of the Commonwealth nations. Some had survived the tragedy; others had been elected in its wake. They were here, like him, to officially dedicate the monument. They all knew of his personal loss, of course, but had so far been either too polite or too reticent to mention it.

Is it time?

The thought surprised him. He'd spent the past three years pushing it to the back of his mind, smothering it with notions of duty and continuity; and yet here it came now, worming its way back.

When he'd first taken the throne, in the immediate aftermath of the battle in the English Channel, he'd done it to avert a nuclear war. He'd always meant to abdicate. He'd promised Julie that he would. But then the Gestalt invaded, and everything changed. He put aside his personal feelings for the good of his country and his Commonwealth, and loyally played the part his people expected; but he had never been of royal blood and bore no right to sit upon the throne. He wasn't even sure he was entirely human. Now, with this dedication, could it finally be time to walk away, to announce his retirement and take himself off to a small cottage on a Greek island, somewhere far from the machinery of media and state? Today seemed as good a day as any. If the crowds and cameras were gathered here in order to draw a line under the catastrophic events of the recent past, then surely now would be the perfect time to put an end to his reign? He had served his people. None of them knew that he had no claim to the crown. He had served and he had suffered, and the people had taken him to their hearts. Surely they would understand and be sympathetic if he announced his wish to step down, on today of all days?

The cracked bell tolled in the damaged tower. He rose to his feet and walked to the microphone. Heads and cameras turned towards him. The upturned faces of the people packed into the square reminded him of a field of sunflowers, turning to greet the day. As they fell silent, he cleared his throat.

"Today," he began, reading from the words projected by the autocue. They shimmered in the air before him like the delusions of a heat-stricken madman. "Today marks a most solemn anniversary. It is a time for remembrance but also a time for hope; a time to acknowledge our grief but also to give thanks for the peace and international cooperation that have followed in the wake of catastrophe. For now, nation stands shoulder to shoulder with nation, united. Our petty and dangerous squabbles have been put aside in the face of strange and graver threats, and in honour of those whom we come here today to remember." He paused, conscious of the bell tower behind him. The words he was reading were his. He'd written them himself, yet still they died in his mouth. He couldn't go on. His throat felt closed up and he couldn't swallow properly. All he could think of was Julie: her face, her smell, the way her eyes would crinkle at the corners when she smiled.

Damn it all.

She'd want him to do it. She'd never wanted to be a queen or princess, but she'd gone along with the charade because he'd convinced her it was necessary. And it had been, at the time; at least, he'd thought so. He'd spent his life being trained to lead, and so who better than him to step in during a crisis? But with that crisis now over, how necessary was it for him to remain? He closed his eyes and sighed. The crowd was silent. They thought he was overcome with grief, and their sympathy stung him even as he was grateful for it. It made him feel like a fraud.

Time to go.

In his imagination, he'd rehearsed this moment a hundred times. Yet, now it was upon him, he couldn't think of anything to say. The only words that came to mind were tumbled, nonsensical platitudes.

He watched one of the vast Gestalt dreadnoughts chug across the rooftops of the city, on its way to Heathrow. Following the Gestalt surrender, the hundred or so dreadnoughts that were still operational had been placed under joint international control. In a world still reeling back from the brink of World War III, no single country could be permitted sole control of such a fleet, and so the vast armoured airships, still operated by their Gestalt crews, had been organised into a defensive force, designed to combat incursions from other timelines. Thanks to Ack-Ack Macaque, Earth's assailants had become its protectors.

Thinking of the monkey, Merovech looked down at his hands.

Why didn't I go with them when I had the chance? How different his life would have been if he and Julie had accepted Victoria Valois' invitation to join the *Tereshkova*'s crew three years ago, in the wake of the so-called 'Combat de la Manche.' They could have travelled the world. Julie might still have been alive.

"I have to tell you something." His voice faltered.

The crowd's wide eyes radiated commiseration and compassion. He gripped the sides of the lectern with his white-gloved hands and took a deep breath. His legs were shaking.

"I have to—"

He became aware of voices behind him, and glanced around. A number of the world leaders arrayed behind him were talking urgently into their phones, or listening to aides. Had they guessed what he was about to say? Even as he frowned at their interruption, he saw Amy Llewellyn shouldering her way towards him from the back of the stage. She had her security pass in one hand and carried a SincPhone in the other. Her dark brows were drawn together and her cheeks were ashen. Reaching him, she placed one of her hands across the microphone and raised herself on her toes to whisper in his ear.

"It's Mars," she said, pushing the phone into his hands. Her breath was warm against his cheek.

"Another message?" Merovech looked down at the handset she'd forced on him. The very last thing he wanted right now was to talk to his mother.

"No." Amy shook her head, expression grim. She gripped his shoulder. "They've launched a missile." She eyed the expectant crowd. "And if our estimates are correct, it's the size of the Isle of Wight."

BREAKING NEWS

From *B&FBC* NEWS ONLINE:

Astronomers detect 'missle' from Mars

PARIS 18/11/ 2062 – Astronomers working for the European Space Agency have observed the launch of a gigantic projectile from the surface of Mars. The shock announcement came earlier today, during a service of remembrance to mark the second anniversary of the Gestalt attack of 2060. The projectile, which is believed to be some sort of weapon, is on a course to hit the Earth, and is due to arrive in less than six months.

At a hastily convened press conference in Paris, Dr. Sandrine Aurand, a spokesperson for the ESA, told reporters that the missile appears to be moving faster than expected, saying, "If our measurements are correct, the only way to explain the object's apparent acceleration is to assume some form of antimatter propulsion."

Antimatter is matter in which the charges of the particles are reversed. When it comes into contact with ordinary matter, the two annihilate each other with a release of energy much greater than that given off during a nuclear reaction. Antimatter is extremely rare, and it is not known where the newly revived crew of the Martian probe could have obtained enough to power a missile of such size.

According to observations, the object is most likely a captured asteroid or 'minor planet' measuring almost two kilometres in length, which makes it comparable in mass to the asteroid that is thought to have wiped out the dinosaurs.

"We're running simulations at the moment," Dr. Aurand warned, "but wherever this hits, the effects will be global."

Read more | Like | Comment | Share

Related Stories:

Government appeals for calm as shoppers stockpile food and water.

Emergency talks to be held in London.

Opinion: Is it time to make peace with Mars?

Today's List: Ten historical impacts that literally shook the globe.

Religious sects proclaim 'End of the World'.

Did H.G. Wells predict all this 160 years ago?

Where will you be when the rock hits? Celebrities tell us their plans for 'Doomsday'.

CHAPTER NINETEEN
THE BELLY OF THE BEAST

VICTORIA VALOIS STOOD in the cockpit door, her pistol pressed into the skin at the back of the pilot's neck.

"So, how come you're still human?" she asked. She had to raise her voice over the noise of the engines.

The Frenchman gave a tight shrug. He was trying to concentrate on his instrument panel.

"I'm good at what I do."

"Okay, prove it." Victoria pointed forward, through the windshield. "Get us as close to that roof as possible, and lower the ramp."

"You want to get out?"

"No, we're picking somebody up."

The hull rattled, as if hit by a handful of ball bearings.

"They're shooting at us!" Paul said.

Victoria ignored him.

No shit, Sherlock.

She kept the barrel of her gun jammed against the pilot's spine, just below his helmet, where it met his shoulders. Her other hand gripped the doorframe and she had her feet braced against either side of the narrow gangway. She watched the horizon tilt and slide as the big helicopter wallowed around, lining its tubby backside up with the old warehouse. A small screen on the pilot's console showed a grainy night-vision view of the roof, taken from a camera at the back of the copter. In its unreal green light, she could see Ack-Ack Macaque crouched by one of the air vents. The gun in his hands flashed, and Victoria flinched as a bullet clanged against the bulkhead behind her.

"Jeez, now *he's* shooting at us," Paul complained.

"What do you want me to do about it?"

"You could call him. Assuming he's still got his radio."

"His radio?" If she could have spared a hand, she would have slapped her forehead. "Of course, he was wearing his link when he fell into the portal."

Paul smiled infuriatingly.

"It's a good job one of us pays attention."

Pocketing her gun, Victoria reached forward and lifted the radio handset from its clip on the console between the seats. She thumbed through the frequencies, and then squeezed the button to transmit.

"Hey, monkey-man. It's us. Stop firing, and shift your derrière."

ACK-ACK MACAQUE THRUST the Desert Eagle into his waistband, and pulled tight the strap holding the chainsaw. Then he ran. He crossed the rusting iron roof on all fours, scampering as hard and fast as he could, careless of the noise he made. Shots came from below but he ignored them. He couldn't see who was firing or where the bullets were going; all he could see was the inviting maw of the helicopter's open cargo ramp. He could feel the blood surging through him and felt like whooping. He had been alone, but now his troupe had found him. With a last, desperate bound, he was aboard, and half-running, half-stumbling up into the belly of the beast.

He found himself in a cargo bay filled with toppled candles. For a second, he thought he might be back in the woods with Apynja, hallucinating, still high on exhaustion, vodka and weed. Then reality kicked in and he forced himself forward, to where Victoria stood, covering the pilot with her weapon. She smiled.

"Damn good to see you, monkey-man."

"Likewise. But I think I hit your fuel tank." He'd certainly stitched a row of bullet holes across the helicopter's flank and seen liquid vent from the base of the rear rotor. Without looking around, the pilot tapped a dial.

"He's right, we're losing fuel."

Victoria swore under her breath. Reunions would have to wait. "Do we have enough to make it through the portal?"

"Yes, but—"

"Then take us through. We'll worry about the rest later."

Ack-Ack Macaque looked forward through the windshield and gaped at the ranks of lumbering machines arrayed before the metal structure. "Are you fucking nuts? You'll be flying us into the middle of an invasion."

"Yes, but at least we'll be home. We can signal the *Sun Wukong* to follow us when it gets here."

Ack-Ack Macaque focused his yellow eye on her.

"Home?"

"That's where the portal leads," Victoria said. "Célestine's planning to invade *our* timeline."

Her words seemed to echo in his ears. *Home.* He hadn't been back to the timeline of his birth in two years, and the thought of all this armour attacking it filled him with a sick kind of rage. The Gestalt assault had been bad enough; the thought of another onslaught so soon...

"What are we waiting for?" He straightened his collar and champed at the cigar still clamped in his teeth. "The *Sun*'s on its way. Tell it to drop all its missiles on these tossers."

"We can't wait for it."

"We don't have to." Bullets clanged against the hull. "We've done all we can. Now get us through that portal before we fall out of the goddamn sky."

TRAILING SMOKE, THEY passed through the portal and burst into sunlight. Ack-Ack Macaque blinked and put up a hand to shade his eye.

"Are they coming after us?" Victoria asked.

He ducked his head back into the cargo bay. The rear ramp had been left open. Behind them in the winter air, he saw nothing more than the faintest suggestion of a shimmer, like a desert heat haze.

"Nope, not yet at any rate."

"Well, they can't be far behind." He watched her pick up the radio and begin flicking through the frequencies, calling for help. He left her to it, inching his way aft, searching for weapons. If a couple of hundred Leviathans were about to breach the portal, he wanted to face them with something more substantial than a pistol and a chainsaw.

"Come on," he muttered irritably, scanning the bare walls and desk. "There's got to be something." He tried the desk's drawers but they were mostly empty, and he didn't think a stapler would be much use against an armoured battle tank.

"Balls."

He slammed the top drawer. As he did so, the helicopter's rear engine spluttered and the craft lurched. They wouldn't be airborne much longer. Knotting his fingers in the cargo webbing fixed to the wall, he braced himself. Candles dropped and tumbled, rolling across the deck. Through the open rear doors, the green and brown French countryside dipped and spun. He heard Victoria shout something, and closed his eye.

With an almighty splintering crash, the chopper hit the upper branches of a tree and tipped sideways. There was an instant of sickening free-fall, and then the whole craft rattled as the rotors battered themselves to splinters against the stony soil of a winter field, and the cabin crunched down like an eggshell.

CHAPTER TWENTY
GET TO THE CHOPPER

"Never again," muttered Victoria Valois. Picking her way from the helicopter's ruined cockpit, she swore that, as long as she lived, she would never set foot in another of these contraptions.

Ack-Ack Macaque stood waiting for her. He offered her a leathery hand to help her down.

"You okay, boss?"

She held onto his shoulder for support. She had a few new cuts and bruises, but nothing serious.

At least we didn't land in the sea this time... She blinked in the sunshine. Beyond the fields, she could hear traffic. To the north, a bulky two-hulled skyliner forged towards Paris.

"We're home."

"Seems like it." Ack-Ack Macaque sniffed the air. "How's the pilot?"

Victoria shook her head. "He didn't make it." The man had been crushed when the cockpit hit the dirt. The monkey shrugged. He didn't care. What was one dead henchman in the face of an invading army?

"Come on," he said. "Let's get the fuck out of here." He shambled off across the ploughed field, in the direction of the road, and she trailed after him, still feeling a little unsteady on her feet. A watery winter sun warmed her face and, after spending so long in the gloom of Célestine's world, she could feel herself drawing nourishment from its light and heat. In her eye, Paul fizzed and flickered into virtual existence. He looked around, taking in everything she could see and hear.

"We're in one piece?"

"Just about."

He frowned.

"Why are we running?"

Victoria slowed.

"Because of the tanks."

Paul scratched his temple. "What tanks?"

Up ahead, the monkey had dropped to all fours. He had a pistol in his belt and the chainsaw over his shoulder. She watched him bound towards the dry stone wall at the edge of the field, and quickened her pace to keep up.

"You know, the big Leviathans."

Paul shook his head. He stuck out his bottom lip.

"Where are we, anyway?"

"Home."

"Really?"

Victoria didn't answer. She was jogging now, and couldn't spare the breath. She saw Ack-Ack Macaque reach the wall and clamber over it. Standing on the other side, he called to her.

"Come on!"

Floating above the hardened muddy ground, Paul's image radiated surprise.

"Who's *that*?"

Victoria felt a stab of pain. "What?"

"The monkey." Paul straightened his glasses. "How come he can talk?"

Victoria felt like crying.

"I'll explain later."

"Why, what's the hurry?"

A couple of steps from the wall, she stopped and turned. Roughly a kilometre away, an arch-shaped section of air roiled and bubbled like a pan of boiling water.

"That's why," she said, panting.

As she watched, a slab of khaki-coloured metal appeared in the air, in the centre of the disturbance. It quickly swelled into the snout of one of the Leviathans. Moving slowly, rumbling forward on great tracks, the huge machine pushed its way into the world as if emerging from an invisible tunnel. Its gun turrets bobbed and swivelled, seeking targets. Even at this distance, it seemed to tower over her, and she could feel the ground shake beneath her feet.

Paul's mouth fell open.

"Ah."

MOVING AT A crouch, staying as low as possible, Ack-Ack Macaque led Victoria along the edge of the field, keeping the wall between them and the advancing tank. They were moving at a right angle to the Leviathan's progress, trying to avoid getting crushed by its rolling treads. The noise it made was terrific: the continuous rattle and clatter of the tread links; metallic whines and screeches from axles and wheels; the powerful bark and thrum of its engines...

As he moved, Ack-Ack Macaque sucked in as much fresh air as he could, trying to clear the fumes lingering in his head.

Apynja had used him. The realisation burned fiery and sore, its flame fed by anger and embarrassment. When she'd found him, he'd been exhausted and hungry, and lost on a strange world. She'd drugged him, riled him up, and then turned him loose against Célestine's compound, on what she must have known would be a suicidal attack. Yes, he'd been angry about the needless deaths of so many people on her world; yes, he'd been upset and tired, and wanting to hit back; but she'd amplified and exploited that anger, and used him as a weapon. She'd aimed him at the target, and then pressed all the right buttons.

What had she been expecting? There was no way he could have prevailed against so many cyborgs. He'd been running from them for days—taking the fight to them had been insane. He might be reckless but he wasn't usually that stupid. Usually, he knew when to attack and when to retreat, but Apynja had found a way to circumvent his common sense. He felt used. He would have died had Victoria not shown up when she did. Despite all Apynja's talk about individual freedoms and the taking down of tyrants, the saggy old ape had manipulated him into doing something stupid for her own ends, and—now he was starting to think clearly again—he hated her for it. She was just one more self-serving bastard in a long line of self-serving bastards, and he was tired of being treated like a puppet.

Motioning Victoria to stay hidden, he risked a peep over the wall. They were out of the Leviathan's immediate path but not out of range of its weapons, and he had no doubt that, if they were seen, they'd be blown to pieces. Grinding relentlessly forward, the tank's front tracks rolled across the wreck of the helicopter, flattening it into the ground like a dead bird caught beneath an elephant's foot. Ack-Ack Macaque ducked down.

"If only I had a rocket launcher..."

"It wouldn't do any good," Victoria said. "They have shields. They're almost impenetrable."

"You're kidding me?"

"No, sorry."

"Damn it!" He looked at Victoria and saw she was red-faced and out of breath. Her eyes were raw and puffy, as if she'd been crying. She still wore the shabby, threadbare clothes she'd used as a disguise, and her hands and knees were filthy with mud.

"Stay low," he growled.

At the end of the wall, a stream cut between the fields. With a curse and a snarl of distaste, he crawled down into the reeds at its edge, feeling his hands and legs squishing into the frigid, cloudy muck at their base. His nose wrinkled with the rank cabbage-like smell of rotting vegetation, and his skin cringed at the icy water's cadaverous touch.

"Ah, fuck it." At least now he was below the level of the surrounding fields, and hopefully hidden from sight. He started crawling, sloshing downstream, towards a small stone bridge that marked where a lane crossed the stream. He heard Victoria suck air through her teeth as she slid herself into the water behind him; then, a clattering crash as the Leviathan smashed its way through the field's boundary wall.

The beast was going to pass them about two-dozen metres to their left. They were running parallel to its course now. All they had to do was get into the shade of the bridge without being seen. Beneath its mossy stones, they'd have the breathing space to hunker down and plan their next move.

His lips drew back in an involuntary smile. Here he was again, running from enemy war machines in the fields of France. It was just like being back in the game, and he revelled for a moment in the situation's familiarity, remembering better days. He'd been unstoppable back then: the best pilot on the Allied side, victor of a thousand dogfights and a hundred ground skirmishes. He'd once gone hand-to-hand against an entire platoon of Nazi ninjas, and emerged with nothing more serious than a few scratches and some singed fur.

No chance of that now.

The cold water swirled around his arms and legs, aching his bones, and he could feel it sapping his strength—but at least the shock of it had cleared his head. His body might be exhausted but he felt mentally fresher and more on-the-ball than he had in days.

He dipped his head, looking back through his legs.

"How are you doing, boss?"

Victoria's coat was sodden and floating out on either side of her. Her shoulders shook with the cold and her lips had turned a deep purple colour.

"Just keep moving," she hissed through her clenched jaw. Ack-Ack Macaque's grin widened.

"Aye, aye."

He began to shuffle forward, but then stiffened as

he heard the boom of a cannon off to his left. Half a second later, a shell exploded on the right-hand bank of the stream, a few metres the other side of the bridge.

"Shit!" He ducked his head as lumps of soil and clumps of grass rained down around him. The gun fired again and the centre of the bridge blew apart. Stones flew in all directions. Heedless of the water, Ack-Ack Macaque threw himself flat. When he emerged a couple of seconds later, gasping and spitting out weeds, he saw that the small structure had been completely destroyed. If he and Victoria had been sitting under it, they'd have been killed by the blast and buried by the debris.

He leapt to his feet and grabbed her by the hand, pulling her back in the direction from which they'd come.

"New plan," he hollered. "Run like fuck!"

SHELLS CRASHED AROUND them as they splashed through the water. The banks of the stream afforded some protection, but not much. Victoria's legs were shaky with cold and fear, and her face stung from the earth and gravel flung up by the explosions. At one point, she and Ack-Ack Macaque were blown completely off their feet, and lay panting in the mud and ooze, ears ringing.

Closing her eyes, she accessed the gelware in her skull. A mental menu allowed her to dial down her sensitivity to pain and fatigue and increase the amount of adrenaline coursing through her arteries.

"Get up." The monkey tugged her sleeve and she stood, coat dripping into the water around her.

"I'm okay." Where a moment ago there had been soreness and discomfort, now she felt only stiffness.

"Ready to run?"

"*Pourquoi pas?*"

"Come on, then." He pushed her forward. Another shell whined overhead and thumped into the ploughed earth of the field on the other side of the stream. Even through her numbed toes, Victoria felt the ground shudder with the force of its impact. She risked a peep at the Leviathan. The enormous, slab-sided vehicle hadn't altered course, and continued to draw away from them, towards the outskirts of Paris. The shells it fired came from two of the smaller turrets towards its rear.

"They're using us for practice," she said indignantly.

Ack-Ack Macaque shoved her onwards.

"Would you prefer they turned around and used their really big guns?"

"No, but—"

"Keep moving," he said. "We need to get across this field." They were back to the point where they'd originally entered the stream. "We'll use the wall as cover again, only this time we'll go on the other side."

"But—"

"They've almost got our range. We have to change direction. If we get behind the wall, they won't know which bit of it we're behind. They won't know where to aim."

"Unless they have thermal imaging."

"In which case, we're fucked whatever we do, so let's act like they don't." He scrambled up the bank and Victoria followed. A shell hit the ground a few metres behind her but she ignored it and kept crawling. The November soil was hard and friable beneath her hands. The wall lay to her left, the portal to her right. The monkey scurried after her, far more comfortable on all fours than she was.

"Don't stop," he huffed. "The only way we're getting out of this is if they don't know where we are."

Two shells hit simultaneously, but they were back towards the stream, further away than before.

Is it working?

She could see Paul's ghost floating in the air before her. He'd taken off his glasses and had his hands on his hips.

"I'm sorry," he said, "but who's shooting at us?"

"Lady Alyssa."

"I thought she was dead."

Victoria didn't answer; she couldn't spare the breath to explain, and she wasn't sure she could talk to him without her voice cracking. For three years, she'd been dreading this moment: the point at which his simulated personality began to de-cohere and fade, and he became progressively more confused. As a teenager, she'd had an aunt with Alzheimer's and had no desire to repeat the experience of watching another human being unravel piece-by-piece— especially one she loved as fiercely as she loved Paul. She reached the section of wall pulverised by the Leviathan's tracks and stopped crawling. The noise of the tank's engines was quieter now, and the shells it fired were going wide, its rear gunners still concentrating on the section of wall closest to the water.

"Why aren't they firing this way?" she asked.

Ack-Ack Macaque dropped back onto his haunches.

"They don't need to."

"Why not?"

"Because of that." Across the field, beyond the crushed remains of the helicopter, the portal shimmered again, and the snout of another huge battle tank appeared.

"*Merde.*"

"You said it."

Whichever side of the wall they chose, they'd be visible to one Leviathan or the other. They were trapped and exposed, with nowhere to hide, and no weapons capable of inflicting damage on the enemy.

She grabbed the leather shoulder of Ack-Ack Macaque's flight jacket.

"What do we do?"

The monkey smacked his lips and drew the large black pistol from his belt.

"I'll distract them, you run for it."

She gave him a look.

"You're kidding?"

He shook his head, and unstrapped the chainsaw. "I'll charge the bastard. You run for it. See if you can get across the field and lose yourself behind the far wall. It's your only chance."

The second Leviathan was only halfway through the portal but its turrets were already zeroing in on their position. Victoria swallowed.

"I can't leave you."

"You don't have a choice, sweetheart." Ack-Ack Macaque jumped to his feet, brandishing a weapon

191 Gareth L. Powell

in each hand, and let out a howl. Then he started to run. Victoria winced. She could see guns of all shapes and sizes turning on him.

"Wait!" But it was too late. She couldn't do anything to stop what was about to happen. She couldn't even bring herself to run. Her body wouldn't respond. She crouched there, unable to move, as her best friend ran at the biggest tank she'd ever seen, waving his chainsaw above his head.

He wouldn't get close, she knew. He'd die and, moments later, she'd follow him. She tried to close her eyes but couldn't wrestle her gaze from the horror unfolding before her.

She braced herself for the inevitable hail of bullets...

THE AIR CRACKLED and the sun went out.

By the time she realised it was the *Sun Wukong* blocking out the sky, the dreadnought had unloaded a clutch of missiles at the tank, engulfing it in a series of gigantic fireballs. The concussions knocked her back on her derrière, and she sat for a few seconds, mouth open at the ferocity of the attack. Ack-Ack Macaque recovered faster than she did. While her attention remained fixed on the Leviathan—still rolling and apparently unharmed as it emerged from the conflagration—he ran back and yanked her upright.

"Cavalry's here," he said.

Looking up, Victoria saw a helicopter spiralling down from the airship, weaving and ducking to avoid the lines of tracer cutting the sky around it.

Oh God, she thought. *Not another helicopter. Not again*.

Hand-in-hand, they started running, stumbling and skidding on the loose, uneven surface of the ploughed field. Above, the dreadnought fired another clutch of rockets.

"The shield," she said. "The missiles can't get through."

Ack-Ack Macaque said nothing. He just kept pulling her onwards. His palm felt as soft and warm as a leather glove, but the tendons beneath were as hard and tight as wire.

Several of the Leviathan's larger cannons swung upwards, aiming at the *Sun Wukong*. As Victoria watched, they fired a volley. She tried to cover her ears. The noise was deafening, and she could feel it in her gut. The tank rocked on its tracks, and angry explosions tore the airship's underside. At the same time, a pair of missiles dropped from the main gondola and punched through the Leviathan's roof. Their combined detonation lit the tank up from within. Flames burst from every hatch and turret, and the upper superstructure blew apart like a tin can filled with firecrackers.

Even as the wreck burned, the air behind it rippled and the bow of a third Leviathan appeared. Legs and feet now almost completely numb, Victoria staggered unsteadily towards the spot where the helicopter was in the process of touching down in a whirl of dust and twigs. To her left, beyond the wall, the first Leviathan also engaged the airship, and they traded shots. She wondered how much punishment the *Sun Wukong*'s armour could withstand.

With all hell breaking out around her, she ran for all she was worth—but Ack-Ack Macaque merely stood contemplating the burning wreckage of the second tank, with its punctured roof and smoking windows. A slight frown creased his face and he rubbed thoughtfully at the patch over his left eye.

"Now, that's interesting," he said.

CHAPTER TWENTY-ONE
LABYRINTHINE AND MOSTLY UNDOCUMENTED

THE HELICOPTER TOOK them up, through a hurricane of explosions and tracer fire, to the upper deck of the *Sun Wukong*. Victoria's knuckles were white on her safety straps and her heart raced in her chest. By the time they touched down, her gelware had been forced to intercede, flooding her bloodstream with sedatives. She stepped out onto the deck feeling dreamy and disjointed. The monkey shuffled along beside her as if suffering the world's worst hangover.

"We have to get to the bridge," he said. A shell struck the bottom of the airship and Victoria staggered as the deck shook beneath her feet. Ack-Ack Macaque looked at her with his bloodshot yellow eye. "Come on." His face had scratches; his jacket had become filthy, ripped and scuffed; his fur had been caked in mud and tangled with brambles and twigs; and his arms dangled loosely at his sides, as if he lacked the strength to lift them. God alone knew how long he'd been without food or sleep.

"No," she said.

He blinked at her. "But—"

"No, I've got this." She rolled her head, stretching her neck muscles in an effort to shake off the drowsiness of the drugs. "You get below. Take a shower. Get something to eat. Have K8 patch you up." He opened his mouth but she cut him off. "Go on," she snapped in her best captain-of-a-skyliner tone, "you're no use to us if you can hardly stand."

Now she was out of the chopper, and not in imminent danger of another crash, she felt better. And this wouldn't be her first battle.

"I'll call you if I need you," she promised. A damaged rocket corkscrewed up into the sky and burst like a firework. Ack-Ack Macaque sagged with relief.

"Yes, boss."

"Good, now get below."

"Just one thing." He lingered. "Their shields."

"What about them?"

"They work both ways. They have to drop them to fire."

Victoria raised an eyebrow. "Are you sure?"

The monkey gave a grim nod. "I clocked it in the field. That's how the missiles got through to the second tank."

Victoria felt her cheeks redden. So, that's what he'd been doing. She'd been too busy running to pay attention to the ins and outs of the battle. Surprising herself, she lunged forward and caught him in a bear hug. He squirmed, and stank like an old carpet, but she held him tight, clinging to his leather-clad shoulders, feeling his whiskers prickle her cheek and neck.

"I'm so glad to have you back," she said. She held him for a moment, then gave him a final squeeze and hurried up the companionway to the bridge, where she found the Founder in the command chair.

The pregnant monkey looked at her through her monocle.

"Thank goodness you're here, dear." She wore a long velvet dress and a miniature top hat.

"What's the situation?"

"Two tanks clobbered, dear, but more keep coming. Every time we hit one of them, another takes its place."

"Keep firing."

"I'm not sure we can, dear. Those tanks are shielded and we're running out of missiles."

The bridge trembled with the force of an impact. Victoria reached over to connect herself to the ship-wide intercom.

"Don't waste your ammo," she snapped, addressing the crew. "The Leviathans have to drop shields to shoot. Wait until they fire, *then* let them have it." She clicked off, and turned back to the Founder. "Now, get out of my chair."

"Yes, dear."

She let the monkey move, and then slipped into place. There was no time to get comfortable. A quick scan of the tactical display showed that the Founder hadn't been exaggerating: they were running out of ammunition at a frightening rate, and damage reports were coming in from all sections of the airship, nearly all of them tagged as urgent.

"We can't take much more of this," Victoria muttered to herself. It was time to call in reinforcements.

"Paul," she said, opening the wireless connection between her cranial gelware and the *Sun Wukong*'s control systems, "get in there and get on the radio.

Send out the following message with a general distress call: *Am fighting invasion from parallel world. Stop. Outgunned. Stop. Send help. Stop.*"

He blinked at her through his spectacles, eyebrows scrunched in puzzlement.

"Huh?"

"Please, I'll explain later. For now, just do it."

"What are you going to do?"

"I'm going to call Merovech."

"The Prince?"

"The *King*."

Paul smiled. "Oh, I like him."

A shell hit the underside of the gondola like a hammer striking an anvil. Klaxons wailed. With a lurid French curse, Victoria initiated the transfer, giving Paul the electronic equivalent of a hefty shove. He tumbled out of her head, his source code transferred from her neural prosthesis to the airship's computer—his 'home' for the past two years.

She hoped he wouldn't get lost in there. The computer's file structures were labyrinthine and mostly undocumented, and Paul's memory could hardly be described as being at its best; still, she didn't have time to worry. All that mattered for now was that he sent the distress signal; everything else could wait. With luck, there'd be one or two dreadnoughts in the vicinity, fully armed and able to assist.

While he called for help on the radio, she accessed the ship-to-shore telecommunications console and typed in a private number, known to fewer than a dozen people. The phone line rang twice, and she found herself facing the image of a young woman in a business suit.

"Captain Valois? You're back?"

"Who are you?" Victoria had to shout over the airship's sirens.

"Amy Llewellyn, His Majesty's private secretary. Are you calling to speak to him?"

The deck lurched again, knocking Victoria sideways. She had to grab the console's rim to avoid being thrown from the chair. The air on the bridge smelled of burning electrical wire.

"This is an emergency."

"I can see that."

"Then stop blithering and put me through!"

"Victoria?" Merovech looked haunted. "Is the monkey with you?"

"Yes."

"Good. I need to see you both, as quickly as possible."

"That's not going to be easy." Victoria flinched as the airship took another hit. "We're sort of busy right now."

The young king narrowed his eyes, for the first time noticing the chaos around her.

"Why, what's happening?"

She gave him a brief summary of the situation. As he listened, his expression grew darker and more troubled.

"I'll send everything I can," he promised. "How long can you hold out?"

"A few minutes at the most. We're taking quite a hammering."

He shook his head. "Then get out of there. You've done your bit."

"But if we're not here—"

"It won't make much difference." He glanced aside, consulting another screen. "We can have another fully-armed dreadnought on site within fifteen minutes; then another ten minutes after that, with a third close behind."

A huge detonation shook the *Sun Wukong*, and it tipped a few degrees to starboard. They were losing buoyancy and the smell of smoke was growing stronger. Victoria put a hand to the scar tissue at the back of her head. She had no desire to be shot out of the sky again, especially so soon after her most recent helicopter crash.

"Okay," she said, "we're leaving."

Merovech stood. He was wearing a charcoal-grey blazer over a black polo neck sweater. The camera followed his motion, tracking his face.

"Head for the Channel," he told her. "I'll meet you en route. I've got something I need to brief you on."

"What about the invasion?"

Merovech shook his head, looking suddenly far older than his years. "Believe me, we've got worse problems."

Ack-Ack Macaque lay on his bunk, wrapped in a towel. He had a glass of rum in one hand and a fat Cuban cigar in the other. He'd taken a long, hot shower and eaten the meat from a whole roast chicken. He'd even sucked the grease from its carcass. K8 stood in the doorway, bracing herself against the frame to compensate for the tilt of the deck.

"How are you feeling?" she asked.

Ack-Ack Macaque took a luxuriant puff on his cigar and blew a line of smoke at the low ceiling. His bones ached and his muscles felt as if they'd been worked over with a meat tenderiser, but at least he'd scrubbed the dirt from his fur and filled the void in his stomach. Apynja's drugs had worn off and he felt almost back to his old self.

"Better." He stretched and yawned, baring his fangs. "I haven't heard any sirens for a while. Are we still fighting?"

"We're withdrawing. There are other airships coming in to take our place."

Startled, Ack-Ack Macaque sat up. "What do you mean, 'withdrawing'?" He couldn't believe Victoria would run from a fight.

"Merovech wants to see us."

"Oh, he does, does he?"

"He *is* the King."

"So?"

"And he's our friend." K8 adjusted the lapels of her immaculate white jacket. "He says we've got more to worry about than a load of tanks in a French field."

"Pah." Ack-Ack Macaque clamped the cigar in his teeth and stretched his legs over the edge of the bed. He wriggled his toes. "How long until we get to London?"

"We're not going to London. We're meeting Merovech in Calais, in about an hour."

"Time for a nap, then?"

"Maybe a quick one."

Something in her voice caused him to pause. He gave her a look. "What's the matter?"

She looked down evasively, like a teenager with a secret. "Nothing."

He grunted. "Hey, K8, come on. It's me you're talking to. I can see there's something bugging you. What is it?"

"You wouldn't understand."

"Try me."

She licked her lips.

"It's the hive," she said. "Now we're home, we can hear them again." She tapped her temple. "In here."

Ack-Ack Macaque narrowed his eye. "But that's what you wanted, wasn't it?"

K8 balled her fists. It made her look like the moody, freckle-faced adolescent he remembered. "We don't know. Being away from them was difficult, but coming back feels like trying to catch the thread of a conversation that's been going on without us. It takes some getting used to."

Ack-Ack Macaque drummed his toes on the deck. "But it's still what you wanted, right?"

She sighed. "We said you wouldn't understand."

Ack-Ack Macaque took the cigar from his mouth and rolled it between his fingers and thumb.

Bloody kids.

He took a deep breath and reminded himself that it was his fault she was as she was. If he hadn't given her to the hive, she wouldn't be in this mess.

"So," he asked gruffly, trying to make conversation, "what are they saying?"

"All sorts." K8 stretched like a cat. "Remember, there are close to a million of them. Some are still on the dreadnoughts, helping train crews from this timeline; others are on the ground, helping the rebuilding effort."

"And what about the Founder?" Ack-Ack tried to keep his tone neutral. "Now Victoria's let her out of her cage, won't she be plugged back in?"

K8 gave a nod, and he scowled.

"What's she saying to the hive?" Despite their mutual attraction, he'd never completely trusted the Founder, and had been deeply skeptical about her release.

"Not much. Just keep cooperating, keep working hard. That sort of thing."

"That's it, huh?"

"Pretty much."

"No insurrection?" The first time he'd met her, she'd been trying to take over the world. This new meekness seemed out of character, and he didn't buy it.

"There is one thing." K8's face split in a sudden grin, teeth squeezing the tip of her tongue, eyes sparkling.

"What?"

She covered her mouth with her hand, trying to stifle her amusement. "We shouldn't say."

Ack-Ack Macaque growled. "What's she planning?

K8 shook her head. "It's not like that, Skipper."

"Then what is it? I know she's up to something. If she so much as—"

"She's pregnant."

Ack-Ack Macaque's head jerked back. The cigar fell from his fingers.

"*What?*"

K8's smile broadened. "You're going to be a daddy."

Ack-Ack Macaque coughed. He worked dry lips but no sounds emerged from his throat. There seemed to be a disconnection between his brain and vocal cords.

K8 stooped to retrieve the cigar. She held it out to him, and he took it, fingers shaking.

"You're shitting me?"

Her laugh was clear and bright, like a Highland brook. "We're afraid not, Skip. It's the truth."

"And it's definitely mine?"

"No doubt about it."

With a groan, Ack-Ack Macaque sagged back onto the bedclothes.

"And everybody knows?"

"Only the hive."

"Why hasn't she told me?"

K8 spread her hands. "You'd have to ask her."

He bared his teeth. "Oh, I intend to, you can be sure of *that*." He glared at the rivets on the ceiling. "Where is she now?"

"She's on the bridge, with Victoria."

Tired stomach muscles protesting, Ack-Ack Macaque sat up.

"Then I should probably go and see her, huh?"

K8's smile faded. "No, not yet. There's something else you have to take care of first."

"Can't it wait?"

"It's Bali. He's been stirring up trouble."

"Tell me something new."

K8 bit the inside of her cheek. "He's serious this time." She started fiddling with her cuffs, then stopped as she realised what she was doing. "We don't like it. He really thinks he should be in charge."

Ack-Ack Macaque huffed. "Well, he can moan all he likes. If he wants to be leader, he'll have to challenge me first. That's the way it works." He gave a snort. "And he's hardly going to be dumb enough to do *that*, is he?"

The corners of K8's mouth pulled back in a nervous grimace.

"Um…"

"You're joking?"

"We're afraid not." She pointed upwards. "He's waiting for you up in Hangar Three. Most of the other monkeys are up there. Some are just curious, but others support him."

Ack-Ack Macaque's exhaustion came flooding back, like a tide reclaiming a beach. "So, I've got a mutiny on my hands?"

"We're afraid so."

"Have I got time for a nap, and to get some clean clothes?"

K8 checked her watch—a habitual and obsolete gesture given the connections in her head. "He's given you an hour. He says you forfeit if you don't show your face by three o'clock."

Ack-Ack Macaque bridled. "Cheeky bastard. What time is it now?"

"Two-thirty."

"Ah, crap." Ack-Ack Macaque pushed himself up, onto his feet.

"What are you going to do?"

"What do you think I'm going to do?" He scratched at his eye patch. "I'm going to teach the little twat a lesson. Give me five minutes and then go and let them know I'm on my way."

K8's brow furrowed with concern. "Are you sure you're up to it?"

He laughed, but there wasn't any humour in the sound, only bitterness. "Not really, but what choice do I have?"

"You could arrest him, and throw him in the brig."

Ack-Ack Macaque opened the drawer containing his spare clothes. He couldn't go up there in a dressing gown. If he wanted to assert his dominance over the troupe, he'd have to do it looking his best.

"No, I couldn't," he said. "His supporters would think that was my way of avoiding a fight. They'd take it as a sign of weakness."

"Monkey politics?"

"It's all about being the alpha male, sweetheart."

K8 rolled her eyes but didn't protest.

"All right," she said wearily, "but be careful."

As she turned to leave, Ack-Ack Macaque pulled a knife from the bottom of his sock drawer.

"Careful isn't a word I know." He held the weapon up to the light, checking the edge for nicks and dents. "Oh, and K8?"

She paused in the doorway, one hand gripping the handle to keep her balance.

"Yes, Skip?"

"It's good to see you."

She smiled.

"It's good to see you, too, Skipper."

LATER, UP IN the hangar, Bali stood at the centre of a helipad, naked save for his necklace of leopard's teeth. His fingers gripped the hilt of a foot-long machete and his feet straddled the crossbar of the pad's large, yellow 'H'. He stood with as much nonchalance as he could muster, with his weight on one hip and his shoulders loose, and an insolent sneer on his face. He wanted the other monkeys to know he wasn't afraid. They stood around him at a respectful distance, fidgeting and glancing at wristwatches. None dared speak aloud. Bali's own timepiece showed there were only three minutes remaining until the deadline. Despite what the K8 child had said, it didn't look as if Ack-Ack Macaque would be making an appearance. Deep inside, Bali snarled to himself. It would be typical of the irresponsible clown to ignore this challenge and risk losing a lot of credibility in the eyes of the monkey army.

"Come on," he muttered impatiently. He didn't want to win by default, and he didn't want to drag this out. A simple, clear victory would be all it took. He'd seen the state of his rival—scratched, filthy and exhausted—and felt confident he could beat him.

And then all this will be mine. He checked his watch again. The monkeys around him were getting fidgety. They knew that, any moment now, the challenge would be resolved one way or another and, unless Ack-Ack Macaque showed his face, they would have a new leader.

Two minutes. Bali could feel his palm sweating against the machete's plastic grip. He tapped the point of the blade against the metal deck. The troupe needed strong leadership. They needed goals, and incentives, and something for which to aim and strive. Now Ack-Ack Macaque had freed them from their various timelines, they needed a *purpose*—and Bali knew he was the one best equipped to provide it.

And what greater purpose could there be than ensuring the survival of the troupe? He would find them mates and a homeland—and not some dreary stockade on an empty world, but a true home, on a timeline with a working infrastructure and plenty of potential slaves. Before being rescued, every monkey here had been the victim of human experimentation. Instead of hiding themselves away in the jungle, they deserved revenge; they deserved the chance to turn the tables on their former oppressors, and use their newfound intelligence for something more satisfying than erecting mud huts and digging latrines.

One minute. He drew himself up. The nervous chatter stopped, and all eyes turned to him.

"Well," he said with a fierce grin, "I seem to have been stood up." He held his arms out to his sides in a theatrical gesture, the machete dangling limply from his right hand. "It seems our erstwhile leader has better things to do than defend his position."

For a second, awed silence reigned. Then the pad lurched beneath their feet. With a mechanical squeal, it began to rise. Overhead, part of the upper deck slid aside, revealing the open sky, and a lone figure silhouetted against it. It was, of course, Ack-Ack Macaque. Bali felt his heart skip. The older monkey stood with his arms crossed and his back to the sun. A cigar smouldered between his fingers and he wore a brand new flying jacket, leather cap and goggles. A pair of chrome-plated Colts gleamed at his hips and he had a pristine white silk scarf knotted around his neck. As the lift drew level with the airship's upper surface, he fixed Bali with a baleful eye, and cleared his throat.

"*Au contraire, mon frère.*"

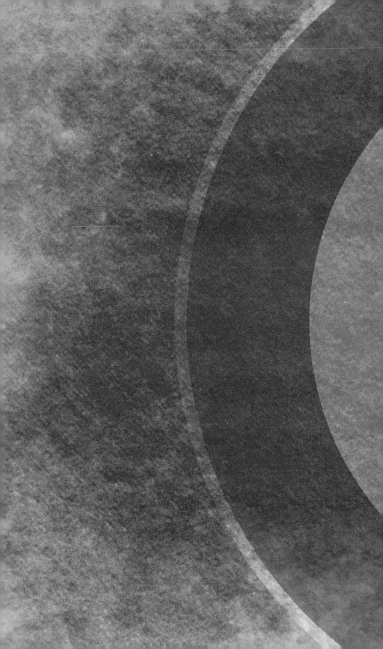

PART TWO

EMBERS ON THE WIND

Gliding o'er all, through all,
Through Nature, Time, and Space,
As a ship on the waters advancing,
The voyage of the soul—not life alone,
Death, many deaths I'll sing.

(Walt Whitman, *Gliding O'er All*)

CHAPTER TWENTY-TWO
NAPOLEON JONES

VILCA'S MEN WERE going to kill him. He tried to lose himself in the improvised warrens of the vertical favelas, but knew it was only a matter of time before they found him. He'd been away too long; his memories of the rat runs and back ways were out of date by at least a couple of decades. In the end, two of his pursuers cornered him on one of the innumerable wire footbridges stretched between the barrios that clung coral-like to both walls of the steep, narrow canyon.

"Stay where you are, Jones." The short one's name was Faro. He was a tough young street kid. His elder brother Emilio blocked the other end of the bridge. They would have both been small boys the last time Napoleon Jones had been here; but now they were in their mid-twenties and armed with machetes. Caught between them, he realised he had nowhere left to run. The springy bridge was less than two metres in width and fifty in length. Half a kilometre below, corrugated metal rooftops patchworked the canyon's rocky floor. Other bridges crisscrossed the gap at various heights. Flyers and cargo Zeppelins nosed like cautious fish between them. Shanties crusted both the canyon's cliff faces, layer upon layer.

Lines of laundry drooped from window to window. Cooking fires filled the air with the bitter tang of smouldering wood and plastic. He could hear shouts and screams and children's voices. Somewhere a young woman sang.

"What do you want?" he said, buying time.

The two kids each took a step onto the wire bridge. Napoleon took hold of the handrails to steady himself.

"We got something for you, from Vilca," Emilio said.

Napoleon tipped back the brim of his Stetson. "Maybe I don't want it."

Faro laughed cruelly. He slapped the flat blade of his machete against the palm of his hand. "Maybe you're going to get it, whether you want it or not."

Napoleon risked a peep over the handrail. This canyon was just one of hundreds arranged in a vast, sprawling delta, carved out over millennia by the patient action of wind and water. Like the tentacles of an enormous squid, the canyons stretched from the mountains at one end of the planet's solitary supercontinent to the sea at the other, providing the only shade in what was otherwise a pitiless, UV-drenched desert.

Looking down, he saw a cargo Zeppelin about to pass beneath the bridge, its broad back like the smooth hump of a browsing whale, and felt the walkway shudder beneath his feet as the street kids advanced, weapons raised.

He should never have come back to Nuevo Cordoba. He should have known better. He looked longingly down the canyon, in the direction of the distant ocean. The wind tugged at his lizard-skin coat. If he could only get back to his starship, the *Bobcat*, floating tethered at the offshore spaceport, he'd be free. He could finally shake this planet's dust from his boots. As things stood, though, it looked as if he'd be lucky to make it off this bridge alive; or at least in one piece.

He glanced at the approaching thugs. They were closer now. Emilio swung his machete from side to side.

"Nowhere to hide?"

Napoleon glanced from one brother to the other. They were almost within striking distance.

"I don't want any trouble."

"Shut it," Faro said.

Below, the Zeppelin slid its blunt nose into the shadow of the bridge. Napoleon took the antique flying goggles that hung around his neck and pulled them up over his eyes. Seeing the movement, Emilio stepped forward with a grunt. He scythed his machete around in a powerful swing aimed at Napoleon's head. Napoleon ducked the blade and came up hard, grasping for the big lad's arm while the force of the swing still had him off balance. He slammed Emilio's wrist against the rail of the bridge, trying to get him to drop the knife. Emilio roared in annoyance and pushed back. The machete came up in a vicious backhand swipe. Napoleon tried to twist out of the way but the tip of the blade caught him across the right forearm, biting through lizard skin, cotton and flesh.

"Ah!" He staggered back, clutching the stinging wound. He saw more of Vilca's men arrive. They began to advance across the bridge, and Napoleon knew this was a fight he couldn't win. As the brothers dropped into fighting crouches on either side of him, ready to hack him to pieces, he braced himself against the handrail.

"Sorry, boys," he said.

Using his boot heel to push off, he crossed the width of the walkway in two quick steps and launched himself over the opposite rail, into empty air.

THE WIND TORE at him. His coat flapped. The fall seemed to take forever.

Then his boots hit the fabric upper surface of the Zeppelin hard enough to jar his spine. He bounced, sprawling forward in an ungainly tangle of limbs and coattails. For a second, he thought he was going to roll right off the side and fall to his death at the bottom of the canyon. Then his hands and feet found purchase against the fabric and he clung spread-eagled, sucking in great raw lungfuls of cold canyon air.

If he raised his head, he could see, over the curve of the hull, one of the engine nacelles, with the blurred, hissing circle of its black carbon impeller blades. Beyond that, nothing but air and rooftops.

Heart hammering in his chest, he clawed his way back up to the relatively flat surface at the top of the Zeppelin. Once there, he rolled onto his back and sat up. He'd skinned his knees and palms. His right arm hurt and his hand and sleeve were slathered and sticky with blood. Worst of all, he'd lost his hat. Still, he was alive. Behind him, Faro and Emilio boggled open-mouthed from the footbridge. He pushed his goggles up onto his forehead and raised a bloody, one-fingered salute.

"So long, fuckers."

The wind straggled his hair. Staying low to avoid being blown off the airship altogether, he crawled back towards the tail fin and found a maintenance hatch set into the fabric at its base. He pulled it open and climbed down an aluminium ladder, into the shadowy interior.

The outer envelope of the airship housed a number of helium gas bags, with walkways and cargo spaces wedged between them. The air was dark and cold in there, like a cave. Moving as quickly as his protesting limbs would allow, Napoleon made his way shakily across a catwalk and down another ladder to the access panel that led to the control gondola slung beneath the main hull. As he dropped into the cabin, the pilot—a scruffy young technician sipping coffee at a cup-strewn computer console—turned to him in amazement.

"Where did you come from?"

Clutching the torn sleeve of his snakeskin coat, blood seeping through his fingers, Napoleon glowered. He pointed forward, through the windshield, at a docking mast protruding from a cluster of warehouses near the base of the canyon's right-hand wall.

"Take us down, boy," he said.

As soon as the Zeppelin's nose nudged the mast, Napoleon Jones was off and running again. He pushed through the narrow stairwells and crowded walkways that formed the streets of the vertical town.

His boots splashed through water and over broken glass floors of shattered tiles. Down here at the base of the favela, water dripped constantly from the upper levels. Strip lights flickered and sizzled; power cables hung in improvised loops. He passed dirty kitchens; tattoo parlours; street dentists. Blanket-wrapped figures slept in alcoves behind steam pipes. He smelled hot, sour plastic from the corner kiosks, where fabbers made shoes and toys from discarded bottles and cans. He turned right, then left, trying to put as much distance as he could between himself and Vilca's men. He moved awkwardly, cradling his hurt arm, trying to keep pressure on the wound.

Reappearing like this, after two decades, had been a mistake. Twenty years ago, he'd been at the top of his game: a celebrated daredevil repeatedly flinging his craft into hyperspace on arbitrary trajectories, just to see where he'd end up. The media called the sport 'random jumping', and it was a dangerous pastime; not all the pilots who took part returned. Those who did, especially those who'd discovered a newly habitable world or the location of an ore-rich asteroid belt, became celebrities. Venture capitalists and would-be entrepreneurs lined up to sponsor them. And in his time, Napoleon Jones had been one of the best and brightest of their number. But he'd been unable to manage the wealth and attention. He fucked up. He developed a tranquiliser dependency and let things slide. He got sloppy. And then one day, he simply disappeared.

Now he was back, he was a fugitive. In his absence, Vilca had gone from a small-time gang boss to *de facto* ruler of Nuevo Cordoba's favelas, and he wanted the money Napoleon owed him; money that should have part-financed another random jump into the unknown, but went instead to supporting an extended stay on Strauli, a crossroads world eight light years in the wrong direction.

Napoleon came to the end of a corridor and cut through a laundry area. Hot wet steam filled the air. He squeezed through the narrow spaces between the vats of boiling clothes, searching for another way out. Spilled detergent made the floor slick and slippery. The workers watched him with dull, incurious eyes. They knew better than to get involved. Eventually, he found a hatchway that led into a narrow service duct between one set of buildings and the next. Thick cables ran the length of the floor, beneath a layer of waste paper and discarded packing materials. At the end of the duct, he emerged into daylight. He was on the floor of the canyon now, looking up at the layers of improvised dwellings that towered a hundred metres up the side of the cliff above him.

A tangle of shacks and warehouses covered the ground between him and the vertical settlements on the far wall, clustered to either side of the melt-water stream that ran from the mountains at one end of the canyon to the sea at the other. Napoleon looked left and right, trying to orientate himself. He wasn't familiar with this part of town. His old stamping grounds were further downstream, towards the port. He'd come this far inland seeking an old flame: the girl he'd ditched twenty years ago, when he'd jumped out of the system *en route* for Strauli, half baked on tranquilisers and intending never to return. He brought his ship down in the ocean off the coast, where the canyons met the water, and left it floating there. Then he went looking for her.

Her name was Crystal. He had found her in a small room off a darkened landing, half an hour before Vilca's men found him.

"What do you want?" she asked.

"It's me, honey. Napoleon." He took off his hat.

"I know who you are."

"I've come to see you. To see how you are."

She looked him up and down with contempt.

"You still look exactly the same," she said.

He forced a smile.

"So do you."

Crystal gave a snort. "You always were a lousy liar, Jones." She stepped back from the door, her heels clicking on the vinyl floor. "You can come on in, if you want."

Napoleon hesitated at the threshold, both hands holding the brim of his hat. The room wasn't much larger than the bed it contained, and dark; and the air smelled of stale sheets.

"I thought you might have been married."

"I was, for a while." Crystal squeezed her hands together. "It didn't take."

"What happened?"

She stopped kneading her fingers and wrapped her arms across her ample chest.

"Why the hell do you care?"

Napoleon shrugged.

"Look, I'm sorry—"

"You're sorry? You stand there all sorry, not having aged at all. While the rest of us have had to live through the past twenty *years*."

He held up his hands.

"I just wanted to see how you were."

Crystal tossed back her mane of red hair.

"I'm fat and middle-aged and alone. Are you happy now?"

Napoleon stepped back onto the landing. While the hyperspace jumps from one star system to the next took the same amount of time as it took light to cross the intervening distance, the jumps themselves felt instantaneous to the crews of the ships making them; so for every light year Napoleon had travelled, a calendar year had worn away here, for Crystal. She'd gone from her mid twenties to her mid forties while he'd only aged by a couple of years.

"I should be going," he said, regretting the sentimental impulse that had brought him to her door.

Her lip curled. She took hold of the door, ready to close it.

"Yes, go on. Leave. It's the only thing you're good at."

Napoleon backed off another step.

"I can see you're upset—"

"Oh, just go."

She closed the door, leaving him standing alone in the gloom of a solitary overhead fluorescent strip. He could hear her sobbing behind the door. The sound gave him a sick, empty feeling.

He replaced his Stetson and, hands in pockets, he walked back to the stairwell. From there, he went looking for a bar; but before he could find one, Faro and Emilio found him.

Now, still on the run after his adventures on the

Zeppelin, and still bleeding heavily from the gash in his arm, Napoleon started making his way through the maze-like shanties on the canyon floor, towards the transport tube that threaded along the base of the far wall, fifty or so metres away. If he could get there and get on a train, he'd be at the port in no time.

He staggered forward. The sky was a thin strip of blue, high above. Flyers and Zeppelins floated like fish in an undersea trench. Down here at the bottom, a thin frost covered everything. The sun rarely penetrated to this depth.

The houses here were ramshackle affairs. Some were two or three storeys in height. They looked like pieces fallen from the cliff-hugging favelas looming over them on either side: minor debris presaging a forthcoming avalanche. The houses belonged to mushroom farmers. Between them lay tended rows of edible fungi, like the fingers of dead white hands thrusting up through the damp soil.

Napoleon picked his path with care, sticking close to the houses, avoiding the crops. The last thing he needed was an irate farmer taking pot shots at him; and besides, he didn't want to get his boots any dirtier than they already were.

He was almost to the river before Vilca's men caught up with him again. This time, it was four of them in a flyer. They came in low and fast, the flyer's fans kicking up dirt and rubbish. Napoleon started running as best he could but he couldn't move quickly while cradling his arm. Bullets ripped into the ground around him, sending up angry spurts of dust; each one closer than the last.

He made maybe ten metres before something punched through his thigh. The impact spun him around in a graceless pirouette.

He landed on his back in the dirt. The flyer's howling fans kicked up a maelstrom of dust and grit around him, and he rolled onto his side, trying to curl into a ball, cringing in anticipation. Waiting for the next shot.

CHAPTER TWENTY-THREE
SUNBURN

THE TRADING SHIP *Ameline* flashed into existence a thousand kilometres above the inhospitable sands of Nuevo Cordoba. The ship was a snub-nosed wedge, thirty metres across at the stern and narrowing to five at the bow, its paintwork the faded blue and red livery of the Abdulov trading family. Alone on its bridge, her neural implant hooked into its virtual senses, Katherine Abdulov looked down at the planet beneath, with its deep, fertile oceans and single barren supercontinent. Even from here, she could see the tracery of fissures comprising the canyon system that gave shelter and life to the planet's human population.

"Any trace of infection?" she asked the ship, and felt it run a sensor sweep, scouring the globe for signs of The Recollection's all-consuming spores.

> NOTHING I CAN DETECT, AND NO MENTION OF ANYTHING SUSPICIOUS ON THE PLANETARY GRID.

Kat heard the ship's words in her mind via her neural link, and pursed her lips. For the moment she was relieved, yet knew such relief to be premature. Even if the contagion hadn't yet spread to this planet, it was almost certainly already on its way, using cannibalised human starships to spread itself along the trade routes from Strauli Quay. She took a moment to remember the other worlds already lost to the unstoppable red tide. Their names burned in her mind: Djatt, Inakpa… Strauli.

She'd seen her home world swallowed by The Recollection, lost most of her family, including her mother, to its insatiable hunger. Now she was out here, at this world on the edge of unknown space, hoping to warn the inhabitants of the approaching threat, and rescue as many of them as she could.

Through the ship's senses, she felt the arrival of the rest of her flotilla: two dozen fat-arsed freighters, each piloted by a crew of Acolytes, and each with the cargo capacity to transport several hundred refugees.

One by one, they reported in.

"Target the spaceport and the main canyon settlements," she told them. "Save as many people as you can."

HER ONLY PREVIOUS visit to the isolated world of Nuevo Cordoba had taken place years ago—whole decades in local time—during her first trip as an independent trader. That had been back before her pregnancy and the birth of her daughter, back before the coming of The Recollection and the loss of her left arm. She remembered the planet as a corrupt, mean-spirited place, the canyon dwellers made hard and cynical by the harshness of their environment, and lives spent mining the rock or grubbing for mushrooms and lichen. She wondered how they were coping without the arch network. She also remembered one Cordoban in particular: a random hyperspace jumper with whom she'd had a brief affair. She remembered his Mephistophelean beard; his long hair tied back in a dark ponytail; his Stetson hat, and snakeskin coat. The way his skin smelled of cologne and old leather.

PROMPTED BY THE memory, she said, "Scan the port for the *Bobcat*'s transponder."

> ALREADY LOCATED. THE *BOBCAT* IS CURRENTLY FLOATING IN THE PARKING ZONE OFF THE CONTINENT'S WESTERN COAST. DO YOU WANT TO MAKE CONTACT?

Kat settled back in her couch feeling winded. She'd been half-joking when she asked for the scan. She hadn't actually expected him to *be* here. Swallowing down an unwelcome flutter, she drummed the instrument console with the tungsten fingers of her prosthetic hand.

"Just see if he's on board."

The *Ameline* opened a comms channel. Through her neural link, Kat felt it squirt a high-density info burst at the other ship. The reply—a similarly compressed screech of data—came a couple of seconds later, delayed by distance.

> HE'S NOT THERE AT THE MOMENT.

"Can the ship patch us through to his implant?"

> I'M AFRAID NOT.

"Any mention of him on the Grid?"

The *Ameline* accessed the planetary communications net and ran a quick search.

> HE'S IN TROUBLE.

Kat rolled her eyes. *Of course…*

"With the law?"

> THERE'S A PRICE ON HIS HEAD.

"Can you locate him?"

> IT SEEMS HE'S BEEN TAKEN CAPTIVE BY ONE OF THE LOCAL GANGSTERS, A MAN NAMED EARL VILCA.

"Show me."

A map unfolded before her eyes: a three-dimensional aerial view of one of the canyons, patched together by the ship from direct observation, public records and intercepted satellite observation. A yellow tag marked Jones' last known location, on the canyon floor.

> THE *BOBCAT* WAS ABLE TO TRACK HIM THIS FAR, THEN HE VANISHED. EITHER HE'S DEAD, OR HE'S BEING HELD SOMEWHERE WITH COMMS SCREENING.

A scarlet circle appeared on the map, near the upper lip of the canyon wall, at the top of the vertical favela.

> THIS IS VILCA'S COMPOUND. IF HE'S STILL ALIVE, CHANCES ARE THAT'S WHERE THEY'RE HOLDING HIM.

"Can I speak to Vilca?"

> I'LL SEE IF I CAN—

The ship's voice cut off. Kat sat forward.

"What is it?"

> INCOMING.

The map of the canyons vanished, to be replaced by a stylised strategic overview of the planetary system. Nuevo Cordoba floated in the centre. Green tags picked out each of the twenty-four rescue freighters.

Off to the left, coming in above the plane of the planet's equator, a flashing red circle highlighted an unidentified ship.

> IT JUST JUMPED IN. COURSE EXTRAPOLATION MARKS ITS POINT OF ORIGIN AS STRAULI.

Kat's heart seemed to squirm in her chest. These days, every unidentified ship was a potential threat.

"Is it infected?"

> ALMOST CERTAINLY.

The intruder seemed to be heading straight for the planet, ignoring the scattering freighters. Kat disconnected her neural implant from the ship's sensorium and reeled her perceptions back into the confines of her skull.

"Are we close enough to intercept and engage?"

> AYE.

She flexed the fingers of her artificial hand. The joints buzzed like mosquitoes.

"Okay," she said. "Let's do it."

UNDER FULL ACCELERATION, it took the *Ameline* an hour and a half to get close enough to fire on the unidentified ship. Throughout that time, Kat remained in place on the little ship's bridge. Housing only two crash couches, the room was too small for her to pace nervously—more of a large cockpit than a ship's bridge in the accepted sense. Instead, she sat impatiently watching their progress via the interactive touch screens on the forward wall.

When they were almost within range, she activated her implant and joined her mind once more to the

Ameline's heightened senses. When hooked in to the ship like this she could feel the thrust as a tingle in her feet; the power of the engines as a growl in her chest and stomach. Her nostrils were full of the cold, coppery smell of the vacuum. The heat of the local sun warmed her. The lights of distant stars pinpricked her cheek.

She opened a line to the weapon pod slung beneath the *Ameline*'s bows.

"Are you ready, Ed?"

Ed Rico lay submerged in the greasily organic entrails of the Dho weapon. Its flabby white wax forced its way into his eyes and ears; it filled his lungs and stomach, even the pores of his skin.

"I'm here." His voice sounded thick, the sound forcing its way up through the alien mucus clogging his throat.

Ed had once been an artist, back on Earth. He had come to Strauli the hard way, through the arch network, and been chosen by the Dho to wield this ancient weapon; to become part of it.

Cocooned within, he had no access to the rest of the ship while in flight. The weapon's tendrils fed him nutrients and oxygen to keep him alive; and when he wasn't needed, it simply put him to sleep.

Now though, Kat knew he'd be fully awake, brain pumped with synthetic adrenaline; all his senses filled with a real-time strategic view of the space surrounding them.

All he had to do was point and click.

> IN RANGE IN TWENTY SECONDS.

"Get ready to fire."

Ahead, the infected craft continued toward the

planet, seemingly oblivious to their approach. Yet deep in her head, Kat felt a strange scratching sensation, as if tiny animals were flexing their claws against the inside of her skull. She knew this feeling, recognised it for what it was. During her first brush with The Recollection she'd been briefly infected by it, and now the dormant nanomachines it had pushed into her body were stirring, disturbed from their slumber by the proximity of an active mass of their fellows.

There could be no doubt now that the ship ahead was infested.

"Over to you," she told Ed. "Fire when ready."

> TEN SECONDS.

The Recollection was a gestalt entity comprised of uncounted trillions of self-replicating molecular-sized machines—each one in the swarm acting as a processing node, like a synapse in a human brain. Destroy one and the network simply re-routed, maintaining its integrity. Let one touch you, and it would start converting your atoms into copies of itself: remorseless and unstoppable. The ship ahead would be packed with them, like an overripe seedpod, ready to spread its voracious cargo across the unsuspecting globe below.

> FIVE.

Kat swallowed. Ahead, the target remained on course, still apparently unaware of the attack about to rain down upon it.

> THREE.

> TWO.

A white, pencil-thin line stabbed from the *Ameline*'s nose: a superheated jet of fusing hydrogen plucked by wormhole from the heart of the nearest star. Still hooked into the ship, Kat saw it on the tactical display. It cut the sky like a knife. The hellish backwash of its scouring light hit her virtual face like sunburn. Where it touched the infected ship, metal boiled away.

The beam flickered once; twice; three times. The target broke apart. The pieces that hadn't been vaporised began to tumble.

Kat pulled out of the tactical simulation, back into the real world of the *Ameline*'s cockpit.

"Did we get it?"

> SCANNING NOW.

Kat blinked. Her eyes were watering. Although she'd witnessed the scouring light via her neural implant, her body's reflexes still expected afterimages on her retinas, and seemed confused to find none.

A wall screen lit, showing a forward view of the planet, which instantly crash-zoomed to a sizeable piece of wreckage silhouetted against the daylight side, tumbling through space wrapped in a cloud of hull fragments and loose cables. Fluid dribbled from a severed tube.

> VESSEL DESTROYED BUT SOME DEBRIS REMAINS.

"Damn. Can we hit it again?"

> IT'S ALREADY ENTERING THE ATMOSPHERE OVER THE CANYONS. IF WE FIRE NOW WE CAN EXPECT CIVILIAN CASUALTIES.

Kat hesitated. She didn't know if she could bring herself to fire on innocent people. Not again. During The Recollection's attack on her home planet of

Strauli, she'd been forced to destroy the orbital docks in a futile attempt to stem the spread of infection. A million people had died, either in the initial explosions or the subsequent disintegration of the structure, and their deaths still troubled her.

She looked down and flexed the fingers of her left hand. The metal of the fingers and wrist had been stained and half-melted during an attack by The Recollection. She could have had the whole arm surgically re-grown months ago, but she preferred to keep this clunky souvenir. It reminded her of everything and everyone that had been lost. It was her scar and she'd earned it.

She watched the tumbling wreck flare as it hit thicker air.

"Follow it down," she said.

CHAPTER TWENTY-FOUR
EMBERS

KAT KNEW STRAIGHT away that she didn't have much time. Standing in the airlock of the *Ameline*, she could see greasy black smoke belching from the site of the crashed starship debris. It had been a big ship, probably a container carrier of some sort. Sliced apart and half-vaporised by the Dho weapon, fragments of the vessel had fallen to the ground, ploughing into the desert that covered most of the planet's solitary supercontinent, flaming like meteors. By the time she'd followed them down, huge tracts of scrubland were already ablaze. Now, surveying the impact crater from a dozen kilometres away, with her eyes on full magnification, she could make out grain-sized specks of red in the smoke: clumps of infected matter from the ship riding the hot air like embers, using the updraught to spread themselves across the landscape.

Embers on the wind.

This was exactly what she'd been trying to prevent. From bitter experience, she knew the specks contained tightly-packed clusters of aggressive nanomachinery. Where they landed, the ground turned red. Spreading stains of wine-coloured destruction bloomed as the tiny machines ate into the surface of the planet, turning rock and dust into more machines, exponentially swelling their numbers.

The ship had been a seed pod: its systems hijacked by the contagion, its hold full of seething red nanomachines ready to split the hull and burst forth in an orgy of destruction.

Kat felt her lips harden. Her little fleet might rescue a couple of thousand people; but there was nothing she could do for the rest of the population. She was five light years from the Bubble Belt. By the time she jumped there and came back, a whole decade would have passed, and this world would have fallen. She thought of the tortured, wailing minds she'd encountered during her own brush with The Recollection; of her mother, pinned like a butterfly in its virtual storage spaces, with nothing to look forward to but an eternity of torment.

She turned back into the familiar confines of the *Ameline*.

"We should have been quicker," she said.

In her mind, she heard the *Ameline*'s reply.

> WE HIT THAT SHIP WITH EVERYTHING WE HAD. THERE WASN'T ANYTHING ELSE WE COULD HAVE DONE.

"We could have rammed it."

> AND WHAT WOULD THAT HAVE ACHIEVED? IT WAS TOO BIG. IT WOULD HAVE FLATTENED US AND KEPT RIGHT ON GOING.

"I know, but still."

> THIS IS A WAR, AND WE'RE LOSING. CASUALTIES ARE INEVITABLE.

"We should be doing more."

> THE FREIGHTERS WILL RESCUE SOME OF THE POPULATION.

"A tiny fraction."

> BETTER THAN NONE.

She let out a long sigh. This was the third world she'd seen fall to The Recollection. First Djatt, then Inakpa, then her home world of Strauli. Now this place, New Cordoba.

Just another apocalypse.

Before it arrived at Djatt, The Recollection had been drifting through space for thousands of years, the relic of an ancient and long-forgotten alien war. Now it had access to human ships, it could spread unstoppably from world to world, consuming everything it touched. And all humanity could do was fall back.

As the airlock door slid closed behind her, she turned for one last glimpse of the redness spreading across the land, the widening circles meeting and merging, growing with obscene haste. She'd seen this happen before. With nothing to stop it, she knew the infection would cover the entire surface of the globe within days.

There was nothing she could do.

Except...

She gripped the gun.

"Take me to Vilca," she said.

THE *AMELINE* DROPPED onto the desert sand a dozen metres from the edge of the canyon, directly above Vilca's compound. The old ship came down with a whine of engines and a hot blast of dirt. As the landing struts settled and the engines whined into silence, Kat unhooked herself from the pilot's chair and made her way down the ladder that led to the rest of the ship's interior.

At the foot of the ladder, opposite the door of her cabin, the ship's locker held a rack of weaponry picked up on half a dozen different worlds. She reached up and pulled a twelve-gauge shotgun from the wall. It was a gas-powered model, fully automatic and drum-loaded, capable of delivering three hundred flesh-shredding rounds per minute. She hefted it in one hand, resting the stock on her hip as she picked up a couple of extra magazines and pushed them into her thigh pocket.

> I HOPE YOU'RE NOT PLANNING ON DOING ANYTHING STUPID.

"Define stupid."

WEAPON AT THE ready, Kat stepped from the bottom of the *Ameline*'s cargo ramp. Her boots crunched into the coarse desert sand. Tough little grass tufts poked through here and there, stirring in the thin, scouring wind. Overhead, the sun burned blue and hot. Ahead, the canyon lay ragged and raw like a claw mark in the skin of the world; and over the lip, Vilca's compound.

She took three quick steps to the edge and looked down. As she'd expected, a metal fire escape led down to an armoured door in the side of the building. A razor wire gate blocked the top of the staircase. She considered cutting her way through; then decided it wasn't worth the bother. The people inside must know she was here. They would have heard the *Ameline* set down, and they were sure to be watching her, even if she couldn't see any cameras.

She held the shotgun across her chest and raised her chin.

"I'm here to see Vilca," she said.

A minute later, she heard the sound of scraping bolts. The heavy door hinged open. A gun appeared from behind it, clutched in the fists of a young kid gaunt with malnourishment.

"Who are you?"

"My name is Katherine Denktash Abdulov, of the Strauli Abdulovs, and I am here to request an audience with your esteemed Capo, the Right Honourable Lord Vilca."

Beneath the rim of his cap, suspicion screwed the kid's face into a wary scowl.

"Huh?"

Kat sighed. *Young people today…* She licked her lips, and then tried again.

"Take me to your leader," she said. The kid's eyes scanned the canyon's lip, alert for treachery.

"You alone?"

"Yes."

He looked at her shotgun, then down at the pistol in his hand, transparently calculating the difference in their relative value and firepower.

"You'll have to give me your weapon."

Kat shook her head. "I don't think so."

The kid scowled. "Give me the shotgun or I won't take you to Vilca."

She looked him up and down: just another armed street thug with bad teeth and delusions of competence. A few years ago she would have been intimidated; now she couldn't care less. She cleared her throat.

"You saw my ship land?"

The kid's eyes narrowed further. "Yeah."

Kat took a step closer to the razor wire gate.

"You saw its fusion motors?"

The barest nod.

"They spew out star fire, son. That's fourteen zillion degrees centigrade. What do you think will happen if I let them hover over your little citadel?"

Behind her, she heard the *Ameline*'s engines whine into life. The ship was monitoring her conversation via her neural implant, and this was its idea of theatrics. Suppressing a smile, Kat took another step forward, so that her stomach pressed up against the spikes on the wire gate. At the same time, she brought the shotgun to bear, pointing the barrel at the bridge of the kid's nose.

"Open up," she growled. The kid's eyes went wide. He knew he was out of his depth. He looked at her, then over her shoulder at the rising wedge of the *Ameline*. She saw him swallow. Without taking his eyes from the looming ship, he reached for a button inside the door and the gate drew back. Kat stepped forward, shotgun now pointed at his midriff.

"What's your name, son?"

"Faro."

She raised a finger and waggled it, telling him to turn around.

"Never try to out-negotiate a trader, Faro."

* * *

Faro led her down a set of pleated metal steps. His trainers dragged on each stair. She kept the shotgun trained on the small of his back.

"How old are you?" she asked. He didn't answer. His vest and jeans hung off him, several sizes too large for his half-starved junkie frame.

"Down 'ere," he muttered.

At the foot of the steps was an iron door. Beyond that, a poorly carpeted corridor that stank of incense. Faro flapped an arm at a pair of rough pine doors that formed the corridor's far end.

"Vilca's office."

Kat gave him a prod with the shotgun barrel.

"Why don't you knock for me?" She followed him to the doors. "Go on," she said.

Faro tapped reluctant knuckles against the wood. From inside, a voice called: "What is it?" Faro glanced back at Kat, his eyes wide, unsure what to do. She nudged him in the kidney with the tip of the shotgun.

"Open the door," she suggested.

Inside, the office was as rough and raw as the rest of the building, but the rugs on the floor were thicker and newer than elsewhere, and there were curtains at the windows. A heavy-set bald man sat behind a scuffed steel desk.

"I said I wasn't to be disturbed. Who the devil are you?"

Kat took Faro by the shoulder and pushed him aside. She drew herself up.

"My name is Katherine Denktash Abdulov, master of the trading vessel *Ameline* and scion of the Strauli Abdulovs. Are you Earl Vilca?"

The fat man frowned.

"You're a *trader*?"

Kat lowered the shotgun so that the barrel pointed at the floor.

"As I said, I represent the Abdulov trading family."

The man eased back in his chair. He gave her an appraising look.

"And what can I do for you, Miss Abdulov?"

Kat took a pace towards the desk.

"That's *Captain* Abdulov, and you have a friend of mine. I want him released."

Vilca chuckled. He folded his hands over the bulge of his stomach. Gold rings glistened on his sausage-like fingers.

"Very good," he said approvingly. "I do so like a woman who comes straight to the point."

According to the profile the *Ameline* had been able to piece together from information retrieved from the local Grid, Earl Vilca was one of the most powerful men on Nuevo Cordoba. His operation dealt in drugs, prostitution and extortion. He had politicians and high-ranking police officers in his pocket, and a seemingly endless supply of teenage muscle. On a world of high-piled shanties and meagre mushroom harvests, he lived like a king. But when Kat looked down at him, all she saw was a white, bloated parasite: a puffed-up hoodlum in a cheaply-fabbed suit.

"I know who you are, and what you are," she said. "And I'm not impressed. So if you'd be kind enough to release Napoleon Jones, I'll be on my way."

On the opposite side of the desk, Vilca pursed his lips. He drummed his fingers against his belt buckle.

"Jones, eh? Well, well, well." He shook his head with a smile. "You've come bursting in here to rescue Napoleon Jones? He's nothing but a two-bit hustler. What do you want with him?"

Kat gripped the shotgun.

"As I said, he's a friend."

Vilca narrowed his eyes. He ran his tongue across his bottom lip. Then he sat forward, hands resting on the desk.

"All right, Captain. I'll make you a trade. Jones for some information."

"What kind of information?"

The fat man waved his hand at the sky.

"I hear things. Rumours. Shipments have disappeared. Scheduled deliveries from Strauli have not arrived. Ships are overdue."

Kat felt her pulse quicken. She knew where this was going and she didn't have time to waste playing games.

"Strauli has fallen," she said bluntly. "Inakpa, Djatt and probably several others."

Vilca blinked at her.

"Fallen?"

"Gone, destroyed. No more."

The man's brows drew together. He plainly didn't believe her.

"I am serious, Captain. I have been losing money—"

Kat stepped right up to the desk and glared down at him.

"They're gone."

"Gone?" Vilca's cheeks flushed. His fingers brushed his lower lip. "But what could do such a thing?"

Kat used her implant to signal the *Ameline*.

"I've asked my ship to download all the information we have to the local Grid. See for yourself. It's all tagged with the key word 'Recollection'."

Vilca gave her a long look. He was getting flustered.

"Go on," she said. "Check it out. I'll wait here."

"No tricks?"

Kat nodded in the direction of Faro, still cowering in the corner of the room.

"Your boy here can keep an eye on me."

Vilca looked up and to the right, accessing the cranial implant that connected him to the vast cloud of data that formed the planetary Grid. Kat stood watching him. She shifted her weight from one hip to the other. After a few seconds, she saw the colour drain from his cheeks. She knew what he was seeing. She'd seen it herself firsthand: the destruction of Djatt, the boiling red cloud that seemed to emerge from the fabric of space itself, closing like a fist around the planet.

His eyes snapped back into focus.

"*Madre de Dios.*"

"Quite."

"What can we do?"

"Give me Jones."

Vilca's eyes narrowed to slits. "What's to stop me killing you and using your ship to escape?"

Kat hefted the shotgun.

"You try to kill me and I'll use my ship's fusion exhaust to scour this canyon back to the bedrock."

Vilca gave a snort. He seemed to have recovered his composure.

"You wouldn't. You're not the type."

Kat leaned toward him.

"Check the data, Vilca. Look at the fall of Strauli Quay."

"Strauli…?"

The man's eyes flicked away for a second.

"You *fired* on the Quay?"

Kat set her jaw. "I had no choice."

"But there were more than a million—"

She raised her shotgun, pointing the barrel at his chest.

"Do you still think I'm bluffing?"

Vilca swallowed. She could see a damp sheen on his bald pate. After a moment, he let his shoulders slump.

"All right," he said. "You win. Faro, would you please fetch Mister Jones?"

Kat realised she'd stepped too close to Vilca's desk. She hadn't kept track of the boy. As she turned, she saw him raise his gun. Her finger yanked the trigger. The shotgun jumped in her hand. Faro jerked backward, chest shredded by three rapid-fire blasts. She turned back to Vilca, and caught the fat man in the act of reaching for the pistol in his desk drawer. She fired into the surface of the desk and he jerked his hand back, eyes wide.

"Okay, that's enough!"

Kat's pulse battered in her head. She didn't know if she was angry with Vilca, Faro or herself.

"Get Jones up here, right now!"

Vilca knew he had been defeated. He sent an order via his implant. Moments later, a pair of wide-eyed teenagers brought Napoleon Jones to the door. They were half-carrying him. He couldn't walk by himself.

They looked down at Faro's smoking corpse and turned questioning eyes on their boss. Vilca waved them away with a flap of his meaty paw.

"These people are leaving," he said.

Kat looked at Jones. His arm and leg were bandaged. His coat was torn. The antique goggles still hung around his neck.

"Kat?"

"I've got a ship up top. We're leaving."

Jones shook his head, as if trying to clear it. He'd been beaten. His lips and eyes were swollen; his moustache caked with dried blood.

"What about Vilca?"

The man behind the desk looked up at him.

"You should not have come back, *señor*. People love a daredevil because they are always awaiting his death. If he lives too long, well," he spread his hands, "they become resentful."

Kat pulled on Napoleon's sleeve.

"Leave him. He knows it's all over." She picked Faro's pistol from the dead boy's fingers.

"What's over?"

"His little empire." She glared at the fat man. "This whole planet."

Vilca put his head in his hands.

"Go now," he said.

Kat put an arm around Napoleon and he leaned his weight on her shoulder. They backed out of the room. When they reached the door at the far end of the corridor, the one that led to the roof, Vilca raised his head.

"Captain?" he said, his voice hoarse.

Kat paused.

"Yes?"

"What can we do? About The Recollection, I mean."

She took a deep breath. She owed him nothing. Further down the canyon, the freighters were filling their holds with refugees. She'd done all she could.

She looked him in the eye.

"Pray it doesn't take you alive."

WITH GREAT EFFORT, Katherine helped Jones up the metal stairs. When they got to the surface, it was snowing. Blood red flakes fell from an otherwise clear and empty sky, whirling around on the warm air rising up from the canyon.

"Oh hell." The outbreak had spread faster than she'd expected. Using her implant, she told the *Ameline* to warm the engines. If they hurried, they might still have a chance.

"Come on, Jones." His arm lay draped across her shoulders. She gripped it and pushed upwards with her legs, taking as much of his weight as she could.

> TOO LATE.

Ahead, at the lip of the canyon, a scarlet slick covered the *Ameline*'s upper surfaces.

"No!"

One of the red flakes stuck against her right thigh. Another hit the back of her hand. She looked at Jones. He already had half a dozen in his hair, more against his shoulders and back.

"Damn it." She let go of his arm and brushed at her trousers. For each flake she dislodged, another three attached themselves. Where they touched her skin, she felt a sting like the bite of a tiny insect. Her movements became more frantic, but to no avail.

No, it can't end like this…

She thrashed impotently at the storm, trying desperately to brush herself clean. As the blizzard intensified, she lost sight of her ship, lost touch with Jones. All she could feel were a thousand needle-like stings all over her body; all she could think of were the millions of dead on Strauli Quay; and all she could see were bright red sparks—billions of them, shredding and consuming her limbs, roaring through her head and heart like a fire. Reducing her every cell to ash and embers.

Embers on the wind.

PART THREE

MONKEY VS MULTIVERSE

All you need in this life is ignorance and
confidence; then success is sure.

(Mark Twain, *Letter to Mrs Foote*, Dec. 2, 1887)

From the *European Review of Physical Sciences*, online edition:

Editorial: Our science is wrong

Two years have passed since our world was invaded by a white-suited hive mind from another dimension, and yet we still have absolutely no idea how they did it.

We have examined the machinery aboard the captured Gestalt dreadnoughts, but have yet to come up with a convincing explanation. The problem is not that these fantastical engines are too complicated—on the contrary, they appear to be of an extremely simple construction—the problem is that they work *at all.*

By somehow moving an airship from one parallel timeline to another, these engines violate almost everything we know about physics. According to all our theories, they should not work; and yet they do. Travel between alternate worlds has become an undeniable reality—a reality that has thrown into disarray everything we thought we understood, and left us with a stark realisation: our science is wrong.

Fitting the Gestalt machinery into our view of reality will necessitate a radical overhaul of both quantum and classical physics. Under current 'laws', they should not be able to do what they do, and yet they do it anyway. Either these airships are a figment of our collective imagination, or the universe (multiverse?) is far stranger than we could ever have expected.

Read more | Like | Comment | Share

Related articles:

Hacking the Gestalt 'Wi-Fi'.

What's it like to be part of a hive mind? The answer may surprise you.

Ten famous people with doppelgangers amongst the Gestalt.

RAF takes command of refurbished Gestalt dreadnoughts.

Are US politicians already negotiating with other time streams?

From the rubble: Berlin's extraordinary recovery.

CHAPTER TWENTY-FIVE
ILLEGAL DUPLICATE

PAUL WASN'T ANSWERING her calls, so Victoria found his projection drone and activated it manually. The tiny machine looked like a cross between a toy helicopter and a complex mechanical dragonfly—much like the surveillance drone they'd used in Nguyen's lab. When she hit the power button, its little fans whirred and it wobbled into the air. The lenses spaced around the narrow constriction at its middle brightened, and a three dimensional image of Paul flickered into being on the bridge before her. He appeared to be wearing his usual Hawaiian shirt and white lab coat.

"Where am I?" He rubbed his eyes and looked around with a puzzled expression. Victoria moistened her lower lip.

"You're on the *Sun Wukong*."

"And who are you?"

"Your wife."

Behind his glasses, his eyes were wide and fearful, like those of a frightened animal. "My wife?"

"Ex-wife."

He seemed to mull this over. A hand came up to scratch the bristles on his chin.

"You're… Vicky?"

"*Oui, mon amour.*"

He frowned again. "What happened to your hair?"

Victoria put a hand to her scalp. "I had an accident, years ago. You saved me."

"I did?"

"Yes. Yes, you did." She felt a lump in her throat; she couldn't swallow properly. "Don't you remember?"

Paul looked pained. He reached up to fiddle with the diamond stud in his ear.

"I'm not sure…"

"Do you remember the *Tereshkova*?" she prompted. "The battle over London?" She stepped close to him. She wanted to touch his face, ruffle his spiky hair.

"I remember a smiling man."

Victoria felt her heart lurch. "You don't need to worry about him," she said hurriedly, blinking away the memory of Berg's reptilian face and the screams he made as the monkeys tore him apart.

"But the rest…" Paul flapped his arms helplessly. "It comes and goes. I get flashes."

Victoria put a hand to her mouth. She wanted so desperately to comfort him.

"It's okay," she said. "I'm here. I'm going to look after you."

Paul clenched his jaw. He glared over the top of his glasses.

"I'm not an idiot. I know what's happening to me."

"Then you also know that I love you, and I'm going to do whatever I can to help."

His expression hardened. "There's nothing that can be done."

Victoria clenched her fists. "I'm not letting you go without a fight."

"But what can you do?"

Victoria drummed her fingers against her chin. "Could we duplicate the original back-up, and integrate your stored memories?"

Paul shook his head. His earring flashed. "It wouldn't work. We didn't keep a pristine copy. The memories I've gathered since being activated have overwritten and updated the original recording."

"So, all we have is you as you are now? No back-up to the back-up?"

Paul looked down at his body, and wiped his hands down the front of his lab coat. "That's the way these things were designed. Nobody wants multiple copies of their dearly departed."

Victoria bit her lip, thinking furiously. If they couldn't get the original, then maybe they could get the next best thing...

"You know, there *is* another copy of you."

"Where?"

"On Mars."

Paul raised skeptical eyebrows. "Mars?"

"Yes." Victoria walked over to the main windshield. Rural France lay below like a winter blanket, a patchwork of browns and yellows. "When you were killed, Berg cut out your brain, soul-catcher and all. He took your official back-up and we never recovered it." She turned her back to the view and levelled a finger at him. "You, the you I'm talking to right now, *you're* the illegal duplicate."

Paul shrugged his shoulders, plainly struggling to follow her reasoning. "If you say so."

"Don't you remember?" Victoria leant back against the glass, arms folded. "Nguyen told us all the stolen souls had been loaded aboard Céleste Tech's Martian probe. And that means there has to be a copy of you up there too, maybe stomping around in one of those robot bodies."

Paul walked over to stand beside her. He looked out at the blue afternoon sky.

"Even if that is the case, I don't see what good it does us."

Victoria knew she was grasping at straws. "If we could get to it and somehow integrate the two of you…"

Paul clicked his tongue behind his teeth. He reached a hand towards the window. "First off, I don't know if that's even possible and, secondly, what does it matter anyway?" His fingers reached the pane, and seemed to sink into the glass. "We can't get to Mars. And, even if we could, the copy might have expired by the time we got there. Most copies last around six months. It might as well be on the other side of the universe." As if to reinforce his point, the image of his hand emerged from the other side of the glass, into the air outside.

"That shouldn't stop us trying."

Paul flexed his fingers in the wind. "What do you suggest?"

"I don't know." Victoria turned her palms upwards. "Perhaps we can negotiate with Lady Alyssa. She could transmit the file containing your copy. It would get here in minutes rather than years."

"Why would she do that?"

"I don't know. Maybe if we had something she wanted?"

Paul opened and shut his mouth a couple of times, as if he'd been about to snap back a retort but had then forgotten exactly what it was he had been about to say. His features softened into an expression of confusion. Slowly, he withdrew his hand from the window, bringing it back into the room, and looked at it. He repeatedly opened and shut his fist as if seeing it for the first time. Then he raised his eyes to Victoria's and smiled apologetically.

"I'm sorry, but who are you again?"

CHAPTER TWENTY-SIX
BIG DOG

THE WIND BLEW across the top of the airship's armour-plated hull, ruffling the hairs on Ack-Ack Macaque's cheeks and the backs of his hands, and flapping the scarf at his neck. His arms were folded across his chest. As he drew them tighter, the brand new leather jacket creaked around his shoulders like a timber galleon. Thank goodness K8 had talked him into buying several spare sets of clothes. She knew his propensity for getting into trouble and, although he'd grumbled at the time, he was grateful now. If he was going to convince this ragtag mob of primates that he was still their leader, it helped to look the part; and besides, in his state of injured exhaustion, it was pretty much only the stiffness of the jacket that was holding him upright.

With a squeal and a clunk, the platform—designed to transport helicopters from the hangars to the flight deck—drew level and the crowd parted around Bali, forming a loose semicircle with the younger monkey at its focus.

Ack-Ack Macaque glanced back, to the gun turret at the far end of the airship's hull, almost a kilometre away, where K8 monitored proceedings through the scope of a high-powered sniper rifle.

"Stay cool," he told her, knowing his words would be picked up and relayed by the throat mike beneath his scarf. "Don't shoot unless I'm already dead."

He didn't have an earpiece, so couldn't know if she replied. Nevertheless, he trusted her. She knew how important appearances were in these matters. If she intervened to save his life, he'd lose the respect of the troupe—not because she was a girl but because she was human, and this was one fight he had to win or lose by himself. He uncrossed his arms, clamped the cigar between his teeth, and cracked his knuckles. Surrounded by onlookers and supporters, Bali did his best to look unimpressed.

"I didn't think you'd come," he said, fingering the blade of his machete.

Ack-Ack Macaque grinned, letting them all see his teeth.

"I didn't." He gestured at the platform. "You came to me."

"A cheap trick."

"No." Suddenly serious, Ack-Ack Macaque blew smoke from the corner of his mouth. "A message." He took a step forward and saw Bali tense. "I heard you wanted to challenge me."

The younger monkey drew himself up. "That's right."

"You don't feel like backing down?"

Bali's blade swiped the air. "Not today, grandpa. We've followed you for two years and enough is enough. It's time things were different. We need to start thinking about ourselves and about what *we* want. Let the humans deal with their own problems."

Careful to keep his face impassive, Ack-Ack

Macaque gave an inward groan. Part of him had been hoping Bali would lose his nerve and retract his challenge, sparing them both a fight—at least until Ack-Ack's bruises had been given a chance to heal.

"The people we're fighting against are the ones who made us," he said, appealing to the onlookers as much as Bali. "They're the ones who turned us into monsters."

Bali laughed scornfully. "Then perhaps we should thank them?" He thumped a hand against his breast. "Just because you hate yourself, old man, it doesn't mean the rest of us have to be wracked with self-loathing."

"Is that what you think?"

"Yes, it is." Bali let the flat edge of his weapon rest against his shoulder. "Now, *compadre*, are you going to bore me to death or are you going to meet my challenge?"

Ack-Ack Macaque huffed. He didn't want to fight Bali—the monkey had been a trusted lieutenant and he honestly didn't know if, in his current state, he could beat him—but neither could he walk away.

"I rescued you," he said.

Bali scowled. "Maybe I didn't need rescuing. Perhaps I *liked* living in that temple. Perhaps I *liked* being a god."

"I didn't hear any complaints at the time."

"You're hearing one now." They stood looking at each other, neither willing to be the first to break the stare. Finally, Ack-Ack Macaque rolled his cigar from one side of his mouth to the other, and gave a weary huff.

"So be it." He flicked a hand at the crowd, and the

circle widened as every monkey in it took a quick step backwards. "Pick your weapon."

Smirking triumphantly, Bali held his blade aloft.

"I choose the machete!" The polished steel gleamed in the cold November sun, and Ack-Ack Macaque shook his head, suppressing a shudder. *Not another knife fight.* Too many memories brawled at the edges of his awareness; his nostrils filled with the jumbled odours of sawdust, blood and shit.

No!

In one movement, he pulled out a Colt and fired. Bali's arm jerked as the bullet snatched the machete from his grip and sent it clattering across the deck.

In the sudden, echoing silence, nobody dared move.

"Pick again," Ack-Ack said.

Bali sucked bruised fingers. "Are you insane?"

Ack-Ack Macaque lowered his revolver until it was aimed directly at the younger monkey's face. The spectators cowered.

"Possibly," he admitted. "I'm certainly sleep-deprived and recovering from some pretty fucking strong drugs."

Bali swallowed, looking truly uncertain for the first time. He thrust his chin forward. "Are you going to shoot me down, just like that?"

For a moment, Ack-Ack Macaque considered it. With his thumb, he levered back the Colt's hammer, clicking a fresh shell into the firing chamber. All he had to do now was squeeze the trigger. One little squeeze, and all his problems would be gone. He could blow Bali's brains all over the top of this dreadnought, and then go and find the Founder and demand to know why she hadn't told him about the baby; and then, after that, maybe he could *finally* go and get some fucking sleep.

His forefinger caressed the trigger. *So tempting...* But would the other monkeys respect him or despise him for taking the easy way out?

With a silent curse, he eased the hammer forward, and slid the smoking gun back into its holster.

"I don't need to shoot you," he growled, "to show everybody here what a jumped-up little piss-weasel you really are."

He took a deliberate step forward. Bali flinched but held his ground.

"You don't frighten me, old man."

Ack-Ack Macaque grinned. "Yes I do." He took another step forward, clawed hands reaching out.

"So," Bali said, raising his fists, "we're going to duke it out like gentlemen, is that it?"

Still advancing, Ack-Ack Macaque shook his head. "Don't be a twat."

The first flickers of real fear crossed Bali's face. He began to back away. "Then what?"

Ack-Ack Macaque rotated his shoulders and flexed his neck. His original plan had been to intimidate Bali into submission, but now his blood was up. Tiredness and irritation gave way to boiling anger. As far as he was concerned, the upstart was a stand-in for every hurt, frustration and set-back he'd suffered over the past few days, and all he wanted now was to stomp the insolent look from the little bastard's stupid eyes.

"We're going to fight like monkeys," he said gruffly. "We're going to scream and leap and scratch and bite. You know, old school. And then, at some point, I'm going to rip your tail off and jam it up your devious, back-stabbing arse."

Bali's hackles rose. He stopped retreating. "Oh, really?" He spoke for the benefit of the audience. "You think you can take me in a fair fight?"

Ack-Ack Macaque laughed.

"Who said anything about fair?"

THEY CRASHED TOGETHER with a screech that seemed to fill the vaulting sky. A kilometre away, the sound chilled K8's blood and prickled the hairs at the back of her neck. Through her rifle's telescopic sight, the two monkeys became a tumbling blur of flailing limbs and thrashing tails. They squirmed around each other, each trying to clamp his teeth around the other's windpipe. She saw flying clumps of torn hair and ripped clothing, and the flash of yellow incisors.

"Aw, shite."

Her index finger tapped against the trigger guard. She wanted to help, but the Skipper's instructions had been very specific. She wasn't to fire on Bali unless Ack-Ack Macaque died—and even then, she was only allowed to do it in self-defence. If Bali's first act as new alpha male was to turn on the humans—K8 and Victoria—she was authorised to put a bullet in his brain. Otherwise, she was just to get the hell off the airship and let the *Sun Wukong* go wherever it wanted.

I don't think so.

K8 jerked upright, startled by the voice in her head. Since returning to this parallel, the voices of the Gestalt had been a low buzz at the back of her awareness, a conversation she could tune in or out at will. This voice, however, was much louder—a sharp feminine voice speaking directly into her mind, and the sudden, queasy sensation of another presence in her head, peering out through her eyes.

"What do you mean?"

If you get a shot, child, you take it.

"Founder?"

Who else?

"But the Skipper, he said—"

I don't care what he said. He's a reckless fool. If you see a chance to end the fight, you end it.

"But the other monkeys…"

You leave them to me.

K8 closed one eye and squinted down the scope. Her cheek brushed the rifle's wooden stock.

"They're moving too fast." She clicked the magnification up a notch. "If we shoot, we could kill them both."

Then wait for one of them to get the upper hand.

Lurking behind the voice like the background hiss of a radio transmission, K8 sensed frustration, concern, and an exasperated, grudging respect for Ack-Ack Macaque and his hotheaded ways. She hunched around the rifle, arranging herself in order to minimise the amount of recoil her shoulder would have to absorb. Despite the cold wind, her hands were sweating. Through the sight, she saw Ack-Ack Macaque pull back his arm and let fly with a punch that sprayed blood and teeth from Bali's mouth.

"Yay!" K8 whispered—but, even as Bali turned with the force of the blow, his foot swept around and caught Ack-Ack off balance. The big monkey went down on his back, and Bali was on him, hands locking around his throat, throttling him. Heart beating hard, K8 tried to focus the cross hairs.

Before she could, one of Ack-Ack Macaque's hands came up to grab the side of Bali's head, and his thumb pressed into the younger monkey's eye. Bali twisted away with a cry of pain, but still the chokehold stayed in place.

Was Bali going to win? From where K8 knelt, he seemed to have the advantage. He was younger and faster, and coming to the fight fresh and rested instead of exhausted and bruised; and with his hands locked around the Skipper's throat, surely it was only a matter of time…

Come on, girl.

K8 swallowed. Bali was still on top of Ack-Ack, who was writhing furiously, trying to throw his opponent off. If they could just hold still for half a second…

Ack-Ack Macaque's thumb stabbed into Bali's eye socket again, this time rupturing the soft jelly within. Bali screamed and pulled back, hands flying to his face. Vitreous fluid poured down his cheek like the contents of a broken egg. Freed from his stranglehold, Ack-Ack Macaque sat up and lunged forward with a vicious head-butt. The other monkey toppled back and they rolled apart. Bali was on his back now, feet in the air, hands clamped to his face.

NOW!

The force of the command swamped all other thoughts. K8's finger twitched and the gun bucked— and a thousand metres away across the curving roof of the dreadnought, Bali's left knee exploded.

*   *   *

ACK-ACK MACAQUE TIED his white silk scarf around his fallen opponent's thigh, pulling it tight to form an improvised tourniquet. Then he turned to glare at the distant figure of K8, who was standing up now, the rifle dangling from her right hand.

"Why the fuck did you do that? I was *winning*, for Christ's sake."

At his feet, Bali moved feebly, one hand on his shattered leg, the other covering his punctured eye.

"Hold still," Ack-Ack Macaque told him. "You'll be okay."

Bali looked up at him, his remaining eye filled with anguish.

"You're not going to kill me?"

Ack-Ack Macaque reached into his jacket and pulled out a pair of cigars. He lit both, and handed one over.

"I never was. I only planned to teach you a lesson."

The other monkeys stood awkwardly around them. Some didn't believe the fight could be over; others were just waiting to see what would happen next.

"A lesson?" Bali's laugh was brittle. The hand holding the cigar shook so violently he almost dropped it. He was going into shock. To keep him focused, Ack-Ack Macaque bent down and slapped him across the cheek.

"I didn't say I wasn't going to kick your ass." He stepped back a few paces, his boots leaving bloody footprints on the iron deck. Bali regarded him with horrified disbelief.

"But, you took my eye..."

Ack-Ack Macaque shrugged. "If you challenge the big dog, you're going to get bitten."

He straightened his jacket, and glowered at the assembled crowd.

"Now, I'm going to let this one live," he said, nodding down at his fallen challenger, "for one reason, and one reason only. And that's because I've seen enough senseless killing to last me the rest of my days. There are too many assholes out there thinking they've got the right to kill and maim and enslave, and I've had a gut-full of all of it. I won't be one of them." He stomped to the edge of the deck and threw an arm out, pointing to the horizon. "If any of you want to leave this ship and live out your days on Kishkindha, you're welcome. I won't stop you. But let me just say this. You remember those tossers we were just fighting? The ones in the big tanks?" He recalled his woodland encounter with Apynja, and bared his teeth at his audience. "Do you know they killed everybody on their timeline, just because they fucking *could*? They murdered eight billion people because they were *in the way*." He shook his head, feeling disgusted with himself, with Bali and K8, and the whole messy fuck-up.

"The woman leading them is called Alyssa Célestine. Some of you may have heard of her. She's a grade-A fucking psychopath." He sucked his cigar until the end glowed like a flare, then spoke through a plume of smoke. "She wants to live forever. She's worked with copies of herself and Doctor Nguyen on a number of timelines, trying to convert people into undying machines. And that's where we came from."

He jabbed the cigar butt at the nearest monkeys. "We're byproducts of their experiments. They didn't want to try uploading people until they'd tried it on monkeys first." He hawked and spat over the edge of the deck, and watched his phlegm get snatched away by the wind. "And so, here we are. We're the cast-offs, the prototypes. The ones sentenced to lives of loneliness and pain, separated from our species and surrounded by humans. And my question to you is this…" He paused, letting his words hang, watching their eyes widen. He was their boss and he was angry. This wasn't a victory speech; it was a call to war.

"Are you motherfuckers ready to do something about it?"

CHAPTER TWENTY-SEVEN
NUCLEAR WINTER

As the Sun *Wukong* approached the glittering ribbon of the English Channel, Merovech's helicopter touched down on the airship's upper deck. As he stepped out, into the downdraught from the rotors, two dark-suited bodyguards, a pair of armed Royal Marines, and a young lady with a briefcase accompanied him. Standing at a safe distance, Victoria watched them hurry towards her, their heads bent and hands shielding their eyes. As this was a royal visit, she'd made a point of wearing the Commodore's old dress tunic and scabbard. She even wore a blonde wig to cover the scars on her scalp. She might not be in sole command of this airship, as she had been with the *Tereshkova*, but she'd be damned if she couldn't look the part.

Once clear of the rotors, the boy-king's pace slowed. He straightened up and fixed her with a smile.

"Victoria!" He took her hand and pumped it, then pulled her into an awkward, backslapping embrace. "I really thought we'd lost you."

"No," she said, gently extricating herself, "we're still here, still alive and kicking."

"But why did you have to stay away so long? Couldn't you have sent word?"

"We've been busy."

"And Ack-Ack?" Merovech looked around hopefully.

"He'll join us later." Victoria glanced past the King's shoulder. "You must be Amy Llewellyn."

The young woman swapped her briefcase into her left hand and extended her right.

"Captain Valois. We spoke on the phone." Her voice was as cold as a Welsh mountain frost.

"Yes, well, I'm sorry if I was rude." Victoria gave a halfhearted shrug. "But needs must, you know?"

"Quite." Amy regarded the windswept deck and wrinkled her nose. "Frankly, I don't even know what we're doing here. But now we are here, is there somewhere a bit warmer where we can talk?"

VICTORIA TOOK THEM down to the potted jungle at the nose of the airship, where they found Ack-Ack Macaque nursing a glass of medicinal rum and talking to the Founder.

"You've finally grown up," the Founder was saying, touching him on the arm.

Ack-Ack Macaque didn't reply. He looked around at the intruders with a guilty start. If Victoria hadn't known him better, she would have sworn he looked embarrassed.

She made five coffees, and placed them on the patio table. The others took chairs. The bodyguards lurked between the trees, and the Marines—who were clearly uncomfortable about the number of armed monkeys prowling the *Sun Wukong*'s corridors—took up positions by the big brass door.

"Right," she said, folding her hands on the iron tabletop, "now, perhaps you can tell me what's more urgent than an invasion?"

Merovech moistened his lips. He looked so much older than she remembered, less angry and more careworn than the mental image of the teenager she'd carried with her for the past two years.

"It's my mother," he said quietly. Among the branches, a parrot squawked. The air smelled of blossoms and rich compost.

Abruptly, Ack-Ack Macaque climbed to his feet and went to lean on the bamboo rail at the edge of the verandah. He lit a cigar and looked down through the airship's glass nose at the waves washing the French coast, his hairy head haloed in clouds of drifting blue.

Victoria frowned at his back, then turned her attention back to the King.

"She's the one leading the tanks."

"No, not her." Merovech tapped his knuckles against the table. "She's an alternate version. I'm talking about the Duchess, the one from this parallel."

"The one who blew herself apart with a hand grenade?"

He gave a nod, wincing at the memory. "She had a back-up, on the Mars probe."

"We knew that."

"Well, the probe's reached its destination, and she's been in contact."

Victoria's eyes widened. "Already?"

"It's taken them three years."

"What does she have to say for herself?"

Merovech's face clouded. "It's not so much what she has to say, as what she's done." He turned to Amy Llewellyn. "Would you mind?"

The Welsh girl pulled a flexible display screen from her briefcase and unrolled it on the table, weighing down the corners with coffee cups.

"These are the best images we've been able to get so far," she said. The pictures on the screen showed two grainy shots of the night sky, obviously taken through a telescope. "This first picture was taken yesterday at 1100 hours, this second one six hours later."

Victoria bent forward to get a better look. The only difference between the two shots was the position of a fat white dot that had been ringed with red marker pen. Between the first picture and the second, it had moved relative to the stars behind it.

"What is it, a spaceship?"

"A projectile."

"From Mars?"

Merovech cleared his throat. "My mother gave the world an ultimatum, to join her or suffer the consequences. When no-one replied, she launched this."

"No-one replied?"

Merovech turned his coffee cup but didn't lift it. "She was trying to turn country against country, but we've been doing a considerable amount of diplomatic work since the Gestalt attack. She couldn't have foreseen that."

Victoria was impressed. How different things were to the way they had been, three short years ago, when the West had been on the verge of nuclear war with

China over the sovereignty of Hong Kong. Times had changed, relations had thawed; and all it had taken to usher in this era of peace and cooperation had been a global invasion from a parallel world.

She tapped the image on the screen with her fingernail. "So, what kind of projectile are we talking about? Is it a bomb?"

Amy enlarged the picture, but couldn't resolve any further detail. The white dot remained a white dot. "As far as we can tell from spectrographic analysis, it's a solid lump of rock, possibly a repurposed asteroid."

"And what kind of damage are we talking about?"

Amy sniffed. "Projections vary, but it's likely to be extensive. Given its mass and speed, it'll hit with anything from several hundred to several thousand times the force of the Hiroshima explosion. There'll be catastrophic damage, earthquakes and tsunamis, and the aftereffects won't be much fun, either. At the very least, we're looking at a worldwide nuclear winter lasting anywhere from ten to a hundred years."

Victoria thought back to the parallel world she'd just left, to the grey skies and dying plants, and the thin, starving and disease-ridden survivors.

"Why are you telling me this?" She shuddered.

Amy gave Merovech a sideways glance. "I've been wondering that myself."

Merovech had been leaning back, listening. Now he sat straight, and reached across the table for Victoria's hands.

"You and Ack-Ack, you've saved the world twice in the last three years," he said. "I guess I'm kind of hoping you'll find a way to do it again."

Leaning against the bamboo rail, Ack-Ack Macaque blew air through his nostrils in a low, animal grunt. Victoria ignored him.

"Can't you fire a missile at it and blow it up?"

Merovech shook his head.

"It's not possible," said Amy Llewellyn. "We don't have anything with that kind of range or stopping power. We could fire a hundred warheads at it and it still wouldn't be enough."

"Then what's the plan?"

"We don't have one." The Welsh girl made a sour face. "If we did, we wouldn't be here talking to you."

Victoria reached up and pulled off her wig. She let it fall to the table.

"You want us to go up into space?" She ran a hand over her bald scalp, grimly amused at Amy's attempts not to stare.

"We don't have a craft," Merovech said. "We've got some experimental engines but nothing to bolt them onto."

"Then I'm sorry, your highness, but I don't see how we can help." Victoria got to her feet. "Unless you need us to evacuate you to another parallel?"

Merovech set his jaw.

"I won't leave my people to die."

"You may not have a choice." They stood looking at each other for a moment, and Victoria couldn't help but admire his bravery and dedication. The boy who never wanted to be king had grown to be one of the finest kings the Commonwealth could ever have hoped for. At the rail, Ack-Ack Macaque took the cigar from between his teeth.

"I've got an idea," he rumbled.

Victoria gave him a look. "Seriously?"

"Yeah." He leant back, resting his elbows on the bamboo, the butt glowing between his fingers. "I'll need to check it with K8, but yeah, I think I know how we can stop that asteroid." He picked something from the hairs on his chest, inspected it, and then popped it into his mouth. "This whole invasion thing, too."

Amy Llewellyn frowned skeptically. "You really think one monkey can make that much of a difference?"

Ack-Ack Macaque stiffened. He stood straight and looked her up and down. "You really think I can't?"

For a moment, there was silence, broken only by the cries of the birds in the upper branches. Then the Founder cleared her throat.

"You have a plan?" she asked, speaking for the first time since the meeting convened.

"That's what I said." Ack-Ack Macaque wouldn't look at her.

"Care to share it?"

He turned back to the view through the airship's glass nose. When he spoke, his voice was gruff.

"Well," he said, "the first thing we're going to have to do is capture one of those tanks."

CHAPTER TWENTY-EIGHT
HEAVY COAT

THE THINGS ACK-ACK Macaque missed most about the *Tereshkova* were its watering holes. He missed hanging out on a barstool, eating peanuts and drinking daiquiris. The old skyliner had been built to transport passengers in comfort and elegance, and most of its half a dozen gondolas had sported at least one lounge area with a fully stocked bar. The *Sun Wukong*, on the other hand, was a warship. It had been built by a hive mind with no real interest in creature comforts. The crew cabins were spartan affairs, with steel-framed bunks bolted to the metal walls. The only touch of luxury was the forest built into the airship's nose, and even that had its uses.

After the humans left through the brass door to return to the bridge, he spent a few minutes swinging through the upper branches, stretching himself, working out the kinks in his back and shoulders. The fight with Bali had left him battered, but he'd been bruised and hurting to begin with.

The Founder watched him from the patio table. She'd discreetly tipped her coffee into the soil at the base of one of the potted trees and replaced it with tea—black, with a slice of lemon—which she sipped as she waited for him. When he finally came down from the trees, she was sitting demurely, monocle in place and hands clasped in her lap.

"Do you feel better now?"

Ack-Ack Macaque growled. "I feel like hammered shit."

"Are we going to finish our conversation?'

"What conversation?" He shuffled over and flopped onto a vacant chair. "You already told me you were pregnant."

The Founder twitched her tail.

"I haven't told you the best part, yet."

Ack-Ack Macaque raised an eyebrow, too tired to move or really give a shit. "What best part?'

"It's twins."

The air drained out of him. He felt like a week-old party balloon.

"Twins?"

"A boy and a girl, as far as can be told."

"Holy hopping hell."

The Founder removed her monocle and polished it with a lace handkerchief.

"Is that all you have to say?"

"For the moment."

"And you're still going through with this idiotic plan to capture a Leviathan?"

"Yah."

She twisted the lens back into place. "I thought that now you knew about the children, you might—"

"Might what?" Ack-Ack laughed bitterly. "Give up this life of adventure and settle down somewhere?"

"Don't be childish."

"Then what? What do you want from me?"

The Founder looked towards the vast, cone-shaped window that formed the airship's nose. The daylight glinted on her monocle.

"When you told me you'd let Bali live, I thought you'd finally started to grow up. I thought you were starting to accept your responsibilities."

Ack-Ack Macaque snarled deep in his throat. "Why the fuck do you think I'm doing this? You think I'm facing off against those tanks for *fun*?"

"Why else? This isn't our fight. We could leave now, leave this world to Célestine and her minions, find a better one, a safer one..."

"Fuck that." He leant his elbows on the table and leaned towards her. "Listen, lady. I saw some stuff on that last parallel, when I was in the woods."

The Founder frowned.

"What sort of 'stuff'?"

"Stuff that opened my eye." Ack-Ack Macaque put a fist to his forehead and mimed an explosion.

"You mean the drugs that *female* gave you?"

"No, it was more than that."

The Founder gave a dismissive snort. "If you don't want anything to do with these children, just say so."

Ack-Ack sat back with a sigh. "You don't get it."

"I'm quite sure I don't. Why don't you explain it for me?"

Frustrated, he ground his right fist into his left palm. "I saw the multiverse," he rumbled. "All of it. Now, whether it was real or a hallucination doesn't matter. I know what I saw."

The Founder considered him with cool disdain. "And what else did you see? What 'revelations' were vouchsafed?"

Ack-Ack Macaque bit down on an angry reply. She could be as sarcastic as she liked, he was still going to say his piece.

"I know that if we run, now, we'll be running forever."

"Not necessarily."

"Yes, yes we will." He scratched his chest. "Because I've seen what happens—I've seen war and suffering. I've seen that wherever you go, wherever you run, there's always some fuck-knuckle thinks he has the right to impose his will on everybody else. Look at Bali." He lowered his voice. "Look at yourself."

The Founder's chin dropped. She squeezed her hands in her lap.

"That was a cheap shot."

Ack-Ack Macaque swore, got to his feet and shambled over to the drinks cabinet. It was a box on wheels containing a few bottles and a stack of glasses, and had once been a minibar in an expensive New York hotel, before he'd liberated it by heaving it through the window into the pool.

"Don't mean it ain't true." He knew he was being petty, but didn't much care. After all, it was her who'd bombed London and killed all those people, not him, and he saw no reason to sugarcoat the truth. He rummaged in the cabinet and fixed himself rum and cola, dumping both into a tall glass without care for drips or spills. Once again, he missed the shabby elegance of the *Tereshkova*'s lounge, and the white-gloved stewards who used to mix his drinks.

Still seated, the Founder said, "So, this is where you've decided to make your stand?"

He stood straight, downed half the glass in a single swallow, and then wiped his lips on the back of his hand.

"I'm tired of saving the world," he said. "If we keep jumping from one timeline to another, we're always going to be butting up against trouble, in one form or another." He took a second smaller sip; swallowed. "There's always going to be somebody that needs their ass kicked."

"You'd rather stay here and fight?"

Ack-Ack Macaque stuck his chin out. "Sure, why not? This is where I'm from. I've got friends here."

"And that's worth dying for, is it?"

He shook his head. "You're not listening."

"And you're not explaining yourself very well." The Founder unfolded her hands and stood. She brushed down the front of her skirt with a gloved hand. "I just want to be sure you know what you're doing, and that you're doing it for the right reasons."

Watching her, and the bulge at her middle, Ack-Ack Macaque drained his glass. He clunked it down on top of the cabinet.

"I belong here," he said. "I can't run out at the first sign of trouble."

"I'd hardly call impending global annihilation 'the first sign of trouble'."

"Whatever." He reached up and snatched off his goggles and leather cap, and tossed them down beside his glass. "I'm talking about Victoria and K8, and Merovech. They're..." He tailed off.

The Founder inclined her head. "They're *what*?"

Ack-Ack Macaque swallowed. He felt foolish, and that only fuelled his irritability.

"They're my troupe." He fixed the Founder with a baleful eye, daring her to laugh, but she only smiled.

"So, you *do* care about something, then? You have chosen a side?"

"Shut up." He stomped back to the rail and leant his weight on it. Through the airship's nose, he could see the distant coastline of England lying like a green smudge on the other side of the Channel. Seagulls wheeled through the air like little white fighter planes. Ships carved long, foamy wakes across the calm waters.

Damn it all, what *had* Apynja done to him? What had happened to the days when he would have simply hopped into his plane and flicked the world the finger? When had he started giving a shit? He glanced back, around his shoulder, at the Founder's pregnant belly and shuddered. It filled him with… what? Not dread, exactly. He wasn't afraid of being a father. No, it was something else, something harder to pin down. For much of his life, as far as he'd been concerned, he'd been living on the edge of death, throwing himself into one dogfight after another, relying on skill and sheer bloody-mindedness to see him through. Now though, for the first time, he felt flutters of apprehension. Where previously he would have been itching to get going—to fly eagerly against the Leviathans in a battle to the death—now a strange fatalism gripped his heart. Mortality weighed on him like a heavy coat. When he thought of the children— his children!—growing in the Founder's womb, he experienced a wave of sadness, almost regret, and knew in his gut that, one day, he'd go off on one of those damn fool missions and never return. One day, he'd leave them fatherless. In that instant, he knew it, and knew the Founder knew it too.

No wonder she's pissed off.

He licked his lips and swallowed. His life had split in two. A crazy, reckless chapter had drawn to a close, and something new was waiting to take its place—an unexplored future with no maps or precedent, where everything to which he'd become accustomed would change. *He* would change. Truth was, he already had. For the first time in his life, death actually meant something.

CHAPTER TWENTY-NINE
INCOMING

With Victoria and Merovech on the bridge, the *Sun Wukong* retraced its steps, back towards the field near Paris where the portal stood. Merovech had stayed on board despite the express objections of his security people. He didn't want to miss this. The only concession he'd made to their concerns was to don a helmet and flak jacket.

As the site of the incursion became obvious on the horizon, Victoria saw at least twenty of the large vehicles spread out in a fan shape, their huge caterpillar tracks having flattened trees, power lines and stone walls with as much ease as the first tank had flattened her helicopter. Above them, four ex-Gestalt dreadnoughts hung like armoured thunderclouds, dispensing volleys of missiles whenever a Leviathan dropped its shields for a split second.

"Looks like a stalemate," she said. "The tanks can't shoot the airships because they daren't lower their force fields in order to fire, and the airships can't hurt them in return while their force fields are in place."

Merovech stood silhouetted against the front window, peering forward.

"So they're just sitting there, looking at each other?"

"Not exactly."

The cannon on the front of one of the Leviathans boomed, gushing smoke and flame. At the same instant, a rain of black torpedoes fell from the nearest dreadnought. Both vehicles rocked with the forces of impacts and explosions.

"It's a war of attrition," Victoria said from the command chair. "They're going to keep plugging away at each other until eventually someone's going to score a lucky hit, or they all run out of fuel and ordnance."

"It seems so pointless."

"Well, nobody ever said war had to make sense." She rose and walked over to join him, right hand resting on the pommel of her sword. "The Founder says there are Gestalt advisors on each of the airships, helping coordinate the attacks."

"I suppose that makes sense."

"You don't sound too keen?"

Merovech let his hands fall to his sides. "I know they surrendered, and I know they've been a big help with the rebuilding and everything." His voice caught. The light shimmered in his eyes. "I just can't forgive them for what happened to Julie."

Without thinking, Victoria reached out and took him by the shoulder.

"It'll be okay."

He shook his head and put a hand to his mouth. "How can you know that?"

"Because I'm going through the same thing with Paul."

"Paul's dead?"

"Paul's been dead for three years."

"But his back-up?"

"It's falling apart."

Merovech swallowed, and wiped his eyes. "I'm sorry to hear that."

"Yeah, me too."

"Is there anything I can do?"

"Not unless you've got a way to get us to Mars." Ahead, one of the dreadnoughts took a hit to one of its engine nacelles and peeled off, side-slipping away from the fight with all the majesty of an iceberg calving. Smoke trailed from its damaged impeller.

"If I had," Merovech said, "I'd be using it to stop that asteroid." He looked sideways at her. "Do you really think Ack-Ack's got a plan?"

"He says he does."

"What do you think?"

Victoria gave an elaborate shrug. "Who knows? But he's been talking it over with K8; I think he's confident."

"He hasn't told you what it is?"

"He will when he's ready."

"But you trust him?"

"Trust him?" Victoria laughed at the absurdity of the idea. How could she trust somebody so fundamentally unreliable?

And yet...

"He's never let me down."

Merovech looked hopeful. "You think he's onto something?"

"Could be."

"He's really going to try to save the world?"

"Or die trying."

The young king gave a nervous laugh. "Well, that's all I can ask."

Victoria gave his arm a comradely pat. She knew she should leave it there, change the subject or walk away, but found she couldn't.

"What happens if he can't save it?" The old journalistic itch was playing up again, and she just had to know. "Is there a plan B?"

Merovech's jaw tightened. "We have the nuclear shelters. A few of us might survive, but only until the stored food runs out."

"What about the dreadnoughts?"

"What about them?"

"They can jump to other parallels. You could load them up with people, use them as life rafts."

Merovech's brow creased thoughtfully. "How many can they hold?"

"I don't know. A thousand each, maybe."

"It's not enough."

"You have six months." Victoria waved her arms helplessly. "You could keep coming back for more, right up until the impact. You'd get tens of thousands out. It would be worth doing."

"But how would we decide who to take?"

"Does it matter?" She barked with incredulous laughter. "Just take as many as you can."

"But where would we go?"

"We'd find *somewhere*. If the monkey army can set up a homeland, we can too."

Merovech looked unconvinced. "But the ones left behind, they'd still be killed."

Victoria took a deep breath, feeling suddenly powerless. However much she tried, there was no way around the scale of the coming catastrophe. She'd seen the damage projections. Whatever she did, whatever any of them did, that rock was going to hit the Earth like a hammer, and when it did, there would be a colossal explosion. Everything in an area the size of Australia would be vaporised on impact. The rest of the world would be battered by secondary impacts, rattled by earthquakes, and drowned beneath tsunamis. So much dust and ash would be thrown up into the atmosphere that the sun's rays would be unable to heat the surface for years, maybe decades. Without its warmth, the remaining plants would wither and die, as would the animals and people that depended on them. The food chains would collapse. Some life might survive, clinging to hydrothermal vents at the bottom of the deepest oceans, but within a few years, the human race would be as dead as the dinosaurs and the ravaged Earth left for Célestine and her army of Martian cyborgs to inherit. It was Armageddon, Ragnarök and the Mayan Apocalypse, all rolled into one, and all Victoria could do was cross her fingers and hope Ack-Ack Macaque wasn't bullshitting when he claimed to know what he was doing.

AMY LLEWELLYN MARCHED onto the bridge, heels tapping across the deck with staccato urgency.

"I'm sorry, sir." She was out of breath. "I have to show you something." Without waiting for a reply, she crossed to the tactical display and pulled out a data crystal. "May I, Captain?"

Victoria waved a generous hand. "Be my guest." She watched the Welsh girl slot the crystal into the console and tap at the glass-topped controls with a painted nail. Above the forward window, the main display screen fuzzed, and then brought up a blurred picture.

"This was taken twenty minutes ago," Amy explained, "by one of our high-altitude reconnaissance planes."

Victoria frowned at the image. It showed a black triangle, obviously an aircraft of some kind, hanging above the curve of the Earth. The sky behind it was mauve, shading to black. Where the harsh sunlight struck its flank, it gleamed a metallic blue.

"What is it?" Merovech asked.

"I don't know." Amy's voice held the brittleness of an icicle. "But it's the size of a house and it doesn't show up on radar."

"Have you checked with the Americans?"

"They think it's Chinese."

"And the Chinese?"

"They think it's American."

Merovech gaped. "Are you telling me *nobody* knows what it is?"

Victoria stepped forwards. "Could it be from Mars?"

They both looked at her. Amy Llewellyn shrugged and increased the magnification, which made the blurred triangle larger but revealed little in the way of additional detail. "It's big and it's fast," she said, "and we have absolutely no idea what it is or where it's from."

"Jesus." Merovech rubbed his knuckles into his eyes. He looked ready to drop. "Can we track it?"

"No, sir," Amy tapped her knuckle against the image. "It outpaced our guys as if they were standing still. They only had time to snap this picture."

"Where were they when they took it?"

"Over the Atlantic, sir." Without seeming to notice, Amy bit the corner of one of her perfectly manicured nails.

"Did they get a fix on its course?"

"Yes, sir."

"Well?"

She blew a fragment of painted nail from the corner of her mouth. Behind her professional façade, her eyes were wide and scared. When she spoke, her accent was more pronounced than before. "Well, it seems to be heading this way."

An alarm sounded on the *Sun Wukong*'s bridge. Victoria shouldered the girl aside and checked the tactical display.

"*Merde*. We've got incoming. A pair of helicopters."

"Hostile?" Merovech asked.

"Without a doubt."

"Can you shoot them down?"

"No, they're wrapped in the same energy fields as the tanks."

"What about when they fire?"

"They're not firing. I think they're a boarding party."

"What do we do?" Merovech looked around, as if searching for a weapon.

"You stay here," Victoria told him. "Post guards on the door. Take command of the flotilla, keep up the attack."

"And you?"

Victoria drew her sword. "I'm taking the remaining monkeys topside. We're going to be there to welcome them when they land."

BREAKING NEWS

From *Curious Occurrences* (online edition):

UFO sightings

American authorities are investigating a series of bizarre UFO sightings, with reports coming in from as far afield as Tokyo, San Diego, and Havana.

At 15:00 hours GMT, observers in Japan reported a large fireball, which moved slowly across the sky from west to east, accompanied by a loud roaring noise. An hour later, the crew and passengers of a Puerto Rican cruise liner watched a 'gigantic' spacecraft pass slowly overhead, again accompanied by a loud roaring sound. One of the British passengers on the vessel, Mr. Richard Lewis from Birmingham, filmed the incident on his mobile phone and uploaded the footage to his social media profile.

"It was incredible," he wrote in his status update, "I've never seen anything like it. It wasn't an airship. I don't know what it was."

In another peculiar instance, the pilot of an airliner called in to report a 'close encounter' over Baja California, describing a craft that looked "A bit like a space shuttle without wings. It was blue, and had these huge rocket exhausts sticking out the back."

Online speculation suggests the appearance of these craft could herald another invasion from a parallel world but, so far, the US Air Force has refused to confirm or deny the validity of the sightings. In a brief statement, it acknowledged that an investigation was under way, urged people not to panic, and promised that the public would be 'kept informed' of developments.

Read more | Like | Comment | Share

Related Stories:

Tereshkova crew reappears in France.

Swiss government reopens Cold War bomb shelters.

Thousands flock to Rocky Mountains to join survivalist cults.

Pope calls for 'six months of repentance'.

Reports of fighting near Paris.

Church of Rock 'N' Roll declares 'Second Coming of Elvis'.

'Pork Flakes' breakfast snacks recalled following spate of heart attacks.

CHAPTER THIRTY
CUDDLES

THE CHURCH STOOD at the edge of the village. Like many churches in that part of rural France, it was small, rectangular and austere, with little in the way of carvings or other ornamentation, just a single stained glass window and a lone bell at the top of a modest tower. In its graveyard, Ack-Ack Macaque crouched behind a headstone and looked out at the tanks lumbering through the fields beyond the village. Even at this range, he didn't need binoculars. The damned things were the size of buildings and he could feel the earth tremble with the vibration of their tracks. Behind him, the village itself had already suffered half a dozen hits, but he couldn't tell whether these had been the result of accident or deliberate attack. The inhabitants, clutching suitcases, children and cats, were fleeing in the direction of the main road. In the village square, two houses and a boulangerie were on fire and the war memorial had been toppled. He could smell wood smoke and hot bread, and the faintest traces of incense and candle wax from the church.

He took a moment to consider the memorial's broken column. How many times had this territory been fought over? The First and Second World Wars had left their scars on the landscape from here to Norway, but there was a history of conflict and dispute in this area stretching back through the Napoleonic Wars, the French Revolution and the Hundred Years War. Europe, which liked to see itself as a cradle of civilisation and enlightenment, had for much of its history been a seething cauldron of blood and death—a rag caught between the jaws of fighting dogs.

"And here we are again," he muttered with disgust, adjusting the strap of the chainsaw he carried on his back.

"What's that, Chief?" Erik the orangutan crouched a little further along the wall, clad in beige fatigues. Beyond him, hunkered low behind a pair of gravestones, the red-faced macaques Lumpy and Fang sat curled around their submachine guns. Fang wore a horned Viking helmet and carried a sword at his belt; Lumpy was naked, save for a leather tunic. Cuddles, the big gorilla, lurked in the church porch. He wore aviator sunglasses, a white vest, and a pair of cut-off camouflage shorts. In his thick arms he cradled the dead weight of a six-barrelled minigun.

"Nothing." Ack-Ack Macaque dragged his thoughts back to the objective at hand. "Okay," he said, "you see the Leviathan on the left by the copse, the burning one?"

"Yes, Chief."

"That's our target."

Erik ducked back into the wall's shadow, resting his back against the ancient, mossy stones.

"How are we going to get down there?"

"Carefully." Ack-Ack Macaque pulled out a cigar

and fastened it between his teeth. "If we get caught in the open, it's all over." He beckoned them closer, and unrolled a printed photomosaic of the battlefield, taken from a camera on the *Sun Wukong*. "There's a culvert running alongside the lane," he said, tracing the ditch with his finger. "We can follow it down the hill as far as the copse."

Lumpy leant in. "What we going to do then, Chief?"

Ack-Ack Macaque rocked back on his heels and glared at him.

"They're trees, we're primates. What the fuck do you think we're going to do?"

"Hey, Cuddles, unless you want your arse shot off, keep it down."

"Sorry, Chief."

They were about halfway down the hill from the village now, moving in the direction of the battle and the ruined tank Ack-Ack Macaque had picked out as the most likely target for his purposes. The culvert along which they were crawling smelled of mouldering leaves and old dog shit, but he was past caring. He'd been running, crawling and fighting so long, all he knew how to do was keep going—keep soldiering on. He could rest when all this was over; until then, nothing else mattered. And, after all this skulking around, he was actually looking forward to getting in among the Leviathan's cyborg crew. He'd had enough hiding; it was time to fight back, and blow off steam by blowing off a few heads.

Ahead, the Leviathan resembled a land-going

warship, its superstructure rising in successive levels, each bristling with gun turrets and missile launchers.

"I figure they're heavily defended at ground level," he said. "But maybe they don't expect enemy troops to come at them from above."

"So," Erik asked, "we're going to drop out of the trees?"

"Bingo." Ack-Ack Macaque stopped crawling. His elbows and knees were sore and the front of his jacket was caked in mud. When he swallowed, his neck still hurt from being throttled by Bali. "I reckon, if we get up onto that second level, we'll find an access hatch or something."

"You reckon?"

"I've studied the motherfucking photos." He started moving again, muttering under his breath about smartarses. Behind him, Erik cleared his throat.

"What about Cuddles, Chief?"

Ack-Ack Macaque turned to glare over his shoulder.

"What about him?"

"Well," Erik lowered his voice. "He's a silverback. He weighs like five hundred pounds."

"So?"

"So, how's he going to climb a tree?"

Behind them, Cuddles let out an aggressive snort. "You see these arms?" he growled. "If I can peel a car apart with my bare hands, I think I've got the strength to pull myself up a damn tree."

Erik cringed. "No offence, big lad. It's just I never heard of a gorilla doing that."

"And I never heard of such an ignorant orangutan."

They crawled onwards in sullen silence. At the bottom of the hill, fresh explosions shook the fields. Handfuls of dirt and stones rained down into the ditch, showering their backs. The ground shook beneath them, and the crunching, screeching noise of a Leviathan grew steadily closer. Motioning his squad to stay down, Ack-Ack risked a peep over the edge of the lane. From the field on the other side of the tarmac, one of the giant machines rumbled in their direction, trying to get out from beneath the dreadnoughts' barrage.

"Oh, balls." There was no time to move. He hunched back into the ditch. "Change of plan, chaps. Get ready to follow my lead."

He stayed down as the vast machine clattered across the road, shattering the tarmac. From above, he heard the sound of its cannons firing. As it loomed over the ditch where he hid, he leapt to his feet and threw himself forwards, into the wide space between the sets of the tracks. With the guns in action, the shield had dropped. Erik, Fang, Lumpy and Cuddles came after him, the latter just managing to clear the culvert before the bank gave way beneath the tank's weight.

Now, they were under the Leviathan, within its protective force field envelope. Everything stank of diesel and wheel grease. The noise was almost indescribable, like being caught in the heart of an exploding steel foundry, and they had to duck as the underside of the vehicle slid past, centimetres above their heads. With no hope of being heard above the din, Ack-Ack Macaque settled for waving his squad towards the rear of the tank. It was their only choice of direction. Running on his hands and feet, he made for daylight, hoping the tank's back end would be lightly armed, and that the gunners would all be facing forwards, looking for targets ahead or to the sides, rather than directly in their wake. If the monkeys could remain unobserved the next time the tank lowered its shield, they'd have time to dart across the field and into the trees.

Before he could reach the back end, the Leviathan squealed to a halt, rocking on its tracks, and figures dropped from the tail to block his way. A quick glance behind showed other figures at the front of the tank—all with the unmistakable tall, slim build of Nguyen's cyborgs.

Ah, crap. They had been detected. If they were going to get out from under this tank, they were going to have to fight their way out.

"Erik! You and Fang take the front," he barked over the din of the idling engine. "Cuddles and Lumpy, cover the rear."

Directly above him, a hatch scraped open, spilling light into the shadows beneath the tank. From the overhead darkness, thin metallic arms reached for Ack-Ack Macaque. He snarled, and slipped his chainsaw from its strap. If the tank's crew wanted a fight, he was going to give them more fight than they could possibly imagine.

With a howl, he bent his legs and sprang upwards, leaping headlong into the belly of the beast.

CHAPTER THIRTY-ONE
JUST FLESH

THE HELICOPTERS TOUCHED down at the *Sun Wukong*'s stern, their wheels kissing the armoured deck only long enough to disgorge their passengers. With no appearance of haste, the willowy cyborgs—ten in all—arranged themselves into a V-shaped formation and began marching towards the nearest hatch, where Victoria stood, flanked by a dozen heavily armed monkeys. As they approached, she raised her sword, levelling the point at the chest of their leader.

"*Arrêtez-vous, s'il vous plaît.*"

To either side of her, the monkeys displayed their weapons—a motley collection of rifles, pistols and submachine guns.

The cyborgs stamped to a halt, just out of reach.

"You are required to surrender this vessel," the leader said, his voice expressionless and devoid of emotion. He had high cheekbones, slicked-back hair and a pencil moustache. The skin on his face looked almost real, but his hands, where they protruded from his utilitarian one-piece overall, had the mirror-like finish of polished chrome. They resembled gauntlets from a suit of armour, and she couldn't help but speculate about the rest of his body. Where had the line been drawn between man and machine—and which parts were still soft enough for her sword to penetrate?

"You're not welcome here," she said. "Get back in your tanks, turn around, and go back to where you came from." Around her, the monkeys chattered appreciatively. The cyborgs, however, remained impassive.

"It's for your own good," said the one with the moustache. "You may fight us now, but you'll thank us in the long run."

Victoria raised her sword slightly, lining it up with his throat, which looked reassuringly organic and vulnerable.

"I don't think that's going to happen."

The half-man looked down at her. His pupils were black dots set in silver irises.

"You have no idea of our capabilities."

Victoria kept her expression neutral, making use of her best poker face. "On the contrary, I've met your sort before."

"Then you should know that we're very hard to kill."

Without breaking his gaze, she turned her chin a little to the side, so he could see the thick scars at the back of her head and neck.

"As am I."

The moustache kinked as the cyborg's mouth twitched up at the side in what was probably meant to be a smile. He held up his fists, and a pair of foot-long machete-like blades slid from recesses concealed beneath his cuffs. A series of *snicks* came from each of the cyborgs behind him as their own blades slid into place—one from each arm. In the winter sunlight, the edges looked sharp enough to cut the air itself, and certainly strong and heavy enough to snap Victoria's thin sword like dry spaghetti.

"You're just flesh," the leading cyborg said, contempt dripping from his lips.

Victoria felt her pulse quicken. Her fist tightened on the grip of her weapon.

"And you're not even that."

Her gelware came online. It reacted to her elevated heart rate by flooding her body with adrenaline. She felt the clarity and speed of her thoughts increase as sections of her consciousness were shunted from her brain's natural cells to the crisp lucidity of the artificial processors in her neural prosthesis. Her thinking became clearer and more dispassionate, and she realised that she was going to have to kill or be killed. These creatures had come to take the dreadnought and slaughter or convert its crew. They weren't interested in negotiation or compromise, and they'd dismissed their helicopters because they had no plans to surrender or retreat. They were here to fight and win, and Victoria was the only obstacle in their path.

Well, that's just fine.

She glanced sideways at the snarling monkeys. "Take 'em out, boys," she said, and lunged forward. Striking with all the accelerated speed her gelware could muster, her first thrust took the guy with the moustache through the Adam's apple. He gurgled and choked, and blood spewed down his chest. But, even as she withdrew the sword, his hands scythed up, gleaming blades describing two neat parabolas in the winter air—and she found herself holding only the grip and guard. With the cut-off point of her sword still protruding from his neck, he came for her, and she backed away. Around her, the shrieking monkeys grappled with the other cyborgs. Shots were fired, blades flashed. She saw one macaque—a gorgeous Japanese snow macaque with thick beige fur and a bright red face—impaled on the end of a cyborg's fist.

"*Merde.*"

Moustache Man swung at her and she danced away. To her left another monkey went down, throat slit. Fast as the monkeys were, the cyborgs were faster, and the blades protruding from their synthetic wrists added half a metre to their reach.

"Retreat!" she called. "Fall back to the hatches!"

MEANWHILE, BELOW:

"Pass us those cables." K8 pointed across the engine room to a bundle sticking from a power socket. She had a lot to do, but the pair of chimps she'd been assigned weren't being a great deal of help. At first, it had been because her habit of referring to herself using plural pronouns, such as 'we' and 'us', confused them; but now they were just plain distracted. Over the past few minutes, more and more of their attention had become fixed on the sounds of combat coming from above. As K8 toiled, preparing the groundwork for the second part of Ack-Ack Macaque's plan, she heard small arms fire, monkey screams, and even the dull crump of a grenade. As the fighting grew closer, the chimps, whose names were Oing and Boing, grew increasingly skittish. They kept chattering to each other and fingering the holsters slung around their waists, leaving K8 to do the bulk of the work herself.

Not that she minded so much. Sometimes it was just quicker and easier to do something yourself, rather than explain it to someone else, and, as the majority of the work here involved wiring—setting up a power feed from the airship's generators, and a six-foot cradle to hold the force field device the Skipper planned to bring back from one of the Leviathans—it was nothing she couldn't handle alone.

She stomped over and picked up the cables she wanted, and hauled one end back to the improvised metal frame she had built in the centre of the room. The design of the contraption wasn't entirely of her own devising. As she laboured on it, she received a constant flow of suggestions and comments from other members of the Gestalt, their minds attuned to her thoughts, seeing the project through her eyes. To a girl used to loneliness, whose only real friend had been a foul-mouthed, unappreciative monkey, their warmth and companionship gave constant comfort, and the reassurance that she would never be alone again. Right at this moment, as she tugged the power leads into place and connected them to a socket hastily screwed to the side of the structure, her thoughts were communing with members of the Gestalt in London, Cairo, San Francisco and Dubai. Their shared awareness stretched like a web of light around the world, binding and bonding them in ways far more intimate than the ties of familial or sexual love. The Founder, with the help and encouragement of her puppet, the Leader, had tried to use the Gestalt's hive mind as a weapon—but K8 thought that by doing so, they'd missed the point. As far as she was concerned, this interconnectedness wasn't a tool to be used to achieve a goal, it was an end in itself. It was a beautiful way to live and work and collaborate—not in pursuit of power or greed, but simply to enrich the lives of all by sharing knowledge, skill and camaraderie.

She picked up a wrench. The noise of battle grew louder still. It sounded as if scuffles were taking place in the corridor outside the engine room. She heard a monkey screech. Something thumped against the wall; there were two gunshots in quick succession, and then silence.

The chimps drew their pistols.

"Hurry up, girlie," warned Oing, extending a hairy arm to level his weapon at the door.

"Yeah," Boing agreed, using his free hand to pull a bayonet from his belt, "make it quick."

ON THE AIRSHIP'S bridge, Merovech watched the computer plot different coloured vector lines across a map of Europe.

"Extrapolating from initial sightings," Amy said, "projected analysis shows the unknown craft arriving in our airspace within ten minutes."

"You definitely think it's coming here?"

"Where else would it be going?" She cast a hand at the forward window, and the battle raging below. "It's too much of a coincidence for it to be going anywhere else."

"What can we do?"

"You could give the order to scramble jet fighters."

"Would they get here in time?"

"They might."

Merovech rubbed his chin. He was twelve hours overdue for a shave. "Okay, do it."

"Yes, sir." Amy signalled to one of the Marines, who began talking urgently into his radio.

"Not that I expect it'll do much good."

"Sir?"

Merovech shrugged. "You say it overtook one of our fastest planes and left it for dust. It's the size of a large house, yet it doesn't show up on radar. Whatever it is, it's an order of magnitude more advanced than anything we can put in the air."

CHAPTER THIRTY-TWO
PURÉED BRAINS

THE LEVIATHAN'S INTERIOR was a maze of noisy steel chambers and cramped, badly lit companionways. It felt like the inside of a submarine. Slashing and stabbing with his chainsaw, Ack-Ack Macaque fought his way deeper. With each swing, sparks flew and severed metal limbs dropped to the deck, twitching and writhing like decapitated snakes. Somewhere along the line, he'd lost his flying cap and goggles, and the cigar he held chomped between his teeth had been snapped in half. The arm holding the chainsaw had become slathered to the elbow in blood and synthetic fluids, and he was down to his last three bullets—yet he felt better than he had in months. He'd never wanted to lead an army. He was a soldier, not a general, and *this* was where he belonged: at the heart of the mêlée, grappling overwhelming odds, with the fate of the world on his shoulders.

The confined spaces in the heart of the Leviathan proved an advantage, as Célestine's cybernetic soldiers couldn't overwhelm him; they could only attack one at a time, which suited him fine. When he swung his chainsaw in the narrow gangways, they didn't have the leeway to dodge, and more than one of them went down with their faces shredded from their skulls and their brains ripped to purée.

His other advantage was that his strategy seemed to be confusing them. They were deploying themselves to defend access to the control room at the top of the vehicle, whereas Ack-Ack Macaque's target was lower, and to the rear. They thought he wanted to destroy the tank, or capture it; that he gave a flying fuck about their nuisance invasion, when, in reality, stopping it wasn't on his immediate to-do list—later maybe, but not right now. Right now, he had another objective. As they moved to block his upward progress, he moved back and to the side, wrong-footing them at every turn.

Behind him, the rest of his squad raced to keep up, fighting off pursuers and pausing only to finish off those wounded cyborgs he'd left in his wake that were still capable of offensive action.

"How much further?" he shouted over the noise and vibration of the Leviathan's engines. Behind him, Erik consulted an infrared photo of the tank, taken via scopes on the *Sun Wukong*, his rubbery-looking fingers measuring the distance from where they thought they were to the large heat source at the Leviathan's stern.

"Five metres. Just the other side of the next hatch."

"Are you sure?"

"No."

"Ah, fuck it." Ack-Ack Macaque spat out the soggy butt of the broken cigar. He was gambling everything on the assumption that the heat source marked the position of the engine room, and that the engine room housed the device he sought.

"Well, it's certainly loud enough. Tell Cuddles to get his arse up here. If what we're looking for is in here, we're going to need him to carry it."

"Roger, Chief."

Ack-Ack Macaque put a hand against the hatch. Like the rest, it was made of thick, uncoated steel, with rivets the size of golf balls, and he could feel it throbbing to the beat of the Leviathan's mechanical heart.

"This has to be the place." Hefting the chainsaw in his right hand, he holstered his Colt and gripped the wheel that opened the door. The steel was shiny with use. He gave it two quick yanks and it spun open. The locks disengaged, and the hatch swung inwards.

Beyond, the engine room was a mass of ducts, pipes and tangled wiring, at the centre of which lay two vast and thundering turbine engines. He sniffed. The air stank of hot oil and choking exhaust fumes, and the racket was so loud he couldn't hear the whine of his chainsaw—only feel it juddering through the bones and muscles of his arm.

"Right," he yelled over his shoulder, hoping his troops could hear him, or at least get the gist, "let's get in and out before they have a chance to figure out what we're doing."

He stepped over the raised threshold, onto a catwalk suspended above the grinding turbines. At the far end, the device he'd come for stood bolted to a bulkhead, looking like an upturned coffin leant against a wall. Between him and it stood a cyborg, and Ack-Ack Macaque sighed. The walkway didn't seem all that secure underfoot, and he could feel it sway with the cyborg's movements. There was no point trying to speak over the din, so he simply bared his teeth and drew his revolver.

"*Adios, muchacho*." He squeezed the trigger and the gun bucked in his hand, once, twice, three times. The advancing figure stopped. The first shot had torn a gash across its temple, exposing the shiny silver skull beneath the skin and biting away a sizeable chunk of ear. The second and third had hit it in the chest, but Ack-Ack Macaque could see no evidence of damage. He'd hoped to hit something vital, but the shots didn't seem to have penetrated anything save for the cyborg's cotton overalls.

"Bollocks," he muttered, tossing aside the empty handgun. Facing him, the cyborg frowned, and put a hand to its ruined ear. Anger flashed across its features. With slow deliberation, it started walking forward, hands grasping at the air. Ack-Ack Macaque swore under his breath. He needed the box at the other end of the gangway. He needed it to save the world—and if that meant going through this robotic motherfucker to get his hands on it, then that was the way it had to be.

"Okay," he snarled, shaking the chainsaw, "you want some more, eh?" He ran to meet his opponent, and they crashed together at the walkway's midpoint, suspended above the spinning turbines. The cyborg parried Ack-Ack Macaque's first swing, using his left forearm to deflect the whirring teeth, while swinging his right fist at the monkey's midriff. Luckily, Ack-Ack was ready for the move, and twisted aside, bringing his chainsaw back and around for another swipe. As he did so, the cyborg smiled, and vicious-looking blades sprang from his wrists. He used one to block Ack-Ack's second attack, and stabbed with the other. Unable to counter the thrust, Ack-Ack Macaque was forced to relinquish the chainsaw and skip back. He only just made it. The tip of the attacking blade ripped a razor-straight gash across the front of his jacket and the leather sagged open, revealing the white sheepskin beneath.

Incandescent with rage but now unarmed, Ack-Ack Macaque screeched at his attacker and did the only thing he could think of. Bending at the knees, he waited until the cyborg took another swing, and leapt, launching himself over the gangway's rail. For a split second, he seemed to hang in space. The turbines spun beneath him, ready to crush and mangle him. Then his tail hooked one of the wires supporting the walkway. He swung down and round, passing beneath the feet of his surprised attacker. His hand grabbed the underside of the gangway, and he let the momentum carry him, so that he came up the other side and hit the cyborg in the head with both feet. The impact jarred every bone in his body and snapped the metal man's head back on its shoulders. Something cracked, and the figure staggered.

Ack-Ack Macaque dropped to the floor. When he got back to his feet, he saw the cyborg tottering, its head dangling behind it, held in place by electrical wires. Ducking under its swiping, blindly scissoring arms, he grabbed its overalls by the knees and heaved. The metal body went up and backwards, and toppled over the rail into the engines below.

For an instant, it seemed to bob and dance on the spinning turbines before getting caught and dragged into the machinery. He saw the head fly in one direction, one of the arms in another. Then its torso must have caught on something, because there was an ear-splitting bang, and the engines whined into smoke and silence.

Looking back to the hatch, Ack-Ack saw Erik and Cuddles were watching him with wide, awestruck eyes.

"Come on," he barked, ears ringing in the sudden silence. "I need you guys to grab hold of this device and get it back to K8 on the *Sun*."

Erik the orangutan blinked at him.

"What about you, Chief?"

"Me?" Ack-Ack Macaque scowled down at his damaged jacket. "I'm going to need my chainsaw and some ammunition. I've got some unfinished business with Célestine." He tried to pull the two sides of the slit together with his hands. "And, while you're at it, see if you can find me some goddamn safety pins."

CHAPTER THIRTY-THREE
AMELINE

TWELVE KILOMETRES ABOVE the battle-torn fields of northern France, the former trading ship *Ameline* slowed to a halt in the air. The ship had been travelling at Mach 4, but now it was stationary, hanging in the sky like an impossible statue. In cross-section, it was a snub-nosed wedge, its sheen of blue and red paint bleached by the light of a dozen alien suns. Jacked into its virtual senses, Katherine Abdulov looked down at the carnage beneath. Even from here, she could see the Leviathans crawling around like tracked armadillos, and the massive airships harrying them from above.

"Any sign of Célestine?" she asked the ship, and felt it run a sensor sweep, scouring the countryside below for signs of their quarry.

> DIFFICULT TO TELL.

Kat heard the ship's words in her mind via her neural link, and pursed her lips.

"But this fits her M.O.?"

> OH, DEFINITELY. THERE ARE A LOT OF CYBORGS DOWN THERE. MONKEYS TOO.

"Monkeys plural?"

> IT SEEMS NAPOLEON'S FOUND HIMSELF A POSSE.

Kat gave a weary sigh.

"And what about our other target, the Valois woman?"

> ACCORDING TO RADIO TRAFFIC, SHE'S ON ONE OF THE AIRSHIPS.

"You're sure?"

> SURE AS CAN BE.

"Have they seen us yet?"

She felt a shiver in the connection, like the electronic equivalent of a sniff.

> WE'RE INVISIBLE TO THEIR RADAR. THE ONLY WAY THEY'LL NOTICE US IS IF ONE OF THEM STEPS OUT ON DECK AND LOOKS UP WITH THEIR EYES.

"Which is always possible."

> MEH.

Kat took a moment to savour the view: the clear blue skies and rolling brown and yellow countryside, the grey urban sprawl of Paris to the north and the sea to the west. All of it alive, untouched, and relatively unspoiled. *Djatt, Inakpa, Strauli...* Those tragedies seemed so long ago, so far away—and yet their pain never lessened, never left her. And so here she was at the other end of the universe, trying to save this world—trying to avert yet another apocalypse.

She opened a channel to the forward weapons pod, where Ed Rico lay cocooned in alien technology, as much a component of the gun as its operator.

"How are you doing, Ed?"

"Hanging in there." His voice sounded bubbly and distorted, forcing its way up through layers of alien mucus.

"Keep an eye on the horizon," she told him. "I'm

going to try landing on the airship, but if this all goes tits-up, we can expect an armed response."

"Don't worry." He sounded like a man choking, pushing each syllable through the glop that filled his lungs and throat. "I'm on it."

"Thanks, Ed." She turned her attention back to the downward view. The airships moved like armoured clouds, raining fire on the tanks, which in turn resembled the restlessly moving buildings of a mobile city.

"Okay," she said, "let's go down there and say hello."

She looked down and flexed the fingers of her artificial left hand. The metal of the fingers and wrist had been stained and half-melted during an attack by the Recollection.

The ship trembled around her as the engines changed their pitch, and the deck skewed forward.

> DESCENDING NOW.

Through the ship's senses, she felt the wind caressing the outside of the hull and the hairs on her arms and neck prickled in response. Tingles in her feet represented the push of the thrust, growls in her stomach the power of the engines.

"Let's *try* to do it gently this time," she implored the cranky old spacecraft as she felt it fire up its fusion motors. "Remember, we want to speak to these people, not incinerate them."

CHAPTER THIRTY-FOUR
WRENCH

OING WAS THE first to die. A tall, golden-skinned female cyborg came crashing through the engine room door. Her mane of bright red hair gave her the look of an idealised Roman centurion, and her shining blades were black with blood and gore. She dispatched the chimp with a single backhand swipe of her arm, gutting him with a vicious slash from right hip to left nipple.

As Oing collapsed in a flood of gore, Boing opened fire with his sidearm. K8 covered her ears. The gunshots were shockingly loud in the confined space, but seemed to have little effect on the gleaming woman. When the gun was empty, Boing threw it at her. It hit her on the chest and fell to the deck.

K8 looked around for a weapon, but the only thing with any heft was the wrench she was already holding—and even that looked pitifully small and ineffectual compared to the half-metre blades extending from the woman's sleeves.

The cyborg looked down at the gun on the floor.

"Is that it, Cheetah?" she asked. Her voice was rich and deep, and only slightly human. Boing snarled. He shifted his weight from one foot to the other and tightened his grip on the bayonet in his other hand.

"That's not my name."

"Do you think I care?"

She raised her arms—one held forward defensively, pointing at him and daring him to rush her; the other pulled back, fist level with her ear, ready to strike.

Boing growled.

Feeling helpless, K8 called the hive for assistance, but they were all too far away to offer practical help.

All save one.

Be strong, my child. The Founder's words emanated an indignant and flinty resolve. K8 squeezed the wrench in her fists. Boing and the golden woman were circling each other.

Help us.

I am trapped on the bridge with Valois and the Marines, but I will come as soon as we can.

We need you now.

I'm afraid that's not possible.

K8 felt anger stir up inside, let it leak onto the communal channel.

Then what bloody use are you?

She crouched beside the metal cradle she'd improvised on the engine room's floor, thinking maybe she could unplug the power cables she'd just connected and use them to electrify the deck. She didn't know whether doing so would affect their cyborg attacker, but was certain it would, in all likelihood, kill her and Boing.

Best leave that as a last resort.

Motion caught her eye. Boing leapt forward, lunging with the bayonet. His long, hairy arm gave him tremendous reach and the tip of his weapon actually touched the golden woman's breast before her arm—moving so fast it was little more than a blur—swiped him aside with all the power of a car crash, sending his broken body tumbling and flopping across the deck like windblown laundry.

Sickened, K8 swallowed hard. Slowly, she rose to her feet, wrench held shakily before her. At this point, her fear and anger had become interchangeable. She couldn't tell where one finished and the other began, but both were firing her with a desperate, insane urge to fight back, no matter how mismatched and hopeless the struggle—the same instinct she imagined filled swimmers and led them to struggle in the jaws of a shark, or compelled doomed cavemen to pit their fists and fingernails against the claws and teeth of a sabre-toothed cat. Whatever happened here, she knew she would not beg, would not grovel, and would not die like cowering prey. She knew that if the Skipper were here, he'd do the same. He'd never give up, never surrender, and never give his opponent the satisfaction of seeing his fear—and neither would she. She took a deep, steadying breath, and gripped the wrench with both hands. Gold eyes flicked in her direction. The cyborg let its head tilt to one side. It looked her up and down, from the ratty baseball boots on her feet to the tousled top of her carroty hair.

"Oh, relax," it said. "I'm not going to kill you."

K8 felt her jaw clench. The golden woman stepped towards her, moving on thin, graceful legs.

"Jeez," the cyborg said, "you look so short."

K8 worked her lips. It took her three attempts to make her voice work.

"Stay back."

The woman smiled.

"I'm not going to hurt you, K8." With a sound like scraping cutlery, her stained blades retracted into her sleeves.

"How do you know my name?"

"How do you think?" A shining hand reached out, plucked the wrench from her grip, and tossed it away. "I'm you, you dumbass."

"M-me?" In her head, K8 could feel the other members of the Gestalt recoiling from her.

"Yeah, girl. I'm the version of you from the other world. You know how this works."

"But I would never, never—"

"Never can be a long time when you don't have a choice."

With her back to the wall, K8 looked around for a way out. Her eyes fell on Oing and Boing, still lying where they fell.

"Why did you have to kill them?" she demanded, cheeks burning.

"They were in my way."

"And me?"

"You can be saved." The gold woman shook her red Mohican, which shimmered in the light like strands of fibre optic thread. "You can come with us, and have a body like mine."

"But, I—" K8 stopped, surprised to hear herself using a singular pronoun. "I…" the Gestalt were still there at the back of her mind, but their voices were quieter now, less intrusive—and where once there had been 'we' and 'us', now there was only 'me' and 'I'.

"Are you listening?" The golden woman reached for her. "I'm trying to save you."

"Well, I don't need saving." Still distracted by the changes taking place in her head, K8 slapped the cyborg's hand away. "I don't need you, or anybody else."

The gold woman cocked her head in amusement. "But you're so lonely."

"No, I'm not." K8 bunched her fists. "I thought I was, but I'm not."

"Because of the monkey?"

K8 felt her heart rattling against her ribs.

"Yes, the monkey."

The golden woman straightened up and made a show of looking around the room.

"Then where is he, eh?" She bent forwards, putting her face level with K8's, and K8 could see her own distress reflected in the polished mask. "Everybody let me down; why should you be any different? Where's this hairy 'friend' of yours when you need him? *And where was he when I needed him?*"

A cough came from the door. They both looked around to see Cuddles standing on the threshold. The big gorilla filled the entranceway with his muscular bulk, the Gatling gun cradled like a toy in his massive hands.

"Ack-Ack sends his regards."

A fat, leathery finger squeezed the trigger and the gun's barrels spun. The cyborg tried to leap aside but, fast as she was, she couldn't outpace a weapon capable of firing fifty rounds per second. The room flickered as fire danced from the gun. K8 let her knees give out and collapsed to the deck, landing on her hip. Above her, her golden counterpart jerked and danced like a marionette as bullets punched through her metal skin, into the flesh and wiring beneath. Stray shots riddled the rear wall. Used shell cases showered around the gorilla's feet. The chattering roar of the gun filled the room.

And then all was quiet.

The minigun's spinning barrels whined into silence and the last spent case jangled on the iron deck. The room stank of hot metal, spilled oil and gun smoke. K8 uncovered her ears and looked up. The perforated cyborg stood swaying. It put a hand up to the smoking holes peppering its chest, and then dropped heavily to its knees.

"You idiots," it wheezed.

Cuddles pushed up his sunglasses and fixed the woman with a sharp-toothed sneer. His feet straddled the end of a long, grey, coffin-shaped box. He dropped the minigun and pulled out a large silver pistol, which he levelled at her head.

"Fuck you, lady."

After the whining din of the Gatling gun, the pistol's shot was a flat crack. The bullet hit the cyborg in the forehead and her head tipped back on her neck. Something snapped in her chest, metal parted and, as if in slow motion, her head and shoulders broke from the ruins of her trunk. They fell backwards with a heavy thud. The rest of her body—sparking wires projecting from the shards of her chest—tottered for a second on buckling legs, and then collapsed in the opposite direction.

STILL FEELING NUMB, K8 helped the gorilla lug the stolen shield device across the deck to the cradle she'd built.

At first glance, it appeared to be a sealed container with no obvious controls or openings, save for a power coupling at the narrow end. As Cuddles kicked the remains of the golden cyborg out of the way, she ran her hands over the edges of the box, searching for seams or hidden catches.

"Any idea how it works?" the gorilla rumbled. Grease and dirt streaked his white vest, and his sunglasses perched on top of his head. The dog tags around his neck clanked quietly when he moved.

K8 sighed and shook her head. Her pulse still roared in her ears and she felt sick. She couldn't believe she'd been talking to another iteration of herself; that the brain in that precious metal physique had once belonged to a girl almost identical to her—a kind of twin sister, but a shadow sister that had turned to the Dark Side, renouncing her humanity and morals in exchange for a shot at immortality. K8 shook herself and decided she'd worry about the philosophical implications later. When all this was over—assuming they lived through the next few hours—she'd have time to freak the hell out. Right now, she had a job to do, and the Skipper was counting on her to get it done. Hell, the whole future of the *world* depended on it.

She coughed and cracked her knuckles. Then she gave the grey box a prod with her toe.

"I guess we just plug it in and see what happens."

She helped Cuddles guide it into the makeshift cradle and was gratified to see it was an almost perfect fit.

Let us help, child. The Founder's voice echoed in the spaces behind her conscious thoughts.

Get lost.

Our minds, working together…

K8 screwed her eyes shut and tapped her knuckles against her temples. She'd yearned to rejoin the hive, craved its comfort the way a raindrop craves the ocean; yet now, a crack had appeared. She could still hear them, still feel them, but they'd let her down in a moment of need. They'd left her hanging, high and dry. A rift had opened and now she wasn't sure it could ever be repaired. She wasn't part of their collective any more. In facing death, she'd found herself.

Shut up and get out of my head.

All that mattered now was the task at hand, and the Skipper's plan.

You can't shut us out.

Leave me alone.

You hate being alone, all by yourself. Don't you remember? Don't you remember how hard it was, how lonely?

She picked up the power cable and rammed it into the waiting socket, twisting and jiggling it until it slid home. The number of voices in her head rose to a chorus, a multitude. A whole congregation of true believers called to her, beseeching her.

Come back to us. Be one with us again.

Tears rolling down her face, she crammed her fingers into her ears. They sounded like disappointed primary school teachers and she tried to drown them out the only way she knew how.

La la la la, she sang to herself, inner voice almost shrieking the words she remembered from a childhood spent as the only ginger kid in her class, the words she'd used to block out the schoolyard taunts.

La la la, I'm not listening.

CHAPTER THIRTY-FIVE
MARY SHELLEY

ACK-ACK MACAQUE LEAPT from the rear of the crippled Leviathan, leaving it straddling the road, and ran on all fours across the field. The fighting had intensified, with the tanks and airships exchanging fusillades in an almost continuous bombardment, and he hoped everybody's attention would be fixed on their opponents rather than scanning the grass for scampering primates.

He didn't know for sure which tank Célestine was in, but he had a fair idea. So far, the Leviathans had arranged themselves in an arrowhead formation, with one at the rear, close to the portal—and that was the one he was running towards. The Duchess might be a deranged and evil bitch, but she was also very keen on self-preservation. She wanted to live forever, which meant she wouldn't be riding in the vanguard with the rest of the grunts; she'd be at the back, close enough to command the battle but sheltered behind the first wave of tanks. And, now he was on the inside of the 'V', he made straight for her.

What he'd do when he found her was another matter. He hadn't given it much thought, beyond the vague idea that he'd rip her arms off and use them to beat the rest of her to death. After all, this was the woman who'd started it all: the spider in the web, pulling the strings. She was the one who'd contacted the various Doctor Nguyens on their respective worlds, and encouraged them in their experiments. If it hadn't been for her, he might never have been uplifted. He might have stayed a semi-conscious monkey, living out his days in ignorance. He and all the other sentient monkeys and apes might have gone on with their lives as nature intended, without being strapped to tables and shaped into aberrant, gaudy monstrosities. If Nguyen had been his personal Frankenstein, Célestine was his Mary Shelley. She was the author of all that had transpired, the mad genius behind his story, and he *really* wanted to kill her. Because who knew what insanity she intended to unleash this time? Three years ago, she'd egged on her counterpart on this world—Merovech's mother—to engineer a nuclear confrontation with China, all in order to further her own desires for cybernetic immortality, and, if Apynja was to be believed, she'd already killed most of the population of her own timeline, sentencing billions to sickness and lingering death for her own foul ends.

Well, fuck that with a long, greasy pole. It was time for a reckoning, and it seemed only fit and proper that he—one of her discarded prototypes— should be the one to dish out the justice.

A stray shell hit the ground a couple of dozen metres to his right, with a force that bowled him over and showered him with earth and stones. He rolled with the impact, taking it on his shoulder, and came back up onto his hands and feet, still running.

It's going to take more than that to stop me today. All his aches and pains seemed to have fallen away, having sloughed off like a dead skin. Adrenaline burned through him like good rum. He felt young again.

Ahead, his target lumbered forward at less than walking pace, the vast tracks barely turning.

She doesn't want to get too far from the portal, he thought. And who could blame her? The last thing she would have been expecting was to have her lead tanks savaged by armour-plated aerial behemoths. She would have been anticipating a world still recovering from the nuclear standoff between China and the West, a world devoted to peace and disarmament; she would have had no idea she wasn't the first to try invading from another parallel, and therefore she couldn't have foreseen the presence of the Gestalt dreadnoughts.

Attacks from other worlds—so far, the Earth had suffered two, and now there was the threat of the asteroid from Mars. Was this the way reality was going to work from now on? Would there be other aggressors, an endless procession of belligerent invaders from an infinite number of parallel worlds, unending strife and conflict?

Fuck, no. Not if I've got anything to say about it.

Veering to the left, he started to circle the great machine. Even in his wild state, he wasn't reckless enough to try a frontal assault. His Colts had been refilled and he'd retrieved his chainsaw, but neither would be much use if the forward machine guns drew a bead on him.

A missile whistled overhead, coming in at a steep

angle from one of the dreadnoughts on the edge of the pack, and exploded against the Leviathan's invisible shield.

"I've got to time this right," Ack-Ack Macaque muttered. He needed to be in position when the tank retaliated; ready to leap through when it dropped its force field in order to fire.

And there it was! The cannons at the Leviathan's snout let loose a volley that rocked the beast on its tracks and shook the earth beneath his feet. Without waiting for the echoes to die away, he hurled himself between its caterpillar tracks. He rolled and kept rolling, until he was right under the main body of the tank and away from the danger of being crushed by its treads. Then he climbed to his feet and brushed himself down. Having already infiltrated one tank, he knew exactly where to find the hatch on the underside of this one. Without hesitation, he marched over and, standing directly beneath, used the butt of his Colt to hammer on the steel.

"Knock, knock, motherfuckers. Guess who."

VICTORIA VALOIS USED the blunt end of her fighting stick to give the green cyborg's head a final series of whacks. When its emerald skull finally caved and she was quite sure it was dead, she turned to look around the *Sun Wukong*'s bridge.

"Everybody okay?"

Three camouflage-painted cyborgs had tried to force their way onto the bridge, but all had been felled. The two Marines were down, one dead and the other injured. Merovech stood by the front window, his arm around Amy Llewellyn's shoulders. He held a French-made FAMAS assault rifle in his free hand, taken from one of the fallen soldiers.

"Are we safe now?"

Victoria walked to her command chair and pressed a control. A loud clunk came from the back of the room, followed by more slams and thumps from further back in the gondola.

"I've locked down the airship. All the fire doors and bulkheads are now sealed. I don't know how many of those metal bastards are still aboard, but that should slow them down."

"What about the crew?"

"What about them? Between screeching, firing wildly in all directions, and flinging their own *merde* at each other, they're doing nearly as much damage as the invaders." She worked her shoulder, which hurt where it had taken a glancing blow from a cyborg's kick. "It'll do them good to stay confined for a while, give them all a chance to calm down."

She watched Merovech help Amy over to a chair. The secretary had been thrown into a wall and cut her head. The King pulled the handkerchief from the breast pocket of his suit jacket and pressed it to her wound.

A light flashed on Victoria's console, indicating an incoming message. She accepted it, and routed the signal to the main view screen above the forward window.

"Victoria Valois?" The woman in the image wore a grey coat over olive green one-piece fatigues. She had short brunette hair and eyes the colour of dried dates.

"Yes?"

"Greetings, from one captain to another. My name is Katherine Denktash Abdulov of the Strauli Abdulovs, late of Strauli Quay, and I am here to offer my assistance."

Victoria frowned.

"I'm sorry, who are you?"

"Katherine Abdulov, of the trading vessel *Ameline*. We're currently two hundred metres above you, monitoring your situation."

"Two hundred metres above…?" Victoria reached out and activated another screen, displaying a composite of feeds from all the security cameras on the upper deck. As she did so, Merovech left Amy holding the handkerchief to her head and came over to stand behind her.

"There," he said, pointing over her shoulder at one of the images. Victoria tapped it, enlarging it until it filled the display.

"Jesus."

The wedge-shaped UFO from Amy's photographs hung in the sky above them, balanced on three jets of pale fire. Victoria glanced from it to the face of the young woman on the main screen.

"Yes, that's us." Katherine Abdulov rolled her eyes impatiently. "Right where I told you we were. And, once again, we're here to help."

Victoria swallowed. A thousand questions swarmed, fighting to be asked. Behind her, Merovech said, "Help? What kind of help?"

Katherine looked at him with frank astonishment.

"With the invasion," she said. "With the tanks you're fighting."

Victoria raised an eyebrow. "You have weapons?"

"Oh yes."

"Well, those tanks have some kind of force field. It's damned near impenetrable."

"Really?" The young woman glanced off-camera for a moment, and then smiled. "Watch this."

For a few heartbeats, nothing happened. Then a brilliant white pencil-thin spear of light flashed from the spaceship's nose, overloading the cameras. Victoria leapt from her position and ran to the front window.

"*Putain de merde!*"

Below, the hindmost Leviathan lay carved in half, sliced down the middle like a log in a sawmill. The edges of the cut smoldered a molten yellow and beneath them, a long, thin strip of grass and soil had been charred down to bedrock. Victoria put a fist to her lips, hardly daring to breathe. The weapon struck again, and another of the giant tanks flared.

"Yes!" She punched the air. "Oh, yes, yes, yes!"

CHAPTER THIRTY-SIX
DEATH IN THE AFTERNOON

ACK-ACK MACAQUE LOOKED up at the blue sky.

"What the fucking, fucking *fuck* was *that*?" He'd been skirmishing his way through the big tank's walkways and chambers when the world turned white and hot, and everything tipped sideways. Now he lay with his back against what, until a moment ago, had been a wall, with his nose full of the stink of burning plastic and singed monkey fur.

Climbing gingerly to his feet, he poked his head above the cooling edges of the room and looked out. The other half of the tank rested on its side a few metres away. Smoke rose from a dozen points, and he could see flames leaping where fuel lines had been cut.

"Holy crap in a hand basket." He had no idea what had happened, only that he'd been lucky to survive the experience. The cyborg he'd been fighting at the time hadn't fared nearly as well. It had been standing directly in the path of whatever had split the tank, and now its body lay on the grass between the two halves of the wreck, cleft into asymmetric and half-melted segments. Its metal body had probably shielded him from the worst of the mysterious attack, but all he felt towards it was the fierce satisfaction of seeing an enemy brought low.

He had to get out of here and find the Duchess. The edges of the cut walls were rapidly cooling. He leapt up onto one, trusting his boots to shield his feet from the residual heat. The tank lay with its innards bared to the sky, its rooms and walkways like the indentations in an empty chocolate box. As long as he kept moving, followed the walls and kept his balance, he'd be okay.

He started running, using his tail as a counterbalance to steady himself. He guessed Célestine would be somewhere towards what had been the top of the vehicle, so he made his way in that direction, and found her lying in the ruins of the Leviathan's control room. She had two cyborgs with her, but both were damaged and disorientated. Crouching on top of the wall, he decapitated them both with his chainsaw, sending their metal heads rolling into the echoing depths of the damaged tank like ball bearings rattling into a sewer.

The Duchess looked up at him.

"Oh," she said. "It's you. What do you want?"

Ack-Ack Macaque curled his lip. "I've got a message for you."

Célestine rose to her feet and brushed herself down with her palms. Her black uniform was rumpled and dusty, and one of the sleeves had been badly scorched.

"You know, I told Nguyen you were going to be trouble."

Ack-Ack Macaque killed the chainsaw's engine, and laid it aside.

"Well." He drew his revolver. "That's one thing you got right."

"You said you had a message?"

"Yeah, from a lady called Apynja."

Célestine blinked and her face tightened.

"Oh, so you're working for her now?"

Ack-Ack Macaque was surprised. "You know her?"

"Of course I know her. She's my sister."

He opened and shut his mouth a few times.

"Your sister? But she's a—"

"I wouldn't expect you to understand." Célestine drew herself up. "Now, what is it she has to say?"

Ack-Ack Macaque glowered at her and raised his gun.

"Just that you shouldn't have killed so many people."

"Me?" Célestine pushed her tongue into her cheek. "That's a good one."

Ack-Ack Macaque snarled. "You killed eight billion people. I don't see anything funny about that."

The Duchess waved a hand. "It's all just numbers." She looked up at the sky. Her breath came in small, almost imperceptible wisps. "You have no idea who she is, do you?"

Ack-Ack Macaque rubbed his leather eye patch. The socket beneath itched.

"She's an ape."

Célestine laughed and shook her head.

"Oh no, no. She may be many things, but she's not remotely an ape. She's not even human."

"Then what is she?"

"I told you." The woman smiled with all the warmth of a shark. "She's my sister. Or rather, she was, before she grew a conscience."

Ack-Ack Macaque growled. "You're not making any sense." He waved the gun at her in annoyance. "Make sense!"

Célestine stuck her chin at him.

"I'm making perfect sense, you vile creature. You're just too stupid to grasp what I'm talking about." She put her hands on her hips. "Aren't you?"

Ack-Ack Macaque took a deep, shuddering breath. "I'm the one holding the fucking gun," he reminded her.

"So you are." Up ahead, one of the other Leviathans sparked and fell to pieces, diced into chunks by a blinding white beam from the heavens. Moments later, the one next to it suffered an identical fate. Ack-Ack Macaque blinked away purple and green afterimages.

"Your invasion's cancelled," he said. "You're fucked."

"Really?"

Célestine brought her hands together and smiled. She seemed to shimmer and her body grew translucent. She was fading, exactly as Apynja had faded from the clearing in the wood.

"Oh no you fucking don't!" Ack-Ack Macaque stood up and fired his Colt into her almost transparent torso. His first two shots seemed to pass through without hurting her, but the third made contact. Célestine screamed with pain and rage, and suddenly she was solid again. She fell back into a sitting position, hands dabbing madly at a bloody wound in her stomach.

"You imbecile. What have you done?"

Ack-Ack Macaque raised the pistol's barrel to his lips and huffed away the smoke.

"I told you, I'm delivering a message." He holstered his weapon and jumped down beside her. "To you and all the other megalomaniacal ball-sacks out there."

"And what message is that?" She was panting, and her skin was pale with shock. He crouched, bringing his snout to within inches of her face.

"That we've had enough of your shit."

He watched her struggle and curse. She tried to pull herself up on the edge of a chair but his bullet had damaged her spine, and her legs wouldn't work.

"Do you even know how many people you've killed?" he asked contemptuously. She gave a snort.

"Do you?" Another bolt sizzled from above, bisecting a Leviathan to their left. With a squeal of brakes and a crunch of abused gears, the remaining tanks cranked into reverse and began backing towards the portal. "After all, you're hardly blameless, are you?"

Ack-Ack Macaque bridled. "I only kill people that need killing."

"And who are you to decide?"

"Who are you to say I can't?"

Célestine coughed, and wiped her lips on the back of her sleeve.

"You can dress it up any way you like, but you're as much of a murderer as I am."

Ack-Ack shook his head. "Nobody's as much of a murderer as you are, lady."

She laughed bitterly.

"Your friend Apynja is. Or she was before she changed her ways, the hypocritical bitch."

"What are talking about?" Ack-Ack shuffled back slightly, to avoid the blood spreading from her wound. "She's just an escaped orangutan."

Célestine shook her head sadly. "She's so much more than that. Yes, I killed a world. I admit it, and I'm proud of it. But her." She coughed again. This time, her sleeve came away red when she wiped her mouth. "She's killed dozens. Hundreds maybe."

"Who is she?"

Célestine's eyes became glassy and her head began to sway. Ack-Ack Macaque took her by the shoulders and shook her.

"Who is she?"

He shook her again, but her head lolled back and her body went limp, and he knew she was dead.

CHAPTER THIRTY-SEVEN
ALL THE FISH

WITH THE INVASION defeated and the Leviathans in retreat, Victoria allowed herself to slump into the command chair. Merovech and Amy had taken the surviving Marine to the infirmary in search of medical attention, leaving her alone on the airship's bridge. The noise of battle had faded, and the only sound she could hear was the constant hum of the *Sun Wukong*'s engines. Her shoulder still hurt, and she had a number of additional cuts and bruises, but her mind wasn't dwelling on her injuries. Right now, she had other priorities.

She couldn't read the words on her computer display, but knew the control sequence by heart. A tap here and a tap there, and Paul's hologram activated. The little drone sailed into the middle of the room and projected his image in all its three dimensional luminosity. For the briefest moment, he remained frozen as the airship's processors booted up his personality, and she took the chance to drink in his appearance without distraction—his bright shirt and creased white lab coat; his spiky peroxide hair and hipster spectacles; the jewelled stud in his ear. This could very well be the last time she'd ever see him, and she wanted a clear picture to remember him by.

"Ah," he said, blinking rapidly and focusing on her. "You again. I was hoping you'd be Vicky."

Victoria felt her heart sink into the pit of her stomach.

"I am Vicky."

"Really?" He peered at her over the rim of his glasses. "My word, so you are. What happened to you, to your hair?"

She didn't feel like going through it all again. "It's a long story."

"And you've aged."

Her hand went to the back of her head. She felt suddenly, stupidly self-conscious. If this was going to be the last time she saw him, she realised, it would also be the last time he saw *her*, and she wished she'd had time to make more of an effort with her appearance. Not that he'd remember once she'd switched him off again, but still she couldn't help feeling she should have done more to create a sense of occasion. After all, how many chances did one get to say goodbye forever to the love of their life?

"It's over," she said. "The invasion. Célestine's dead."

Paul's face creased. He was obviously struggling to make sense of her words.

"Does that mean we can go home now?"

Victoria felt something stick at the back of her throat. "We are home, my love."

He took off his glasses and looked towards the large window at the front of the gondola.

"We are?"

"Come and see." She climbed to her feet and

trudged over to the glass. He followed, the soles of his feet never less than a centimetre above the deck.

"Look," she said, "that's Paris over there on the horizon. You can see the skyliners over Orly Airport."

He peered down his nose.

"If you say so."

"This is where we came from, Paul. We're back." She put out a hand to touch his arm; stopped herself. "I just wanted you to know."

Paul stroked his chin, squeezed his lower lip.

"I wanted to go home, to my apartment." His voice was small and lost.

"That's in London."

"And we can go to London?"

"Of course we can. Just not right now." She turned her back on the view, squaring up to him and gathering her resolve.

"Why not?"

"Because we need to talk."

"That sounds serious."

"I'm afraid it is." She clapped her hands together and squeezed. "*Je suis désolée.*"

His eyes looked into hers, shifting nervously from one to the other.

"What is it?"

Victoria opened her mouth but nothing came out. Her throat had gone dry and the words wouldn't form. She turned her face away and exhaled. She couldn't seem to breathe properly.

"I'm afraid this is goodbye," she croaked at last.

"Goodbye?" Paul frowned. He didn't understand. "Where are you going?"

"I'm not going anywhere." She waved her hands in a helpless gesture. "It's you. I have to turn you off. I've got no choice."

He shook his head and she saw the diamond stud twinkling in his ear.

"You're pulling my plug?"

Victoria winced. If she was going to get through this, she had to be firm.

"You're falling apart," she said.

"So, what?" His eyes were wide, his expression alarmed. "Does that mean I get put down like an incontinent old dog?"

Victoria shook her head. This was hurting way more than she'd imagined. "It takes longer every time I switch you on," she tried to explain, "and there's less of you here each time. One day, I'm going to switch you on and you'll be nothing but a drooling electronic vegetable—that's if you even boot up at all."

Paul's mouth was a hard line. "I see."

"I can't do it, Paul." Her eyes prickled. She felt her poise crumbling like wet sand. "I can't go through that. I don't want to see you reduced to such a state."

"And what about what I want?"

She ran an agitated hand back across the top of her head. "I don't know. It seems... kinder to say goodbye now." She walked back to the command console, feeling his eyes on her the whole way.

"But I love you."

Her vision blurred. "I love you too, and that's why this is so hard for me. Believe me, this is the most difficult decision I've ever had to make." She activated the touchpad that would cut off the power to his projector and confine him to an inactive file in the computer's storage. All she had to do was tap the final command and he'd be gone—probably forever.

"We've been through so much." His tone was pleading. She had to fight back tears.

"I know, and I'll always treasure every moment."

"But now you're going to kill me?"

Victoria felt like weeping. "Don't say it like that."

"How else should I say it? I don't want to die."

A tear brimmed over her lower lid and dripped onto her cheek. She didn't bother wiping it away.

"You died three years ago, Paul. You just haven't stopped talking yet."

Another tear fell, splashing onto the black glass console. Her finger hovered over the cut-off switch. Her hand shook.

"Please," he said.

She bit her lip. "I'm sorry. Goodbye, Paul. *Au revoir.* I'll always love you." She looked up and their eyes met.

"Vicky, wait…"

She sniffed, fighting back sobs.

"What?"

He looked down at his feet for a long moment. When he looked back up, his expression had changed. He looked bemused. He frowned at her in puzzlement, as if trying to remember who she was.

"I'm terribly sorry," he said. "What were you saying?"

Victoria swallowed back her grief. If she had to do this, it was better he was confused rather than terrified. She forced a watery smile. In her heart, she wanted him to be reassured, to be happy—and sometimes, ignorance really was bliss. She looked him in the eye.

"I was saying goodbye, my love." Her finger touched the control and he disappeared. One instant he was there, blinking owlishly at her; the next, he was gone, switched off like a light, leaving only the tiny drone to mark where he had been standing.

VICTORIA STUMBLED FROM the bridge with tears cascading haphazardly down her face, falling onto her chest, and soaking into the fabric of her tunic. She didn't care. She'd had enough of being strong. The grief she felt wasn't grief for her husband, the flesh-and-blood man whose funeral she'd attended three years ago; the grief burning a hole in her heart right now was for the Paul who'd been her constant companion since that dark day—the electronic ghost who'd become something so much more than the sum of his parts; the back-up who'd ended up getting closer to her than anyone else ever had, or ever would. She was crying for him, and for herself. For with him gone, who did she have left? She had friends, yes, but who would love her; who would comfort her in the night, and stay up talking with her until the dawn? Paul had spent time literally living in her head. How would she, could she, ever be that close to anybody, ever again?

Heedless of her appearance or the worried stares of the monkeys she passed, she made her way topside, seeking fresh air, wide open spaces, and a fresh sense of perspective. However, as she stepped out onto the flight deck, her eyes fell on something she hadn't been expecting to see. In the centre of the airship's back, resting on three extended landing struts, sat the *Ameline*.

Two figures were walking towards her, clad in identical green fatigues. One was the woman from the transmission, Katherine Abdulov. She walked with a shotgun balanced on her hip. The other figure was... familiar.

"Cole?" Victoria's heart leapt at the prospect of a friendly face, a sympathetic ear.

The man raised his eyebrows. "Pardon?"

She wiped her nose on the cuff of her tunic. This wasn't her former comrade, the alcoholic sci-fi writer who'd helped her uncover the Gestalt conspiracy. This was merely another iteration of the same man—a stranger with a similar face.

"Sorry, love," he said, scratching the side of his nose, his accent betraying traces of time spent in both Cardiff and London. "My name's Ed." He shrugged again. "Ed Rico." A grin split his face and he pointed two fingers at her, miming a ray gun. "Take me to your leader."

Katherine Abdulov elbowed him in the ribs. Then they both frowned. Katherine stepped forward and placed a hand on Victoria's shoulder.

"Why are you crying?" she asked.

SCIENCE NEWS

From *Physics? Fuck Yeah!* (online edition):

Is our Universe a hologram?

TOKYO 18/11/2062: Scientists in Japan claim to have found the clearest evidence yet that our universe—that's you, me, and everything we can see and hear around us—is a hologram. If true, this breakthrough could be a vital stepping-stone on the path to reconciling Einstein's theory of relativity with quantum physics, and paving the way for a so-called 'Theory of Everything.'

According to calculations made by the team at Ibaraki University in Japan, the three dimensions we're familiar with—length, breadth and depth—are illusions, and the universe is simply a projection of information encoded on a two-dimensional 'cosmic horizon' in the form of vibrating, one-dimensional 'strings'.

Although it sounds complicated, the idea can be visualised by imagining a balloon full of smoke, with pictures drawn on the outside. When a light shines through the skin of the balloon, the pictures cast seemingly three-dimensional shadows through the smoke.

While the theory has been around for some years, this is the first time a team claims to have simulated the process in convincing detail, by using extra dimensions implied by the proven existence of multiple, co-existing timelines.

The next step will be to widen the idea to incorporate a fundamental theory of the structure of the multiverse. Whether or not that project is successful, or even possible, today's news provides an important boost for string theory, which had rather fallen from fashion of late.

Read more | Like | Comment | Share

Related Stories:

Quantum computers 'borrow' processing time from their counterparts on other timelines.

Gestalt engines reverse-engineered to power alternate world 'probe'.

Incursion in France? Reports of King leading airship task force.

Plea for 'responsible' approach to deep-water mining of seabed resources.

Jet stream change to cause colder winters in Europe.

CHAPTER THIRTY-EIGHT
FOLLOWING ORDERS

AMY LLEWELLYN LOWERED herself into a sitting position on the bunk, back resting against the pillows.

"So," she asked, "what are you going to tell the reporters?" Since the cessation of hostilities, news copters had been circling the dreadnoughts, desperate for a shot of the King.

Merovech unhooked the submachine gun from his shoulder and laid it on the side table. They were in one of the crew cabins, which he had requisitioned. The infirmary had been filled to overflowing with wounded, irate monkeys, so he'd only stopped there long enough to grab some dressings.

"I don't see why I have to tell them anything." He perched on the blanket beside her and used his finger to push a strand of hair from the gash in her forehead. "It doesn't look too bad," he said, squinting at it in the dim overhead light. He went to the cramped bathroom, tore off some toilet tissue, and moistened it under the tap.

"This may sting a little," he warned, and began to lightly sponge the wound. During the scuffle on the bridge, she'd fallen and hit her head against a steel bulkhead. She'd been stunned by the blow, and there was no doubt she'd have a painful bruise. However, it appeared the cut wasn't nearly as bad as he'd feared. Once he'd cleaned away the blood that had run down her face, the wound turned out to be little more than a deep graze.

"You have to tell them something," she insisted. "You're the King, for goodness' sake. You shouldn't be riding into battle."

Merovech smiled with one side of his face. "I don't see why not." He opened the bag of supplies he'd lifted from the infirmary and emptied them onto the bed. "There are precedents, you know." He peeled apart a dressing and pressed it to her head. "Now, hold this in place while I get some tape."

She touched her fingertips to the bandage and he picked up a small roll of white surgical tape and some scissors, and used four short strips to fix the dressing securely to her skin. When he was done, he sat back to inspect his handiwork.

Amy cringed. "How do I look?"

"It's a bit crooked, but you'll be fine."

She coughed and looked away, cheeks flushed. "I feel such an idiot."

"There's no need."

"You're too kind." Her voice held a sarcastic edge. Irritably, she tried to stand. "But I've got work to do. Somebody's got to sort out this mess." She got upright and swayed, and Merovech caught her by the hands.

"There's no hurry," he said, supporting her. "Take a moment. You've had a bang to the head; you're going to be a bit wobbly."

Her fingers felt cold, so he blew on them. It seemed like a natural thing to do, but Amy snatched them away as if he'd bitten her.

"What's the matter?"

"Nothing, I'm sorry." Her face was flushed and she wouldn't meet his eye. In the cramped cabin, they were standing face-to-face, almost touching.

"Did I do something inappropriate?"

"No." She brushed a lock of hair behind her ear and straightened her jacket. "Not at all."

"Then what is it?"

Amy rolled her eyes and tried to turn away, looking mortified. "Nothing, forget about it." She brushed down the front of her suit. Her hand shook, and Merovech thought of his dead fiancée.

As a young prince, he had met his share of eligible society women. The royal matchmakers had tried to pair him with rich girls from all over the Commonwealth—the daughters of industrialists, presidents, oil barons and sultans—and yet none had fascinated and challenged him like Julie Girard. He'd loved her from their first meeting on the Paris metro. She'd been a breath of fresh air. The girls he was used to were all ambitious, would-be princesses. They were obsessed with gossip and horses, and dazzled by the glamour of the throne. Julie wasn't anything like them. For a start, she favoured a republic. She believed in causes and direct action, and thought the world could be made a better place through protest. She was the most *real* person he'd ever met. She hadn't cared for power, fame or prestige. The things that concerned her were honest, tangible things. Things he hadn't considered until she showed them to him. Poverty, social justice, animal rights... She had opened his eyes to a world of inequality and injustice, and he'd planned to abdicate and spend the rest of his life with her, fighting for her causes.

Only, of course, things hadn't worked out that way—and now here he was, standing in an airship's cabin with a girl from Wales, feeling emotions he couldn't name. He missed Julie so much that her absence had become a physical need. His skin cringed at the lack of her touch; his lips were raw where he'd been nervously dragging them over his teeth, missing her kiss. He hadn't let go, hadn't grieved. He'd kept everything bottled up inside so he could do his duty to his country and Commonwealth.

And now...

Now, he just wanted to be held. He wanted to rest his head on Amy's shoulder and feel her arms around him. He wasn't in love with her (at least, he told himself he wasn't). He had no family, no close friends. She was the nearest he had to either, and he wanted her to stroke the back of his neck and whisper comforts to him as he wept into the fabric of her jacket.

It felt right. She felt right.

He coughed and looked at his feet.

"Amy, listen—" He wasn't sure exactly what he was going to say, but it didn't matter. Before he could continue, K8 knocked smartly on the open cabin door.

"Hey, Your Majesty." She looked curiously from Merovech to Amy. "Not interrupting anything, am I?"

Merovech gave a silent, exasperated curse.

"What do you want?"

The girl raised an eyebrow at his aggrieved tone. She jerked her thumb at the low metal ceiling.

"We've got a couple of visitors upstairs you *really* need to meet."

ACK-ACK MACAQUE SHUFFLED across the field. He was bone tired and his jacket hung in ribbons. A pistol dangled from one hand, the recovered chainsaw from the other. Around him lay the remains of the Leviathans. Some of the wrecks had been cut in two; others had been diced into fat metal cubes with drippy-looking melted edges. A couple of the tanks were on fire, and their smoke stained the autumn air, hanging thick and languid across the battlefield.

A damaged cyborg clawed its way across the turf. Its legs were missing and it was using one arm to pull itself forward while the other brandished a fat machine gun. Ack-Ack Macaque walked up behind it and pressed the chainsaw to the wrist of the hand holding the weapon. Sparks flew and there was a noise like someone feeding a set of steel railings into a wood chipper. He felt the vibration rattle his teeth. Then the hand fell to the earth and the chrome fingers writhed in the dirt like the tentacles of a beached sea creature.

"Where do you think you're going, eh?" He reached down and flipped the cyborg onto its back. Part of its face had been torn away, exposing the wires and circuits beneath the stretched skin and dull armour.

"Please," it whispered through its mangled mouth, "please, I don't want to die."

Ack-Ack Macaque's lip curled. "You start a war, sunshine, you have to be prepared to lose it."

"No."

The monkey frowned. "What do you mean, 'no'?"

"It wasn't me. I didn't want any of this." The thing was begging for its life. Ack-Ack Macaque pocketed his revolver and rubbed his eye patch.

"Were you on one of those tanks?" he asked.

"Yes…"

"Then you're the encmy." He took a firm grip on the chainsaw.

The cyborg wriggled back on its elbows, trying to squirm away from him. "I was only following orders."

Ack-Ack Macaque snarled. "That's the oldest bullshit in the book." He raised the chainsaw over his head and the cyborg cowered.

"But it's true! I didn't want to be *this*." It thumped the stump of its arm against its chest. "I didn't have a choice."

Ack-Ack Macaque showed his teeth. "Oh, really?"

"People were dying." The metal figure stopped wriggling. "They offered me a chance to live."

Ack-Ack Macaque lowered the saw and nudged the metal body with his boot. "You call this 'living', do you?"

"I had no choice."

"Horse crap. You had a choice. When they turned you into a robot, you had a choice. When they told you to get into a tank and invade my world, you had a choice." He bent low over the recumbent figure, growling his words. "If we hadn't stopped you here and now, how many innocents would you have killed before you grew the balls to say 'no'?"

The cyborg's eyes had become misaligned. One looked up at him imploringly while the other lolled drunkenly in its socket. "The Duchess, she would have killed me."

"The Duchess is dead."

Something seemed to sag in the cyborg's posture. "Then it's over?"

Ack-Ack Macaque shook his head. Overhead, the dreadnoughts were dispersing like clouds after a storm, moving away in the directions of Paris, London and Berlin—large ports where they could refit, repair and resupply. Their engines thrummed, stirring the still morning sky like the broodings of a billion disgruntled bees. The only one not moving was the *Sun Wukong*.

"These things are never over," he said. "There's always some other ruthless bastard out there, with an army of gullible cowards." He stepped forward and placed one booted foot on the cyborg's chest. It struggled beneath him.

"What are you going to do?"

"I'm going to put you out of your misery."

Its stump flailed and its hand clawed at the soil, trying to heave its legless torso out from under his foot. "No, please! It wasn't my fault! I just wanted to live."

"Everybody wants to live." Ack-Ack Macaque raised the chainsaw and levelled the point of the whirring blade at the cyborg's throat. "But you chose the wrong side. You chose to stand with the killers." He stabbed downwards, leaning his weight on the handle. With a metallic screech, the chainsaw bit through the cyborg's neck. It buried itself in the earth below and juddered to a halt, motor stalled. Disgusted with the whole incident, he left it where it was—sticking up like a grave marker—and stood upright. His back ached. He brushed his leathery palms together and spat into the dirt.

"There's always a choice."

CHAPTER THIRTY-NINE
STOP THE ROCK

VICTORIA GATHERED THE crew of the *Ameline* and the command crew of the *Sun Wukong* on the verandah at the airship's bow. Several of the armoured glass panels had been cracked or broken during the fight and cold wafts of fresh November air curled through the greenhouse warmth of the potted jungle, agitating the parakeets and other birds that twittered and squawked among the leaves on the upper branches. A utilitarian trestle table had been set up on the verandah, overlooking the rail, and her guests were seated on either side, perched on folding chairs and stools borrowed from the galley. Katherine Abdulov sat at the far end with Ed Rico on her right, while K8, Merovech, and Ack-Ack Macaque occupied the remaining chairs.

The monkey's solitary eye glowered around the table.

"Okay, does anybody want to tell me what the fuck's going on? Who are these people, and why does this guy look like William Cole?"

Victoria stood up. "These are the people who helped us against the Leviathans."

"Yeah, I saw. As a matter of fact, I was in one of those tanks when they cut the fucking thing in half."

Victoria sighed. Her tears were gone, but they'd taken most of her strength with them.

"They stopped the invasion," she said.

Ack-Ack Macaque huffed. "I could have handled it."

"I'm sure you could. Nevertheless, try to be polite."

Victoria turned her attention to the woman at the far end of the table. Katherine Abdulov sat with her hands in the pocket of her thick overcoat, and the ankle of her left boot resting on her right knee.

"You're not out of the woods yet," Katherine said.

"How so?" Victoria cocked an eyebrow. Célestine was dead; the assault had failed.

"The asteroid."

"Ah, of course…"

"Do you have a plan to deal with it?"

Ack-Ack Macaque stirred, and raised a paw. "I do."

"Care to share it?"

The monkey took out a cigar, bit off the end, and spat it over the bamboo rail, into the airship's glass nose cone. "I figured we could fly up there and twat it."

K8 smiled. Merovech shook his head. "We don't have anything that can make the journey," he said.

"Of course we do." Ack-Ack Macaque struck a match and lit up. Smoke curled around his muzzle. "And you're sitting in it."

"An *airship*?"

"Why not?" The spent match sailed after the cigar tip. "We use the Duchess' force field to keep in the air and keep out the radiation, and we bolt your ion drive to the back."

"That's insane."

"Yeah, but it's gonna work." He moved his one-eyed gaze around the table, daring those present to disagree. Finally, his attention settled on Katherine. "What do you say, space lady?"

Katherine Abdulov rubbed her chin.

"Don't look at me," she said. "I've got no idea. All I'll say is that if you're going to try riding in it, you're a damn sight braver than I am."

The monkey scoffed. "And I suppose you've got a better idea, sweetheart?"

Katherine and Ed exchanged looks.

"You could come with us."

"On your ship?"

"Of course. You've seen what it can do. Ed can carve lumps off that rock. Chop it up into little pieces."

"That'll stop it?"

"No." Katherine looked regretful. "But it'll help. Make it a bunch of smaller targets, and easier to destroy."

"And then what?"

"Then your kludged-up space Zeppelin can finish the job." She uncrossed her legs and set both boots on the deck. "We can break it up into glowing rubble but we can't stop it. Our weapon isn't designed to take down big targets. It would take us too long to pick the rock apart with our narrow beam—but, if we dice it into little enough pieces, a couple of nukes from you should be enough to vaporise the remains." She looked up at the cracked panes in the glass ceiling, high above. "That's if you can get this heap put back together, armed and launched in time."

As one, Victoria and Ack-Ack Macaque turned to Merovech. The young king's manicured nails tapped the table's Formica top.

"How long have we got?" he asked.

"A couple of weeks, a month at the most." Katherine gave a one-shouldered shrug. "It depends how fast your ion engines are."

"I'm not sure." Merovech looked thoughtful. "Not very, I think."

"Then the sooner you can launch, the better."

Merovech stopped tapping his nails. He met Victoria's eyes. "Set a course for Gibraltar."

"Gibraltar?"

"The ESA has a test facility in the Straits. It's an old, repurposed oil platform. That's where the engines are."

"Aye, sir." Victoria glanced at K8. "Do you mind?"

"I'm on it." The girl sprang to her feet and vanished into the jungle, hurrying in the direction of the bridge.

"What else do we need?" Victoria asked. Ack-Ack Macaque removed his cigar and tapped ash onto the deck.

"Nuclear weapons," he said.

Merovech nodded. "Well, I may be able to help you there. We have a number of submarines in the North Atlantic. I'll have one meet us there. What else?"

"Food and water, enough for the whole monkey army."

"You're going to take them all to the asteroid?" He raised his eyebrows. "Surely a skeleton crew would suffice?"

Ack-Ack Macaque shook his head with slow deliberation. "No, we're going to need as many soldiers as we can carry," he said.

"Soldiers?" Victoria scratched the ridge of scar tissue at her temple. "What do you need soldiers for?"

Ack-Ack Macaque sucked the end of his cigar. The tip burned brightly. He exhaled at the high ceiling and smiled.

"After we've dealt with the asteroid, I'm taking them to Mars."

"That's your plan?"

"Yah." He smacked his lips together. "We're going to go up there and kick some butt. Otherwise, what's to stop the Robo-Duchess chucking another rock at us?" His face darkened. "And besides, we've got a score to settle."

Victoria felt her heart quicken. The breath caught in her throat. There had been a copy of Paul's 'soul' on the probe, along with the stolen personalities of all Cassius Berg's victims. They had been taken to form the basis of a cybernetic slave army, toiling to build Célestine's utopia among the cold Martian rocks. There was even a copy of Victoria that had been ripped from her skull during her first encounter with the murderous Smiling Man.

"I'm coming too," she said. She'd seen firsthand the kind of twisted sexual depravities Doctor Nguyen had foisted on a different copy of her 'soul', and knew she couldn't leave herself or Paul at his mercy.

Paul... Could there really be a way to splice the remains of his crumbling psyche with the 'fresh' copy in the Martian probe? Even now, at this late stage, could some part of him still be salvaged?

She became aware that Ack-Ack Macaque was squinting curiously at her.

"Okay," he rumbled, reading her face, "that's settled. Merovech and K8 can fit this beast out. Vic and I will ride with Kat here to the asteroid. Once we're there, we'll do what we can to whittle it down to a more manageable size. Then we'll meet up with the monkey army, nuke what's left of the rock, and go on to Mars."

"And what if it doesn't work?" Victoria could hardly bring herself to believe any of it was possible. "What's the contingency plan?"

Ack-Ack Macaque scowled around the red cherry of his cigar. "There isn't a contingency." He sat back in his chair with a growl. "If this doesn't work, that's it. Game over, folks. End of the fucking world."

ISSUED BY HM GOVT.

PROTECT AND SURVIVE

This pdf tells you how to keep your home and family safe during an asteroid strike.

1. Taking shelter

In advance of an asteroid strike, warnings will be broadcast on all television and radio channels at the following times:

i. Twelve hours before impact.
ii. Six hours before impact.
iii. Three hours before impact.
iv. One hour before impact.

Warnings will then continue at fifteen-minute intervals.

When you hear the warning, please make your way immediately to a place of shelter.

Your shelter should contain:

i. Enough food and water in sealed containers to last your family for 14 days.
ii. A portable radio and spare batteries.
iii. Warm clothing, and changes of clothing for the entire family.
iv. Bedding or sleeping bags.
v. Torches with spare batteries, matches and candles.

vi. Sturdy refuse sacks and packing tape.

Read more? Y/N

CHAPTER FORTY
SURFIN' FROGS AND PUNCHING GODS

As THE SUN *Wukong* powered south towards the Spanish border, Katherine Abdulov took Victoria to see the *Ameline*.

"Call me Kat," she said, buttoning her coat as they stepped out onto the airship's flight deck. "Everybody else does."

Victoria tried to place her accent but couldn't. There were hints of Spanish and Arabic influence, but nothing she could pin down. To starboard, the sun was a red ember on the horizon. In the darkness below, the lights of Bordeaux and Toulouse slid past on either side like the raked coals of glowing campfires. Feeling the cold, she tugged at the hem of the Commodore's military jacket, straightening it. It had been tailored for a skinny old man, not someone with breasts, and so had a tendency to ride up at the waist.

"Everybody?"

"My family."

"And where are they?"

Kat scuffed the sole of her boot across the metal deck. "All dead."

Victoria thought of Paul. "I'm sorry."

The young pilot shrugged. "Don't be. We all are."

She stopped walking, and the wind ruffled her hair. "Dead, I mean. You and me." She craned her neck to peer over the side. "Everybody down there."

After her recent experiences in helicopters, Victoria preferred not to look down. Instead, she let her hand rest on her scabbard. Her head felt cold and she wished she'd brought a hat.

"We're not dead yet." After all, wasn't that what this was all about? Weren't they trying to save the world?

Kat clicked her tongue regretfully. "Yeah, I'm afraid you kind of are."

Victoria was confused. "But you said the plan would work, that we could stop the rock."

"That's not what I'm talking about."

"Then what is it, *s'il vous plaît?*"

The younger woman faced into the wind for a moment, and took a deep, savouring breath.

"Come inside," she said, nodding at the *Ameline*'s open cargo ramp. "I'll explain everything."

KATHERINE STALKED UP the ramp and Victoria followed. She found herself in a hold that had seen better days. The walls were covered with scuffs and dents; much of the webbing had been torn or tangled, and graffiti marred the doors and bulkheads. The air smelled musty, with hints of solder and old sacking.

"This way," Kat said, leading her forward, through a hatch outlined with yellow and black warning tape, into a passenger compartment lined with rows of threadbare seats, their plastic covers split and frayed, the foam insulation ratty and discoloured beneath.

"Everything happened a long time ago, and far away," Kat said without lingering. She stepped through into a short corridor, at the end of which was a ladder leading upwards. Victoria stood at the bottom and watched her climb, then followed. At the top lay the *Ameline*'s bridge. It was a small cockpit, with a low, readout-covered ceiling and a pair of well-worn couches. Kat took the couch on the right and motioned Victoria to the one on the left.

"Where?" Victoria asked.

"Back in the real world."

"This isn't the real world?"

"No, sorry."

Victoria twisted around, trying to get comfortable as she processed the statement. "We've seen a few timelines," she said, "and they all seemed remarkably real and solid."

"None of them were, I'm afraid."

"I don't follow."

Kat exhaled through her nose. "I'm trying to explain this as gently as I can." She brushed back her hair. "Take your monkey friend, for instance."

"What about him?"

"He used to be a character in a computer game, didn't he? And when he was in there, he was locked into the virtual world."

Victoria didn't like where this was going. "We rescued him. We got him out."

"But did you?" Kat moved her cupped hands as if weighing up invisible bags of flour. "Did you really rescue him, or did you simply bring him from one simulation to another?"

Victoria narrowed her eyes. The old journalistic instinct twitched. There was a story here and, whether she wanted to know the truth or not, she needed to uncover it.

"You tell me," she said.

Katherine gave her a frank look. "I don't think I have to, do I? I think you've already guessed."

"You're implying all the worlds we've seen, the whole multiverse, they're all part of a game?" Victoria was beginning to wish she had a martini.

"Not a game, as such, but a simulation nevertheless."

Victoria gave a loud tut. "*C'est ridicule!* There isn't enough computing power in the world."

"Not in *this* world, no."

Victoria took a deep breath. "Okay," she said reasonably, "let's backtrack a couple of steps. Why don't you explain to me again who you are, and how you got here?"

Kat sighed. She crossed her booted feet at the ankle and tapped at a couple of overhead readouts.

"I was born on Strauli," she began, "which is a planet a hundred light years from here, in the year 2360."

"The future?"

"More like the distant past, now."

Victoria shook her head. "I don't understand." She was missing something, but wasn't sure what it might be.

"I'll get to it." Kat promised. "But, to start at the beginning, my family were traders, and I captained one of their ships."

"This one?"

"Yes, the dear old *Ameline*." Katherine gave the bulkhead an affectionate pat. "We've been through some scrapes together, I can tell you."

Victoria reached over and touched her sleeve. "But how did you get *here*?" she insisted.

Kat made that clicking noise with her tongue again. "Something got loose," she said. "Something horrible. We weren't sure if it was a weapon or a deranged filing system, but it was sentient, and it called itself 'The Recollection'." Her shoulders quivered as she tried to repress a shudder. "It rolled over world after world, breaking apart everything it touched, and storing it all as information."

She was telling the truth. Victoria could tell; she'd had enough practice interviewing politicians and other professional liars.

"What did you do?"

"We ran." Kat punched one hand into the palm of the other. "We gathered together as many survivors as we possibly could and we made for the stars." She stopped talking, eyes focused on the pictures in her head—a thousand light-year stare.

"So, why are you here, now?"

"It caught us." The words came out tinged with loathing. Kat's fists were clenched. "The Recollection's whole purpose was to gather intelligent beings," she said, "to harvest them and deliver their stored minds to the end of time, to a point it called 'The Eschaton'—the ultimate end of all things."

"But why?"

"Because its builders believed they'd be resurrected, brought back to life in the infinite quantum mind-spaces of the ubercomputer."

Victoria frowned. "*Je ne comprends pas.*"

Kat tipped her head back against the chair's rest and rubbed her eyes. "At the end of time, as the last stars guttered and died, they believed there would be a final flowering. That their descendants—or the descendants of whichever race survived until the end—would have the means and wherewithal to construct a huge computer of near infinite complexity, powered by the very dissolution of the universe itself. And having retreated within this computer, they'd then be able to play out the entire history of the cosmos, over and over again with endless permutations. As the final seconds of the real universe ticked towards their conclusion, the builders would be able to live out aeon after simulated aeon, cocooned within their virtual worlds."

Victoria looked at the main view screen, which currently showed a crystal clear, light-enhanced image of the *Sun Wukong*'s deck and the darkening sky beyond. "And that's where we are now, in this simulation?"

"Yes." Fingers laced over her midriff, Kat closed her eyes. "When The Recollection came for us, we fought and we ran. But, as I said, it caught us." She shivered again. "All of us."

Victoria lay back and considered her reflection in the touchscreen panel above her head. Not everything Kat had said had made sense, and she had plenty of questions. They were part of her default response: if she didn't understand something well enough to explain it in a newspaper article, she just kept chipping away at it until she had all the facts.

"If all that's true," she asked hesitantly, picking her words, "how come you remember it and I don't?"

"Because it never happened to you." Kat gave one of her one-shoulder shrugs. "You were long dead by the time The Recollection reached Earth."

"Then what am I doing here?"

The young pilot glanced sideways at Victoria. "The ubercomputer's vast and powerful. It recreated you from the DNA of the people it had. From them, it extrapolated every person who ever lived, anywhere, and brought them back to life."

Victoria wanted to laugh or cover her ears. It sounded like the most muddleheaded New Age tomfoolery, and she really wanted a drink. This wasn't, she felt, the kind of conversation one should have sober.

"I'm sorry, but all this, everything you're telling me, it all sounds crazy."

Kat sat upright. "It is crazy, but that doesn't make it any less true."

"And what about you?"

"I had a brush with the Recollection. It infected me with its spores but only at a low level. I had protection." Her artificial hand went to her throat, as if touching a pendant that wasn't there. "The changes it made to the structure of my brain enabled me to retain my memories. There are others like me, just a few of us who know the truth, who remember."

"And you're just flying around, spreading the word?"

"No." A grim shake of the head. "We're fighting a war."

"Against the computer?"

"Against its builders." Kat pressed a control, and a rotating three-dimensional display blinked into existence in the centre of the cockpit, showing a tactical representation of the surrounding airspace, from ground level to the upper stratosphere. Possible threats, such as ground vehicles and large buildings, were picked out in red. "I told you they retreated into their own simulations to escape the death of the universe. Well, some of them went native in a big way. Instead of being content to live out their lives in recreations of the past, they decided to change it to suit themselves, to carve out little empires and stamp their domination on the timelines."

"Like Célestine?"

"Bingo." Kat clicked her fingers. "She's one of the builders. A long time ago, she cast versions of herself across all the timelines, and now she sits behind the scenes, working through them to achieve her ends."

"Célestine built the multiverse?"

"Yes, in part. But there's another out there, another of the architects of the simulations, and she's more dangerous than Célestine could ever be."

"Who is she?"

"A criminal, responsible for a million atrocities." Kat's fists clenched. "We've been tracking her for years but she's recently gone quiet. Most of her alternate selves are dead."

"And you think she's here too?"

"I know it."

Victoria swallowed. Her mind raced. Then she froze. Something cold squeezed her stomach and her mouth went dry.

"Is she me?"

"What?" Kat's eyebrows shot up. "No!" She laughed. "No, you can relax, you're fine. It's not you." The laugh dried like a puddle in the sun. "No, you already know her. She built the airship we're riding on, using her knowledge of glitches in the programme to move it between the timelines."

"The *Founder*?"

"The clue's in the name, I guess."

"But she's a monkey."

Another shrug. "It amuses her to take animal form. She might be a monkey on this world and an ape on the next. And she goes by many names— Founder, Architect, Apynja…"

"You're here to get her?"

"Her and Célestine." Katherine Abdulov drew herself straight and Victoria saw her lip curl. "We're here to stop them before they do any more harm; to bring them to account for the billions who've died in their little games."

"Virtual beings?" Victoria thought of the world she'd visited most recently, laid waste by Célestine's drive to build a cyborg army. All those ghosts…

"Sentient beings nonetheless, and fully capable of suffering."

"Why are you telling me all this?"

A mischievous smile glimmered behind Kat's dark eyes. "Because you and Ack-Ack Macaque have been fighting them and, if you don't mind me saying, doing a damn good job."

"And you want our help?"

"Not help so much, but maybe we should pool resources. What do you think?"

Victoria took a deep breath and let out a long, draining exhalation. "This is a lot to take in."

"I know." Kat chewed her bottom lip. "It was tough for me too, to start with. But please think about it. I could do with someone like you. There are very few who can move between the worlds, and you've been doing it for the past two years." Her expression became wistful. "And besides, I've been looking for Ack-Ack for a long time now."

"You have?"

"Yes." Kat smiled. "You see, I know who he really is."

ACK-ACK MACAQUE STOOD with K8, on the viewing platform at the top of the Rock. The Strait of Gibraltar lay before them like a sparkling azure carpet. At the foot of the Rock, the hotels and apartment complexes of the town clustered close to the shoreline. Waves broke against the beaches. A westerly breeze blew in off the Atlantic, bringing a chill to an otherwise unseasonably warm November day, and he turned up the collar of his coat. Fourteen miles away, across the water, the stony Rif Mountains of Morocco loomed brown and purple through the haze—the uppermost tip of a whole new continent that stretched eight thousand vertiginous miles to Cape Town, and the spot where the waters of the South Atlantic ran into those of the Indian Ocean.

"Make the most of it," he said, watching as K8 took photographs of the view with her SincPhone. She didn't reply, just kept snapping. She knew as well as he did that they might never get another chance to come here, and that their forthcoming journey to Mars could very well end up being a one-way trip, even if they somehow defeated Célestine and her minions.

He was pleased to see that she'd finally changed out of her white suit, into a pair of jeans and a black t-shirt, both purchased on the ride here from the airport. The suit jacket and skirt had been abandoned in the back of the taxi and were now somewhere in the city below, off on adventures of their own.

Ack-Ack turned to look into the wind, at the vast dark bulk of the *Sun Wukong*. The airship rode at anchor above the airport, its impellers spinning sporadically to keep it in place. From here, he could see the damage it had suffered during its confrontation with the Leviathans. Its armour had been blackened by flame and smoke, and pockmarked by shells, which had, in a handful of places, penetrated through into the rooms and spaces within.

The *Ameline* sat atop the larger vessel like a frog on the back of a surfboard. Its three landing legs were splayed to provide maximal balance, and the sun glinted from its various sensor blisters and intake valves. In a few short hours, he would be riding it into space. He glanced up, at the seemingly impenetrable blue of the zenith.

"To shake the surly bonds of Earth," he misquoted, "and punch the very face of God."

K8 looked around. "What?"

"Nothing." He patted his jacket pockets. He wanted another cigar but the last one had left his throat raw. On the other side of the viewing area, a couple of wild Barbary macaques perched on a railing, watching him with dull, suspicious eyes. They were used to the tourists that came up here during the year, but this was the first time they'd seen one of their own parading around in clothes and boots, taking in the sights like a human—and standing as tall as one.

He flipped them the finger. *Fucking yokels.* What did they know about anything? Here he was, about to launch himself into the void in order to save their hairy backsides, and all they had on their minds was food. They sat up here year after year, looking down on the town with its cars and motorbikes, luxury hotels and airport... and scratched themselves. They were curious, but their curiosity seemed limited to the contents of handbags and litterbins; none of them had ever ventured downslope to steal a car or attempt a little credit card fraud. Their worries were immediate and mostly revolved around eating and fucking, and they'd go on to spend their whole lives up here on this rock, sandwiched between Europe and Africa and knowing nothing of either.

He envied them that, he realised. They'd never have to fight a war or save a planet. If he'd been given the choice, he'd have stayed like them. He'd have been far happier to have been spared the upheavals of the past few years, and instead have spent his life as a simple, half-aware simian, passing his days in the rough and tumble ignorance of monkeydom.

They glared at him, and he glared back, showing his teeth.

"You want to swap places?" he asked them. "Be my fucking guest."

*   *   *

LATER, HE AND K8 rode the cable car back down to street level. They caught a cab to The Macaca Sylvanus, a small pub adjacent to the main airport terminal, and a place popular with visiting skyliner crews.

All eyes watched them as they walked from the door to a table by the window, where they had a view of the runway and the looming underside of the *Sun Wukong*.

"It's hard to imagine," K8 said when they were settled with drinks, "that all this might be gone in a few months."

Ack-Ack Macaque swirled the rum in the bottom of his glass. The ice cubes cracked and clinked. "Only if we fail."

"And how likely is that?"

He didn't really want to think about it. "We're trying to fire a two-kilometre-long airship into space using experimental engines and a force field we don't really understand," he said. He raised the glass to his lips and sniffed the contents. "Your guess is as good as mine. For all I know, the whole fucking thing'll blow up on take off."

"But you won't be on it, will you? You're going ahead with Abdulov."

"Fuck yeah." He'd flown all sorts of aircraft in his time, from his beloved Spitfires to lumbering transport planes. Now, he was itching to get inside the *Ameline* and see what she could do. If the size of the fusion exhausts at her stern was anything to go by, that crate could really *move*. He tipped a little of the drink into his mouth, savouring the sting of the alcohol on his tongue. "That's the plan."

"What about me?"

"You can come if you want."

K8 visibly perked. "Really? I thought you'd want me on the *Sun*, looking after the machinery."

"Nah." Ack-Ack Macaque glanced around the room. Most of the patrons had gone back to their own conversations; those that hadn't were trying not to stare. "If it works, it works; if it doesn't, it doesn't. I can't see how you being on board will make a damn bit of difference." He drained his glass and set it down. "Besides, you didn't think I'd go off and leave you behind, did you?"

K8's cheeks coloured.

"I did wonder. Things have been a little... weird between us."

Ack-Ack Macaque gave a snort. "I did what I could. You wanted to be brought back to the hive, so I brought you back."

She fiddled with the straw in her bottle of Pepsi. Without the white suit, she looked younger and somehow more alive.

"Yes," she said slowly. "I did. That's true. For a time, getting back was all that seemed to matter—but I think I'm getting over that now."

Ack-Ack Macaque put down his glass. As well as the change in her outward appearance, he'd noticed the change in her speech patterns. Every time she opened her mouth, she sounded less like a blissed-out automaton and more like her old self.

"Good." He reached up and scratched his eye patch. "Because there aren't going to be any Gestalt on Mars."

"What about the Founder?"

Ack-Ack made a face. That was a subject he *really* didn't want to discuss. He tried to shrug it off.

"It's complicated," he said, voice gruff.

"I know Victoria's got her locked in the brig."

Ack-Ack picked at the hairs on the back of his hand. "Abdulov thinks she's some kind of alien."

K8 took a sip of cola. "What do you think?"

"I think I knocked her up." He signalled to the barman for another round.

"Awkward."

"No shit."

Outside, a supply helicopter rose from the tarmac. He followed it with his eye as it wheeled upwards, towards the vast airship. Another followed, and then another. Merovech had been as good as his word. Food, water and other consumables were being loaded onto the *Sun Wukong*, along with enough spacesuits to allow the monkey army to operate on the surface of the Red Planet.

The suits had been hastily churned out by the *Ameline*, and were little more than transparent inflatable human-shaped balloons with sleeves for arms and legs, and large fishbowl helmets. They were designed to protect the old trading ship's passengers in case of accidental hull breach and cabin depressurisation. They were flimsy and vulnerable, but they'd do for now. As long as they kept out the vacuum long enough for him to defeat the last copy of the Duchess, he'd be satisfied. He could start thinking long-term survival later, with the fight over and both worlds safe.

"You know," K8 said hesitantly, "I never blamed you for what you did to me."

Ack-Ack Macaque scowled. "You didn't have to."

A fourth helicopter lumbered skywards. He watched it wobble into the air, the downdraught from its rotors kicking up a swirl of dust and sand. K8 reached over and grasped the cuff of his jacket. "And you shouldn't blame yourself, either."

"Easier said than done." At the height of the final battle against the Gestalt, he'd given her to the hive. It had been a tactical decision and had played a big part in their final victory, yet the guilt had been immense. For the past two years, as they'd traipsed the multiverse freeing uplifted monkeys from laboratories on a hundred different parallels, he'd watched her suffer withdrawal from the rest of the hive, knowing all the time that he was the cause of her pain and discomfort, that it was all his fault.

"Forget it," K8 said. The barman brought more drinks. Ack-Ack looked around at the people on the other tables. There were about a dozen of them, all told, in a room designed to hold around three times that number. Some were crewmen and women from visiting skyliners. You could tell them by their uniforms. The others were a mixture of fans—former gamers bedecked in vintage leather flying coats and decorative brass goggles—and wannabes here to find work. A small knot of tourists lingered by the counter, throwing the occasional glance his way, and more were arriving all the time, sidling into the room in ones and twos as news of his presence spread over the social networks.

K8 leant across the table and whispered, "And since when have you had a conscience, anyway?"

Ack-Ack Macaque didn't want to meet her eye. He toyed with his glass instead.

"It's a recent development," he said.

CHAPTER FORTY-ONE
NOT BEING ONE

When Ack-Ack Macaque and K8 returned to the *Sun Wukong* an hour later, Victoria was waiting for them. She sniffed the air.

"Have you been drinking?"

Ack-Ack Macaque grinned. "Just an eye-opener, boss."

"Good." Victoria rubbed her hands together. A good night's sleep had done wonders for her; she felt brisk and alive for the first time in days. "Because we need to talk." She led them to the bridge. With the craft stationary, the control room remained deserted. Those crewmembers that weren't ashore were busy aft, helping repair and refit the vessel for its upcoming voyage.

"About anything in particular?" Ack-Ack Macaque flopped into the pilot's couch and put his feet up on the console.

"About your girlfriend."

"What about her?"

Victoria swallowed down her irritation. "We need to decide what to do with her. We have her locked up, but should we turn her over to the authorities, or take her with us?"

The monkey took hold of his tail and started halfheartedly grooming it, his glove-like fingers picking through the scorched and frazzled hairs at the tip.

"I don't think it matters," he said. "Because if she's what Abdulov claims, I think she can escape any time she wants."

Victoria poked her tongue lightly into the side of her cheek and exhaled a long breath.

"We've had her locked up for two years."

"Have we?" Ack-Ack Macaque didn't look up. "Because I met her in the forest, right before I stormed Célestine's compound. Who do you think gave me all those guns?"

"Are you sure it was her?"

"Of course I'm sure. Abdulov said she sometimes went by the name Apynja, and that's who I met. Only she didn't look like a monkey then, she looked like an orangutan." He let the tail drop. "And when we'd finished talking..." He trailed off, and coughed. If Victoria hadn't known him better, she would have sworn he was embarrassed. She stepped over and put her hand on the console, next to his feet.

"What happened when you finished talking?"

He coughed again, and his yellow eye glowered up at her. "She went all see-through and vanished, like a ghost. There, are you satisfied?" His stare dared her to disbelieve.

Victoria frowned. "So, all that stuff the Founder told us about who she was and where she came from—"

"All horseshit."

"But if she can come and go as she pleases, why's she stayed in our custody for the past two years?"

Ack-Ack Macaque took his boots from the control panel and put his hands on his knees.

"She's a talking primate. Where better to hide than in an airship full of them?"

"So, we just let her go?"

He stood, and straightened his coat. "The way I see it, it doesn't matter. If she wants to go, she'll go. If she wants to stick around…"

"Abdulov wants to arrest her."

"So what? A lot of people in London want to arrest her. You saw what a mess the Gestalt made."

Victoria raised her chin. "Julie died in the Gestalt attack, or had you forgotten? Merovech will want her to answer for that."

Ack-Ack Macaque made a peculiar growling noise deep in his throat. His breath smelled, as it so often did, of rum. "Well, Merovech can go whistle. Whatever else the Founder is, she's carrying my babies." He stomped towards the door. "I know she's done some bad shit, but the babies come first. If Merovech or Abdulov or anybody else wants a reckoning, they'll have to wait."

"And what if they won't wait?" she called after him.

He paused at the door.

"They'll have to come through me first."

AFTER HE'D GONE, Victoria went to stand at the main floor-to-ceiling window, looking out across the Strait in the direction of Tangiers. She wanted to talk to Paul, wanted to hear him make one of his smart-alecky quips to defuse the tension; only Paul was gone, and she had nobody. The inside of her head felt empty and echoing, like a cabin without a passenger—an emptiness mirrored by the dull, hollow ache in her heart.

Pleasure craft bobbed on the ocean; ferries cut back and forth. To the west, a civilian skyliner rode the prevailing wind, plying a coastal circuit that would take in Rome, Athens, Istanbul, Alexandria and Tunis. Victoria watched it pass, imagining the passengers lounging on its observation decks. At that moment, she would have given anything to be one of them, to have seen the whitewashed coastal towns and ancient ruins of the Mediterranean for herself, while she still had the chance.

Such a cruel irony, she thought, that she would have to leave the world in order to save it.

She felt the butterflies flapping in her chest. How would it feel, she wondered, to fail? To see the world reduced to ash and darkness and know it was partially her fault? Against such horror, the hope of making it to Mars and finding a way to resurrect Paul seemed a selfish and petty yearning, but right then, it was all she had to cling onto. For three terrifying, wonderful, dangerous years, he had been her whole world and she could never be whole again without him.

She sniffed. Sometimes, she wished the gelware had replaced more of her brain. It would be a relief at times like this to retreat into the emotionless clarity of machine thought, untroubled by fear or sentiment. And yet, wasn't that precisely what Célestine and the Founder had been trying to do, in their own peculiar ways? Each had wanted to 'improve' humanity by freeing it of its emotions and its dependence on frail flesh and greasy animal neurons—not realising that, as they did so, they were sacrificing the very individualism and eccentricity that made humankind so unique.

Am I turning into a monster? Looking at her faint, translucent reflection in the glass, she touched her fingertips to the ridge of scar tissue on the side of her head, and felt the various input jacks inlaid into the puckered skin.

No.

She still felt uncertainty, loss and pain. However much she might want to escape their weight, she knew deep down that her feelings were the only proof she had that she was alive, and more than simply a reanimated corpse with a computerised brain—that she was, on some deep and fundamental level, still human.

She wiped her eyes on the gold brocade at her sleeves, and allowed the gelware to pump a mild sedative into her blood. She couldn't afford to fall apart today. She had work to do. She turned from the window to find Merovech standing in the corridor outside the room, his knuckle raised, about to knock on the open door.

"Are you all right?"

She waved away his concern.

"You don't have to knock," she told him. "You're a king."

The young man looked self-conscious. "Actually, that's what I'm here to talk about."

"Being a king?"

"Not being one." He came over to join her in the light from the window. His tie was loose, his collar open, and his suit rumpled as if he'd slept in it—which, she realised, he probably had.

"I'm going to abdicate," he said frankly, hands in pockets. "I've been thinking about it for a long time. I promised Julie I would, and I think the time's finally come."

Victoria opened her mouth to speak, then realised she didn't have anything constructive to say. Somewhere at the back of her mind, a small part of her cursed. Before her accident, when she was still a journalist able to read and parse written text, she would have done almost anything for a story like this. Getting advance notification of an abdication direct from the monarch, having exclusive access to him before the event, would have made her career; and, for a moment, she allowed herself to imagine how it would have felt to break news of that magnitude.

"Why are you telling me?"

Merovech tapped his shoe against the metal deck. "Because I want to come with you."

"Are you serious?"

He looked up at her. "Of course I'm serious. I've given this a lot of thought. I know exactly how I'm going to do it." He turned his head to the sea, and the huge union flag painted on the roof of the airport terminal. "I've got a speech ready." He tapped his head. "It's all in here. I've been rehearsing it all night."

Victoria felt curiosity drown her other feelings. She couldn't help it. "What are you going to say?"

Merovech wrinkled his nose. "That I'm stepping down for personal reasons, and appointing a committee to oversee the functions of the monarch until such time as a referendum can be carried out, and the citizens of the Commonwealth decide for themselves how they want to be ruled."

Victoria felt her eyebrows rise. "Wow."

Merovech smiled guiltily. "Well, what have we been fighting for, if it hasn't been freedom from dictators and autocrats?"

"And you really want to come with us, on the *Ameline*?"

His face grew serious again. "I think it's best. If I stayed, I'd only be a distraction." He raised his eyes to the sky. "And don't forget, that's my mother up there on Mars, which makes it my fight as much as yours."

From *The London and Paris Times*, online edition:

Abdication!

PARIS 20/11/2062 – The world's media were caught off-guard this morning when, in a shock statement, His Majesty King Merovech I stepped down as ruler of the United Kingdom of Great Britain, France, Ireland and Norway, and Head of the United European Commonwealth.

Declaring his intention to step down with immediate effect, the King is believed to be accompanying the dreadnought Sun Wukong as it prepares to leave Earth.

Citing "personal reasons", the King expressed his gratitude to his citizens, and said he hoped they would forgive him.

So far, there has been no official statement from either the Palace or the Prime Minister, but Downing Street sources have indicated that His Majesty's last act as regent was to appoint an interim committee to oversee the functions of the monarchy. The committee's primary task will be to prepare a referendum in which the people of the Commonwealth will vote for a new head of state. Whether this new head will be a king, queen or president remains open for discussion, and it is rumoured that His Majesty hopes his former subjects will opt for a republic.

In the meantime, little is known of the King's plans, although credible sources in Gibraltar say he is planning to lead the fight against the Martian aggressors, who are led by the reincarnated 'soul' of his mother, the Duchess of Brittany.

In an ironic postscript to the announcement, polling organisations report that the King's approval rating in the wake of his resignation has soared to an all-time high of nearly 97 percent.

Read more | Like | Comment | Share

Related Stories:

Democracy or populism?

King's cousin, Princess Isabelle, to be next monarch?

Referendum to be held 'early next year'.

World leaders pay tribute to Merovech I.

Ten famous historical abdications.

Our last, best chance: the Sun Wukong prepares for lift-off.

Internet billionaire opens underground 'asteroid shelter' in Kenya.

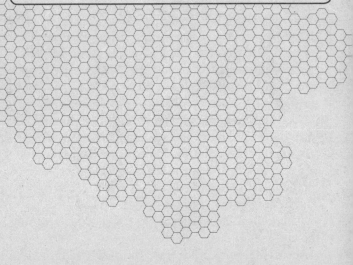

CHAPTER FORTY-TWO
SHOTGUN

KATHERINE ABDULOV LED them into the *Ameline*'s passenger lounge and showed them where to sit.

"Stay buckled up until we're clear of the atmosphere," she warned. "The inertial dampers aren't what they used to be, so you might get thrown around a bit if things get bumpy." She watched K8, Merovech and the monkey strap themselves into chairs, then caught Victoria's eye and nodded upwards, towards the bridge.

"Do you want to ride shotgun?"

Victoria looked at her friends. Merovech seemed preoccupied, looking down at his thumbs. His thoughts were quite obviously elsewhere, and who could blame him? She knew he took his duty seriously. He was probably tearing himself up inside right now, wondering if he'd made the right call, done the right thing. Beside him, Ack-Ack Macaque kept taking his Colts from their holsters and spinning their barrels. If he was nervous, he was hiding it well. He looked restless and eager to fight, as if he couldn't wait to get going.

"Come on," he muttered. "Let's get this kite in the air."

Across the room, K8 seemed the most reassuringly

normal of the three. Clad in jeans, trainers and a hooded top, she looked like an average teenager, and her wide-eyed apprehension filled Victoria with an unexpected rush of protectiveness.

"Are you okay?" she asked.

The girl smiled bravely. "Oh, aye. Never better."

ONCE UP ON the bridge, Victoria settled into the co-pilot's couch. This time, all the displays and overheads were alight, showing data on ship systems and atmospheric conditions. She tried to make sense of it but couldn't. The diagrams were unfamiliar and the letters and numerals, thanks to her head injury, were nothing but squiggles.

"How are we doing?" she asked.

In the pilot's chair, Kat smiled. Her dark eyes seemed to shine.

"The ship says we're ready to go."

"It can talk?"

"Yeah." Kat tapped the side of her head. "I hear it in here, through my implant."

"But, it's intelligent?"

Kat made a face. "I wouldn't go that far... Hey!"

"What?"

Kat seemed to be listening to something Victoria couldn't hear. After a couple of seconds, her eyes refocused.

"The ship thinks it can tap into your gelware, if you'd like to be able to interact with it."

Victoria looked dubiously at the bulkheads and instruments surrounding her.

"Should I?"

"Your choice."

"Okay, then." As soon as the words left her lips, she felt a tingle at the back of her skull, and then sensed an odd, silent hiss, like a carrier wave.

> HELLO

She jumped. In her head, the voice felt loud and unmistakably synthetic.

"Uh, *bonjour?*"

> AH, YOU'RE FRENCH. I'VE ALWAYS LIKED THE FRENCH. MY NAME IS THE *AMELINE. JE M'APPELLE L'AMELINE*. WELCOME ABOARD.

"Thank you."

> *MON PLAISIR*. NOW, MAKE YOURSELF COMFORTABLE. WHEELS UP IN FIVE.

"Five minutes?"

> SECONDS.

The cabin lurched. A rumble came from below, deep but rising in pitch. Instinctively, Victoria gripped the armrests, and her heart raced as her mind flashed back to the helicopter crash. Through the link, she could feel the edges of the ship's excitement. It was like an eager dog scenting an open field. The sky above was its playground and it wanted to leap up and run forever.

> HERE WE GO.

Victoria felt the seat shove against her. The thrust was less violent than she'd feared but still insistent. Through the forward view, she watched the top of the *Sun Wukong* fall away as if snatched downward by a kraken's claws. The *Ameline* went up like an elevator, rising swiftly until the land shrank away to a green and brown blur and the horizon took on a distinct and visible curve. Then the old ship tipped on her tail and pointed her nose at the stars.

"A short jump and we'll be there," Kat said.

Victoria didn't reply. She had no words. Ahead, the stars lay strewn across the sky like scattered pearls, so close she felt she could reach out and let them run like sand through her fingers.

Oh, mon dieu, she thought. *This is really happening. I'm in space!*

Through her gelware, she could feel the ship straining at its leash. Titanic energies gathered in its jump engines, building and building until the whole hull seemed to shake with unbearable energy and impatience. Her body itched with a fire that felt almost sexual. She opened her mouth to ask whether they were going to wait to see if the *Sun Wukong* had successfully taken off but, before she could, she heard Kat issue a mental command. The ship whooped. All the gauges spiked at once. All the lights went red. There was a flash of intense, dazzling white light and an instant of shocking cold—

CHAPTER FORTY-THREE
SPACE MONKEY

VICTORIA SAGGED FORWARDS against her straps, gasping.

"Is it always like that?"

Beside her in the cockpit, Kat smiled. "You get used to it."

"I don't know if I want to."

Ahead, the screens pictured a grey rock, rounded and scarred like an old potato. Reflected sunlight lit one side of it. Its craters were little wells of impenetrable shadow.

"There it is," Kat said.

Victoria leaned forward, staring. "That's it? That's the 'missile'?" She narrowed her eyes. "It looks tiny, like a pebble."

"Don't let the visuals fool you." Kat was busily tapping away at controls and readouts. "Everything looks sharper in a vacuum. There's no dust or haze to indicate distance, so it all looks closer than it is."

"How big is it?"

"About the size of the Isle of Man."

"*Putain.*"

"And I know it doesn't look as if it's moving, but trust me, it's coming on like God's own freight train." She tapped a communication panel. "Hey, Ed, how are you doing?"

Ed Rico's voice burbled from the speaker. He sounded like a bad ventriloquist choking on a glass of water.

"Ready when you are, Captain. Only—"

"Only what?" Kat asked.

"Only, maybe we should let the monkey take the shot?"

"Any particular reason?"

Rico gurgled. "It's his world we're saving. Also, I'd like to see how he handles it."

There was a moment's pause. Kat had a rapid, silent conversation with the ship, and then shrugged. "Fine, whatever." She broke the connection and turned to Victoria. "You'd better tell your hairy friend to get suited up."

As the airlock door swung open, Ack-Ack Macaque found himself face-to-face with eternity. Beyond the curve of the fishbowl helmet, the sky fell away in all directions, receding to infinity wherever he looked. His panting sounded loud in his ears, and he felt his toes contract as if trying to tighten their grip on a branch—an automatic primate response to vertigo.

"Holy buggering shit," he muttered. Every instinct he had screamed at him that he was falling—falling between trees forever—but he tried to ignore them. Heights had never bothered him all that much. He wouldn't have made a very good pilot if they had, but this boundless infinity was something else again. With an effort of will, he tore his eyes from the sky and tried to concentrate on spying out the handholds inlaid into the ship's skin. Designed to facilitate extravehicular maintenance, the little recesses were spaced evenly around the hull, allowing an astronaut to 'walk' around the outside of the ship with their hands. Every fourth one had a clip for tethering a safety line. Using them felt similar to rock climbing, only without any sense of weight or appreciable notion of either up or down.

Moving one hand at a time, keeping the other firmly gripped, Ack-Ack Macaque worked his way forwards, towards the *Ameline*'s blunt prow.

When he got there, he saw the alien weapon was a pod grafted beneath the bows. It looked like a cocoon made of melted candle wax. As he drew near to it, one end of it peeled apart like a banana and a helmeted head emerged. Behind the faceplate, sunlight flashed on Ed Rico's roguish grin.

"Come and have a go," he said, his voice sounding distant and scratchy in Ack-Ack Macaque's headphones.

Ack-Ack watched the man drag himself from the weapon's embrace like a butterfly pulling itself from a ruptured chrysalis. Then, holding the lip of the opening with one gauntleted hand, he beckoned.

"Just slide your feet in," Rico said.

Moving slowly, Ack-Ack pushed himself forward. Ed took hold of one of his boots and guided him into the pod's sticky-looking maw.

"I'm not sure about this," Ack-Ack grumbled.

The thing resembled a hungry maggot trying to latch onto his feet.

"Relax," Ed said. "It's not nearly as gross as it looks."

"Yeah?" Ack-Ack Macaque made a face. "Because it looks pretty fucking disgusting from here."

He allowed Ed to feed him into the hole, until his head sank beneath the lip and he was looking up at the sky through his helmet.

"What now?" he asked.

Ed maneuvered himself so that he was looking down at Ack-Ack. His head obscured the stars.

"Wait until the top closes, and then take off your helmet."

Ack-Ack Macaque eyed the walls around him. They reminded him unpleasantly of pictures from a colonoscopy. "And what then?"

"Breathe in the liquid. Stay calm."

"Easy for you to say."

"Ah, you'll be fine." Ed backed away as the edges of the opening began to pucker. Slowly and silently, they crinkled shut, leaving Ack-Ack Macaque swaddled in darkness. Huffing and muttering, he reached up and un-dogged the neck of his helmet. Raising his arms was tricky in the confined space—kind of like getting undressed in a coffin made of slime—but he managed to prise the glass bowl off his head.

Now that his eye was adjusting, he could see that the walls of his prison shone with a faint green luminosity. They glistened with white, gloopy sweat. His nose wrinkled in revulsion.

"This place smells like feet."

Pressure on his boots and legs told him the gloop had begun to collect in the bottom of the cavity, gradually rising to fill the cramped space.

"Fuck." He wanted to get out. As the rising liquid reached his waist, he began to struggle, instinctively trying to claw his way upwards to avoid drowning. As it reached his chest, he took a deep breath.

Come on, monkey. If a scrawny tosspot like Rico can do this, so can you.

He screwed up his eye and his courage, and clamped his lips together. The gunk came up over the neck of his suit and over his chin. Then it was exploring his face. Involuntarily, he jerked backwards, trying to reach clear air, but the stuff had already found its way into his nose. It seemed to flow with purpose. Within seconds, it had pushed its way into his lungs, invaded every opening, from ears to pores to arsehole. And he could breathe. Somehow, miraculously, the muck was feeding him air. Even as he choked on the obstruction in his throat, his lungs were drawing oxygen from the liquid.

Slowly, chest heaving, he began to calm down.

I'm not dying, I'm not dying...

He opened his eyes, cringing at the touch of the peculiar gel against his eyeballs.

Oh, holy fuck, this is disgusting.

Then he saw the hair-fine filaments extruding from the walls like the tentacles of albino sea anemones. He tried to flinch away but the walls of the fissure contracted like a sphincter, squeezing against him and holding him in place. He tried to snarl, but the filaments pushed their way into his mouth and nose and he gagged as he felt them slither into his throat. Another insinuated itself into his left ear, and another two drilled into his eyelids. For a second, every nerve in his body flared with intolerable pain.

And then he saw *everything*.

The walls of the chamber were replaced with a three-dimensional tactical view of the surrounding volume. He saw the rock ahead, his target, outlined in red. He felt the caress of the solar wind, the touch of its warmth against his cheek, and he felt the weapon like a Spitfire beneath him—responsive, keen, and ready to do as he bade. He felt its power like an electrical shock to his spine. He'd seen what it had done to Célestine's Leviathans and now, as the weapon integrated itself with his frontal lobes, came the knowledge of how it worked. Suddenly he knew, as if he'd always known, that the weapon displaced plasma from the heart of the nearest star and squirted it in a tight beam at its target. That pencil-thin line of brilliant white, crackling energy he'd seen in France had been raw fire from the core of the Sun. Thirteen million degrees centigrade. No wonder it had carved metal like butter and eaten through the bedrock beneath.

And now that insane destructive beam was his to control!

Heart beating, he opened himself to the weapon's interface. All he had to do was think of the target and the gun would do the rest. Like a god, his will would be made manifest; a single thought would be enough to unleash a lightning bolt of pure, sizzling energy.

"Oh baby," he muttered to the system swaddling him, "where have you *been* all my life?"

* * *

ON THE *AMELINE*'S bridge, Victoria watched as the white line stabbed out, spearing the oncoming asteroid. Where it hit, the surface turned a livid molten yellow. If the ship's cameras hadn't automatically polarised, she would have been blinded. As it was, the line was reduced to a dull grey laceration in the fabric of reality. On the asteroid's surface, dust and loose rock blew away from the boiling incision. Then the beam moved. Slowly, it tracked upwards, slicing though the stone like a hot wire through a block of cheese. Then it blinked off. When it reappeared, it moved laterally, cutting from left to right. Then it jumped again, and now it moved from right to left. Faster and faster it slashed, hacking back and forth, up and down, until it became a flickering blur.

Under its assault, the asteroid seemed to fall apart. Glowing chunks broke away into space, only to be skewered and reduced still further. Within a couple of minutes, the potato had become a mass of cooling, tumbling fragments, each no bigger than a basketball.

Kat said, "Your monkey did well."

Victoria let herself smile. "He likes blowing things up." She felt a strange kind of pride. "It's kind of what he does."

"I can see that." Kat tapped the screen. "But those fragments will still do a lot of damage if they hit the Earth like that. Let's hope your airship can mop them up. They're small enough that a nuclear blast should vaporise most of them. The rest can burn in the atmosphere."

"So, that's it?'

"If the plan works, yes. Actual surface hits should be minimal. All we have to do now is track this cloud of debris and wait until the airship gets in range."

"Where is the *Sun Wukong*?" Victoria asked, looking at the inscrutable instruments above her. "How's it doing?"

Kat consulted the ship. "Almost in orbit. It's had a bit of a shaky ride, apparently, but the thing's more or less intact. They should be firing up the ion engines at any minute."

Victoria let out a breath she hadn't realised she'd been holding. Something eased inside her.

"Well, fingers-crossed they work."

Kat's face remained grim. "We'll soon find out. I'm plotting in a course to jump back there now." She jerked her head towards the hatch at the back of the bridge. "Why don't you go below and share the good news?"

CHAPTER FORTY-FOUR
EMPIRE STATE

LATER, STANDING ON the verandah inside the *Sun Wukong*'s glass nose, Ack-Ack Macaque looked out at a dark sky filled with stars. His fur was still damp from the alien goo of the weapon, and his throat and eyes were sore from the intrusion of its questing fibers; but despite all that, he felt good. The demolition of the asteroid had been an almost religious experience for him—an act of epic cosmic vandalism that dwarfed all his previous accomplishments. And the best bit was that there was more fun to come, as soon as the lumbering, slowly accelerating airship got close enough to unleash its nuclear torpedoes.

Yes, he thought, *an airship. Here I am riding a goddamn Zeppelin through the motherfucking universe.* Even to his own ears, it sounded batshit insane—and it had been his plan! He took a deep puff on his cigar and glanced around at his comrades. They had gathered here to toast their success with the rock, and the airship's successful launch. Even Apynja had been let out of the brig, once he'd convinced Victoria that mere walls couldn't hold the female monkey if she decided to do that teleport trick he'd seen her do in the forest.

"So," he rumbled, "what should I call you? Founder or Apynja?"

She looked up at him through her monocle. She wore a specially made black corset and skirt, and a top hat with a black veil that angled down across her face, covering her other eye.

"Does it matter?"

"I suppose not." He returned his gaze to the void beyond the windows. It would take weeks until they reached the remains of the asteroid, months after that until they reached Mars and the final confrontation with Célestine. He huffed smoke at the stars. Beside him, the Founder clicked her tongue and ran a protective hand over the bulge at her middle.

"You shouldn't be smoking around me, you know."

He looked down.

"Sorry." He dropped the butt to the deck and ground it out with the toe of his boot. The truth was, he hadn't been enjoying it anyway. Smoking had become a habit that had outlived its pleasures. Maybe now, with the babies on the way, it was time for him to quit.

He felt the Founder move closer along the rail, until their elbows were almost touching.

"You're an old soul, monkey man."

He fixed her with his good eye. "What?"

She smiled and shook her head fondly. "You don't remember at all, do you?"

"Remember what, lady?"

"All the times we've done this before."

He looked incredulously at the walls of the airship and the star field beyond.

"Lady, nobody's done *this* before."

Her smile broadened, but he thought he caught an edge of sadness in her eyes, and something else in the way she drew a ragged breath through her nose.

"You're an old soul, Napoleon. One of the oldest, just like me, just like Célestine. You've been here from the beginning, in one form or another."

"What in holy hell are you talking about?"

The Founder raised her chin. "When we built the multiverse, there was one resurrected soul who opposed what we were doing. He was a man named Napoleon Jones—a human brought to our time by The Recollection. He thought we should embrace the chaos instead of hiding from it. When we took shelter in our creation, he plagued us with his sabotages and pranks for millennia. Somehow, when we were copying him into our virtual creation, he found a way to embed himself in the very warp and weft of the world. However many times we caught and killed him, he always resurfaced, always came back to cause trouble, and usually in the form of a talking beast."

"Wut?"

"A thousand times I've tried to build a paradise, and a thousand times you've thwarted me, Jones." She waved a bony finger in his face. "The Gestalt was only my most recent attempt."

"My name ain't Jones." Ack-Ack Macaque glowered. "And this paradise of yours sounds more like slavery to me."

The Founder glared defiantly. "I didn't say it would be a paradise for everyone."

"Just for you?"

She turned slightly and indicated the rest of the assembly with a twitch of her lace-covered hand.

"These people aren't real, you know."

Ack-Ack looked at Victoria and K8, who were engaged in earnest conversation with Merovech and Cuddles. "They think they're real, and that makes them real enough for me."

Leaving her where she stood, he stalked over to Katherine Abdulov, who was leaning against one of the giant pots at the edge of the jungle, nursing a glass of white wine.

"What are you going to do with her?" he asked.

Kat looked at the Founder and gave a one-shouldered shrug.

"She's done unspeakable things. All we can do is try to lock her up."

"Even knowing she'll escape?"

The young pilot gave him a curious look. "We can't kill her, if that's what you mean."

"Why not?"

"Because that's the sort of thing she would do."

Ack-Ack Macaque growled in his throat. Then he looked down at his arm. The fur stood on end. Static sparked from teaspoons. He felt his hackles bristle.

And there was Célestine, standing in the centre of the room. A few final blue flickers of static danced down her metal legs. The air smelled of ozone.

Ack-Ack Macaque went for his holsters. He had both guns pointing at her head before she'd fully finished materialising—but when he pulled the triggers, nothing happened. Célestine held up a hand and the metal grew hot. With a screech of pain and annoyance, he dropped them both.

"I'm tired," Célestine's voice boomed. "Tired of being interfered with. Tired of playing by the rules. Tired of playing these stupid games."

She clicked her fingers, and they were elsewhere.

SUNLIGHT DAZZLED HIM. A cold wind tugged at his jacket.

"What the fuck?" Ack-Ack Macaque put up a hand to shade his eye and squinted into the early morning light. He was back on Earth, on top of a building. A city stretched beneath him, all glass and stone. Vapour steamed from rooftop vents. The sound of traffic drifted up from street level.

"Where are we?"

"New York." Célestine stood ten metres away, beside a telescope mounted on a metal pole. "At the top of the Empire State Building."

He blinked, eye still adjusting. The Founder was here too, standing away to the side like a referee in a boxing match.

"How?"

"I told you." Célestine's voice was loud and dangerous. "I'm sick of playing by the rules. We built this world. If we have to, we can change whatever we want."

"Then why have you waited this long?"

She glared at him. "Because I was trying to do it properly. I was trying to build an empire that would last a hundred thousand years."

"But you've fucked it up now, yeah?"

"Because of you, you loathsome fleabag."

His Colts were gone. He had nothing except the

knife in his boot, and he didn't think that would do much good against her titanium skeleton—especially if she could change the laws of physics at a whim. He looked desperately around the viewing gallery.

"But why bring me here?" he said, playing for time, hunting for a weapon.

Célestine laughed, and it wasn't a pleasant sound.

"Have you ever seen *King Kong*?"

Ack-Ack Macaque shrugged. "I've never been to China."

"She means," the Founder said, interjecting at last, voice sour with exasperation, "that she's going to kill you."

Ack-Ack huffed. He didn't like the look of this at all. In the space of an hour, he'd gone from glorying in the power of the alien weapon to standing helpless and unarmed in front of his greatest enemy. The turnaround seemed far too fast, and tipped in favour of the wrong party.

"She can try." He took up a fighting stance. He knew he was outgunned and outclassed, but that wouldn't stop him. If the metal bitch wanted to end him, she'd have a fight on her hands. He wasn't about to go gently into any goodnight, no sir, and he'd rather go down fighting than give her the satisfaction of admitting defeat.

In fact, screw her. Screw the lot of them.

With a yell, he flung himself forward. Célestine didn't even try to dodge. She stood her ground as his fingers clawed for her, and slapped him away at the last minute with a backhand that felt like a blow from an aluminium baseball bat.

He tumbled over and over, fetching up against the wall at the foot of the rail.

"Ouch, fuck." Stunned, he shook his head, trying to clear the red mist that interfered with his vision. Dimly, he saw the cyborg striding towards him. He grabbed a railing and pulled himself unsteadily to his feet.

"Had enough?" he asked her, and hawked a wedge of bloody phlegm into the dust. "Because I can do this all day."

Her lip curled. With a gesture, she parted the railings behind him. Off-balance, he teetered on the edge of a drop that seemed to fall away beneath his heels forever. The cars four hundred metres below looked like ants; the people like bacteria.

Hey, that's cheating!

He windmilled his arms to keep his balance, and had a sudden flash of another time and place, of a metal bridge over a deep canyon, and an airship passing beneath.

Célestine stepped forward. She had her hand pulled back, ready to shove him over the edge. As she lunged towards him, he grabbed her wrist and heaved backwards. If he was going over, he was going to take her with him. He heard the Founder yell, "No!" But it was too late. He was already falling, and Célestine's body toppled after him. He kept a death grip on her arm. If she tried to teleport, he'd go with her. If not, well...

Let's see how her metal head survives when it hits the pavement from this height.

The observation deck fell away behind them. The wind roared in his ears.

Oh crap, this is it...

He stared at death, in the form of an onrushing sidewalk.

Then the view blurred. A mirage shimmered beneath him. He felt himself buffeted up, banging his head against Célestine's metal chest. With a bang of displaced air and a flash of white light, the *Ameline* levered itself into existence, hanging in the sky metres from the wall of the skyscraper, jet thrusters whining.

Ack-Ack Macaque and Célestine hit its upper surface and rolled apart.

> HELLO!

Ack-Ack lay gasping for breath.

"What?" The voice had been speaking to him in his mind.

> I'M THE SHIP. I'M CONNECTED TO YOUR GELWARE BRAIN.

He shook his head. Close to the vessel's nose, Célestine clambered awkwardly to her feet and looked around, seemingly dazed.

"Shut up." He glanced around for a weapon, but found none. The alien pod lay beneath the bows, and he couldn't get to it from here.

> I'M THE *AMELINE*, MONKEY. I'M TRYING TO HELP YOU.

"Then kill this metal bitch."

> CAN DO. BUT YOU'RE GOING TO HAVE TO HELP.

Célestine fixed on him and started walking forward, hands grasping like claws. Ack-Ack Macaque danced backwards, staying out of reach.

"How?"

> MY WEAPONS ARE UNDERNEATH. I NEED YOU TO THROW HER OFF SO I CAN GET A CLEAR SHOT.

"I can't, she's too strong."

> THEN FIND SOMETHING TO HANG ON TO.

Without further warning, the old ship rolled. Ack-Ack Macaque lunged for one of the handholds he'd used earlier. He wrapped his fingers around it and clung. Less nimble, Célestine toppled. She lost her footing and fell, over and over, towards the ground. Ack-Ack Macaque felt his arm being torn from its socket. He snaked his tail through the next handhold along, using it to help support his weight.

The *Ameline* was still at ninety degrees to the ground when the weapon at its tip fired. A burning shaft of starfire speared the falling cyborg and, as she tumbled, diced her into glowing chunks. Still dangling precariously, Ack-Ack Macaque watched the burning debris rain onto Fifth Avenue.

"Yeah!" he yelled into the wind. "Take that! You see what you get when you mess with my friends?" He sent a gob of spit sailing earthwards. "Try teleporting your way out of *that*!"

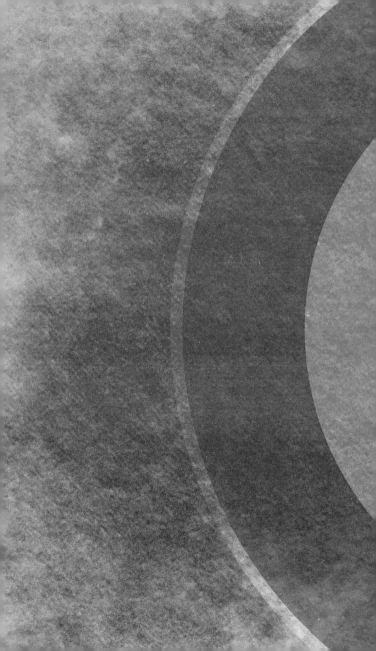

EPILOGUE

GONE

Farewell dear mate, dear love!
I'm going away, I know not where,
Or to what fortune, or whether I may ever see you
again.

(Walt Whitman, *Good-Bye My Fancy!*)

EPILOGUE
GONE

ACK-ACK MACAQUE CLAWED his way around to the airlock. When he got there, he found Victoria and K8 waiting for him. They pulled him inside and helped him to a chair, then let him catch his breath as the old ship powered up, away from the city.

"Thanks," he gasped when he could finally speak.

"Don't thank us," Victoria said. "We had nothing to do with it. One moment we were standing on the *Sun Wukong*, the next we were here, on the ship."

"But I thought—"

> AND DON'T LOOK AT ME, EITHER. I WAS MINDING MY OWN BUSINESS BEFORE SOMETHING ZAPPED ME INTO *THAT* HORRORSHOW.

Ack-Ack Macaque frowned. He scratched his eye patch.

"The Founder," he said quietly. She must have used her powers—her knowledge of the simulation—to teleport the ship and his friends here, the same way Célestine had brought him. "I guess she wasn't as bad as everybody said, huh?"

K8 gave him a skeptical look, one eyebrow raised.

"You really have lousy taste in women," she said.

Ack-Ack Macaque gave a snort. "You're talking about the mother of my babies."

"That's as may be, but I'll bet you that's the last we'll ever see of her."

The ship gave a couple of final bumps, and then steadied. Katherine Abdulov appeared from the hatch leading to the bridge.

"Célestine's dead," she said. "We scanned the wreckage. There wasn't a piece of her left that was bigger than an orange."

"So it's over?" K8 asked.

Victoria shook her head. "There are still the cyborgs on Mars. If we don't deal with them now, who knows what they'll throw our way next time."

The young Scot pouted. "And how long's it going to take us to get *there*?"

"Six months."

From the ladder that led from the ship's bridge, Katherine Abdulov cleared her throat. "Perhaps I can help?"

They all looked at her.

"I've been doing some calculations with the ship," she said. "We think we can tow you."

"Would that be faster?" Ack-Ack Macaque asked.

Kat grinned. "I reckon we could get you there in six weeks."

Ack-Ack Macaque sat bolt upright. "Hot damn! That's more like it. I'd go nuts rattling around that airship for half a year."

"And then, after that," Kat continued, "maybe you could help us?"

"In what way?" Victoria's eyes narrowed suspiciously.

Kat's smile turned serious. "Napoleon and I go back a long way," she said. "And it's good to have him back, even if he is a monkey now. Besides, there are other builders out there. What say we go and throw a wrench in their plans?"

K8 laughed. "A monkey wrench?"

Ack-Ack Macaque fixed her with his most withering scowl.

"Not funny."

He turned his stare on Katherine. "Do you think we can track down the Founder?"

"Possibly." Abdulov stuck out her bottom lip. "I mean, we've done it before. She'll know we're looking but, in theory, yes."

"Good." He shifted himself on the seat, getting comfortable. "Because I want my babies back."

His arms and legs felt as if they were made of wood. The accumulated aches and pains of the last few days—the barks, bruises and grazed knees; the multiple punches, kicks and bites—had taken their toll. As Victoria and Kat continued to plan their next move, he let his solitary eye fall closed.

With the *Ameline*'s help, they could be on Mars in a matter of weeks. And then the real fighting would start: monkey versus machine in a battle to the death, on the red sands of a dying world, with all the other worlds of creation at stake and an infinite playground stretching out all around them.

All they had to do was seize it.

SIX MILES ABOVE New York City, the *Ameline* readied her engines. Her course was set: first, a jump to rendezvous with the *Sun Wukong*, and then onwards, ever onwards, through all the billions of possible worlds.

Her fusion reactor came online, generating power for the jump engines. Deep in her belly, the engines began to spin up until the old ship felt she could leap the length of the universe in a single orgasmic bound.

> HOLD ONTO YOUR HATS, she warned her passengers. Her scanners took a final, almost lingering sweep over the blue and green marble that was the Earth. Then all the readouts on her bridge spiked at once. The *Ameline*'s engines tore a hole in the walls of the multiverse. There was a blinding flash of pure white light, and then they were all gone and elsewhere—humans, monkeys and spaceship alike.

THE END.

ACK-ACKNOWLEDGEMENTS

HERE, AT THE end of the 'Macaque Trilogy', I'd like to take the opportunity to thank the following people for accompanying me on the journey:

Jon Oliver, Ben Smith, Mike Molcher, Lydia Gittins, and the rest of the team at Solaris Books, for giving me the chance to write these novels in the first place. My agent, John Jarrold, for all his advice and support. My wife, Becky, for giving me the time and space in which to write, for reading and editing the first drafts, and for keeping me going when all I wanted to do was crawl into a hole and never come out again. Jake Murray, for his excellent and inspiring covers. Jetse de Vries and Andrew Cox, for publishing the first 'Ack-Ack Macaque' short story in Interzone, way back in 2007. Matt Smith and Tharg The Mighty, for allowing me to fulfil a boyhood dream by writing an 'Ack-Ack Macaque' comic strip for 2000 AD. My sister, Rebecca, for her excellent and incisive critiques. The rest of my family, for their constant and unflagging belief. Su Hadrell, for useful feedback on early drafts of Hive Monkey and Macaque Attack. Neil Beynon, for his insights on the first draft of Hive Monkey. And Danie Ware, Desiree Fischer and the team at Forbidden Planet, for book launches, signings and other events.

And, lastly, I want to say a big thank you to all the people who've read, reviewed, discussed or recommended these books over the past three years; all those who came to readings or book launches; all those who voted for *Ack-Ack Macaque* in the 2013 BSFA Awards; and all those who've engaged with the monkey on Facebook or Twitter. Your response has been terrific, and this trilogy/quartet wouldn't exist without you.

Thank you all.

Gareth L. Powell
Bristol, June 2014

ACK-ACK MACAQUE

'Fizzes with wild ideas... A ripping yarn about murder, mayhem and monkeys'. *Philip Reeve*, author of *Mortal Engines*

GARETH L. POWELL

In 1944, as waves of German ninjas parachute into Kent, Britain's best hopes for victory lie with a Spitfire pilot codenamed 'Ack-Ack Macaque.' The trouble is, Ack-Ack Macaque is a cynical, one-eyed, cigar-chomping monkey, and he's starting to doubt everything, including his own existence.

A century later, in a world where France and Great Britain merged in the late 1950s and nuclear-powered Zeppelins circle the globe, ex-journalist Victoria Valois finds herself drawn into a deadly game of cat and mouse with the man who butchered her husband and stole her electronic soul. In Paris, after taking part in an illegal break-in at a research laboratory, the heir to the British throne goes on the run. And all the while, the doomsday clock ticks towards Armageddon...

 WWW.SOLARISBOOKS.COM

Follow us on Twitter! www.twitter.com/solarisbooks

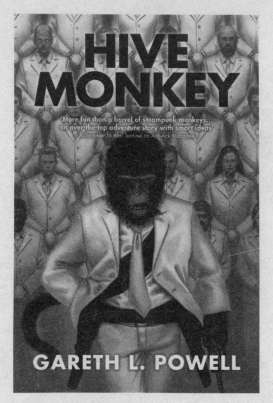

HIVE MONKEY

'More fun than a barrel of steampunk monkeys...
an over-the-top adventure story with smart ideas'
Milwaukee Journal Sentinel on Ack-Ack Macaque

GARETH L. POWELL

In order to hide from his unwanted fame as the Spitfire-pilot-monkey who emerged from a computer game to defeat the nefarious corporation that engineered him, the charismatic and dangerous Ack-Ack Macaque is working as a pilot on a world-circling nuclear-powered Zeppelin.

But when the cabin of one of his passengers is invaded by the passenger's own dying doppelganger, our hirsute hero finds himself thrust into a race to save the world from an aggressive hive mind, time-hopping saboteurs, and an army of homicidal Neanderthal assassins!

 WWW.SOLARISBOOKS.COM

Follow us on Twitter! www.twitter.com/solarisbooks